White

Rabbits

Pinch, punch first of the month...

Dawn Llewellyn-Price

White Rabbits

ISBN 979-8-86-339174-8

Cover design by the Author.

Photographs Copyright © Dawn Llewellyn-Price 2023

(E/1)

For lucky ladies everywhere. Buy the shoes.

With thanks to

Hilary in Wales, there at conception, through to delivery, who suffered endless DMs & screenshots at ridiculous times of the day and night.

Ali & Jean in Spain, who put up with plot lines under a baking sun. With one or two glasses of cooling Cava along the way.

'Chef Jeff' who fed and watered me throughout.

Lee for #toegate

Cat Sollis-Rickwood for property advice.

Staff at Swansea Marriott, Dylan Thomas for his fishing boat bobbing sea, & La chica española en el chiringuito con los zapatos.

&

The women of Wales. Every one a beaut.

Saying 'White Rabbits' on the first of the month has been attributed to the Middle Ages in the British Isles. A place where the fear of witches matched against the purity of the creatures, brought good luck. But only if they were the first words spoken. The saying survives today, along with 'pinch punch first of the month, can't pinch back.'

Chapter 1

Spring, 1st March.

A handwritten letter rested between French manicured fingertips, thumb obscuring the stamp, brutally scuffed by a black ink postmark. Someone put pen to paper, slipped it into an envelope, and suffered the tart taste of the glued edge. At the sorting office, it navigated speeding machinery, before a whistling *postie* carried it up the path and pushed it through the letterbox, where it spiralled innocuously onto the raffia mat. Spring sunshine filtered through leaf-etched door glass, the paper warm and pliable as a glossy fingernail ripped the seal.

Who on earth sends letters these days, and in a bubblegum pink envelope?

A tearing sound broke the stillness of morning as one folded, rose-tinted page offered a few lines of spidery handwriting in thin-nibbed black ink.

I thought you should know that your husband is having an affair. I don't know who she is, but he's told someone he works with at the factory.

Elegant hands trembled as pursed lips mouthed over the words. Leaden liquid splashed along the now blurred and indecipherable line as moist eyes glanced to the ceiling.

Is that porch roof leaking again? But it's not even raining.

Salty droplets created the stinging sensation as they spilled down her cheeks. Wiping them away with a free hand, she focused on the writing until it became legible.

He hasn't mentioned a name. Just that she's young and blonde. Sorry, you don't know me, but better coming from a stranger.

A friend of a friend

Savagely stuffing it into a jacket pocket, she bent sharply to snatch the envelope which had fallen in a spiral to settle on the mat.

The same inelegant scrawl formed her name and address, while a local postmark grazed the Queen's head. With an angry crumple, it followed the contents swiftly out of sight, blighting the outline of last season's navy pinstripe trouser suit. Bright rays highlighted dust and a few fingerprints marking the glass door, and the broken tufts of raffia harbouring a few dead insects on the ceramic floor tiles.

I must give that mat a shake this weekend. Seems like it's time for some Spring cleaning.

Snatching up her briefcase, she checked the fresh daffodil was securely pinned to her lapel, murmured 'White Rabbits' to the morning, slammed the door behind her, and stepped out into a world spinning with such severity, she no longer knew which hemisphere she was in.

♥

Chapter 2

'Start the day with a smile, and finish it with champagne'

Anon

Beating a swift staccato with a pen against her flamingo-patterned eco cup, Grace scanned an almost autumnal flurry of emails cascading down her laptop screen and shook her head. The headline act seen frequently in recent months, topped the bill above work-related messages.

'We have news about your Lottery ticket. Please log into your account.'

Velvet Teddy coloured lips formed the words 'Three quid or a lucky dip? At least it pays for the next one.'

Where my dreams will shatter like Christmas baubles in the January sales.

With a gentle sigh, she sipped the coffee, breathing in the steamy aromatic coils.

Smells so lush, just what I need.

Glancing at the wall clock which ticked towards half-past eight, she wondered why her colleagues weren't in. On a desk strewn with invoices and sales quotes, Grace set down the cup, allowing a tapping index finger to reveal the full-length display of her screen. It drifted away into the distance, as yesterday's sweltering August bank holiday weekend, along with summer, ebbed with it.

'Let's see what delights I'm dealing with today,' she announced to an empty office.

The phone asleep on her desk yawned, before stretching into vibrating, blinking wakefulness, drawing her attention to its screen, as she slid down the notifications bar. One text, an unread WhatsApp, and more infuriating news items brought a further mutter.

'I thought this was supposed to be *Great* Britain? How *any* of us stay sane these days is beyond belief.'

The coffee was slow to kick in and the weekend was tiring. *Girls' Night Out* on Friday, and *date night* on Saturday, meant Grace was delighted to sit down with her mother for lunch the following afternoon, gaining some respite from the unusual heat in the interior of the 17th Century *No Sign* wine bar.

'What are you doing tomorrow?' her mother asked, laying down her cutlery for the last time and leaning back in the chair with a replete sigh.

Bank Holiday Monday would roar in the following day and with it the traffic-snarled roads leading to the packed beaches of the beautiful Gower peninsula.

'I'm going to grab a Joe's' ice cream and take myself off to the beach while this sunshine lingers and laze on the sand like a teenager. I bought that book you mentioned on *How to manifest your dreams*. Let's see if it can do anything for us.'

They laughed as Grace savoured the last velvety cherry drops from a glass of Caracara Chilean Merlot and breathed in the aromas of roast potatoes, cauliflower cheese, and gravy which wafted past as large trays slalomed around customers in the race to reach the other tables. The Dickensian atmosphere of the historic pub, with its slate floors and open fireplaces, was well-loved on Sundays in Swansea, whatever the season.

'Sounds like a plan, love. Make sure you take a hat. You

don't want to get sunstroke in this heat and your Gran always used to say. 'Be careful what you wish for.'

'I only remember her saying 'You can't plan anything' and I'd say 'Gran, if you don't *plan* anything, you'll never *do* anything.'

Grace sighed and rubbed her abdomen.

'Maybe we shouldn't have planned a roast dinner in this weather.'

'You can't beat a Sunday roast whatever the weather,' her mother signalled for the bill 'and we need to get used to hot summers. No need to go trotting off abroad anymore.'

Grace reached for her handbag and laughed. 'You're a fine one talking, Mam. Can't see *you* holidaying in Wales, North or South. Imagine you down in Tenby for a week. It's full of fishing boats, not cruise ships. No gorgeous Greek captains for you and Amanda to chase.'

'I love Tenby.'

'Doesn't everyone? Even Wally the Walrus stayed for weeks. Maybe this bestseller I bought will manifest a world cruise, and I'll come too.'

'You better wade through it then, love. I'm getting older, not younger. I can't believe it's the first of September on Thursday. The months are flying by.'

Monday afternoon's solo visit to the curved sweep of the Bay, with suntan lotion and a small picnic, brought the last bank holiday weekend of the year to an end. Late afternoon, as the distant tide crept in, the sparkles and white effervescence of cool water relieved parched skins sprawled aimlessly across the sand. Jet skis played offshore, their droning loud above the shouts of swimmers, and squeals of children as the beach of the second-largest tidal range in the world revealed endless golden sand.

While a dash into the cool but sparkling water wearing a bikini for the first time in years lifted her spirits, the salty waves splashing around her thighs sprayed her as shore-breaking sea trickled around her ankles. Dropping back onto her towel, the damp, darkened sand plastered along her limbs and between her toes, the sounds of beach life lit up her features with end-of-summer smiles.

Next summer, I promise I'll do this every weekend. Sea water is so therapeutic.

The pages of the book soon found her studiously memorising gems of advice; release your desires to the universe, and the universe can take it from there. Be patient, for big changes seldom happen overnight. The overload of suggestions continued.

Five minutes of daily daydreams? Easy. Say what you want out loud. No problem. But I want changes now. This is complete nonsense. Do they think we're fools? I suppose I am, for buying it.

While the sun and pounding of the waves tricked her into drowsiness, she lost heart halfway through and tucked it into her beach bag, knowing the next time she set eyes on it, a holiday would loom and it would reappear from a darkened cupboard recess, a souvenir of this rare visit to the city's beach, spilling sand onto the bedroom carpet.

Settling back on the sand, lids lowering, she reminisced over careless summers with school friends on the dunes; of bus tickets, sneaked cider bottles, packed sandwiches, chatting up boys, and arriving home late plastered in the sticky golden grains of Swansea's five-mile-long, perfectly curved beach.

It's been a delight of a day. Oh, the joys of untroubled youth. I miss you sometimes.

Leaning back in her swivel chair, Grace tried to focus. A Tuesday start to the working week was tough. With an ongoing conflict in a corner of the continent, which, according to a fretful media, was the sole cause of everything wrong with the nation, she avoided thinking too far ahead. The desire to keep these last visions alive, before days shortened, and summer clothes hid from audacious moths seeking residence in their folds, was strong. September was two days away, driving them towards an autumnal change of season, and ahead lay an energy crisis everyone was fated to suffer. The thought drew her attention back to the top of the screen and the lottery email.

Oh, come on, let me win a million. Then we'll be able to

turn the heating on in November instead of Christmas day.

A screeching, jovial command pierced the silence, making her jump. 'Grace Lewis, sales meeting, ten minutes!' Angela from accounts, stuck her head around the door, laughing.

'Very droll. You should be on the stage. Is that where everyone is?'

The voice dropped to a normal level. 'Yes, didn't you get the memo? Hope you haven't got a hangover. It may go on a bit.'

'Clear head. My big night out was Friday.'

'Mine was *all* weekend. Manic, it was.'

Angela's speech patterns and Welsh lilt were in full flow, but she looked in need of a hairbrush and fluids, having drained the last of the summer wine. The unusual August heat and dehydration dulled her skin.

'Drink some water girl, you look like poo.'

Angela pushed back stray strands of fine blonde hair from her tired face. 'Ta *Mammy,* I feel like it.'

 Grace laughed. 'Why do we do it?'

'The boozing? A Brit thing. All done in the hunt for a man, and they *definitely* look better through rose-tinted glasses.'

'Not found anyone on those dating apps?'

 Angela grimaced, nose wrinkling, and shook her head slowly. 'Too many left-swipes from me.'

'Well, keep kissing the frogs.'

'*That* pond is overflowing.'

Grace picked up her coffee and took a gulp.

'See you down there. I need a refill.'

The door whooshed shut. *Count yourself lucky, Grace. At least you're not in Angela's position.*

With the cup still warm in her palm, she sighed, remembering the lottery email. What would it be like to win a decent sum of money? It was a simple slide into the realms of Instagram lust, to revel in the throes of red-soled Louboutin shoes and Zimmerman frocks. Easy to imagine negotiating the narrow streets of Monaco in a low-slung open-top car, pulling up outside the Hotel de Paris, hips swaying under a tightly fitted white suit, *avec* matching floppy hat, and enormous sunglasses. How effortless to emulate Grace Kelly as she floated into Reception in the wide wake of bellboys bearing matching luggage in all shapes and sizes, a tsunami of drapery spilling up against the desk.

'Je suis arrivé, j'ai réservé une suite!'

'I've arrived, I have a suite!'

But I'd never get out of anything low-slung. My heel would get caught in the pavement and I'd twist an ankle. What is it with heels and pavements?

She saw herself splayed in the road, hanging onto an open door, heels clattering as she struggled inelegantly to right herself, bringing a twitching smile to the corners of her mouth.

Naturally, some handsome Marquis or Duc poised nearby, appalled at her impropriety, would turn away in disgust as he adjusted his silk cravat, instead of coming to her aid. Grace laughed and raised perfectly groomed brows, eyes closing as the daydream continued and she sank further into the swivel chair, swinging it playfully in a gently creaking semicircle. *I must get John to spray some WD40 on this old thing.*

Next, she wafted down a wide, spiral marble staircase, adorned in a voluminous, diaphanous frock, smiling graciously as she floated past an eclectic floral display in an enormous glass vase while cameras flashed in her glowing, cosmetically highlighted face, dark hair curled and filled with beautiful extensions tumbling princess-like around her elbows.

Charity balls and polo matches flickered in full cinematic reels, followed by sunbathing on far-flung beaches, while she cooed, 'Hello dahling! Anyone want champers?' to the beautiful people draping the decks of sleek bowed yachts. Such a grandiose daydream. Spectacular for a quiet morning in a deteriorating building on the edge of Swansea Docks.

I love the word frock. It's so evocative. Now, get on with your day.

Outside was the once Welsh Principality, far removed from the Mediterranean version, featuring a monumental vista of cranes, merging the scent of the sea with malodorous whiffs, while the sound of vehicle reversing beeps broke through any peace still offered by an ageing, grime-edged window on the world outside. Where ivy and weeds thrived, but Bougainvillaea and Jasmine failed to grow. *At least we still have a Prince and Princess, depending on your viewpoint.*

Grace studied her brightly patterned coffee cup as she topped it up. A couple of years ago it would have been a breezy pop-in takeaway with a bagged side order from one of the higher-priced coffee chains where people lounged with cakes and computers, cradling their branded mugs. These days she utilised the office kettle, a mini cafetiere, and a bag of filter coffee. People were changing habits to survive the tough months predicted. Her attention moved to the top line of lottery ticket news, speculating on how much money she'd need to graze the surface of the lifestyles of the super-rich. Five million, fifty million?

I wouldn't know where to begin. But I'd have a bloody good go.

Collecting up a mound of paperwork she tapped it into order against the desk, producing a satisfied sound, the thud of paper against old, wearied wood, indented by the wounds of work.

Whence you came, my A4 friends. You could have been a desk, but fate stepped in, and look at you now, all shiny, white, and new. I wish I was shiny and new again. But at least this summer, I'm tanned and glowing.

She slid a jacket sleeve up to her elbow and admired the results of a rare hot summer, the skin soft and oiled beneath her fingertips. It produced a fleeting joyous pleasure before the desk phone rang.

'Grace Lewis. Oh, hi John. Just found out. Yes, on my way down.'

Now in a minute. Our infernal 'Welshism' where time is flung in the air with dramatic abandon, and only we natives 'get it.' Only I shouldn't be in meetings. I'm supposed to be jamming up highways, seeing customers, yelled at by white van men as I block their commercial bays. Why don't they just put more visitor spaces? There are never enough.

Reversing the chair away from the desk, she stood near the window as a movement in the car park below caught her eye. Among the disorderly staff cars slumped and slathered in degrees of dirt, a driver's door opened, and out stepped a man from a perfectly linear parked, clean, matte red sports model.

Her own backache-blue saloon, pockmarked with fortnight-old raindrops and suicidal summer insects, obscured the L&B Industrial Services *Visitor Parking* sign. *Shouldn't have parked there, Gracie. You've blocked the top-tier space again. And look who needs it.*

Sahara wind dusted her tongue as Marcus from Head Office moved around to open the boot, effortlessly withdrawing a heavy laptop bag with a swift, elegant movement. Seldom seen in this neck of the woods, he swooped in and out of nationwide branches like a rare red kite, seeking his prey, then migrated for months at a time. Grace saw him turn towards the sleek convertible, point his keys, and as the mirrors inverted, head towards reception underneath her window.

He strode purposefully towards the entrance, long muscular legs encased in the latest deep charcoal Italian slim-fitting suit, its short jacket revealing areas others are designed to hide, the luminous sheen of luxe living reflecting the morning sunlight. A tumble of blond hair touched his suntanned brow, a chiselled jaw well suited to someone with a role higher in the company bent towards a striped shirt collar as he studied his phone screen. He oozed Corporate Class. Dark-lashed eyes followed him across the car park until he slipped a pair of Gucci-style sunglasses into a pocket and vanished from view.

He must have got up early. I doubt he'd give up his bank holiday to drive to Wales alone, bored in a hotel room overnight. Unless he brought company.

It wouldn't be long before staff on all three floors of the ageing building would grow excitable over his arrival. Grace was rarely in the office when Marcus visited but was witness to all gossip the following morning.

'He was wearing a light grey suit.'

'He's so bloody gorgeous.'

'No sign of a wedding ring, either.'

'He's down here *loads* these days, every three weeks at least. Do you think the company is in trouble?'

'Who knows, Covid didn't help, did it?'

'We seldom saw him before.'

Angela took pleasure in her own words, behind the queue of responses. 'He was asking about you, Grace, but I said you were only in first thing, then gone for the day.' *Which is why I park in the visitors' space. Nobody needs it this early.*

'Maybe he wants to sack me, and he's going through my sales figures with a fine-tooth comb. I was the last one in. I could be the first one out.'

Angela smirked and winked.

'Depends which *sack* and which *figure* you mean!'

Grace raised a brow.

'Hey, I need my job. Mortgage to pay, government to support.'

'It takes two to tango. Don't you fancy him? Everyone else does.'

She placed a playfully thoughtful finger on her lips and waited a moment in deep consideration.

'Hmm, good looking, but young.'

Angela studied her closely over rustling invoices.

'Only a handful of years, surely?'

A flurry of chatter debated his age over the sounds of a phone ringing, keyboards tapping, and drawers closing.

'Around thirty-one, I reckon.'

'Everyone's thirty-one to you, Gloria.'

Angela picked at the thread again. 'Besides, you two would make a beautiful couple. Didn't he sit next to you at the Spring Ball?'

Grace jiggled her left hand in Angela's direction, exaggerating her ring finger with a few rapid jerks. Her colleague shrugged. 'Any port in a storm.'

How does she know there's been a storm? A category three hurricane? Their eyes locked for the briefest of moments before Grace looked away.

'Well, I'd give him one. Or two, if I could find the energy.' Graham volunteered, causing a peal of raucous laughter to race around the office.

Marcus was a man to tango with on any slippery surface, and she remembered the touch of his hand low on her back as they merged on the dance floor. And the expression in his eyes when he'd taken her hand to lead her onto it only moments before.

Don't go there, Grace. It's only Tuesday.

8.45 am

'OK, hope everyone's weekend was good? Anyone overindulge?' John, the branch manager asked.

'Not me!' Norma, I.T.

'Yes, totally.' Angela, Accounts.

'Failed.' Alan, Marketing.

'No chance with the kids, and the in-laws staying.' Gareth, Rep. for West Wales.

Please get on with it. I've got customers to see, traffic to argue with, and hours in solitary confinement behind a steering wheel, talking to myself. Not to mention the endless swapping of heels for driving flats between calls.

Grace glanced at her engagement ring as the conversation dissipated into the background. The meeting drew to a close as she studied the luminous stone, nestled up against a diamond-studded wedding ring. Not quite Tiffany, square-cut, pear-shaped, or even her best friend these days, but it still sparkled.

What's that Marilyn Monroe song about losing your charms? Get the diamonds, always get the diamonds.

Twisting her hand back and forth, she watched the tiny embers flicker in the sunlight through the boardroom window and wondered if they would ever ignite into a blaze again.

'OK, that's me done,' John's voice broke into her thoughts. 'Thanks, everyone. Time to get on with the business of the day.'

The sound of scraping chairs and sighs signalled time to leave. Grace tiptoed away via the rear loading bay doors, her feet moving lightly across weed-strewn broken concrete around the side of the building. Easing elegantly behind the steering wheel, laptop case flung onto the passenger seat, her heart raced as she dropped the sun visor to hide her face. Moments later she was out onto the main road, slipping into traffic towards appointment number one, a short drive to Thomas and Williams Industries.

Why didn't you wait and say hello? One quick, courteous hello? Well, I didn't. Get over it.

11.30 a.m.
WhatsApp/Mam

We've finally booked that last-minute cruise. I'm going with Amanda on Saturday, two weeks around the Med. No more of that testing either. Things are getting back to normal out there. Divorcees on tour can resume.

That's great Mam, chat later, bit busy here.
Don't forget your Euromillions ticket tonight.

She would buy her own while hearing peaceful birdsong through an open sunroof beneath a canopy of trees in her favourite pit-stop. As she loaded orders on her laptop, under a mirroring sky, it was a place of respite to retrace the events of the past months and replicate those arguments in her head.

'You'll never forgive me, will you?'

'I'm trying.'

'We have to let go of the past.'

'So I forget? Just like that?'

'It's the only way forward. If we can't, what do you expect will happen? We carry on living together because of marriage and mortgage certificates? I don't think it works that way, Cariad.'

You're probably right, Rhys. It doesn't work that way. It just doesn't.

Chapter 3

The previous Saturday Grace and her mother explored Singleton Hospital Car Boot Sale. They'd wandered along trestle tables set up to relieve people of unwanted tat, and giggled their way around a myriad of strange items people part with for cash. Her mother pointed to a chipped, fruit-covered dish someone once loved.

'I wouldn't pay a fiver for that!'

'Shh Mam, they'll hear you.'

'Well, that's ridiculous. Five quid. It's a Boot Sale not *'Bargain Hunt.'*

They'd wandered around for well over an hour buying nothing until her mother leaned over one table for closer inspection.

'Oh look, a lucky rabbit's foot!'

'A what?'

Her mother pointed out the once popular gambler's charm; a scrap of brown fur, nestled among a Pandora's box of old jewellery, formed into a brooch, with a thick metal clasp. There were other tarnished items, tangled necklaces, and a broken but elegant watch, ideal for evenings out if you didn't need to know the time. Alongside the box, a plethora of ancient items spilled across the table, seeking new homes.

'Let me buy it for you. It may bring you luck.'

Grace pulled an uncertain face.

'Is it real?'

'Of course it is. Ancient. Dead for decades. These things fell out of fashion years ago. It's no different to those fluffy things you girls buy to hang on your handbags, and most of them turn out to be real fur.'

Grace tentatively touched the softness of the pelt, sad to see this unloved sacrifice desolate at the bottom of the box.

'But Mam, I'm not superstitious.'

Her mother's face registered surprise.

'When you were a kid, you always whispered *White Rabbits* on the first of the month.'

She grinned and nodded.

'I still do!'

'Blame your Gran, she taught you. She was so superstitious. Ladders, magpies, birds, broken mirrors, new shoes on tables, everything. She had one. Do you remember? You played with it when you were little. She swore it brought her luck at Bingo, and to be fair, she often won a house or a line.'

Grace laughed, layers of childhood memories, and her blue-eyed, blonde-haired, good-humoured grandmother rushed back.

'I can't remember being that small, Mam.'

'Well, you loved that furry foot. You used to dance around the living room with it after you'd taken it off her coat.'

'I'll take your word for it. Go on then, you can buy it for me. It will be a family heirloom for us women. Gran owned one, you're buying one, and I'm getting one. I'll treasure it.'

The woman standing behind the offerings jumped in. 'Two quid love, else it's in the bin before I leave here. Just don't let the vegans see you with it. I've heard a few choice comments from one earlier.' An East-End accent burst into jovial laughter.

'Really? But it's ancient,' her mother pointed out, 'and you can't change the past, only the future. We can all help with that.'

The woman shrugged and nodded.

'In your Gran's day, everybody ate rabbit, it was plentiful after the war until myxomatosis broke out. Most organic, free-range meat you can get.'

The seller nodded in enthusiastic agreement.

'You seldom see it here, but in Spain, it's in all the supermarkets.'

'Most people on holiday are in hotels, though. They wouldn't need to shop.' Grace pointed out.

'Right luvvies, everything's gotta go today. I'm sick of dragging this stuff out every weekend. That's the trouble with the older generation. They keep everything and expect you to sort it after they're gone.'

Grace's mother laughed and nodded sagely. 'Yes, they make programmes about it!'

'It's my in-laws' stuff. Both of them gone within six months. Funeral déjà vu, I swear. Life's too short. *Do* things is my new motto. You never know when your world will turn topsy-turvy.'

Grace had been upside down for months.

'At least it will be a talking point, but it doesn't look much like a foot.'

Her mother smiled and held out a two-pound coin from her purse.

'If you don't know what it is, no. It's too old and compacted.'

'Here you go. Who knows, maybe she'll win a million on the lottery.'

The seller took the coin and tucked it in her money belt which hung weightily around her waist. She was having a good day.

'Blimey, luvvies, good luck with that!'

'You're far from home.' Grace's mother suggested. 'What brought you down from London?'

The woman smiled happily, tendrils of greying hair visible beneath a shady golf cap.

'We've been down here five years. Best move we ever made. We love Wales, and Swansea's our little secret. We don't ask the family down too often, in case they want to move in.'

The three women bonded briefly over shared laughter as Grace gingerly took the ancient charm from the jewellery box and studied it closely.

'Hang on!' her mother stopped her as she was about to attach it to her handbag strap.

'I think you're supposed to kiss it for luck.'

Grace pulled a wry face and shrugged.

'Oh well, in for a penny, in for a pound. Or in this case,

two.'

She lifted the furry charm to her mouth and pressed her lips briefly against it.

'Oh, I forgot I'm wearing red lipstick!'

'On second thought, I think that's dice you kiss. Never mind, it can't harm. I've got a tissue and some sanitiser in my bag. That should do the trick.'

Grace clipped it onto her handbag with a less than admiring glance as they strolled towards the next set of treasures displayed on trestle tables behind rows of parked cars.

'Cheers, gals!' the seller waved them off.

'Oh, I do love a Car Boot Sale!' her mother laughed, catching her daughter's elbow as they skipped forward. 'Shall we head down to Mumbles and grab lunch? And a Verdi's *Rustica* afterwards?'

'Lunch and dessert? Why not? It's all we ever seem to do these days.'

Parking was difficult in the village of Mumbles, a short drive from the city centre. Weekends, when the sun showed up, were always busy, attracting visitors from across the United Kingdom, particularly water sports enthusiasts. Small boat sailors filled the car parks and slipways. Windsurfers, fishermen, walkers, and cyclists descended on the once small fishing village turned trendy. With its bars, boutiques, and recent addition of Oyster Wharf, which housed Croeso Lounge and the eclectic Gin and Juice bar, its candy floss cocktail created a sunset in a glass; pink to match the vivid dusks across the Bay.

Popular Italian ice cream parlours Joe's and Verdi's drew crowds, while Dick Barton's fish and chip shop at nearby West Cross had been names on families' lips for decades. The once infamous Mumbles Mile, host of stag and hen parties, where totters became staggers along the route from pub to pub, covered hostelries of past and present.

Those days were in the distant past, and Mumbles maintained its upmarket feel despite its late-night venues. It captured a bijou mood, with boutique-style shops scattered among the fishing village streets, including Goose Island, Joules, and Sea Salt, with the eclectic art of Grey Dog Gallery tucked away behind the shops, and The Lovespoon Gallery, selling carved Welsh love tokens on a seafront corner.

With parking impossible in the shadow of twelfth-century Oystermouth Castle, her mother drove them towards the refurbished Victorian pier and lifeboat station and found a roadside space near the yacht club. Crossing the road with haste, they headed to Verdis, plundering a free outside terrace table before anyone else swooped in.

'Phew, that was lucky!' her mother laughed, settling into a chair and picking up the menu. 'What are we having?'

They ordered a light lunch to leave some room for dessert, taking in the view of Swansea Bay from the opposite side of the city. In the distance, the seafront blocks of residential buildings and townhouses of the maritime quarter mingled with the vista of the hills behind. The low-slung, youthful Secret Beach Bar and Kitchen lounged at the tide line, close to the clock tower of the elderly Brangwyn Hall, its interior filled with exquisite Empire panels, while the large Meridien Tower the latest high edifice forming the more modern seafront to the one written about by the city's famous poet Dylan Thomas.

While a light wind whipped around them, occasional drifts of Italian food and the scent of the sea filled their nostrils. Her mother's question came out of the blue.

'So, how are you two getting along these days?'

Grace shrugged and took a sip of wine, glancing around to see how many people were close enough to overhear. With the sounds of children, dog walkers, and cyclists passing, and the chatter from nearby tables, she felt at ease enough to answer quietly.

'It's not that easy.'

'It never is love. It's not something to flick off like fluff on a lapel.'

A motorbike revved further up the promenade, interrupting the moment.

'No, I'm just trying to get past it and see how it goes.'

'That's the wonder of choices, and without children, you're better off. Far more difficult to end a marriage when they're involved.'

Grace thought of her father, living in Thailand with a never-ending procession of girlfriends, but said nothing. Her

22

mother didn't need reminding of his exodus.

'I really don't know how I feel about him these days.'

'I know. It shows, love.'

'Does it?'

Her mother nodded, and a sad expression clouded her eyes. Her daughter's marriage was no longer on firm ground.

'By the time I get ready for work, do my calls, the paperwork, refuel the car, pick up shopping, and get home, I barely have time to think about it. If I worked in one place all day, I'd be stewing over it endlessly. I'm not sure if that's a bonus or delaying the inevitable. I'd love some 'me' time. To rent a house for a month, or even a caravan. Somewhere *different*. But that's all added expense.'

'Just don't rush into it. Although it's been four months, hasn't it?'

'Yes. Four endless miserable months, bang in the middle of summer, the best weather in a few years. All ruined by Rhys. If it wasn't for my nights out with the girls…' her eyes drifted off towards the promenade.`

'It isn't easy finding new love nowadays, Gracie, and you're too young to spend your life alone.'

Thoughts of living a single life, trying to meet someone using the dating apps which dominated her friends' lives, and of breaking apart a marriage of twelve years with the resulting upheaval, crowded in.

'I have a group of friends who would agree with you wholeheartedly. They've been looking without luck.'

And it's Rhys dismantling it.

'Have you been looking Gracie?' her mother longed to ask.

I might have taken a peek.

Chapter 4

Grace's takeaway coffee reached her through the window of the McDonald's drive-through, close to her penultimate call. Taking the offered cardboard cup, she nestled it into the drinks holder, then pulled into a space on the quiet edge of the car park.

I should have grabbed something to eat with this. I'll have a rumbling stomach in my last calls. I hate these make-up-for-Monday Tuesdays.

With time for some idle phone scrolling as she sipped, the sunshine filtered through the clouds, casting leafy shadows from nearby trees across the windscreen, and forcing a breeze to tickle her cheek through the half-open window. As the wafting aroma of ground beans tantalised her senses, the birdsong of a text notification broke her reverie.

Chirp/Rhys.

Sorry luv, asked to do Nights 2nite. Machine probs. This place gets more lethal by the minute. Curry 2moro?

Grace sighed. Nothing unusual there. These extra nocturnal shifts appeared with regularity in their married life. With a gentle knead of her forehead, she realised how lovely it would be to have the bed to herself tonight. As she'd lost him to the Bank

Holiday Monday, and he'd declined the Sunday lunch invite, he might as well be missing in action once again. *Bridget Jones, Singleton. One night only.*

Desperate to add *'behave yourself'* to her simple 'OK' response, she paused and left those two emotive words pricking at the tips of her fingers.

Ping
WhatsApp/CocktailsGroup

Who wants to go out on Saturday?

Dare I go out again so soon after last weekend? Do I even want to go out? It's summer's end. Make hay. He's seldom home, anyway.

Soon the savagery of winter storms would arrive to whip up the coastline and make one glance through the window a simple answer to any invitations. Visions of colder nights struggling in and out of rain-lashed taxis, wiper blades spraying faces, heels wobbling in the wind, dresses soaked below coat hemlines, while umbrellas hurled themselves to their death on leaf-strewn puddle-pooling pavements, made the decision easy. Winter was on its way, and it would be long and condescending. With a subverted smile, she tapped her response.

Count me in.

A host of red hearts and drinks emojis flooded the screen. Grace smiled broadly. It was great to have friends, even if they weren't *really* close. The option to get out and forget daily routine with a beguiling mix of fantasy and escapism was ever tempting. With busy lives, some with children and their endless after-school activities, it was no wonder they needed each other's company. And cocktails. *Porn star Martinis. Espresso Martinis. Mojitos. Negronis. Margaritas. Whatever happened to a glass of red or half a lager?*

The phone rang, and the office number flashed.
'Hi, Angela.'
'Can you talk?'

'Yes, coffee break outside MaccyD's'

'Lush. Burger?'

'No. I whiz through the drive-through and drink it in the car park. Saves time and money, and keeps me buzzed.'

'You're so organised, Grace.'

'I have to be with the traffic these days. What's up?'

'Can you go price up an extractor hood and trunking clean tomorrow?'

How exciting. Clipboard and measuring tape, mini stepladder, greasy residue, trouser suit day. Thank god the boys in overalls do the dirty work.

'Oh, and drop a brochure into a prospect today? It's near your last call. Make yourself known, flirt a bit, flutter those baby blues, and flick those tresses. I'll drop you *pins* for both.'

'What are you after with all these compliments? As if my job's not glamorous enough.'

'A prince. If you find one en route, give him my phone number.'

'Thin on the ground on industrial estates.'

A vision of bumping into a hunk from the history books wearing a crown, shoulder-length curly wig, and bejewelled velvet coat popped into her head.

Who knows, maybe he'll get his sceptre tangled in my briefcase in reception?

Angela carried on talking. 'Hey, Marcus is still here, and we're not *exactly* on Hollywood Boulevard, are we? He's going through loads of paperwork, and he's asked about you *again.*'

'Maybe he thinks I'm fiddling the figures.'

They chortled conspiratorially.

'Wasn't he on your table at the Ball?'

You know he was. Even though yours was at the opposite end of a long, disco-dark function room.

'Yes. He probably wants to say hello again. What do you expect with my sparkling wit and personality?'

'And those boobs in that green dress. You stole the show that night.'

'You've made my day.'

'It's your Catherine Zeta-Jones vibe. Dark and mysterious.'

'Right city, wrong gene pool. Catch you later.' Grace hung

up before Angela had time to respond.

He's been asking about you. Again.

Grace sipped her coffee, scrolling as she pushed away thoughts of how many it took to tango before an alarm sounded on her phone. She reached up and dropped the sun visor, pulled out a packet of pills from the hidden pocket, and with a quick swig from a water bottle, swallowed one, before sliding the foil away and flipping it back into place.

Ann's daily dramatics brought a Facebook grimace.

'I've got a sodding parking fine and I can't get into their system to appeal!'

A range of rude suggestions followed in the comments.

'Buy a bicycle.' Grace longed to write, finger poised, then dropped her hand. Beautiful, willowy Ann pedalling around the streets of her locality was a sight never to be seen. What would she do with Carys, tow her behind in a kiddie carrier? Ann wouldn't suffer helmet hair, waterproof jackets, and locking her transport to railings with those beautifully jewelled nails.

Grace studied her own fingertips. A classic French manicure only during work, sometimes Big Apple Red at weekends, or Flip Flop Fantasy coral for summer days. But never jewels. They wouldn't last a day slinging briefcases and handbags in and out of her car. Or swapping over shoes.

Skipping to Instagram, she scrolled down the page to watch a couple of cosmetic tutorials and some luxury travel reels. The longing to see any location apart from the regular views on her route weighed heavily. Her last beautiful overseas holiday was to the Maldives with Rhys, who grumbled about the travel time, and was utterly bored, stuck on an island walkable in ten minutes. Grace managed to survive the snorkelling, and some learn-to-scuba-dive sessions, but Rhys rarely paddled, fearing varieties of nasties touching his feet, preferring to sleep in the sun with a spy novel gathering grains of sand in its page creases as it toppled onto the beach once his eyes closed.

'The food was lush, and the sky was blue.' his only compliment when questioned.

Should have gone by yourself, Grace. Don't fall into that trap again. Although he looked great tanned.

Letting out a disappointed sigh, she switched to camera

mode and snapped a photo of the takeaway coffee with the steering wheel in the background. Adding a black and white filter, she posted it with the hashtags #ontheroadagain and #workinggirl. Scrutinising the angle, she smiled, pleased with her moody, creative result.

'Very Lee Miller.'

Then returned to her emails. Visions of deep blue oceans and beach bungalows drew her focus to the lottery message now back at the top.

Better check it and buy another ticket. It might be a few hundred pounds. I've never won that much. I better get Friday's ticket too. Have done with it.

Opening the App she logged in, and contemplated the morning's meeting. There was the usual pressure for better sales and more calls per day. Grace noticed Gareth looked uncomfortable throughout the half-hour as he covered a huge rural area, where making extra calls was impossible without nights away from home.

There was a notification in her inbox.

'We have news about your account. Please call us as soon as possible.'

Hmm. That's odd. Maybe there's a problem?

Half-heartedly checking the *account status* she found twenty pounds still showing. *Not short of funds. Maybe my card needs updating? I'll ring them anyway after I buy the tickets.*

Grace selected the Euromillions game and selected her lucky *Capricorn* number combinations of sixes, nines, and eights.

Five million. I can live with that. But someone's won a jackpot for it to be that low.

'One day you'll win big and it'll be too late to claim.' Rhys once chided her on finding an out-of-date ticket wedged among old shopping receipts at the bottom of a carrier bag.

'I'm juggling a thousand things. If a tiny scrap of paper escapes, it's no big deal. We're never going to win more than a tenner, let's be honest. It's all a pipedream. People like us never win big.'

'Well, others do, Cariad. Somewhere up and down the land, people are winning millions a few times a week.'

Eyes shining with mirth, she placed the palms of her hands on either side of his cheeks. 'Somewhere up and down the land, Rhys, millions are winning zilch every week.'

There was a laugh and a slow nod.

'Touche!'

'OK, I'll use the App. No lost tickets.'

Hope springs eternal and all that.

Do you want to play your numbers? flashed across the screen. Grace ticked the box, selected two games to cover the week, then remembered the lucky rabbit's foot. Reaching for her handbag, she gave the ancient dangling charm a quick stroke for luck, before pressing *confirm.*

Come on furry thing, I'm counting on you. Start manifesting, and fast. Fridays and Tuesdays are two of my lucky days.

You're in the draw! dropped into her inbox.

Thinking back to the meeting, she pictured Gareth's face; with two small children, his wife wouldn't be happy knowing he'd spend more nights in hotels, to be on his territory first thing, in an area often ninety minutes away. Wales wasn't easily accessible along the west coast and inland areas, yet plenty of customers lurked in those counties.

With her own area spreading from Swansea to the capital city of Cardiff, Newport, and the towns in between, fed by the M4 motorway, she seldom suffered winding, vision-limiting, hedgerow-high lanes.

Grace marvelled at how Gareth coped on those dangerous meandering routes, with razor-sharp bends where livestock appeared regularly in the road. Fewer calls but more driving, early starts with longer days, his week was man-made in her vision of hell. The scent of manure and farmyards was almost perceptible as she dialled the number.

OK, let's see what they want.

Fighting the notion that L&B may consider swapping their territories, Grace shuddered. John knew that Rhys often worked nights and there were no kids or pets to worry about in their household.

Oh no, surely not? That would be the final straw from the bale. Stop it, Grace, they wouldn't do that. Send a woman out to a lonely area, visiting desolate farms up rickety tracks. But even farmers need chemicals. I'll need wellingtons for the mud.

Rubbery, loose, cold flapping-calved boots.

It took a few moments before someone picked up. A woman's low, soft voice murmured down the line. 'Miranda, how can I help you?'

'Oh hi, there's a message in my app to ring this number?'

'One moment, please.'

Grace waited, overhearing sounds of conversation and phones ringing in the background.

'My name is Miranda Bayliss, I'm at head office. This is Grace, right? Your details are showing up from your phone number.'

'Ah, the wonderful world of technology and data protection,' she laughed. 'Is there a problem with my account? I've just bought two tickets for this week with no issues.'

'Yes, I can see that.' Miranda began 'I need you to answer a couple of security questions set up when you created it before I can discuss any details.'

'That's fine.'

Changing territories doesn't bear thinking about.

Winter nights in cold B&Bs with over-friendly landladies in the blast of the Irish Sea winds. Alone most of the week, suffering low-hanging branches, reversing in narrow lanes, cattle lorries, and tractors, and irate farmers waving sticks as her car blocked the pig pens.

How on earth will my marriage survive on top of everything else? Maybe I'll meet a rural man who smells of the fields, or a selkie will walk from the sea to bewitch me. I'll end up in the back of beyond wearing Laura Ashley prints and eating Perl Las cheese until I burst. While Rhys? Well, Rhys will be Rhys.

Miranda was speaking.

'Right, that's all good. Do you mind if I call you back on this number?'

'Great.'

Oh, please don't ask me to change territories. I think I'd have to leave.

The pitch of the ring, compounded by the car's interior,

captured in that metal-encased space, rang tinny and urgent. Grace almost dropped the phone in the urge to shut off the din, an edgy foreboding rising inside.

'Grace, I have news I'm sure you'll be very pleased to hear.'

Her responding laugh was anxious. 'Are you going to tell me I've finally won a hundred quid instead of all those *threes* I keep getting?'

Miranda's voice was calm.

'Yes, definitely better than three pounds… you're not driving are you?'

I foresee miles more in the future.

'No, I'm in a car park drinking coffee.'

Tingling apprehension amplified a notch.

Did I even buy a ticket last week? I was so busy, and I met the girls straight from work on Friday.

Miranda chose her words carefully.

'Are you alone or with company?'

'Alone.'

'Can I ask your location?'

'McDonald's car park, Fabian Way, Swansea.

Bit of a daft question. Why is my voice all croaky?

'Good. Please take a deep breath and put your coffee down, as we definitely have a hundred in winnings for you.'

Grace drifted somewhere above her body. Maybe it was a hundred thousand pounds?

A hundred thousand? Oh, my god. They can stuff their territory change if it is. I can afford to leave and find a job I'd love. Something not involving an industrial environment. Anything not involving an industrial environment.

'Oh, my god' she hissed and put the coffee in the holder. Pressing the speaker, she lowered the phone to waist level, hand vibrating.

'OK.'

'Grace, I have the absolute pleasure to inform you that you won one hundred million pounds on the Euromillions game last Friday. I assure you this information is correct.'

A hundred what?

There was a deep, thick silence followed by a heaviness in

her head and neck as a drifting sensation settled about her. Birdsong outside the partially open window frittered away into the distance, an imperceptible eerie rustle of leaves in nearby trees made the only tangible noise.

While her body sank deeper into the seatback, which morphed into a rising marshmallow wrapping its doughy arms around her, she clutched at the handbrake with her free hand.

Oh my god, I can change jobs. I can pay off part of the mortgage.

'We've been waiting to hear from you, Grace. Are you ok? Give yourself a few moments to let it sink in. I'll still be here when you're able to speak. Just breathe deeply for a few moments.'

Tick Tock, Tick Tock, time passes.

I never noticed how lovely coffee smells in a confined space. The woman…what's her name? Didn't she mention a hundred thousand? No? What was it she'd said? A million? Half a million? A hundred million? No way. They don't have prizes that big, surely? Yes they do, you know they do.

'Did you say a hundred million, a hundred *million?* Not a hundred thousand?'

'Yes, a hundred million.'

Breath filled the interior in short, gasping rasps.

I'm going to have to faint now. Or have a heart attack. Women have heart attacks, even younger ones. That's why she wanted my location. For the ambulance. But they take hours these days. I'll be dead. Dead with a hundred million.

A hefty Herring gull landed on the bonnet of the car with a dull thud and studied her with pale yellow, beady eyes through the windscreen. Birds are unlucky, her Gran always said.

But that's birds coming indoors. 'They bring bad luck and death.' This is just a seagull, and they're everywhere in Swansea. It's a seaside city. Go away, boyo. I don't have any chips. Check out the bins. You may be lucky. Just like me.

❧

Chapter 5

With a hefty flap of wings, the gull left the bonnet and the sound of Miranda's voice brought Grace back to the moment.

'Grace? We've been waiting to hear from you all weekend.'

A fretful Mambo rhythm began in her lungs, rising and falling to furious drums in her ears.

'Oh my god, oh my god.'

'Grace, please breathe slowly. Nice and deep, and slow, and keep listening to my voice.'

I am. Honestly. I just can't breathe.

'Grace, I'm going to call someone from McDonalds to check on you.'

'No, wait. Give me a minute.

Time passes, Tick-Tock.

'OK Grace, do you have any health issues?'

'No. Just stunned.'

Both of them heard a deep sigh.

'It's big news to take in.'

Breathe again, and again. That's better.

Now try to speak. Slowly.

'I never check emails over the weekend. I refuse to drag work home.'

Fuck, is this actually true?

'Quite wise, I'd say, these days. Especially over a bank holiday. You won the jackpot on Friday, with the only ticket. Therefore, the prize is yours in its entirety. Congratulations from us all at the Lottery.'

That's a precise answer. Businesslike. Not like a prank call.

'Fuck. Thank you. Sorry for swearing. But I don't think I believe it.'

Hot tears threatened, then vanished as she swallowed hard.

'Oh, I've heard much worse than that down the years, Grace. How are you feeling now? I need you to keep calm, and when we've finished our chat, I want you to sip your coffee until you feel able to drive.'

What is this woman's name?

Why can't I think straight?

'A room is being booked for you by my colleague, at your nearby Marriott hotel. Your home location is still Swansea?'

'Yes.'

'It's under my name, so for security reasons, please don't mention the Lottery. It's yours until tomorrow. This is what I suggest: you drive there and book in. Spend a few hours or the night. It'll be a quiet space for you to read the information I'll email shortly, and to mull over what's happened before you tell people. I *strongly* urge you not to do that yet, including partners, husbands, parents, and friends, but of course, that's your decision. You really need some hours alone to process this, and everything that will come with it. If you're working, I urge you to ring your boss and say you're ill.'

'Yes, I'm working. I'm a Rep. I've stopped for a coffee. But I think I need a drink now, a proper drink.'

'If you don't feel like driving, I'll call a taxi to collect you. Would you like me to do that Grace?'

Grace managed a mumble. 'A hundred million? Are you one hundred per cent certain? A hundred million?'

Miranda remained completely calm and confident.

'Yes, one hundred million. You are one of our top-level winners. Not our largest prize, but the record for Wales. Because of the amount involved, I will arrange for a team of financial advisors to assist you tomorrow. We can have them with you at the hotel by two o'clock. It is imperative for your own safety that you keep this to yourself until we explain the options to you. Do you have children Grace?'

'No, no children.'

'You need to think about publicity and if you want any.'

Grace sat up from her slumped position in the driver's seat, and screwed her head around, studying the car park for nearby customers. None near enough for conversations to be overheard, but she turned the ignition on and closed the window, regardless.

'No publicity, definitely no publicity.'

This is seriously scary.

One. Hundred. Million.

'Miranda, can you order me that taxi, please? I don't feel safe enough to drive.'

'Yes, of course. What colour and model is your car?'

'It's a blue Focus. Parked near the entrance.'

'No problem.'

As Grace listened to Miranda repeating instructions, she studied her partially drunk coffee, cooling rapidly, her body heat dissipated with it, softened, and she started to shake and chill despite the sun now toasting the windscreen. Closing her eyes, she tipped back her head and tried breathing deeply.

This is surreal. In a moment I'll wake up and find I've dozed off in the car. I must stop daydreaming.

Miranda broke the safety of silence.

'OK Grace, your driver will be with you shortly.'

'Drive'

'Sorry?'

'We call them 'Drive' in Swansea. Taxi drivers. Bus drivers. Cheers drive, thanks drive, drop me *by here*, drive.'

Grace shut up, you're talking complete bollocks. Miranda doesn't want to hear your 'Welshisms.' But we do. We call them 'Drive.'

Miranda's amusement was tangible. 'That's interesting to know. I suggest you turn off your phone for a few hours. I'm sending you the information to read through before tomorrow. I will be your co-ordinator, there'll be a cash package of ten thousand pounds delivered within the next couple of hours, in case you decide to run out tonight and buy yourself a new handbag.'

Miranda laughed and for the first time, so did Grace.

'There's nowhere in Swansea that sells ten thousand pound handbags.'

'The room is under my name, and it's paid for. It's up to you if you want to spend the night there, but with a prize this large, you really need to process this before telling anyone. I need you to absorb that. Now, what's my name?'

'Miranda. Is it Bayliss?'

'That's right Grace. Now, I'll call you back later, and if you need to speak to me this evening, I'll be on my mobile which is included in the email. This is a very exciting moment for you, but with such a large sum, I will reiterate yet again. You *really, really* need to hold back on your instinct to tell anyone, even husbands, partners, or close family. Please wait until you've found time to assess your circumstances. Don't worry about calling me anytime tonight, that's what I'm here for, so you can have a sounding board. You can wake me at midnight, I really won't mind. Are you ok?'

'I think I'm in shock.'

'Of course, you are. This is such a significant life event.'

'It's ludicrous.'

'And it's why people play. Lucky you, it's a dream come true. I'll stay on the line until the taxi arrives, then you can try to relax on the journey to the hotel. Don't forget to take your handbag and valuables and lock your car door. And if you feel at all ill later, please seek medical attention.'

'Thanks, Miranda, I think I'm ok now. By the way, I've just bought two tickets for this week's draws.'

'I can cancel them. Give someone else a chance?'

Grace let out a long, relieved breath.

'Yes, that might be a good idea. You may as well close my account too. I think the taxi is here.'

There was a brief silence and some faint background keyboard tapping.

'All done. Say hi to '*Drive*' for me.'

Oh, how embarrassing.

❦

The ride to the Marriott wasn't silent, not with a Welsh driver behind the wheel. When asked what was wrong with her car, he suggested which parts may have failed, and discussed the weather, and the state of the city's roads.

'I swear we have more bloody potholes than anywhere else in the country. We're famous for it. And the rain.'

Grace mumbled a few febrile responses as she switched off her phone, clutched her laptop and handbag close to her chest, and was relieved to raise her wobbly legs outside the vehicle as it stopped under the hotel's exterior canopy. She remembered to lock the car, and pick up those valuables but forgot her heels and the coffee, which sat three-quarters full in the cup holder, and the small bag of groceries bought between calls remained forgotten in the boot. The trapped heat would ruin the raspberries by the morning, and the milk would be undrinkable.

How did you forget them? What a waste of money.

As she scrabbled in her bag for change, the driver smiled.

'No need love, all paid for including a nice little tip.'

'Cheers, *Drive.*'

As she skittered into the foyer, a newborn quadruped taking those frightening first steps, Grace was indebted to her driving shoes and sunglasses. Little chance of toppling onto the tiled floor and ending up prostrate before the reception desk wearing flats.

Maybe next week I'll be tipping out of sports cars onto the cobbles of Monaco. Oh my god, oh my god, oh my god. Did my flights of fantasy really create this? Is this what Manifesting does? After five minutes on a beach? Or is it the rabbit's foot? What did my Mam say that day?

'Maybe she'll win a million?'

While her laptop and handbag transformed into mutilating creatures attacking her legs as she tottered toward the desk, Grace was beyond any sphere of control.

I really need to pee. Soon.

The receptionist smiled warmly.

'I have a room booked under Miranda.'

Grace raised a hand to her forehead, perplexed. 'I'm sorry, I can't remember her surname. She booked it in the last half hour.'

'Let me look. Ah yes, Miranda Bayliss. Room 316. You have a marina view. Here's your key, there's a lift to your left, third floor. Do you need a dinner reservation?'

It's barely three o'clock. Dinner reservations? I don't know what bloody day it is, never mind if I need a dinner reservation.

'I'm not sure.'

'Ring down when you decide.'

Another guest approached, luggage in hand, and his attention moved away. Grace continued her uninebriated stagger towards the lift and pressed the silver button, the urge for the toilet growing stronger. The door slid open, then closed behind her in one swift motion. Her reflection in the rear mirrored wall proved a shock. This wasn't the Grace reflected in the bathroom mirror this morning, with glowing skin, and muted lipstick. Below the unflattering downlights of this juddering metal rectangle, stared a pale, hollow-eyed doppelgänger. Pressing floor three, her eyelids dropped, as she fidgeted from one leg to the other.

I really need to pee. Like now.

Chapter 6

Spring.

The village pub on the edge of the city was lively on a Saturday night, the bar thronged with pint-holding males and screeching females, the jovial chatter rising high above comfortable levels. Spring was on its way and soon, the beer garden would open and the bar would become a quick stop to order and hand over money before drinkers would return outside to sit on wooden benches, hearing birdsong and basking in sunshine after a long winter.

A sleek bob-haired woman nursing a gin and tonic used the cocktail party effect to tune into a conversation between two men standing near her own little group, paying particular attention to the shaven-headed man giving his opinion to a younger tattooed companion standing alongside. Her ears strained when she heard a name and she focussed to listen over the cacophony.

'His wife's name's Grace. Beautiful girl, longish dark hair.'

'If it's the bloke I think you mean, he lives around the corner? The guy who works in the plastics factory?'

'Yes, that's him, he's often down the rugby club. Dark-hair. She drives a blue Ford Focus. Always wears a suit, I think she's a sales Rep. or a drug Rep. Something like that.'

'So what's been said, then?'

'He's shagging some young blonde. Single, got her own house.'

'Sounds ideal.'

The raucous laughter muted if only to avoid the women nearby overhearing, but being audible to the only one paying attention, now one-handedly swirling the G&T in annoyance.

'Yeah, but he's the one saying it on the factory floor. Stupid to admit that.'

'Is he telling everyone?'

'If he is, he's bloody daft. He told my mate. Gossip gets around.'

'What a twat.'

'Shame, really. They make a lovely couple.'

'Not for much longer by the sound of it.'

'Not if she finds out. He'll be out on his ear. Doesn't strike me as the type to put up with any nonsense.'

The woman contemplating the soggy half-moon lemon floating listlessly in her drink knew exactly who they'd been discussing. With a lift of a single eyebrow, she turned towards the bar and stuck out her glass. 'Can you chuck a few extra chunks in there please, beaut?'

A huge peal of laughter circled the bar from a large group of young drinkers as a loud blast of music shrieked from the wall-mounted jukebox nearby, drowning out the tinkle of ice hitting the glass.

Bloody hell, it's a small world. She raised the drink to her lips, took a sip then turned back to join her circle of conversation, mind in overdrive.

❦

Chapter 7

Grace chose a fabulous emerald satin gown for the Conference and Ball, which highlighted her eyes perfectly. *Blue and green should never be seen, unless there's red lipstick in between.*

Nimble, searching hands found it hanging elegantly on a rail in the Morfa branch of TK Maxx, hiding among a wafting selection of black evening dresses and gold lame bargains which spilled their netting and frills onto the dark flooring below. Marked down to the red label, lower in price than she'd hoped, it was a special find, a glowing treasure among the darker shades, perfect for a special function but too much for a *'girls' night out.'* Studying herself in the changing room mirror, she began a rare conversation with her inner voice.

'You look amazing. Those heels you grabbed off the rack work well.'

'They're only for trying on. I'll find something better before the Ball.'

'Lucky Rhys isn't going. You'll blow all the fellas away.'

'Think so? I could blow a few of them away. Hope that didn't sound crude.'

'A girls' gotta do and all that. Nothing wrong with a bit of vengeful humour, even if it's served hot.'

'You think I should get revenge?'

'Maybe if the chance comes up?'

'Give myself permission for a one-nighter?'

'Why not? He managed a few.'

'Four months' worth, but they were all with the same woman.'

'A lot more, then.'

'It don't amount to a hill of beans in this crazy world…'

'Please don't quote Casablanca. It's black and white and this is How green was my valley.

'That was in black and white, too.'

Grace gave a flounce, enveloping the satin folds around her.

'I can do Gentlemen Prefer Blondes? At least that's in colour.'

'Will you be Marilyn Monroe or Jane Russell?'

'Jane, I'm not blonde.'

'What have you got?'

'I like a man who can run faster than I can?'

'Love that line, but I'd have to tell him, to get real revenge.'

'Why? You'll know *and* keep the whip hand. Plus, have fun along the way. Go prepared, waxed, ready for action. Spray tan, just in case.'

'I'd never waste money on waxing. I couldn't stand the pain. The tan's easy, a Swansea necessity for posh events.'

'None of those Bridget Jones enormous knickers. Buy condoms, capiche?'

'You speak Italian?

'I speak the language of love. Now, buy it, hide it, and don't mention the Ball. Didn't you say it's masked?'

'We won't keep them on all the time.'

'No matter, but no gossip among the jabbering classes. Very *Bridgerton.*'

'Someone will remember me wearing this colour.'

'Make sure you're discreet. Leave at different times, different lifts. Oh, you're a big girl, you know how it works.'

'Thanks for your help.'

'The pleasure was all mine. If we can't empty his pockets between us, then we're not worthy of the name woman.'

'My favourite line. What a fab film that is.'

'I know. I've seen it as many times as you, remember?'

'Yes, of course, you have. We could do a song?'

'You and your celluloids. I don't have time for duets. I have to get home.'

'We could sing it in the car?'

'I'll be gone by then. You do both parts. Sing it for me.'

'OK. It's been great chatting, thanks for your input.'

'As long as you don't make talking to yourself too much of a habit. You know what they say about that.'

Grace bought the gown. It was far too elegant to be called an evening dress. Even the girl at the till was delighted to coo about its *gorgeousness* and how *fab-u-lous* she was going to look. Grateful it was a one-off, perfect fit that didn't cost the earth, and green and red were the finest of nature's complimentary colours, the online hunt would begin for scarlet or cherry accessories that evening. They would be stunners, head-turning, sequinned sparklers.

Real Ruby Slippers. Very Bougie.

We're not in Kansas now, Toto.

A mask, something exquisite and feathery, would follow. Perfect for a Spring event, and while red berries poked their heads through the hedgerows in autumn, the splash of vibrancy was going to make a stunning ensemble on the dance floor.

If anyone wants to dance with me. Surely someone will? Am I too old to wear this? Oh god, I hope I don't end up sitting alone all evening. Not in this frock. Maybe I should keep the receipt?

On the tail of the 1920 pandemic, dancing the Charleston awakened and ushered in the roaring twenties. Grace shuddered at the memory of 2020. The news updates, the three-word slogans, the distancing, testing, vaccines, and shuffling queues outside supermarkets. And the complete lack of social life suffered by everyone.

Rhys, however, came alive in the return of post-pandemic socialising. Well, and truly.

Chapter 8

When Grace opened the door to room 316, the first thing she set eyes on was an impressive vase of black orchids, orange-blooming chrysanthemums, black and sunset Calla lilies, roses and freesias. An ice bucket holding a bottle of champagne and a tray spread with edibles with no time to absorb before racing to the bathroom and sitting with a thump on the white toilet seat.

Relief came quickly, but as she stood up, unfamiliar rumblings in the pit of her stomach found her rushing towards the bath, where a moment later, she vomited into the base and fell to her knees on the tiles.

'Oh god, oh my god!'

Then the tears came, huge droplets adding to the mess below her head. She struggled up, ignoring the pain from her knees, a hand to her forehead, before emitting a wail towards the heavens.

'What the actual fuck? This can't be real. It can't be!'

You're swearing well today, Gracie.

But this is the day to go for it if you must.

I really think I must.

Grabbing the showerhead, she rinsed the contents of her stomach down the plughole with such attention to detail that she wondered moments later if she'd imagined it. Turning on the taps, she washed her hands and splashed her face as the tears stopped, and she glimpsed her mirrored reflection.

'You've won the lottery. You've won the lottery. You. Have won. The Lottery.'

She attempted delight. It denied the request. The shocked expression remained and regarded her grimly from above the washbasin.

Mirror, mirror on the wall, who's the richest of them all? You are, fright night, you are.

Smile.

The Joker from Batman scowled back. Velvet Teddy lipstick smeared her lower face, skin alabaster, suntan magicked away. Wiping it with a pristine white flannel adorning the washbasin, it resembled a muddied rag when she discarded it over the sink edge.

Nothing.

Common sense quashed the overwhelming urge to phone her mother or Rhys and tell them. Grace padded towards the bedroom and flopped on the edge of the bed, studying the flowers. Lovely flowers. Big, expensive flowers, but nothing resembling the ones she pictured that very morning. Her eyes mirrored the stainless steel ice bucket.

Condensation from the champagne trickled down the bottle into the ice below, a flow of icy droplets performing a slow dance along the dark glass. Two to Tango. Moet & Chandon stared back at her.

Drink me. Get one of those flutes and open me up. Do it. Now.

Grace did as the bottle insisted, shakily fumbling with the cork, exploding into a boisterous pop. Both hands held the heavy base as she poured a glass, and then took a sip. Which became a gulp. Followed by another. She drained it then refilled it with haphazard pizazz, the taste of liquid gold on her tongue, the sensation of lively bubbles caressing her throat as it swept into the depths, firing her insides.

There were chocolates. Smoked salmon and cream cheese sandwiches. Strawberries, grapes, and other goodies draped themselves temptingly across the tray, like the Rokeby Venus on her bed. She tasted a sandwich, then picked at the fruit, sipping more of the bubbly, twirling the glass. *An entire bottle of champagne to myself.*

Slipping off her shoes, she kicked them away. The laptop bag rested alongside her handbag, the rabbit's foot facing front. It seemed to look at her. A thudding ache spread across her forehead. *Pull yourself together, girl, you're losing it. Lay down and take a nap.*

As Angela cleared away remnants of the day's paperwork her eyes peeped once more at the corner desk, where Marcus was still going through files on his laptop.

He's certainly handsome, so well put together, yet not unapproachable.

'Would you like another coffee, Mr Bolt? Or are you heading off soon?'

Tantalising eyes looked in her direction, followed by a brief but informal smile.

'No thanks, coming to the end of it now. I won't be here much longer.'

Classy accent, expensive aftershave, a crouching tiger in the corner. He can jump me anytime.

'You're heading home, then? Long drive, is it?'

He stood up and stretched his arms above his head, stifling a yawn, that Italian jacket rising high above his slim hips, drawing her eyes down to his taut thighs and zip fastener. His masculinity was distracting, especially without a boyfriend on the scene.

'It's a long trip to the West Country in the morning. I'll probably drive as far as Cardiff. I know a few hotels there. I've never stayed the night in Swansea before. It never occurred to me. Any suggestions in case I change my mind?'

Don't even suggest showing him the town.

'There's quite a few in Swansea, depends if you want to be in the centre or not. The Dragon or Morgans are handy if you want a few drinks on Wind Street. There are a couple of travel lodges, or if you want to look at the sea, take a stroll on the seafront to stretch those legs. ' She paused. *'Your* legs, on the beach, the Marriott is right on the seafront and really near. Do you want me to have a quick peek online?'

'No need, but thanks for offering. I'll look once I've shut this down. Good to see you again. Until the next time. Laters.'

Angela watched him as the light blinked off, the lid was closed with a soft click and slid into his briefcase. He scooped it up and headed out of the office towards the car park.

That was it. Gone in a trice. But the casual way he one-handedly tapped the screen of his phone as he walked away impressed her. Effortless. Flexi hands. Flexi fingers. Angela shivered.

Bloody nice to see you again, too.
Until the next time.
Laters.
So English.

An hour later, Grace opened her eyes to the sound of rapping at the door, and with a meandering shuffle across the carpet, opened it. On the threshold rose a courier as he raised a package from a pannier at his feet. Clad in red and black padded leather, his helmet, visor upright, allowed his steely eyes to regard her dishevelled appearance, while one hand proffered an electronic device.

The wooziness was in full flow.

Ah, a knight in armour offering me a ring.

He should be on his knees.

'Here my lady, take this symbol of my eternal undying love for you, perchance some other prince appears with profound offerings to steal away thine eye and make ye his bride.'

You have GOT to stop daydreaming.

'Grace Lewis?'

'That's me.'

'I have a package for you.'

He held out a buff colour packet with his glove-free hand.

She received the offering gingerly.

'Sign here, please.' He pushed the device with its swinging pen towards her and she scrawled a slow signature on the tiny screen, avoiding his gaze.

'Thanks.'

He swept majestically away to his steed, leathers creaking. *Bloody hell, girl, just how much of that bottle did you drink?* Grace lifted the champagne to inspect the contents. Three-quarters gone. No lunch, only tiny nibbles of the goodies.

Oh well, in for a penny.

It was still chilled, despite the demise of the ice. She refilled the glass and set it on the bedside table before lowering herself onto the mattress and opening the package. Ten thousand pounds in cash fell to the floor. Picking it up, she studied the single bulky packet. Took another sip of champagne. Sat back against the decorative cushions. Slid off the large elastic band holding the notes together. Fluttered the pile as they do in seedy movies, creating a hefty, comforting noise; thick, airy, and rich.

Why does this feel so furtive? Like a drug deal? Brown paper packets stuffed with cash, in hotel rooms filled with champagne and flowers.

The gulls were busy outside, their muted cawing audible through the double glazing of this seafront hotel. As the lowering sun sparkled through the wide window, bouncing off the ice bucket and the discarded neck foil, the edges of her mouth twitched.

In one fleet gesture, the notes were high in the air, her arms outstretched to follow them, then cascaded around her head, fluttering onto the carpet, the bed, and settled around her like giant confetti. Some nestled jubilantly among the sandwiches and cakes. Yes, there were cakes. She could see them now.

Fairy cakes, with little angel wings, tipped with pink icing. Spectacular biscotti-adorned doughnuts, Red Velvet cakes, smothered in ermine icing. They were all there, disgusting, delicious carbohydrates designed to hook you for a lifetime with their artistic exteriors and enslaving taste.

Grace reached for one and studied its intrinsic beauty. This was going to be her life. Beautiful. A Fairy Cake. A fantastic old-fashioned fairy cake. Taking one glorious bite, she realised what lay ahead.

And there'll be icing on the cake. My life will be deep in icing, sugary sweet.

She smiled. And laughed. Flopped backwards on the bed. And cried again, all the time the mutter of her new mantra filled the room.

'Oh my god, oh my god, oh my god.'

When the tears finally stopped, she switched on her phone and documented the moment. The first was a selfie above her as she lay sprawled among the money. Next the cakes, the banknotes, the bottle, the cork, zooming in on alluring areas of the label, and the decorations on the icing. If there was ever an Instagram Moment, this was it. None of these would appear but she'd been desperate to save the memory before tomorrow stole the magic and they crumbled like a wedding reception at midnight.

Call me Miss Havisham.

What the Dickens?

Me and my crumbling wedding feast.

My crumbling marriage.

Then she filmed it, zooming in on the smaller details, capturing it all for posterity, the aftermath of being told she'd won the lottery. Plus one more photo, for luck. The last, a full length of the room, littered with notes, from the bathroom doorway. *Before someone finds the mistake at Lottery HQ. Before Miranda calls and apologises, asking for the ten thousand to be returned. But she promised it wasn't. Promises are made to be broken.*

You know that, Grace. Better than anyone.

'Maybe I could post the cakes? They won't be a giveaway. Everyone buys cakes.' She sought permission from an invisible audience, from the noisy seabirds outside. Selecting the red velvet, she lifted it, opened the Instagram camera, took a close-up, and posted it with the hashtags:

#redvelvet

#haveyourcakeandeatit

#inseventhheaven

Then she switched it back off again, fearing missed calls and messages. Ten minutes later, Grace gathered herself together enough to open her laptop. There'd been no need to phone in sick, she'd only missed her last call of the day. It was as the emails opened she realised she wouldn't respond to any of them. They would pass to the office, to be handled by her one-time colleagues, doubtless during endless gossip around the kettle.

'It was so quick. She just phoned in one morning and we never saw her again.'

'I wonder what happened, then? Maybe they've split up, and she's starting over?'

'She must have something lined up.'

'She didn't even drop the car off, got some bloke to deliver it and the laptop, and Voila, gone.'

'I'll miss her, though.'

'I got on well with Grace.'

'I wasn't so keen. All that makeup and those heels. Who looks that perfect every day?'

'Oh, come on. She was in front of customers all the time. She could barely face the punters looking like we do. Dress for success, isn't that the saying?'

'Well, that's nice, isn't it?'

'It's true. I can't be arsed to get up every morning, and make all that effort, just to come in here and answer a phone.'

Imagining the peals of laughter going around the first-floor office, she wondered if she'd miss the day-to-day banter.

Only I was never there for most of it. Alone on the road.

Me, myself, and I.

Grace settled down to read Miranda's lengthy email and understood why she was told to say nothing for the time being.

The phone at the bedside rang. It was Miranda. 'Hi Grace, how are you feeling?'

With a relieved sigh to be breaking her silence, Grace slumped back against the pillows.

'I've been better. I was sick in the bath. But now I'm surrounded by banknotes and drinking champagne. Please tell me this isn't a mistake. I'm petrified it's a computer error.'

'Grace, it's not. Can you switch your phone back on, and I'll call you on it in a couple of minutes? We don't want to chat on a switchboard system.'

'Of course. Give me a second.'

With the room phone resettled and the mobile rebooting, Grace topped up her glass and waited for Miranda's call, adding a single strawberry to the champagne and watching it fizz. The phone effervesced into life as she took a hurried sip and pounced on it.

'Hi.'

Miranda's smile shone through her words. 'Have you danced around the room yet?'

'No, but the money has. I did a *throw it in the air* moment.'

'Well done. I hope you're enjoying the champagne and feeling calmer?'

'I took a nap. I think I needed it.'

'Good. Now, have you read through the email and understood it? '

'Yes. It's terrifying.'

Miranda's sigh was audible.

'Well, there's an awful lot to go through. People think winning the lottery will enable them to make many people's lives better, but the reality is any gifts to people come with huge tax implications for those on the receiving end. Of course, you will need to open a few bank accounts in London. You daren't bank anything local. People talk, even those supposed to be under the Data Protection Act. One million might be a topic of conversation at a local bar for a night or two, but your win would be something else, don't you think? It can break friendships, and result in divorces where spouses can walk away with half. Especially those who might be close to leaving, anyway. That's why you need to meet with our financial advisors tomorrow.'

Grace listened as Miranda offered further advice, but her thoughts drifted to Rhys.

Divorce where spouses are ready to leave. Would he go now, if he knew about the money?

It finally dawned on her she couldn't possibly admit the amount she'd won. Even if she told him it was two million, he may still leave, taking half, to fund another lifestyle. From a legal aspect, the full amount would become known. Difficult to hide that sort of money in a divorce settlement. *Offshore? In another country? But how do you do that?*

'OK Grace, you'll meet the advisors at the hotel at two o'clock tomorrow. I've booked a small conference room for you, the Oyster Suite, just ask at reception. It's under my name, so don't mention the lottery. Once the meeting ends, they'll leave the area without speaking to anyone. No one will know your address or area. That's the way we operate for security reasons. Now, I think check out is at noon, so if you stay tonight, have lunch in the dining room before the meeting or relax in the lounge areas.'

'Thanks, I will.'

'Either way, don't say a word to anyone until after the meeting, and you're over the first shock. I can't be clearer on this. If it were only a couple of million, I'd tell you to go yell it from the rooftops, but with such a large sum, you must put your safety and security first. One of our advisors can help you make a Will tomorrow if you'd like. He'll have paperwork with him. You don't have to, however, I would advise it.'

Grace realised Miranda failed to ask if she was married.'

'Yes, of course. Thanks for your help.'

'Good night Grace, but remember, I'm here through until morning if you need to talk. Have no qualms, it's what I'm paid to do. Can I just ask how old you are, I think we sound about the same age. Plain curiosity on my part.'

Grace laughed. 'Let's say mid-thirties. No longer eighteen, but not the big 4-0 either.'

Miranda sighed. 'Yes, I thought so, although I'm closer to blowing out those forty candles than you.'

They both laughed.

'Thank you, Miranda, you've been amazing.'

It must be awful, dealing with all these huge wins. How do you handle it? Most people would be green with envy and fed up to the back teeth with it, especially when we're about the same age.

Alone with the champagne bubbles, Grace checked the time. Not yet a quarter past seven. *I could go down for dinner. On my own? Why not? You've done it in the past on training days. Go eat something decent, see some strangers, face a tiny corner of your new world. This is something to celebrate, after all.*

A table was available in fifteen minutes. Pulling on the despised driving shoes, she grabbed her handbag, collected up the banknotes, and folded a few hundred pounds inside the zip pocket. The rest went into the envelope, tucked in her laptop case, and placed in the wardrobe. The room, unlike her life, was orderly again.

Grace repaired her face, raiding her emergency collection of handbag miniatures, applying lipstick, and foundation from a sample pot, dusting her cheeks with an ancient bronzer. The small eyeshadow palette with the tiniest brush and travel-sized wand of mascara rescued her tired eyes, and she smiled to herself.

Be prepared. Waste not, want not. It's all in the little things.

Studying the results in the mirror, she decided she looked pretty good considering the red eyes and pallor of the past few hours. With a last brush of her hair and a spritz from a perfume sample, she headed for the lifts, wondering what Rhys was doing, and imagining his reaction if she called him.

'Rhys, come home. I've won more money on the lottery than you'd ever imagine. But don't say a word to anyone. No one.'

She saw him taking two minutes to find a quiet place to think, pacing the gents' toilets, or an unoccupied length of corridor, before the joy of the news would overtake him and he'd be bursting to tell someone. He'd grab his closest colleague from the factory floor.

'Don't breathe a bloody word to anyone, but we've won the lottery. Big time'

Then he'd bolt for home, but not before stopping at his mother's house, where his sister lived, with the same caveat.

'Don't tell anyone, and don't tell Grace you know, either!'

They would tell friends, and fellow workers, with the same admonition: 'Don't let on that you know! It's a secret!'

On it would go, the pact of promises, until it petered out into the general population with no connections to the original betrayer, and found its way into the local press.

'Record Welsh Hundred million lottery winner lives in Swansea.'

As she stepped into the lift, Grace realised with impending doom, none of this was going to stay quiet unless she did. This would need so much thought. The prospect was daunting. Rhys's imagined conversation, and his use of *'We've won the lottery!'*

irked as the lift door opened and she stepped into the foyer, almost completely under the control of Jean Moet & Pierre Chandon.

'No, Rhys,' she muttered as she tottered away to find the dining room. '*We* didn't win the lottery, *I* won the lottery.'

Just like WE didn't have an affair with the girl in the nightclub.

You did.

Chapter 9

'Whenever I drink champagne I either laugh or cry, I get so emotional! I love champagne.'

Tina Turner

The champagne worked its magic, enhancing her mood, as bubbles infused the spring returning to her steps, and the endless shaking of her legs dissipated, the knee pain unnoticeable. When she headed towards the restaurant at half past seven, it was with a calm smile and a hundred million reasons to be delighted despite the bland flatties and navy pinstripe work suit.

I wish I was wearing my confidence heels.

Grace steered towards the seats in the foyer, sat, crossed her legs, and unlocked her phone while her right foot twirled gently as she began an online search.

Kat Maconie shoes. This is a start. It may take a few days for delivery, but what the hell? And I love them. Buy British girl, at least for your first foray into exclusivity.

With her head bent in full attention to the screen, a gentle smile touched her mouth as her lips wobbled in muted conversation with the footwear sliding past her eyes, her fingers flicking through the webpage.

Up, down, up, down, back, stop.

'You'll do nicely, Rafi, in white and gold. Oh, and you too, Ola, dragonfly pink leather, and ribbon ties. In you go.'

Shh Grace, you're talking to yourself. Well, today I'm going mad. It's the proverbial first sign.

Add to basket. Go to checkout. Grab credit card. Pay.

Oh, my god, Gracie girl, you've spent over five hundred quid on two pairs of wild shoes in a couple of minutes. Ferocious, beautifully different.

Just like you're going to be. All new and shiny again. But now you need to eat.

'Your table is this way, madam.'

Beaming at the waiter in the Cast Iron Grill, she followed his outstretched hand, and stepped in the suggested direction, a brave Shakira swing to her hips, and a sparkle intensified her eyes.

My hips aren't lying tonight.

A whole new future was about to reveal itself before her, stepping onto the red carpet of happiness as it unrolled and flowed ahead, wearing those prized shoes. Life was about to become incredible, exceptional, wonderful, marvellous, a thesaurus of wonderland, and it began with two pairs of seven-centimetre heels and a rectangle of numbered plastic.

'Grace!'

The gait carrying her forward ceased to function. The muscles in her legs seized wilfully, and she came to an unexpected stop.

Oh hell, I know that voice.

Her eyes closed as butterflies beat their wings inside her chest. They fluttered slowly at first, which in a nanosecond turned into a ferocious flapping that rose into her throat, and as she lifted her lids and scanned the restaurant, she knew this place of respite, this secret corner where like Shylock, she should weigh her pound of flesh, was no more. There, at the far corner table, her eyes settled on a bemused, and surprised visage.

Not here. Not now.
Yes, here. And now.

In retrospect, it should have been obvious. The face smiling at her may not have stayed at a hotel *last* night but would book in somewhere tonight, following a full day at the office. The Italian suit trousers barely encasing those long muscular legs stood briskly upright. Her heart hammered loudly as they stepped in her direction, and in moments she was below a chin tilted towards her from a couple of inches over six feet, peppered with golden stubble from a long day.

Can he hear this thunder in my chest?

It's bonkers loud.

Snippets of sentences reached her through the whoosh of pulsating sensations making her sway.

'Grace. *Finally.* What are you doing here?'

It was a ridiculous response, and she wondered if the words really left her lips.

'I was supposed to meet a friend, but her son fell off his bike.'

Bloody hell, Grace. Where did you come up with that?

'Join me then, if you're not waiting for anyone else?'

He glanced towards the entrance.

Maybe he's expecting a husband. My husband.

'Just me now.'

He led her towards his table with a gentle hand and eased her into the spare seat before slipping back into his own. Grace stared, further words obsolete. Those eclectic blue-patterned, black-edged beauties crammed in her throat, her mouth, choked off speech.

'Grace, are you OK?'

What the hell day am I having? I'm likely to collapse with all these shocks.

With a rapid nod sending the flutterers retreating into her chest, tiny wings flapped slowly as they roosted around her ribcage.

Breathe. Or you'll faint.

Seek medical attention, Miranda said.
I might need the kiss of life.
And I know where from.
Just look at him, Gracie.
Look.

The airy flutters allowed breath to flow.

'I'm fine, honestly.'

The waiter returned with a place setting, menu and wineglass, and a warm smile which provided a brief distraction, before leaving them to face each other.

'It's so good to see you, Grace.'

This isn't happening. Not tonight of all nights.

'Good to see you, too. You're staying here?'

Great. You managed a statement and a rhetorical question.

'Yes, I'm off down south tomorrow. Far easier to book in here and get an early start. It's been a long day. Wine?'

He lifted a half-carafe of white on the table, smiled, and waited for her nod of agreement.

'Just enough here for us both. Two glasses is my limit during the week.'

'That's fine, thanks.' She took a deep gulp.

I must have missed him by the lifts. Would I have followed him if I'd seen him?

'How've you been?' he asked.

'OK. How's life in England?'

Marcus turned off his phone and slipped it into his jacket pocket.

'Constantly clocking up the miles, but no matter how far I drive, I seem to keep missing you. You vanished again today.'

'I didn't know you were here, or I'd have said hello.'

He raised an eyebrow, a flash of uncertainty in his eyes. Gentle heat tinged her cheeks.

Being bold with the truth, Grace? But it's lovely to be this close again.

'Are you sure you're not avoiding me?'

'I'm not in the office much.'

'So I keep hearing. I hoped to see you today.'

'Really?

'Yes, Grace.' There was a visible breath as he prepared his

next words. 'Since the night of the Ball, I can't stop thinking about you.'

This is quite an announcement. Does he know what he's saying?

Hopeful eyes looked into hers, like a child standing by a Christmas tree, flickers of fairy lights dancing in their depths.

'It was an amazing evening, wasn't it?'

'Yes, it was.'

Grace downed another gulp.

Slow down, you're going to choke, cough, and spill it down your front. Not a good look.

'Never heard of Alexander Graham Bell?'

Marcus leaned in, green eyes mesmerising.

The butterflies prepared for rapid take-off.

'Ouch. I didn't think you'd appreciate a call. I've been hoping to bump into you every time I come down here.'

'You could have sent me a friend request?'

'I don't do socials. It's frowned on for management and I edge on career driven.'

'I thought there was something wrong. Last one in, first one out syndrome kicked in.'

Marcus sighed and sat back, watching her reaction to his next comment.

'No, nothing to worry about on that score. Excuses to come to Swansea.'

'Really? Hoping to see me?'

His head tilted as he pulled a wry face and spoke slowly. 'Every single time.'

Mirroring his body language, she sat back.

'I don't know how to react to that.'

Yes you do, you liar.

You're bloody chuffed.

Marcus took a sip of wine and rolled his tongue around his teeth, looking thoughtful.

'I heard a few comments about my monopolising the Green Goddess that night.'

Grace looked perplexed.

'Your amazing dress.'

She pulled a face. 'And the fitness woman?'

He laughed. 'It's also an ancient fire engine. But that's a joke, honestly.'

Remembering Angela's earlier compliment, Grace smiled.

'You could have called me *Sam Tân,* so I guess Green Goddess is an improvement.'

His brows furrowed above his nose.

Grace giggled. 'Welsh for Fireman Sam. He has his own TV series.'

His face burst into a relieved smile, but his voice grew serious.

'I hoped you'd make contact, Grace.'

He's using my name repeatedly. Like he's enjoying saying it. I haven't used his once.

Blue eyes switched up to glaring high beams as she looked directly into his, and her voice took on an edge to match. 'Your last words were *'Drive safely.'* I remember them well.'

Marcus grimaced as a hand stroked his rough chin.

'Sorry. I could see the staff newsletter headlines: *National manager predator of married sales staff.'*

Grace dropped her head, sweeping a gleaming curtain of dark hair around her shoulders.

'I get it. I really do.'

His voice lowered, and his eyes followed.

'I've also heard a rumour that things aren't so great for you at home?'

How? How has he heard a rumour? Angela? The office gossip? Has it shown on my face?

'Well, we're here now.' She deftly changed the subject and picked up her glass, agitation obvious as she lifted it to her lips.

'Are you OK, you look pale?'

'It's been the strangest day.'

'Sounds ominous.'

'Completely the opposite, and now you appear.'

'I hope that's meant in a good way?'

Grace studied his face, those handsome masculine features, as the mix of wine and champagne tempted her towards gold-flecked eyes. Her annoyance vanished, and she wanted only to lean across and touch that taut summer-tinted skin with her fingers, her lips, before autumn faded all trace of that glow.

'Yes, in a good way.'

I'm sitting with him again. This can only be good.

His teeth caught his lower lip gently. 'Glad to hear it. Now, I'm paying for dinner on expenses. We're both employees, are we not?'

For today, at least.

Until I make the call.

'Thanks, I'm starved.'

Marcus studied the menu, eyes moving with speed over the flicked pages. 'Endless options. Why don't they offer you three things? We have too many choices these days. Give me a cave and a mammoth to chase, such an easier way to live.'

'But you'd need a spear, and there wouldn't be a chef putting it in front of you.'

He shrugged, nodded, and between them, they settled on steak and chips.

'I'll get us a bottle of champagne.' Grace began. 'I've heard some good news and I want to celebrate.'

'Anything you can share?'

'Maybe later.'

I doubt I can ever share this with you. You'll walk out that door tonight and we'll never meet again, and it won't matter how many times you visit the Swansea office, I won't be there. But at least you can use the visitor space. I won't be needing it.

'OK, fair enough. I can't drink too much, and we're both working in the morning. You're getting a taxi home?'

'That's how I arrived.'

Fleeting curiosity flickered across his face.

'Well, it's nice to see you in your working clothes, instead of that satin number. Who could cope with that on a weeknight?'

Grace laughed vivaciously, relaxing, a sound that brought a lingering smile to his face.

'You're gorgeously normal tonight.'

'I sell industrial products. Completely normal. Super glamorous.'

'With your lovely Welsh accent, you can charm the sales out of thin air. Industrial products *need* you. You know they did a survey once that said the Welsh accent was the most trusted in the UK?'

'But can they understand us? We speak *fast.*'

'Yes, you're hard to follow now and then, but if I miss something, I'll just gaze into your eyes and hazard a guess.'

'You're such a *player,* Englishman. I'd forgotten how cutting-edge your chat is.'

Marcus laughed, perfect teeth visible, white and gleaming, jawline firm.

'Englishman.' He considered the description. 'I like it. But two can play that game, Welshwoman.'

'Hmm. I see what you mean. I like it too.'

They fell into a natural pause and sipped the wine, while the waiter brought the champagne. Marcus watched her closely as the cork popped and the fizz hit their glasses with that delightful sound heard by brides and grooms worldwide. Grace raised her glass.

'Cheers, and you're right, things aren't great at home.'

Careful girl, this is the booze talking.

'They've been dire.'

Well, that's too much info. What are you thinking? Doesn't matter, you won't see him again. Spill the tea and ease your aching heart. You have someone to talk to. Talk.

A hand reached out to rest on hers. The touch of his warm skin created an exhilarating fizz of its own. His eyes dropped to examine her fingertips.

'I'm sorry to hear that. Hopefully, I can cheer you up.'

'Go for it.'

A smile touched the corners of those magnetic green eyes.

Why is he so bloody attractive?

'I keep thinking about that night. We had such a great vibe.'

His hand remained in place. She breathed deeply and slipped her fingers to interlace with his in a tingle of excitement.

Bloody hell champers, what are you making me do now?

'Me too.'

'Really?'

Why lie? You thought about him endlessly. It eased you through the troubles.

'I think you're lovely, but I told you that.'

Firm fingers tightened around hers, as his thumb gently stroked the back of her hand, creating delightful sensations. She lounged back provocatively, eyed him up and down purposefully, and winked.

'You're not so bad yourself. Do you have a licence for that lot?'

The moment collapsed into frivolity as they burst into loud laughter.

'You're funny. I love that about you. And those eyes. Incredible.'

'Why thank you, kind sir.'

Marcus let go of her hand and leaned back resolutely in his seat, matching her body language.

Thank god. I've drunk so much champagne, I can barely keep the edge off all this excitement. And he 'loves' something about me.

'Now, would you like a starter? Gigantic, wildly expensive prawns, hand caught by shimmer-skinned mermaids in the south seas and smothered in buttery garlic?'

The vision of a plate of delicious shellfish appeared as hunger grew beneath the alcoholic shield. Despite nibbling on cakes and filling up on fizz, lunch failed to materialise following a miniscule breakfast. A distant rumble growled in her stomach.

'Only if we both have them.'

A subtle lift of an eyebrow traced his face, as their eyes met. Was that a knowing smile he was hiding?

'Deal.'

'Marcus.'

I've used his name. It felt good.

'Yes, Grace.' His face beamed.

'I'm resigning in the morning.'

Well, that was a cracker.

You don't half pick your moments.

❧

Chapter 10

Grace studied Rhys carefully in the weeks following the letter's arrival while telling herself incessantly it was a covetous neighbour peeking behind curtains, someone who despised seeing her dressed in a smart suit, driving a company car, and wanted to tear her life apart.

It's not true. It can't be true.

Yet her seldom-heard deep inner voice, the natural instinctive whisper, would come close to her ear at unexpected moments, with words of warning and questions.

Why haven't you asked him outright? Because he'll lie. He's a man. They lie when cornered. It's nature's way. To fool women.

He's up to something. You know he is.

The way his back turned towards her each night in bed. A scarcity of enthusiasm on those occasions when she invited intimacy, a dearth of reciprocal interest, deprivation of contact and the immediate release of embrace any woman would know. Rhys was absent from their union for many weeks.

Checking his text messages was simple, and for close to a month, revealed nothing. He was frequently tired after work, and asleep on the sofa alongside her, his phone in full view on the coffee table, empty beer glass alongside. All she needed to do was reach out and gently lift it, scroll through quickly, and replace it before he woke up. The screen pronounced its innocence nightly.

Then came a message of consequence. It arrived while Wales Captain Gareth Bale was on the local late-night news, as celebrations of his double-winning goal in the Welsh football team's World Cup Play-Off the previous evening continued. Amid images of celebrating fans in a sea of red flickering across the screen, Rhys' phone mirrored the reflection. The briefest flutter, but enough for Grace to reach over furtively and pick it up.

Sorry I couldn't make it tonight. Are you OK for tomorrow? I miss you already.

Grace read the dropdown screen. The physical text remained unopened. Rhys wouldn't know she'd seen it. There was no time to scribble down the number as he stirred and she slipped it gently back into place. He woke fully, stretched, and yawned.

I miss you already.

My god, this is serious.

His original plan of going to the pub on Friday altered unexpectedly.

'I'm staying in tonight, Cariad. I think I had enough to drink last night.'

She forced a response. 'I think everyone in the country did.'

The previous evening they'd walked to the 'local' to watch Wales' World Cup qualifier against Austria and celebrated among a bar full of loudly singing and cheering people, the noise, excitement and pure *Hwyl* as the country's dream of qualifying for the biggest football event in the world drew a step nearer.

As Grace returned from a halftime visit to the *ladies,* someone said a brief *'alright'* to her, then asked how she was. He didn't seem familiar, but she acknowledged with a nod and a smile.

'You're Rhys' wife, aren't you?

'Yes, sorry, I don't know you, do I?'

'Nah, love, but my mate works with him. Everything OK, is it?'

It was an odd thing to ask, but she made light of it with a distracting comment and passed him by.

'Yes, with Gareth Bale at the helm, everything will be fine.'

Grace found Rhys in ribald conversation with some local men and caught the tail end of his sentence as she stood at his side.

'... off that programme, have you seen the shape on her? She's had loads of work done, but fair play, boys.'

Grace flinched as his companions shuffled awkwardly. Rhys placed a guilty arm about her waist, a rare behaviour. The comment hung tenuously in the air. Wives weren't supposed to hear their husbands discussing the sexual attributes of other women, not even in jest.

He turned his attention back to her. 'One more game, and we're through Cariad. Exciting, isn't it? Just think, the last time Wales was part of it, neither of us was even born!'

Her reply was wooden as the sting of his celebrity swooning hung in the air. 'I don't think even our mothers were born in 1958.'

He'd sung a few tuneless lines from *'Yma o Hyd'* as they headed home through the lamplit streets, elbows interlinked to hold them upright, red scarves keeping them warm on the walk.

'Ah, it's a great official song, isn't it?'

Yes, but who decided on those awful bucket hats?'

'I'll give you that, but fans will buy anything to look tribal.'

As Rhys stretched on the sofa, rubbed his eyes and made noises about going to bed, Grace remained motionless.

He's having an affair. My husband is unfaithful. What do I do now? I can't confront him. I need to think. Why do I feel sick? Because he's sleeping with another woman. Gracie, he's not sleeping. You can't call it sleeping. Not until the aftermath.

Her hands dug tightly into the corners of the cushion alongside as she visualised him, arms wrapped around some faceless woman, eyelids closed, snoozing in unfamiliar bedding, in an unknown bedroom.

The cushion, a beautiful Klimt-Esque print in rich tones with the texture of brushed velvet, comforted her in its soft mound. The fibres, dense with the aroma of upholstery and perfume residue, softened as she hugged it tightly to her chest. Grace caught sight of her face, framed above the single closed eye and golden flowing tears on the material, in the mirror on the opposite wall.

Oh my god, it's me. I'm the woman with the golden tears, still waiting to be shed.

If she tackled him now, furiously demanding he call the number on speaker so she could hear the responses, the *four horsemen* would bolt free and ride her down into despair. Despite the rising panic growing from the seat of her chair, which coiled its way up through her shaking body, and forced her hands into tight balls ready to punch the cushions, or the coffee table, she held her ground.

This needed a considered response before the furore of retaliation took over and scored an own goal to end their marriage. The ensuing screaming and throwing of items into the street at midnight, while neighbours appeared on their doorsteps to watch, needed avoiding.

He scooped up his phone. 'Don't be too long.'

'I just want to hear the weather forecast.'

Did he notice the tightness in her voice, how firmly her jaws clamped together as she spoke? Was he aware of the terror and fury building inside?

Why would he? How long has he been getting away with this? At least two months, maybe longer. It takes time for affairs to become common knowledge and the letter arrived a month ago. Everybody's laughing at me. Do my friends know? Was it a friend who sent it? Are the neighbours discussing it over coffee?

And who is she?

Grace dropped her head into her hands. Were there sympathetic glances from people in the street? Odd comments on nights out? Nothing came to mind. Tears refused to fall and her cheeks were still dry when she finally padded softly towards the bedroom three-quarters of an hour later.

With a Medusa-like glower in his direction, she found him deeply asleep beneath the watchful glare of the red-eyed laser ceiling clock above the bed. The fork-tongued serpent coiled on charge along her dressing table, its black tail side winding along the glass top, undulating with a virulent malignant slither towards the wall socket. With stealthy steps she pounced from above, a silencing palm forcing it flat as her free hand jerked the tail from its body. Sliding silently away, she held the hissing, spitting, venomous viper firmly by the neck at arm's length, until snared in the darkened cage of the en-suite.

Everything had vanished. No record of numbers received, a clean call history and notifications deleted. She opened his photo gallery and flicked through. A few from rugby matches, a couple of joyous victory scenes from the pub the night before as the final whistle blew, and some much older shots. Rhys wasn't a recorder of events, neither humdrum nor prolific. Nothing to see here. Move along now.

Grace barely slept, creeping downstairs as the ceiling creature shone 02.47 into her restless eyes, to hide under a sofa back throw, her only company the twenty-four-hour newsreader at whispering volume.

You never lock your phone. Hidden in plain sight. On the ball, boyo, you're on the ball. But you may have just blown the whistle for the end of our marriage.

Chapter 11

Discovering his destination needed the help of an unused smartphone, still up to date and nestled in its box in her wardrobe. A tracker app, the mute button, and a secretive slide into the rear of the driver's seat sleeve, followed by days of checking for unusual journeys finally produced an evening where it revealed an unknown house on a street unrelated to their lives. Rhys always casually refused the 'find my phone' option. Now the reason was obvious.

With the shakiness in her legs growing, a sneaking vibrato with a hollow sensation in her abdomen joined in. Not knowing if she would find the right house, or if he parked directly outside, she hoped his car may lurk somewhere nearby. She'd sit and wait further along the street for him to come out of a door. Any door.

Finding the property in a suburb of the city was simple with her own Sat Nav, but there was no sign of his car nearby. Pulling up outside and garnering the courage to get out and walk those few weed-covered steps to the flaking front door was more difficult.

What would she say? What if a man answered the door? This woman may be married too. Maybe they were having a tête-à-tête when the husband was at work? Maybe it *was* innocent, and he'd gone to pick up an engine part spotted in the small ads. Deep inside, she knew there was no part. Just an aching void where a rhythmic piston should be pumping.

Grace stepped out of the car, her hated flats flung into the passenger footwell, the confidence-boosting heels fumbled into place. Breathing deeply, she smoothed down her jacket and strode purposefully towards the door, silently counting 5-4-3-2-1 before she pressed the dirty white plastic doorbell and took one unsteady step back, the grey heels wobbling beneath her.

The silence was profound. No birds, no traffic, no voices.

No answer.

Are they upstairs? In bed? Am I going to interrupt them in the act?

She pressed it again, a sharper intake of breath, and held her finger there, as one leg jiggled dangerously on a heel. It was Friday. With her hair smooth, make-up perfect, a favourite light grey suit dressed her shapely frame.

Once her morning calls were complete, and Rhys took the day off, this would be a perfect opportunity for daylight cheating. Unless this *Aphrodite* worked Fridays, too. With no way of knowing anything about this creature, Grace stood defenceless on the doorstep of the goddess of affairs.

Pressing the buzzer once again, she peeked up at the bedroom windows, seeking the twitch of a curtain. No visible movement. *They must be together now. Surely they'd make use of every given minute together? Perhaps he's taken her for lunch, spending our hard-earned cash?*

As she turned to leave, a weak, breathy voice came from the house next door. 'There's nobody there, love. She went out earlier.'

A much older woman stood on her front steps, arms crossed, smiling at her. 'Do you want to leave a message with me?'

Grace's lip wobbled. Tears stung her eyes and then tipped

into a deluge, overflowing onto perfectly blushed and contoured cheeks, hot and salty as they dripped over her top lip into her mouth, streaking her immaculate foundation as the washing machine in her stomach grumbled towards full spin.

The woman's expression altered, and she held out a beckoning hand. 'Oh dear, are you alright? Do you want to come in and have a cup of tea with me?'

Then came the briefest of moments, the time needed to raise a hand, and rub it across a wet nose before loud wracking sobs released themselves into the quiet of the street. Words followed, poured out in great gulping cries amid a flood of relief.

'I think whoever lives there is having an affair with my husband.'

There. I've told a stranger. Oh, my god. So much easier than breaking it to a friend.

The neighbour's smile faded, and she edged slowly towards Grace, reaching out a fragile hand to encourage her forward. The woman took her elbow and steered her towards her own door.

'Come on in love. We'll have a cup of tea and a chat. I'd offer you something stronger, but I can see you're driving.'

Grace nodded.

'Just let me get my handbag. I'm going to need to repair this mess.' She stepped towards the car.

I could murder a double gin.

I could murder.

Grace found herself sitting in a comfortable, if ancient, purple armchair, holding a shaking mug of tea. It arrived in a china cup and saucer, but the tremor rattled it so badly it spilled into the base, and a fresh brew followed in a sturdier option. The faded face of Elvis Presley drew level with her own with each sip.

I'm all shook up.

'You've got the best mug in the house, my dear. I love Elvis, he always cheers me up. Now, tell me what's happened. My name is Deidre, but don't feel you have to tell me yours. Your secret is safe with me.'

Settling herself into the matching velour chair opposite, Diedre gave a sympathetic smile, smoothing the soft pile of the armrest with a veined hand. Grace appreciated the kindness shown by this stranger, who lived next door to the woman who was probably sleeping with her husband.

The absurdity is complete.

'I've tracked his movements and we don't know anyone in this area, yet he was there yesterday for four hours.'

A single tear dropped into her tea while she caught the other one with the edge of her hand.

'You can do that these days?'

Grace's head bobbed.

'There's not much you can't do these days, with technology.'

'I wish I could have done the same when I thought mine was having an affair. He was, by the way.'

She looked closely at Deidre. Somewhere among the white hair and lined, thin skin was a pair of bright blue eyes that once looked out from a face not dissimilar to her own. A youthful, attractive face, which laughed, winked, and once went dancing. A face which loved and felt all the jealous hurt Grace now writhed within the throes of.

'Did you stay together?'

'Only for the sake of the children.'

Deidre nodded towards an ageing framed photo of a boy and a girl in school uniform.

'But he's been dead for over a decade now. And if it helps, I caught him out a few more times down the years.'

'How awful. I'm sorry to hear that.'

This wasn't good news. Not at all. Grace studied the backs of her hands. Still youthful, clear of mottling and age spots, unlike Deidre's.

'Yes, dear, some men get caught and don't do it again, knowing they were lucky to get another chance. Others? Well, I think it's built into them. Serial womanisers can't help themselves. My Jim was the same until he fell ill and needed me to look after him.'

'Yes, seems that way, doesn't it?'

'Have you had it out with him yet?'

'No, I wanted to see where he's been first, just in case it was something else, like buying a lawnmower.'

Grace laughed as she heard how utterly preposterous it sounded. Deidre gave a sympathetic nod. Clutching at straws was easy when these things happened. How well she remembered *that* feeling. It never went away, despite forgiveness.

Grace was fervent. 'Does a woman live there? Is she married?'

'Yes, a young woman lives there. No husband, or children, but there was a boyfriend who left last autumn. She's been on the loose ever since. Out at discos till all hours, men back and forth. I swear I have no idea how many boyfriends she has. Obviously looking for the best of the bunch.'

Grace looked shocked.

'Really? So he's not the only one?'

'Fraid not. She's the talk of the street. Times may change, but gossip never does in an area like this. When houses are close together, people see everything.'

Grace slumped back in the chair and set Elvis down on the coffee table.

Heartbreak hotel.

'Oh my god, what's he got himself into?'

And worse still, what might he have caught? And passed on to me on the rare occasion he comes anywhere near.

A Spring chill caused a shudder.

'Well, put it this way dear, if he's got you, and he's seeing her, he must want his head read.'

The words soothed her momentarily.

'Does she work? What can you tell me?'

'Yes, in a local supermarket, and her name's Sian. I don't really see much of her. Shame really, her boyfriend was a nice chap. I think there were a couple of kids already, but between you and me, I think he went back to her. Money worries and those kiddie payments they make all got too much. They think younger girls will take them back to their youth. He used to mow my back lawn now and then, if the Age Concern people weren't due. I like it looking neat. I think he was miserable in the end, so he upped and left. Never even said goodbye, but I suppose in the heat of the moment, the last person you're thinking of is the old woman next door.'

Grace nodded repeatedly, absorbing her words.

'But that's all I can tell you about her. Pretty girl, slim, but not a patch on you. You've got class, dear. She's not in your league.'

Grace stood up quickly. 'Thanks for the tea and chat, Deidre. It's helped me immensely. Can I use your bathroom? I'm a mess.'

Deidre led her to the downstairs toilet.

'I don't know what to tell you, my dear. It's difficult to know what's best. If you don't have any children, then maybe teach him a lesson and throw him out. Trouble is, you could drive him straight into her arms, and there's a ready-made house there for him. Or just pretend you don't know and see if it fizzles out. But whatever you do, do what's best for *you*. There really are plenty more fish in the sea, you know. Great big shoals of them.'

The words rang true as Grace left the house, make-up refreshed from her handbag miniatures. No trace remained of the torrent of tears. She waved for the last time as she slipped into her car, but Deidre was gone, no doubt to get the king washed and back onto his throne on the middle shelf of the Welsh dresser taking up the best part of one living room wall.

Wondering if she would ever end up living surrounded by chintz, china cat figures, and superstar mugs, she pressed the ignition and lowered her sunglasses down from their place on her head. As her finger pulled back, she caught sight of a blonde girl walking towards her along the pavement, carrying a small plastic supermarket bag, and immediately pressed it a second time to turn off the engine.

Is this her?

The tingling sensation creeping along her neck and arms suggested it might be. Grace watched until she saw the telltale lean of her body towards the steps leading to the house and jammed the window button. Leaning her head out, the shakiness and bravado coming so fast it was surprising, she called out. 'Sian?'

Her voice rang croaky and high.

The blonde turned towards the car, smiled, and stepped in her direction.

'Hi yes, that's me! Are you the Avon lady?'

No, I'm not the fucking Avon lady.

Pretty? Yes. Exceptional? No. Blonde hair a mess. Short and a too-on-trend style to suit her own preferences. Ripped jeans, a hoodie top with white trainers were her fashion choices. This would be a short, clear exchange. Crystal clear, spoken with confidence.

'Sian, my name is Grace, and I believe you're having an affair with my husband.'

Did I just say that out loud?

I bloody well did.

Sian stood to attention. Grace watched this information being processed. If she juggled many lovers, how would she know which one she meant? Were they all married or some single?

'I don't know any married men.'

'His name is Rhys. And you know him. He drives a blue Toyota.'

The look of awe on Sian's face provided some satisfaction. 'You mean John?'

'No, I mean this man.'

Grace swiped calmly through her photo gallery, flicking her manicured nails exaggeratedly in search of a picture of them together, and stuck it out of the window with one arm to show her, clenching hard so it didn't shake in her trembling fingers.

Do I look OK? I need to look good right now. Thank god for sunglasses.

Sian studied it, trying to remain collected, except for giveaway twitches around her lips.

'That's John,' she agreed.

Confirmation.

Hell.

'I'd like you to stay away from him, please.'

Grace was winging it, hoping she sounded authoritative despite the mass of quivers pulsing through her body.

'And find another plaything. I'm pregnant again.'

Grace! Where did THAT come from?

She smoothed her flat stomach visibly.

'Our daughters could do without their dad leaving home at this point in their lives.'

Sian stood statuesque despite her distinct lack of height. Invisible thoughts flashed in her eyes.

'I'm so sorry. I had no idea he was married. He said his name was John.'

It was at this point Grace realised Rhys was using his middle name.

In the wisp of a moment, Sian was crestfallen. It was difficult to tell the depth of her hurt, but it was doubtful she was madly in love if there were other boyfriends. Or doubtful Rhys was going to allow it to go as far. Why else use his middle name? If it were to become serious, explaining why wouldn't be too difficult in the future.

'I hate my first name. My mates call me John. '

Grace heard his excuse as he stood at the altar and smiled down at his new blonde child bride while the vicar's confused eyes watched over them.

'The bond of marriage brings two hearts together in ways unseen.'

Sian didn't need to know this. It was time to step out of the car, and she was still wearing her confidence heels.

'Where did you meet him? How long has this been going on?' She asked, standing tall on the pavement.

Tousled blonde hair shook from side to side.

'I'm so sorry. It was December. I was at a work Christmas party. We met then, before Christmas. He was with a load of blokes from the factory. They were all pretty drunk. I didn't know he was married, and he never mentioned kids.'

Grace felt a tiny twinge of sympathy, but not enough to forego this chance. It was a night which went down as unusual in her memory. Crawling home at four o'clock in the morning. Throwing up in the bathroom. Falling into bed fully clothed.

I should have checked his pockets and phone. My god, he must have gone to her house, no wonder he was so late.

'You really have kids?' Her voice was tinged with sadness.

Fight or flight, Grace.

'Yes, two girls and one on the way. We're hoping for a boy this time.'

'Nice.'

'Sian, if this is serious between you, and I'm in for a load of heartache,' she rubbed her belly again, 'then I need to know now. You can have him if it is. Otherwise, I have to tell you, you're not the first, and I daresay you won't be the last.'

This lying is easy. Once you get going.

It surprised Grace how cool and in control she sounded, despite the interior earthquake.

Sian's face peered back, an expression of shock and curiosity.

She's wondering why I stay married.

'He'll stay with me for my family's money.' Grace moved on, not allowing time to voice further questions. This was a sales technique. Keep pointing out what Sian needed to hear. All those training sessions down the years were coming to the fore.

Only ask open questions, no closed questions. What are the customer's needs?

Grace peered pointedly at the house. An unkempt front garden, weeds growing among the steps, rusted iron railings on the low wall rising from the pavement, window frames in need of replacement.

Rhys living here? He hates D.I.Y.

'I'm mortified.' Sian said simply.

Grace studied her face. With all the accoutrements of youthful beauty. Lash extensions, the perfect cat eyeliner, matte lipstick, not dissimilar to her own, but a decade younger. A decade fresher.

Grace propagated the lies, fighting on.

'Do I tell him to pack his bags and come to you? What do you want, Sian? Because I can tell you now, he won't be ruining my life. I'll be the one lounging in spas on Saturdays, while he takes the kids and pays maintenance from his factory job. Do you have room for kids at weekends?'

She purposefully allowed her eyes to drift upwards toward the bedrooms. Sian's face clouded as Grace hoped memories of her ex's commitments came to mind. She silently thanked Deidre, hoping the neighbour may take a peek from behind the curtains as events unfolded.

This was obviously not the future to which Sian aspired. A repeat scenario. She didn't appear to be a pushover, but then love was unpredictable. Grace hoped one of her other boyfriends may better suit her needs.

'I won't be giving up my life so he can have it easy with you. I'm not one of those mothers who will refuse access because he lives with a girlfriend. I will NOT be giving up my well-paid job to take care of three children while he gets all the time in the world with you. I'm tougher than that. Bear in mind he gets called into work some weekends. How are you with kids?'

Sian shook her head.

'I don't know, I don't have any.'

But you have a second-hand husband.

My husband.

Sian stood, visibly shaken. Confronted on her doorstep by a pregnant wife, in full view of the neighbours. The girl's voice wavered.

'No, please don't throw him out. It's nothing serious. Honestly. Just sex.'

Plummeting sensations overwhelmed her, sailing south with speed.

Stand tall, don't sink.

Just sex.

The mainstay of relationships. You complete and utter bastard. I hate you right now.

'Wait.' Sian pulled out her phone and put a silencing finger to her lips.

What's she doing? She's calling him? No.

Nimble fingers put the phone on to speaker and held it out so Grace could overhear. Her heart fluttered fearfully as the ringtones shrilled through the air.

Don't answer, please don't answer. This isn't true. There's been a mistake.

Rhys answered.

Loud and clear.

'Hello, gorgeous!'

The deep voice she knew so well. The timbre which said 'I do' and 'For richer or poorer.' The voice which said 'I love you' with overwhelming frequency. Grace closed her eyes and fought the tears behind her sunglasses. The fluttering became a battering ram, beating against her ribcage.

'Hi, John.'

'How are you today, sexy?'

Sexy.

Young.

Blonde.

Sexy.

The rise of despair, the sick sensation, engulfed her. Black and heavy, it heaved on her eyelids, tugged them low, lashes touching her cheeks. Sinking, end-of-the-world dejection. Gloom, melancholy, a thesaurus of misery swamped her. Still, the battering ram added to the burden.

Here was the man she shared her life with, her bed, her vows, the mundane everyday chats. Choosing paving slabs and pet-friendly weed killer. The same voice down her phone asking 'Korma or Pasanda, Pilau or Mushroom?' as he stood at the counter of an Indian takeaway. The vital life conversations- what car, what holiday, what insurance? Are we having children?

No. We're not.

Here he was, the same Rhys, calling another woman sexy and gorgeous. Under a different name. Under her nose.

Full and utter betrayal.

'I'm OK, John.'

The sound of Sian's voice raised her eyelids.

'But I'm ringing to tell you not to come around later.'

'Oh, why's that?'

His voice took on a hard edge.

'Because I'm getting back with my ex. The one I told you about'

There was a rigid silence.

'I'm sorry, I know we've had fun, but it wasn't meant to be serious, was it?'

As she asked, her eyes locked with Grace's. Sian was doing her a *favour.* Allowing her to listen to the raw truth of reality, in the hope it may help. A seed of appreciation germinated within her.

Rhys spoke, his voice wavering. 'Well, I know you're much younger than me and I do like you a lot, but I knew at some point you'd probably find someone else. I just didn't think it would be this soon. But hey, if you're happy, then I'm pleased for you. Sorted.'

'Yes, I'm happy, thanks.'

'OK, then nothing left to say is there? I've enjoyed our time together, really. You made me feel like a new man. I hope it all works out for you.'

A new man.

A new, unmarried man.

Minus his wedding ring.

'Thanks, John, you too. I mean, I hope you find someone to settle down with.'

'No problem, my lovely.'

Even in the throes of its death knell, he was still using typical terms of endearment. Grace struggled to breathe.

He was letting go easily.

No big deal.

It hadn't been serious.

'But hey, if it doesn't work out, let me know. I'll miss you.' The thunderclap was inaudible to Sian but Grace was certain she felt the non-existent crash. The blonde hung up and looked towards her.

'Now do you believe me?' she asked searchingly, those Russian lashed lids so still she wanted to reach over and rip them out. Holding fast, fighting tears, Grace managed a response.

'You've had a lucky escape.'

Sian's eyelids flickered as she studied the pavement, composing a reply.

'I'm sorry for what you're going through.'

Grace's chin rose slowly, moving her face into a swift burst of sunlight through newly formed clouds. Her skin glowed, and she hoped she resembled the Virgin Mary in Sian's eyes.

Don't let my halo slip, sunshine. I know I'm looking good in this light.

'Not your fault by the sound of it.'

'No.'

Sian faced her, eyes meeting, and shrugged gently, signalling defeat. 'I've gotta go in now. I hope it all works out with the baby. Bit of a nightmare for you, really.'

With a sharp turn, she strode up the steps, a youthful curvy bottom swaying with natural sass.

His hands have been all over it. Cupping those cheeks, smoothing those curves, holding on tight. Fucker.

Was it a tear Grace saw her wipe away as she reached her front door? Maybe not so casual on her part after all. Slumping deep into her driver's seat, she uttered a juddering, tear-filled sigh as the door slammed tight to her side.

It's April Fool's Day. Exactly one month since the letter arrived on Saint David's Day. Red Letter Day. Deliverance Day. Oh god, I forgot to say 'White Rabbits' first thing. Well, it couldn't get any worse than this.

Daffodils still swayed in the front gardens and pots throughout the street and city. Swansea's roundabouts and embankments burgeoned with breeze-blown bright yellow, from mini tête-à-tête, with their tiny, wind-safe heads, to full trumpets and double-coloured narcissi, fighting the wild winds off Mumbles Head, cheering residents and travellers from Swansea Vale to Bracelet Bay and beyond.

The South Wales Evening Post delivered full-colour supplements of schoolchildren dressed in Welsh National Costume, boys and girls whose mothers bought their outfits, dragged them off to school on the first of the month wearing daffodils and leeks on their lapels, shone from the pages, all smiles for the camera.

Grace loved seeing them as she passed by schools on her calls or wandering along supermarket aisles with their parents at the end of the afternoon. So many children in National dress. Her working day, crumpled letter in a pocket, passed in a daze, driving from customer to customer, thoughts playing on a repeat loop, eyes never wavering from the road ahead.

No pleasurable glances at bus stops, pavements, or schoolyards where they would have massed in their black hats with tall, tapering crowns, white frilled brims, red skirts, white aprons, and shawls. Her focus was only on averting disaster as tears repeatedly blurred her vision. Their national day passed her by for the first time, even though she'd worn her fresh daffodil, traditionally pinned to her lapel.

Rubbing her empty midriff, astounded by the ease of the lies she told her rival, she knew they'd achieved the desired effect.

Fait accompli.

Half of December, through January, February, and March, of surreptitious visits to a lover, endless sex, and lies. Of showering, shaving, applying aftershave, freshly laundered shirts, and newly polished shoes. Time enough to grow affection, and marriage threatening emotion.

Grace pressed the starter and drove around the corner, out of sight of both houses now so hugely instrumental in her life, before she pulled over and nudged the kerb with a soft bump which jolted her back against the headrest. Overwhelmed by another outburst of tears, she thumped the steering wheel until her wrists hurt.

'You fucking, fucking bastard.'
She made you feel like a new man.
You made me feel like an old woman.

82

Chapter 12

'Champagne is the only wine that leaves a woman beautiful after drinking it'

Madame de Pompadour

It was ten past two in the morning when Grace and the champagne bubbles floated back to room 316 at The Marriott. After telling Marcus the taxi was outside, she rushed to dress as he lay naked and dozing, taut muscular thighs wound in a tangle of sweaty bed sheets. Leaning over she kissed him softly on his damp forehead before whispering:

'Call me if you want, but now you need to sleep.'

Placing her business card on his pillow was symbolic. Easy access to her number came through his database, and this token of encouragement accented her throwaway comment.

I really want you to phone me.

Really.

I do.

A murmured goodbye mumbled through the cushioning, as a hand caught gently around her wrist, holding her still. He sighed heavily and lifted his head.

'I wish you could stay till morning.'

'So do I, but I have to go.'

'I can't believe you're leaving us.'

Please don't do this, not at this ungodly hour.

'You've got a long drive tomorrow. Don't think about it now.'

The soft whoosh as the door closed saddened her. The night was over, the madness complete. Grace stepped into the lift, punched the third-floor button, and leaned against the mirrored wall, the fizz, exhaustion, and excitement abating.

Oh my god, what have you done? Are you completely insane?

Rabid, I'd say, at this point in the morning.

Following an inept struggle with the keycard, she stumbled through the door, kicked off her shoes, stripped, and drifted towards the shower, hoping the shock of hot water would bring clarity. As she analysed the evening, trails of soapy suds ran down her back, arms, thighs, and abdomen as the heady scent of him washed away. She wondered then, why she'd stepped under it so soon.

These last twelve hours have been surreal.

That's all it's taken.

Half a day to change my life.

They'd gorged on the prawns, the luscious taste and aroma creating delighted smiles as rivulets of butter streaked down chins, tucked into Welsh Black ribeye blood-rare steaks, and skipped dessert. Grace drained the champagne while they flirted endlessly.

'I'm gutted you're handing in your notice.'

Disappointment hung thick in his voice, his tone grew serious as his cutlery laid flat against his plate.

'I know. Sorry to be the bearer of bad news, but I need to be upfront with you.'

'You've obviously had a job offer?'

Caught off-guard by this ready-made reason, Grace nodded averting her eyes.

'Yes, I found out this afternoon.'

'Still a Rep? Or a complete change?'

Lie. Make it up. Get creative. After all, you can't tell him you've just won a hundred million. Tell him what he'd like to hear. Men do it all the time.

'Still on the road, with more territory, so parts of England too. Lots of nights away, probably a godsend at the moment.'

Hinting?

Marcus visibly cheered, which was more than gratifying.

'But let's not talk about this anymore, and just enjoy tonight?'

'OK, Welshwoman. Cheers anyway, to your long and happy future.' They clinked glasses for a second time.

Why is this so scary?

Because spending it alone isn't an option. Not for me.

Grace struggled to remember who suggested going to his room. Him? Her? The fizz hissing and bubbling in her ears? Did she remember them leaning against the small bar, his arm around her waist, nuzzling like teenagers or was it imagined? Was the barman drying his glasses with a cloth, watching them discreetly, or was it a scene from a film, a snippet of a dream in the rare minutes they dozed between orgasms and erections?

Of all the hotels in all the world he has to walk into mine.

The alcohol proved potent as the night meandered on and she remembered the walk outside into the night air, crossing the road to show off the LED display on the walls of the new arena, where a myriad of stars winked across its golden exterior. Of all the wildly flashing show advertisements which frequently lit up the evening sky, it was the inky dark background with thousands of sparkles that shadowed them. Their conversation flooded back.

'Excellent venue, have you been yet?'

Grace giggled.

'I went with my mother in May to see Alice Cooper, just after it opened.'

'Any good?'

'Amazing. Wild. My Mam waited since she was sixteen to see him, so I couldn't let her go alone, could I?'

'No indeed. She's your mum.'

'No, they're mams in Wales. Welsh mams.'

Marcus laughed loudly.

'Wales is intense, it's so different, yet we're close neighbours.'

'We don't roll cheeses down hills and chase them, we have more sense.'

'Just practice for finding wives and girlfriends. Anyway, you eat seaweed bread. Who *does* that?'

Grace laughed.

'Rubbish. Where did you get such an idea?'

Marcus thought for a moment.

'You do, it's called laverbread. Seaweed.'

'Hey Englishman, get your facts straight. It's not bread, it's actual seaweed. Green and yucky-looking and fried up with cockles, bacon, and sausage. A luxury version of your Full English.'

He pulled a face. 'Sounds gross.'

'It's lush. Puts lead in your pencil.'

Marcus roared with laughter. 'You have no filter with champagne, methinks.'

Grace shrugged. 'Welshwomen say what they mean.'

'So is your mam a wild rocker and do you take after her?'

'All the way. Although not much rocking these days.'

'Res ipsa loquitur'

'What the hell is that?'.

'A remnant from school room Latin. The thing speaks for itself.'

'You're a posh boy, then?'

'I wash my own socks.'

They walked up the incline to the new coastal park alongside, set above the multi-storey car park, where Marcus pulled her gently onto a bench, in view of the sparkling exterior.

'Romantic, or what? Did you organise this?'

'I'm extremely im-fluential around here.'

'*IM*-fluential?' He laughed softly. 'I think you're extremely pissed. But thanks. I love *Starry Night*.'

'Van Gogh. You're not the only one who studied Art.'

Then he'd scooped an arm around her, tipped her head back gently, and kissed her full on the lips for a long linger of a moment.

Now I'm seeing stars and not the ones covering the Arena.

The same steadying arm remained close around her waist as they returned to ground floor level and wandered through the arches which lined the edge of the marina, to look at the boats and the reflections of the lights on the water from the surrounding buildings.

'That's the highest residential building in Wales, that is.' Grace told him, accompanied by a sequence of hiccups.

'I love the way you talk.' Marcus nuzzled her neck. 'I could impersonate you all day but you'd think I was teasing. It's so musical, like when you give everyone goosebumps singing your anthem at the rugby.'

'I'll teach you some *Welshisms* later.'

'Only if you must.'

'The view from the Grape and Olive at the top is amazing, but it's a long ride in the lift. I hate heights.'

'This place looks good.' Marcus narrowed his eyes to read out the name of a restaurant near the base. '*El Pescador.* What a great place to live. This city is compact. I didn't realise the marina was close to the beach and the centre. This is cool. Do you live around here, Grace?'

There followed a mumbled negative response, as he steered her back inside, laughing as she attempted to walk without swaying, the flat shoes keeping her safe from toppling over.

'I think you've overdone the champagne.'

You have absolutely no idea.

She finally remembered her giggles and her own fizz-fuelled suggestion. 'Take me to your room, Marcus.'

He studied her face for a long moment. 'Do you want me to show you my etchings?'

'Cut the posh stuff, even I know what they are. Now take me to your room.'

'Are you sure?'

'Before I lose my handbag, or change my mind. I *persist.*'

His powerful arm monopolised her waist as they fell into an irregular step.

'I think you mean insist and I've got your handbag, and its dangly thing, nice and safe.'

'It's my rabbit's foot.'

He grinned and scrutinised the charm as they headed

towards the lift.

'Who carries a rabbit's foot about their person?'

'Me. My mam bought it for me so I couldn't say no. They're very lucky.'

Stealing another kiss his voice lowered.

'For both of us, hopefully.'

As the lift door opened onto his floor, he gripped her hand until the room door swung shut behind them. Then he seized her bag, cast it to the floor, grabbed both hands, pulled her towards him, nuzzled her neck, kissed her ears, found her lips, and forced them apart with his probing tongue until they were both pulling desperately at each other's clothes.

Shoes bounced around the carpet, suits scattered over the chair, the desk, and the floor, until they fell onto the bed, wrapped in each other's corporate nakedness.

'Oh good god, Grace,' he murmured, as his hands caressed her breasts, her buttocks, his erection desperate. 'I've wanted you so much!'

Oh, my god Marcus.

I need you now.

Tonight.

Grace concentrated only on the events of those late hours, basking in his masculinity, inhaling the heady aftershave, smoothing his soft but taut skin, and biting into muscular shoulders while his hardness led her repeatedly back to intense pleasure. A deep voice, close to her ear, offered crude, provocative words designed to increase passion, as he pinned her tighter and harder while they thrust together, pushing her clambering to peaks of long-lost euphoria.

Then the words altered, as he told her how wonderful she was, how he longed to be with her, this younger, fit, honed male now occupied every curve of her body, his tongue invaded every space, his excitement to be intertwined with her limbs showing itself repeatedly through those darkening hours.

Finally, exhausted in an entanglement of hips and arms, they gently recovered from the overpowering array of sensations that ushered them into the post-witching hours. Under his unyielding command, and the influence of the champagne, Grace regressed to life before the letter dropped onto the mat, a life where she still felt attractive and seductive. Mesmerised, she lounged on the edges of the lottery win, creeping back to reality only during the lulls where they'd fallen breathlessly apart, to be pushed away again as Marcus' youthful endless desire reawakened and he'd raised her back to passion. A passion that finally faded after their last frantic entanglement sent them both into a deep slumber.

Summer's end was a spectacular burst of fireworks across the length of Swansea Bay, lost in the heat of bodies to a magical inner soundtrack. Forever *may* just start tonight.

Grace slipped out of the shower, swathed herself in a fluffy towel, and allowed a wry smile to rise on her face.

Bonnie Tyler, you'd be delighted to know your song has run through my head all night. Swansea girls in imagined harmony. Unfurled red chiffon, smoke, running through empty hallways, choirboys, bright eyes. I must stick to champagne, it gives the wildest dreams.

It was the sight of the empty bottle in the ice bucket that broke through her reverie. Reaching for a fairy cake, she flung herself on the bed and smiled. With the first bite, she swallowed the luscious cream top, as a blob of frosted icing stuck to her top lip.

'You're definitely not a cupcake, you're a fairy cake. A butterfly cake. Oh, it's nice to be thoroughly drunk and rich. Thoroughly rich. Thoroughly drunk. And thoroughly satisfied.'

Giggling as dizzy sleep began its journey, the cake slipped through her fingers onto the carpet, and she slid semi-naked between the sheets, and reclined there with a smile, eyelids drooping, sliding her hands down the length of her body, she remembered the touch of his own which held and caressed her through their hours together, and made her feel wanted, desirable, and safe.

Marcus slept naked in his bed, while she sprawled *déshabille* in hers, just floors apart. Her younger lover would soon leave on the long drive to the West Country. However incredible this merging, promises made in the dead of night between men and women often fell apart. Alcohol and attraction were a dangerous combination. Distance and lifestyle, a fatal coupling.

And I'm leaving the company.
I'm changing everything.
What might have been?

Overwhelmed and abruptly distraught, champagne soaked, in the afterburn of heady passion, mammoth transitions waited ahead as Grace grasped what may be a life of distrust, a lonely luxurious existence fending off gigolos and scammers. Fierce tears slid down her cheeks, which she wiped away in anger.

Big girls don't cry, Gracie. No. They howl like she-wolves. And nobody likes change.

Grace scrabbled for her phone as it flashed and tweeted its bird sound. Unknown number.

Chirp.
Champagne with foaming whirls, as white as Cleopatra's melted pearls. Lord Byron. You are so lovely. Miss you already. Check your pics. Xxx

She squinted at her photo gallery against the harsh light of the screen.

Champagne poetry? For me? But please don't be rude. I know all about dick pics. Ffion showed me. Repeatedly.

A series of sharp hiccups slowed down the opening process, but then she was squinting at her photo gallery. An image of them both, heads close on a pillow, smiling in the tousled afterglow, filled her screen.

A blanket of calm snuggled around her. No secretly captured nudity, simply a moment of delightful lunacy as he'd used her phone to centre them within the lens. A beautiful memory of an illicit moment.

'Your phone, Grace. Keep or delete, it's up to you.'

Didn't he joke about showing it to our kids one day? I can't delete this. A memory of the night I hit two jackpots.

Grace's laughter drifted back to her before she'd smothered deeply into his snowdrift of a pillow. She screwed her eyes as the screen dimmed, then tapped a hazy response.

90

Room 316 3rd floor Pls come now. Can Xplain.

Add to contacts. MarX. *Oops, typo. Champagne, you have much to answer for. With your devil's bubbles. One hundred million. One hunk of man.*

Chapter 13

'I only drink champagne on two occasions. When I am in

love and when I am not'.

Coco Chanel

2.40 a.m. Ten minutes passed before the soft tapping on her door grew audible, the same amount in seconds before she welcomed him in, nervously naked apart from her unbuttoned white shirt. The tray and ice bucket shovelled noisily into the wardrobe alongside her briefcase, with barely time to empty the melted cubes into the sink and wash away the remnants of trodden-in sponge cake wedged between her toes. Only the flowers remained on display.

Bleary-eyed, wearing his misbuttoned shirt, trousers, and a pair of towelling hotel slippers, Marcus stepped inside and caught her around the waist, mid-yawn. 'What's going on Grace, why are you here?'

In response, she led him to the bed, a silencing finger against his lips before undoing his shirt, an alien pleasure at the feel of the material slipping over his shoulders and arms. He stripped off his trousers, and they slid under the duvet, his chest against her back, arms wrapped around her, knees bent perfectly together.

'Tell me.' He nuzzled, exhausted, into her neck.

Here we go again, Gracie girl. Little white ones. Line 'em up.

'Rhys and I argued, a real big one, and I booked in here. I said nothing because I didn't want to spoil things.'

Marcus sighed deeply, his cooling breath tickling the nape of her neck. It was the first time she'd used her husband's name, the first time he'd heard it.

'So things are bad enough, you need a hotel room?'

'They're not great. I wanted to be alone tonight. Thinking of you just floors away when we could be cwtched-up together till morning seemed stupid.'

'Cwtched-up?'

Grace pulled his arms tighter around her waist, the heat of his thighs against her buttocks.

'It's Welsh for hugging, holding. *Cwtching.*'

'OK Welshwoman, cwtch me. Really tight.'

'Marcus, what is this?' She whispered into the darkness.

His sigh was heavier than the duvet swaddling them. 'I don't know, Grace. Ask me one on sport.'

Despite the tired solemnity in his voice, she let out a swift girly giggle. Silent moments passed before Marcus choked back a chortle. An ephemeral hush grew into hysterics as he pulled the duvet over their heads to muffle the noise.

'Shh Grace, we'll wake up next door.'

Their bodies juddered into paroxysms.

'I think we already did that in your room!'

They drifted into unwelcome sleep as laughter sank into lassitude.

At six o'clock, he awoke her with a kiss so passionate her head spun, his words mumbling heavy with regret against her lips. 'Wake up gorgeous, I have to leave you soon.'

'Stop it stop it stop it' she murmured, lips fighting back as his tongue probed deeper, while her willing hips slid beneath him, and sleepy thighs curled around his back.

'Not in a million years…' became lost in a tangle of sensual sounds as he slid inside her, arms and shoulders clutched so tightly together there was no escape for their moaning.

Marcus, you're killing me.

I'm drowning in you.

Pull me up.

At half-past six, still joined and exhausted, fingers entwined in her tangled hair, his breath came heavily. 'I think I should stay here with you. Exeter won't miss me.'

'You can't.'

Marcus noted the slight edge of panic in her voice. 'It won't take much persuasion.'

'I have a heavy day today, and my brain is soaked in burst bubbles and garlic.'

'At least we both have dog breath.' He panted playfully around her face.

'Dragon breath. Ych a fi!'

'What?' he laughed as she pushed his head away.

'It means disgusting.'

Slowly they slid apart. He rested his chin on her shoulder, his breathing steady, his tone lowered. 'Would you reconsider resigning? If it's the money, I can try to do something about it.'

I'll never need to worry about money ever again. There's ten thousand in the wardrobe right now. Ten thousand. I've never seen that much cash.

'No, I can't.'

Marcus nodded, signals of defeat as his stubble pricked her skin.

'Sorry, I shouldn't have said that. I hate the idea we won't be working for the same company and I was too stupid to reach out sooner.'

'It's just time to move on.'

'I know. My apologies.'

'What should I do now? Is telling you enough, or should I call John? I really don't want to go in again. I can't face any of them.'

'I'll let them know we're letting you go immediately for personal reasons.'

Grace wriggled backwards into his all-enfolding arms, the stickiness of their sweat moulding them together.

'I can't do farewells. I feel pathetic this morning.'

'I'll sort it, I promise.'

'I'll send the car and laptop back Monday?'

'I'm sure it'll be fine, sweetie.'

Sweetie. That's nice.

'Thanks.'

He squeezed her tighter, his face nestled into her hair.

'I can't believe you walked in there last night. Talk about luck or chance, or whatever you want to call it.'

Of all the restaurants in all the towns in all the world, I had to walk into yours. Serendipitous.

'Do you believe in luck, Grace?'

'I have my special rabbit.'

An amused expression crossed his face.

'I have heard Duracell's a girl's best friend.'

Marcus vibrated with laughter. Grace covered her face. *Oh god. How embarrassing. But at least he has a sense of humour.*

'I met your dangly thing last night.'

I met yours, too.

'Yes, but I was slightly drunk.'

'Sweetie, you were a *lot* drunk and now I know why.'

'We older women can't hold our drink.'

'That's why you have a young stud to look after you.'

Marcus checked his phone, nose wrinkling with irritation, and ran a nervous hand through his tousled hair.

'Grace, don't let this be farewell. I don't want to disrupt your marriage if you're trying to save it. But if not, then I'll gladly come to your rescue.'

'Is this just morning after talk, toy boy?'

Does he really mean it?

'I mean it. This chemistry is fierce.'

Leaning over he played with the lengths of hair spilling around her face.

'Look, we can meet as and when. I just want you in my life, and I'll take whatever you can offer.'

Grace waited a moment, then wriggled around to face him, placed both hands on either side of his face and kissed him full on the lips.

Here it comes, the road to rack and ruin.

'Hey Englishman, I think it might work.'
'We reek of sex, Welshwoman.'
'Sex and garlic.'
'Well, they're both good for you.'
'Next time shave. My chin is sore.'

Newsroom, South Wales Evening Post

'Looks like Wales has got a big winner!'
'How much?'
'One hundred million.'
'Publicity?'
'No.'
'North or South?'
'Dunno.'
'Get on it then, we may get lucky.'

Chapter 14

By seven o'clock Grace was alone, exhausted, and drifting back into a deep slumber. At eleven o'clock she'd awoken, showered, dressed, and walked across to the nearby Tesco superstore to buy paracetamol, toiletries, underwear, a pair of jeans, and a summer top from the end-of-season rail in the ladies' clothing section.

Am I mad, buying off the reduced rail in a supermarket? I'm too tired to walk into town. Barely any clothes shops left now Debenhams has gone.

She casually cast a phone charger into her basket, plus copies of the latest Vogue and Harper's Bazaar magazines, and as she wandered among the aisles, the memory of last night replaying itself in her head, a Mona Lisa smile touched her mouth. As she toyed with items on shelves, she imagined his hands on her buttocks, pulling her tighter towards him, as salmon leapt upstream inside her.

You've won a hundred million. Forget the sex. But even rich people need sex. And the joy of closeness and feeling wanted. Those eleven hours were incredible.

At the checkout, a voice called out.

'Hi Grace, haven't seen you in ages, is all OK with you?'

A neighbour living a few doors away waited two tills along, a half-full trolley ready to unload onto the conveyor belt. Fighting back a guilty blush creeping up her face, Grace returned her cheery wave.

'Yes, thanks. Hope your summer was fun?'

'Great, thanks. We haven't seen much of you two around, though?'

'Oh, both busy as usual. There's never a spare minute.'

There wasn't last night. No time wasted then. I can barely walk. I'd forgotten what lengthy sessions do to a girl.

While her items were whizzing through the scanner, she knew she would be out of the doors before any exit chat held her up. It was as she reached for her purse, that Grace realised the rabbit's foot was missing. The ancient scrap of scruffy fur which dangled off her bag since the Boot Sale, was gone. With a sinking heart, she rummaged inside for the fluffy charm, knowing full well it wasn't there.

I can't lose you now. Where the hell are you? In my room? Somewhere on the pavement?

The checkout girl turned the card reader towards her. 'Anything wrong?'

'I've lost my rabbit's foot!'

Aware of the rising panic in her voice, Grace retrieved her card and tapped to pay.

She handed over the paper receipt. 'What is it?'

'A charm my mother bought me.'

All the time her hand groped inside until she realised she must pack and make way for the next customer.

'I hope you find it.'

'Me too!'

Her feet sped towards the exit. Outside in the sunshine, she paused. Marcus took her bag and cast it on the carpet as passion rose between them. Could it have fallen off then? Pulling out her battery-blinking phone she searched for the hotel number. If he'd found it, he would have messaged her, surely?

'Reception? Housekeeping please.'

Bloody phone, you can't die on me now.

Following a hasty request for a search, power failure cut her off mid-flow. Grace raced the few hundred yards past the marina basin with its Dylan Thomas fishing boat bobbing sea, her eyes scanning the cobbles and pavements already trodden. *Please don't be lost.*

Marcus parked in the visitors' space at the Exeter branch and relaxed against the headrest, rolling his shoulders, stiff following the long drive down. Traffic and roadworks meant an extra forty-five minutes on the journey, nothing unusual with conditions along the M4 and M5 motorways, and his muscles ached with tension.

It was some night. Letting out a deep breath, he was grateful to have chosen the Marriott over other hotels, and Kismet seemed to have played a part in his last-second decision to try Swansea instead of heading to Cardiff.

Fluke resolved unsuccessful visits, along with a lucky rabbit's foot. Despite a complete lack of superstition, last night felt like a celestial sphere formed a zenith above them.

They'd moulded into each other with an intensity long missing from his life. For endless weeks he'd pictured her, wound in his arms, lips, and bodies meeting. Chance finally placed her where his imagination only dreamed.

Closing his eyes he relived the sensations which kept him alive and potent for hours. They'd loved, laughed, *cwtched,* and he'd inhaled her beautiful essence until forced into parting by a lightening sky.

Everything comes to he who waits. I've waited long enough. Good start and I'm not giving up now.

Whereas the night of the Conference and Ball proved a crystalline occasion, there'd been no reason to believe she'd wanted further contact as she wandered away from him wearing *that* green dress. The ethics issue was about to vanish and the onus was on him to make the call to arrange it.

If only she wasn't married.

The best things are rarely easy to attain.

His business brain began its lecture.

Life changes, sometimes dramatically. You should know. That's why divorce exists.

The rest of the working week lay ahead, and it was time to

focus on daytime activities, not the exertions of the darker hours. But first, time to send a text, to let her know he'd arrived. Would it seem pushy, or to be expected? Women liked messages. And it *had* been one hell of a night.

A smile spread across his face as he remembered the photograph he'd taken with her phone around midnight, as they'd settled into a comfortable cwtch and wondered why, when he'd tapped on it, he'd opened a photo of a room strewn with money and champagne. A few fleeting seconds passed before he'd held it up again, pressed the flash symbol, and said:

'Smile, gorgeous, it didn't take.'

The flash blinded them in the semi-lit room, and he'd kissed her again with such passion she moulded into the pillow, her eyes closing, the champagne bubbles and exhaustion sending her off towards dreamland.

'We can show it to our kids.' he murmured, convinced she wouldn't hear the words.

A tinkle of laughter emitted from her beautiful, bare lips before she fell completely asleep. There was no sign of money or champagne when she let him into her room hours later. Perhaps he'd been dreaming too, wrapped up in the headiness of a rare sexual marathon, more alcohol than planned, and the lateness of the hour. Despite the fleeting glance, it *looked* like the same room.

His mood dropped as he remembered one major thing he needed to do concerning this glorious goddess who graced his presence. It would be hard to let her go. But he'd promised. Her life was tough at the moment. Anything to help ease the way.

'Call Head Office.' He instructed his phone, followed by 'Human Resources' as a voice answered.

Fifteen minutes later he sent the text. He'd already saved Grace to contacts and wondered if she'd done the same.

At hotel reception, Grace begged for a pair of scissors to free the new charger from its plastic stranglehold and queried news from housekeeping. Checkout was at midday. Time was ticking.

'I'll find out and let you know, madam.' the receptionist replied.

She headed back towards the lift.

Please find it, oh please find it. Don't panic, you're getting hysterical. It's been a tough night, what do you expect? It's just an old piece of tat, and you've already won the money. But things may go horribly wrong without it.

Twenty minutes later, as her phone began its rise to resurrection, and she'd searched every inch of the room, a uniformed woman knocked on the door, presenting the scruffy bit of brown fur in the palm of her blue latex gloved hand.

'Is this what you're missing, madam?'

'Oh, thank you so much, that's it.'

'The clasp has come open, but I don't think it's broken.'

Grace examined the charm, delighted to agree, her face beaming with relief and happiness.

'Where was it?'

She lowered her eyes.

'Just out of sight under the bed in your friend's room.'

'I'd better keep it inside my bag in future. You're a lifesaver, please, take this.' She offered a fifty-pound note.

Any embarrassment vanished, it didn't matter as long as the charm was back.

'Oh no, there's really no need.'

'Please, take it, buy something which will bring you luck, like this. It's worthless really, but I couldn't bear to lose it. Better still, buy some lottery tickets. You've held it in your hand, it may rub off on you. Pob lwc!'

'Oh OK, if you insist. Glad to help.'

'It's very special. To me, anyway.'

Giving Grace a knowing smile, she walked away. As the door closed behind her, she sank against it holding the rabbit's foot snugly in one hand, tears pricking her eyes, before they spilled in a merciless salty torrent down her cheeks.

Let it out, Gracie girl. There's an awful lot to let go of.

Chapter 15

Two hours later, at the lottery counter inside the superstore where Grace discovered her loss, a woman bought a handful of scratchcards, twenty cigarettes, and a glossy women's magazine. At the last minute, she treated herself to a bunch of brightly coloured flowers. A mix of cheery blooms wrapped in plastic, with a *reduced* sticker made them too hard to resist. It wasn't often she could afford flowers, but today was an exception.

Ten minutes later, inside a small green Toyota in the car park, the same woman began jiggling up and down with excitement, the car body moving with her. The scratchcards in her hands rested lightly against the steering wheel, her knees covered with flakes of silver foil, the ten pence piece she'd used to scratch it off, fallen by her feet.

'Bloody hell, ten thousand quid! I don't believe it. Ten thousand! Oh thank you, you beaut, wherever you're from, thank you and your little rabbit's foot.'

Chapter 16

September's glossy Vogue magazine featured supermodel Linda Evangelista in a red hat, shiny red headscarf, and a mock croc metallic red coat. Inside this *big fashion issue,* Grace became overwhelmed with colour, print, graphics, and designer names on every vibrant page she turned.

'Oh my god, what do I buy to make me look rich?'

Should I even be looking rich? Isn't it crass? No point in having money if you can't look expensive. Why bother entering if you didn't hope to win?

Grace flicked through the magazines and a couple of other glossies strewn around Reception, skimming over the fashions and jewellery ads while lounging in a foyer armchair, briefcase at her feet, awaiting the financial wizards.

Patek Philippe timepieces? Geneva, Switzerland. Even more expensive than Rolex and TAG Heuer.

Wow, people spend this on watches? But will you spend this on a watch, Grace? It'll hold its value. It says here it will actually increase in value. But I've never even heard of them. Doesn't matter. It's the top brand. Not even sold in Harrods.

'I could fly there and back in a day, a quick solo mini adventure. Buy it at source.'

A quick search of flights found Cardiff airport flew directly to Geneva. Scrolling over the map of the city, she found a Patek Philippe salon, a museum dedicated to the brand, and endless designer shops nearby.

Chloe, Gucci, Prada, and Dior, vaulted off the lustrous pages as she continued flicking through the slick sheets, she found Graf, Azzedine Alaia, Celine, La Perla, Jada Dubai, and so many exclusive adverts beautifully designed to tempt the eye and brain into releasing pleasurable endorphins and dopamine.

'Oh my god, this is unreal!'

Order more champagne to keep you in the zone, Grace. Keep the buzz of these twenty-four hours going. Can't you just taste it now?

No. I'll need a clear head for the Oyster Suite and the pearls about to be shucked. They're going to make one hell of a necklace. And maybe a matching bracelet. Plus, I have to collect the car.

She moved back and forth through the thick glossy pages, loving the quality feel as they flicked beneath her fingertips and the rich sound as they thwacked together. An exclusive world of unfamiliar names and places unheard of before now, with the occasional heady whiff of perfume uncovered by tiny peel-off sticker samples.

As her phone charged alongside, the need to eat grew. A skipped breakfast sitting amid her visitors with a foggy brain and an undernourished, complaining stomach may prove an embarrassment. Checking the battery level one more time she smiled and unplugged it from the foyer power point.

'I'm fed up with you. I'm going to buy one of those fancy folding things with better battery life. In rose gold.'

The hotel's position tucked at the edge of the maritime quarter, made it rare for locals to gather for anything except functions. With direct beach access, it was the usual choice of visiting football teams, including the Premier League clubs when the city's team basked in the top tier, and kids with their fathers waited for autographs in the car park on Saturdays, hoping *the Special One* would sign an autograph as he wandered around the marina, players in tow.

Those heady days were over for the moment, with a slip down to the Championship, but Grace remembered the celebrations just over a decade ago when much of the city turned up to greet the open-top bus parade, with the crowds and media coverage. It was a monumental moment. She was twenty-six. Not far off Sian's age.

Stop mentioning that girl's name, even in your head. Forget her. She has no reason at all to be in your mind now.

For one moment, mid-fork to mouth, Grace realised there was a possibility she matched the fortunes of the club. This brought a mischievous grin to her face, breaking through the gravitas that settled over her. A singular amusing thought led her into the *avoirdupois* of the afternoon ahead.

As the effects of the champagne dissipated and memories of Marcus' athletic body eased, her thoughts grew chaotic, helter-skeltering into fall-out and consequence.

'This is lunacy' she uttered to the condiments in her direct eye line. 'I should be home with my husband celebrating. Ridiculous, this is completely ridiculous.'

But you can't Grace, because he's likely to leave you and run off with the young blonde, taking half the money. And you've got your own young blond now. You can't tell him, either. You can't tell anyone at all for the moment. Now that's what's ridiculous.

At her table in the bar, her phone lay in lazy repose between the salt cellar and the dessert spoon. Grace caught sight of her hall of mirror's reflection in the metal's curve. Distorted, inside out, upside down, she recalled the last time she stood in front of magic mirrors at the Waterfront Winterland one chilly December night, where the garish Christmas lights reflected all around and the riotous sounds of fairground rides, music, and ice skaters formed the soundtrack to the evening, while the aromas of flame-grilled burgers, toasted marshmallows, and alcoholic hot chocolate giddied the senses. Grace laughed as Rhys popped up behind her like a meerkat, as she scrutinised her reflection. Tiny head, enormous body.

'Oh my god love, is this what you'll look like when you're seventy? I'll have to find a younger model by then.'

Grace's smile lit up the gloomy corner.

'Still a few years before that happens, *boy bach*, wash your mouth out.'

Only there weren't.

How was I to know he wouldn't wait?

Chirp
MarX
Vibe check. Cloudy in Exeter. Hope you're recovered.

Green Goddess
Vibe good. Drinking water like a Grand National winner.

That's some visual.

         I'm Welsh, we're descriptive.

OK, all sorted. You won't get any calls. Car & kit back Monday.

         Ta. In no fit state to deal with them today.

I know. Laters Xxx

This is decent of him. I must correct the spelling. But what if it's unlucky, like putting your clothes on inside out? Change them back and it vanishes. Oh, my god what's wrong with you, girl? You've never been superstitious. Except for White Rabbits. I really should brush those grains of salt away. They're making a mess on the table.

Grace watched as they fell to the floor, then picked up the salt cellar and threw a pinch over her shoulder like her Gran used to do.

But that's not being superstitious. It's just a 'thing' we all do. Force of habit. Like saluting magpies. And I'm dreading this meeting.

Chapter 17

When a taxi pulled up outside the Marriott reception at half past four, Grace was relieved to sink into the back seat alongside her flowers, their dry stems now entwined in paper, and wave goodbye to the most monumental day of her life. The last day of August, the sunset of everyday existence.

Now I just have to go home to my husband of twelve years and pretend nothing significant has happened since yesterday morning. Where I left him drinking tea in his ancient blue dressing gown at the kitchen table, hair skew whiff, eyes barely open, the smell of singed toast permeating the morning, with nothing more than a casual comment about seeing him later. And then I'm going to have to tell lies. So many lies.

With her fingers moving nimbly over her phone, she sighed. *Wikipedia. Goddess of Deceit. Call me Apate.*

Settling quietly in the back seat, bright sunshine mingled with clouds as they waited at the traffic lights to leave the maritime quarter. As she gazed out of the window to her right, the quiet ticking of the engine soothed her thoughts as her eyes wandered towards the new Copr Bay area with its high-level still to be named coastal park, so different in daylight. The incline where she and Marcus wandered in a heady state of intoxicated, euphoric attraction last night, now busy with people and children entering and leaving, some strolling, some skipping, and a couple of cyclists, their daffodil-coloured lycra weaving slowly among them.

Grace glanced to the left, where the Civic Centre spread its concrete wings at an angle along the seafront, banks of greenery, trees and flowers intermingled with the Brutalist style of post-war rebuilding which left nothing to the imagination, and laid bare endless bands of glazed windows, a slumbering concrete dragon resting on a grassy knoll, its image on the flagpole at its feet, facing the Victorian prison on the opposite side of busy Oystermouth Road.

Oystermouth Road. Leading to Mumbles Road. We do have some lovely street names, even if it takes forever to get where you're going when the sun is shining.

The lights turned green as the *Yellow Cab* headed on the straight road out of the city, the diffused daylight glow of *Arena Abertawe* on her right-hand side, the new swan-inspired bridge leading pedestrians and audiences directly into the newly created leisure area.

Grace smiled, it did indeed resemble a Crunchie bar, a taco, and many inventive social media offerings when it was lowered into place. However it came to be known as years passed, it was still a golden, origami-inspired work of art, illuminated with colour-changing LED lights.

This city is developing fast. My life is altering with it. I don't think I want all this so soon. Even though I begged for it.

With the ebb and flow of rush hour, they were soon passing the LC2 wave-making water park, the modern slate and glass waterfront museum, and the four-pillared Neo Classical museum, along Victoria Road, while The City Gates lazed on the left, waiting for the evening crowds to enter the bottom of Wind Street.

'Sorry about the lights, love. We seem to have caught all the red ones today.'

'That's alright, *Drive*, I'm not in any rush. It's nice to look at all the buildings. I'm usually behind a wheel myself and don't really take it all in. There's never time. I probably need a few history lessons.'

At the next set of stoplights, Morgans Hotel sat to the right with its Harbour Trust frontage, social hub and champagne bar where the colours of the French flag lit up the edifice on Beaujolais Day in November as partygoers filled the car park marquee, suited and booted for a day of celebrating throughout city venues.

Then they were out of the centre, and over the River Tawe bridge where the university rowers passed alongside the Copper Jack tourist boat which sailed up to Copper Quarter, once home to the largest metal production centre in the world.

With the sunlight touching her face through the warm glass, Grace closed her eyes as they passed the SA1 Waterfront area and imagined what the city would have been like a couple of centuries ago. Certainly not the watersports and student magnet of today.

It would have lain beneath a pall of smoke from tall stacks as the Cape Horners brought their cargoes to be smelted on the banks of the Tawe, the masts of tall ships would be visible from all around the city once nicknamed 'Copperopolis' as they sailed up the river bringing ore needed to produce it under the watchful eye of Kilvey Hill above. In Welsh, Abertawe. In English, Swansea. In Viking, a sword-wielding *Sweyne's Ey.*

What am I worrying about? Having too much money? Women back then led horrendous lives.

But Grace was in the present, where the air was cleaner, the hills were green again, and the city was undergoing its first major revamp since the three-night blitz destroyed so much of the centre.

It was *'all change'* and Grace lived in the suburbs of a city now fourth in a list of desired places to live in the United Kingdom. *Why would I want to live anywhere else? This is home. 'Cwtched up' among my fellow Taffs. I adore this little city.*

A short distance passed before she was paying the driver and the taxi pulled away, leaving her studying the back of her dusty company car.

I should have put you through the car wash a week ago. You're completely filthy. Luckily, I'm not wearing white, like a virginal bride.

Well, that's a hoot, Grace.

Taking a deep breath, she raised the boot and placed her bags inside, peeked at the shopping left overnight, then closed it firmly. Checking the windscreen, she smiled.

No ticket. Another stroke of luck or a benefit of 24-hour opening?

Slipping into the driver's seat, she checked her face in the mirror. No outward signs of her wayward night and the decision to change back into working clothes meant she'd arrive home as Rhys would have expected her to have left. As she tipped yesterday's coffee onto the ground, and replaced the stained, empty cup into the holder, she knew nature would handle the liquid, and the recycling bin would deal with the container. And she needed to text Marcus.

Green Goddess
Hope you're having a good day. I had an amazing night.xx

        I'm having a great day thanks to your amazing night.Xxx

I can barely sit down lol

        I wondered how you were faring. Did we break records?
        Xxx

Wasn't counting. Xx

Two kisses? Jesus girl, a couple of typed Xs after what you two were doing? Besides, he put three. Is this sexting, Grace? I doubt it. Too tame. Ffion can teach you. No, she can't. Ffion can never know.

As the engine started, Grace pressed the radio button. The familiar drumbeat to Toto's *Africa* filled the car. Turning up the volume, she sang along, one tuneful Welsh voice unconcerned with any amused passersby, as a world of travel, endless skies and the cruel nature of the bush opened up before her eyes.

I love this song.
I could go on safari?
Or killed in a tribal uprising, as Gran once said.
Don't be daft. You sound just like her.

Leaving the car park as the music faded, the DJ began his

chatter at the turn towards the main junction, where the Mercedes dealership on the left-hand side was still open. With a swift clunk of her indicator, she pulled across and into the visitors' area outside the glass-fronted modern exterior of Sinclairs, and parked.

Ten minutes. I'll have a quick look at what's on offer. I don't even know what I want yet. But it might be a Mercedes. A top-of-the-range, with all the extras. In metallic red. If they do one that colour. To go with my weekend lipstick. But Gracie, you can wear that lipstick every day.

Chapter 18

The house seemed quiet from the outside. Rhys must have gone out since waking, his car was nowhere to be seen. Grace picked up her belongings, but left the emergency bag in hiding, a fretful tension rising in her stomach.

Please be out, please be out, please be out.

The key slid into the lock, and the door opened into stillness. The house was quiet at a quarter to six. No need to face him yet, lugging two scandalous secrets the size of milk churns. She checked the lounge and kitchen, then stood at the foot of the stairs and called his name. Silence. Dropping onto the sofa, she sighed.

What now, Gracie? Where do you go from here? Unpacking the shopping and hiding the cash might be a start.

Wondering where to stow away ten thousand pounds, she unzipped the built-in arm cushion beneath her resting elbow. Rhys never sat on this side. This was her territory in the lounge's landscape. With it safely stashed inside the padding, she sat and contemplated her surroundings.

A three-bedroom detached house, with decent furniture and comfortable seating, well decorated, a normal home for an average couple without kids or pets. A garage without a car, lawn, neighbours on either side and part of a leafy street with modern houses a couple of miles outside the city centre. It served them well as a home, with a large garden for summer, and enough interior rooms to spread out in comfort. Sitting there, Grace detached herself from her environment with unexpected ease.

This was not a dwelling for an exceptionally rich woman. This was for yesterday's Grace. Faithful, devastated, lonely, hardworking Grace. Devastated slid somewhat. Faithful slithered serpent-like under the unruly raffia mat in the porch, the same one the letter landed on, the dirt scraper that needed kicking back into place every time the door opened or closed.

Hardworking? Well, that's dead and buried.

Pass me an apple and call me Eve.

In an instant, all connections to her surroundings dimmed. The furniture planned so carefully around their chosen colour scheme, the soft furnishings to pull it all together, the lighting, the wall art, none of it mattered now.

I don't think I want to live here anymore. I want all this behind me. Maybe in a few weeks, I'll tell him I want a divorce. Or a few months, once I know what's what.

But don't you still love him, Gracie?

I might. But then I might not. Things are changing fast.

Surely not after one night, though?

One?

Rhys Lewis spent the afternoon walking around Morfa shopping park, alongside the Swansea.com stadium, home to the 'Swans' football team with its 'Jack Army' of followers, shared with the Ospreys rugby squad. He browsed the gift shop, scouring the rugby jerseys, scarves, and mugs, leaving with an oval-shaped souvenir keyring, and continued his amble from shop to shop, killing time, stretching his legs. The trouble with shifts was most of your mates were still at work when you were free to come and go at leisure on weekdays.

It was also the trouble when life became mundane, and unexpected offerings appeared to tempt you. Today wasn't one of those days. Today was a boring, get out and pick up some stuff to *top up* the man drawer type of day. Ideal for wandering, grabbing a solo coffee, and chilling before heading home to the wife of twelve years, not even tempted by chocolate.

He didn't expect to see Sian in the distance, coming out of Boots the Chemist, carrying a small shopping bag, and heading in his direction. The last thing he wanted was to bump into her. Five months later he was over it. He didn't think she'd noticed him, head bowed, while examining a receipt.

With a swift stride, he turned sharply and arrowed straight towards B&Q at the end of the block. Sian wouldn't be going in there anytime. Not a *man's* shop. He could kill some time in among the lengthy, high aisles filled with selections of blokeish paraphernalia before escaping to his car, parked among dozens of others alongside her route.

You should never have gone there, boyo. Left well alone. You won't be free of this, not in a city as small as Swansea. Rhys boy, you're a twat. A twat who almost lost his wife. And probably the wedding album too.

In the kitchen, Grace found a vase for the flowers and placed them in a discreet corner of the lounge. Returning to work her way through the bag of groceries, she was thankful there was enough milk in the fridge to last until morning, as yesterday's carton was poured away and rinsed ready for recycling. The raspberries remained perfect, good enough to sample one by luscious one, savouring every burst of flavour on her tongue.

If only there was cream. Or champagne. Or naked buttocks.

The image of Marcus' bare bottom made her close her eyes as she imagined pouring those liquids over his perfect skin.

Hey, you can't have everything.

She laughed raucously to the empty room.

'Actually, girl, you just did!'

As quickly as euphoria took hold, it dissipated as gloomier thoughts arrived. Is this how it felt for Rhys? The joy of pursuance, or being pursued. The bliss of discovering someone new, delirious, pliable, and yielding in your arms. All those minglings of lips and thighs and sweat and fluids, of peaks of pleasure, and troughs of misery. No wonder people have affairs, partners suffer, and families tear themselves apart.

Mother nature's made it addictive.

To push people on.

Grace closed her eyes, jaw tightening, and forced back the sting of tears beneath her lids. This was going to be tough. She studied herself in the full-length mirror after discarding her suit. Even in the new cheap supermarket underwear, her reflective scrutiny agreed she didn't look *too* bad for her age. Marcus found her alluring. Catching sight of her bruised knees drew a brief smile; if the girls saw these, there would be a tirade of comments cavorting through her WhatsApp group.

What've you been up to, beaut? Got a few carpet burns?

Whoop, whoop Gracie girl, been surfin' the shagpile, have you?

Bundling her shirt into the wash basket, Marcus' expensive aftershave wafted upwards into her nostrils. They'd slept nestled in her room as she wore it, their sweat, fragrance, and pheromones soaked into the fibres. Grace lifted it and buried her nose into the material, breathing in the aroma before squirrelling it away at the bottom of the pile.

As she worked her way through the casual side of her velvet-covered hanger filled wardrobe, she found a brightly patterned soon-to-be-packed-away sundress, and slipped it over her head with a sigh.

'There, house, I'm done. Working girl no more.'

The house didn't respond. Not a creak, nor a tick from a clock, or a whirr from the fridge.

'Aren't you listening? I'm done. It's over.'

This revelation became an apocalypse, and she flopped quickly on the edge of the unmade bed, head swimming, hand on her tilted forehead. Things were formidably real now Marcus was gone. She was home and the events of yesterday were in an imagined past. At the hotel, under the intensity of darkness, a pair of muscular arms held her throughout the long night, safely cocooned. In the company of the financial advisors, she remained muffled from her new reality.

If Rhys worked a normal shift, leaving the hotel, and going home to face him before nightfall in a flurry of emotions, meant keeping her secret under those conditions was impossible. Another furry-footed stroke of luck? Rising, she looked at the crumpled bedding and frowned.

I'll make the bed, shall I? Seeing as you didn't bother.

Downstairs, she opened a chilled bottle of wine from the fridge and settled on the sofa with both glass and bottle on the coffee table. Going to the supermarket following the lengthy financial meeting wasn't an option. The sense of shock and excitement, tinged with awe as they'd gone through everything, serious faces peering over reading glasses, briefcases open on the table, was acute. When they left, Grace remained alone for half an hour before gathering up her things and leaving the table to meet the taxi.

Now, curator of an enormous sum, she considered how rich financiers and corporations would be well versed in handling multi-millions. But would a thirty-six-year-old woman who worked for a branch of a nationwide product company have enough of the required skills to manage it?

I don't want to run a business. I want to travel the world wearing beautiful clothes. I want to wake up in different countries and watch sunsets from the strangest places. I want to enjoy my luck, not fret about every move I make and its tax implications. And I want to be someone's one and only.

Picking up her laptop, she re-ordered an online shop from the supermarket for an evening delivery. Averting annoying conflicts over the fridge and food cupboards was a vital move for the evening ahead. Those mundane aspects of her life would soon be in the past. There were easier ways to feed yourself when you owned a bottomless pit of money and all the endless online delivery options anyone may want. She added two extra items to the basket, an expensive bottle of champagne and a box of high-end Belgian chocolates. There would be no arguments over what to eat and what occupied the freezer and cupboards.

Chirp/Rhys.
Back soon, having a wander around B&Q. Want anything?

Wife
A pink power drill.?
Lol. OK Barbie.

Grace rolled her eyes and imagined a conversation when he walked in.

'Hi, where've you been?'

'Only for a walk and to pick up some electrical tape. Good day, Cariad?'

'Yes, a meeting with my financial advisors'

'Oh yeah? What did they have to say?'

'My one hundred million pounds win needs to be managed carefully.'

'Cracking. Cup of tea?'

'I *rather* thought we'd have a bottle of Taittinger instead.' She stressed the second word with a cut-glass accent.

'Whattinger?'

'Champagne, Rhys. The good stuff.'

'Whatever you fancy. Any news?'

'Someone in Wales won big on the Euromillions.'

'Probably someone like you love, left the slip buried in an old handbag.'

Grace remembered those fleeting times, imagining revealing a lottery win. There was screaming and whooping, the phoning of friends, champagne corks popping, the pulling of party poppers cascading into the air, a mini paper firework extravaganza.

An extraordinary cake would arrive, they'd pay off the mortgage, go new car shopping, book a fabulous holiday. But this was when dreams were unlikely to come true, and swiftly forgotten as the next episode of the latest thriller settled them onto the sofa for the night.

This was the opposite. The harbinger of sullen worry, of endless secretive decision-making. A colossal sum to control.

And it's my albatross. *Tight around my neck. Gran never did like birds in the house.*

A large glass of chilled white already touched her lips. The need for Dutch courage to manoeuvre through the upcoming contact growing urgent. This was the man she married. They were a legal force, a pair-bonding, living under the same roof, with interconnected families, mothers-in-law and a rarely seen sister-in-law, friends long and short term. Photo albums. Cars. Strimmers. High thread count Egyptian cotton bedding.

The sound of the back door opening caused a jerk of her hand, spilling droplets down her chin. Urgently wiping them away, she waited pensively to hear his footprints on the kitchen floor. The noise of a turtle choking-single-use plastic bag rustled on the countertop. Then his deep Welsh voice called out.

'Do you want a beer, Cariad, or have you got wine?'

I'd miss his voice. I'm so used to it.

She'd left the corkscrew in full sight on the draining board. With rising annoyance mixed with fear, she found words faster than expected.

'I've got wine. If you want some, bring a glass.'

The sound of a bottle top cascading onto the floor and Rhys cursing in Welsh as he bent to pick it up was her answer.

'Nah, I'm having the grain.'

Yesterday's Evening Post was on the coffee table. She grabbed it and opened it to a random page, pretending to read whatever the print offered.

Her eyes rested on the horoscopes.

Then he was behind the sofa, leaning to peck her on the top of her head before settling at his end and sipping his beer straight from the bottle. There were no direct glances, simple everyday body language for a struggling marriage of twelve years.

'What's that smell? You've been buying flowers again?'

'Yes. Reduced. A bargain.'

'Nice. Waste of money, though, when there's still some in the garden.'

Inside, a pulsating tremble rose through her abdomen up to her vocal chords. These weren't blue butterflies taunting her. These were black bats thrashing in a darkened cave.

'Just get in, did you? Put the news on?' He nodded towards the remote control. Grace was relieved to introduce a third person into the environment as the newsreader regurgitated yet more political misery across the nation.

'Yes, not long.'

'Bloody hell, just look at that.' he groaned, pointing at the screen ticker tape. 'Rail strikes. Lucky we rarely use the train.'

Grace glanced at the ceiling, forcing a slow, soundless, calming breath.

'How was your day, Cariad?'

She took a choking gulp of wine. Rhys always used the Welsh term for love when speaking to her, rarely using her name. She loved hearing him say it. The hangover lingered despite endless sips of water poured from cool, heavy glass pitchers in the Oyster Suite. Grace swallowed hard.

'Million pound orders fell through my hands. I'm rolling in money.'

Does my voice sound normal because it's shaking? Actually shaking.

'Oh good. Don't forget to fling some my way, then. I've shelled out three quid for new batteries today, and paid over a pound for the Evening Post. Just to see who caught the biggest fish, who died, and what John from the Uplands thinks of the latest planning decisions. It's lucky I don't buy it every day.'

Too many words, Rhys. I can't deal with this conversation right now.

'You look like you could fall asleep on a chicken's lip. Still up for a curry?'

Grace looked him full in the face and wondered if her life-changing event was visible. He glanced back, quizzing brows in animated motion.

Can he sense something's happened? Have Marcus' kisses bruised my face? Have I covered up my red stubble-rashed chin? Don't be stupid, he never notices a thing about you.

'Stop moaning. You love the Evening Post. Where would you be without Dave from Sketty moaning about dog mess on pavements? Let's stay in and get a takeaway, or a boy on a bicycle. I've got a delivery van coming at ten, anyway.'

With the vibrato rising in her voice, she persevered.

'We can watch that new film you fancied.'

'Sounds alright to me. I'll ring it in. Same as usual?'

No. My boat's being pushed out.

'Something with prawns, please, off the chef's suggestions. It's been a tough day.'

'OK, your ladyship, fancy shellfish it is. You put your feet up. Have you been eating garlic?'

Grace swallowed. Rhys despised garlic. He could smell last night's, which meant the financial advisors must have too.

'I ate some at lunch. Sorry.'

Why am I apologising for eating something I love?

Rhys shrugged. 'No big deal. By the way, nice of you to make the bed for me before you went to work, not a crease in it. You'd think it hadn't been slept in.'

Grace took a slow breath.

Of course it hadn't been.

'I was off with a younger man, messing up *his* sheets.'

The words slipped off her tongue as she struggled to halt a sardonic smile. Rhys held his beer bottle up to the light, scrutinising the contents. 'Good, was he?'

'Very athletic. Now maybe you can whip upstairs and make it again, as you left it in a heap?'

He took a swig, tutted at something the newsreader reported, and shook his head. 'Airing, Cariad, airing.'

Rhys bounced back to the kitchen to find the menu and phone in the order. Having him a few spaces away to her side, quietly engrossed in a drama, instead of directly across a restaurant table making inquisitive conversation and eye contact, was the better option until she felt equipped to cope with the charade ahead.

Turning her attention back to yesterday's horoscopes, out of curiosity she read what *should* have happened for The Goat star sign.

Capricorn: Dec 22-Jan 21

You need to take a pause on any investments. Be patient enough not to hurry and enjoy your current financial stability. You may have a wonderful evening with someone near, and dear to you. Continue doing something which will prove great for your mental health. In professional matters, your boss may not be too happy with your decisions.

Jesus, Grace. You never look at these things. It's always Angela in the office reading everyone's star signs. Bloody hell.

That was bang on.

Rhys reappeared, today's paper folded under an elbow, a fresh beer bottle in hand.

'It's coming in half an hour. Means I can have another beer. Chill time.'

'Can I have the paper for a minute?'

'What for?'

'What do you mean, *what for?* I want to look at my horoscope.'

Rhys sat, put his bottle on the table, and ceremoniously opened the paper wide, clearing his throat.

'OK, let's see, Capricorn, isn't it?'

Grace rolled her eyes.

'You may now find it easier to climb the ladder to success with a renewed sense of energy. It's an auspicious day to make maximum financial investments. There are chances you'll make some beneficial high-expense plans today… well, that bit's true, your prawn curry was an extra fiver. You're high maintenance, Cariad.'

He settled back and started reading the front page, as Grace mulled over the words and turned her attention back to the News.

The Patek Phillipe watch?

10.15 pm
Chirp/MarX
Hope all's OK. Thinking of you. Will be awake a lot tonight. Xxx

Green Goddess
Thanks. Unpacking late shopping delivery. Xx

Grace barely slept too. Instead, she remained downstairs while Rhys recovered from two long shifts with a few more bottles of beer and a deep, soundless sleep. She was online for much of it, suspended between excitement and agitation, searching for lottery winners and the downsides of wealth.

Warren Buffett, the fifth richest person in the world, still lived in a house he'd bought in 1958 for thirty-one thousand dollars and Bill Gates wore a ten dollar watch, despite their insane wealth.

'*Spend, spend, spend*' was Viv Nicholson's motto, before she lost her husband's football pools winnings, scattering them like autumn leaves in a cyclone of squandering. Three million was nothing compared to Grace's win but was a newsworthy prize decades ago which still appeared in online searches. Welsh winners fared worse, with serious acts of violence on lucky partners by jealous lovers.

As the night wore on, she drifted in and out of sleep while the laptop burned brightly, bruised knees tucked beneath her on thick sofa cushions and the occasional discomforting reminder which came with too much intimacy in too short a time.

She dreamed of unwanted publicity, reporters hounding her in the street, scammers taunting her on her phone, her inbox, begging letters falling through the letterbox, loud hammerings on the door, pleading voices echoing through the frame. Throughout weaved thoughts of Marcus.

Green Goddess
3.00 a.m.
Hope this doesn't wake you up. Can't believe 20 hrs have passed. Xx

MarX
3.30 am
On silent & black screen. Checked anyway. This time last night we were in your room, Xxx

Green Goddess
4.20 am
Awake again. On the sofa since the TV went off. xx

MarX
5.20 a.m.
Don't know if good or bad? Don't want to ask. Rubbish night's sleep. Two in a row lol. Xxx

The argument with Rhys.
Remember the lies.
There'll be loads.

Chapter 19

Autumn, 1st September.

Waking late, her first thought was seventy per cent of lottery winners ended up broke, with a third declaring bankruptcy. *Just statistics. Not you, you're well organised. You'd never spend all that money. Unless someone takes half of it.*

Checking the time on her phone, and seeing the date, Grace whispered *'White Rabbits'* before she moved through the silent lounge towards the kitchen and the cafetiere. *Coffee. I need so much coffee. Oh god, Marcus. I wish you were nearby. I'd race out to meet you, drag you to lunch, and sit looking at your face, your suit, your shirt and tie, and breathe in your daylight essence.*

Rhys appeared, surprised to find her perched on the edge of the table, waiting for the aromatic liquid to reach peak perfection.

'Not going to work love, it's past nine?'

'Coffee?'

Rhys shook his head, filling the kettle for his morning cup of tea.

'I'm not feeling great, I think it was the prawns.'

A hand touched her shoulder. 'How bad do you feel? Bad, bad, or OK to come upstairs for half an hour, bad?'

He looked hopeful.

He's feeling horny? Now? He's got work in an hour.

'Bad, bad.' She stood up and pushed the plunger into the grounds, infusing the kitchen with nutty, caramelised, toasty whiffs.

'OK. He turned away, then paused for effect.

'I dreamt last night Oliver Twist told me the winner of the Rugby World Cup.'

Grace poured a cup and raised it to her lips.

'How?'

'He said 'I want Samoa."

She groaned, trying to stop the tiny twitches at the corner of her mouth. *Don't encourage him. But it's hilarious. Did he laugh Sian into bed with his rugby jokes too?*

For fuck's sake, Grace. Stop it.

10.10 am.

Her mother was on the phone.

'Hi Mam, are you OK?'

'Yes, love. Just letting you know we're heading up to Southampton tomorrow morning. Going to spend a night there before we sail. I've got us a nice little deal in a boutique hotel and we're taking the half-past eight train. Amanda will meet me at the station.'.

'Are you packed already?'

'You know me. Mention a cruise and the case is full before it's booked. Will you water the plants? The keys are in their usual spot. Stay over if you want some peace.'

'Yes, of course I will.'

'OK love, I'll leave you to get on with your day, speak later.'

This is a useful twist.

No need to face her before she left, and time gained to work out a strategy. A full two weeks plus an extra day of travel on either side meant there was somewhere to disappear. Private, nearby thinking space.

'OK Mam, enjoy. Don't let Amanda get drunk and fall over the balcony.'

'Will do. I'll text you when we get to Southampton, love you.'

'You too, Mam. Enjoy the cruise.'

Grace pondered over how to get some money over to her before they sailed. Putting a thousand pounds in an envelope and dropping it through the door with a *'buy yourself something nice'* note was perfect, but it was a substantial amount of money for any daughter to part with during a cost-of-living crisis. Mothers being mothers, she would doubtless return it.

11.30 am. The estate agent's window display showed properties for sale and rent around the city, including the two popular coastal areas she adored, Caswell and Langland Bays. Forcing back a nervous gulp, Grace pushed open the door.

'Hi, can I help you?'

The willowy mid-twenties blonde with a warm smile, stood up from behind a desk.

'I'm interested in properties for sale or rent in Langland or Caswell.'

The girl nodded, and Grace noticed a quick flicker of her eyes taking in the light blue denim jeans, white shirt, and navy blazer she'd pulled on in her rush to leave home. A white bag and loafers completed the ensemble. *I look like I'm going boating. Cowes Week here I come.*

'Yes, we do, but not too many, as I'm sure you're aware. It's the premium area of Gower and the Bays. Properties don't come on the market with any frequency.'

'Yes, that's why I'm interested.'

Grace was aware her voice sounded defiant with a strength rarely present in her daily sales negotiations.

'If you take a seat, I'll show you what we have, to date.'

The agent motioned to a chair, and Grace sat, placing her bag on the floor. The sounds of shuffling papers came from across the office as a selection of information sheets from the large banks of filing holders set out across the walls. She returned and took the opposite seat, behind a plastic screen still visible in many businesses with face-to-face contact, a pandemic leftover invested in and not easily let go.

'These are what we have at the moment.' she spread some sheets in front of Grace 'Would you like a coffee, tea, or a glass of water?'

Grace shook her head quickly, speed-scanning the sales literature. Flats, mainly.

Then the one house, raised above the sea, on a hill overlooking the beach.

'This one. I'd be interested in viewing this.'

Grace noticed the questioning eyes running through her responses.

'Do you need a mortgage? Can you actually afford this? Are you messing with me?' remained unspoken, and she nodded quickly, long shiny blonde hair moving like silk around her shoulders. Grace noticed there were a few stray hairs caught along the sleeve of her black jacket, and her enamelled name tag which read simply 'Emma.'

Emma smelled like a department store perfume counter, expensive and glorious.

'I'm sure we can get you a viewing this afternoon if you'd like? The house is currently vacant but furnished, and for sale, possibly available for rent in the short term. Now I have to go through a few questions with you first and create a file if that's OK with you?'

Grace nodded, and they began with the intrusive financial questions needed to allow a viewing of what may become a dream home. Ten minutes later, Emma was happily announcing there was an appointment for Grace to view the property at half-past one in the afternoon, and she would meet Miles, who would greet her at the driveway with the keys and the security code to open the electric gates.

Emma glanced at Grace's ring finger.

'Will your husband be viewing too?'

'No, it's just me today.'

The blonde smiled happily. The scent of commission filled the air, and Grace wondered how they'd share percentages on a sale this size. By the smile on her face, Emma would indeed sniff the aroma and be in with a chance of reward even if she wasn't doing the actual house showing.

'Are you comfortable with a male agent showing you around?' came the ultimate question.

'Yes, completely happy, thanks.'

'He'll look forward to seeing you there later. Here, take the details and the address is at the bottom. Thanks for coming in, please let me know if you need further help.'

Grace smiled, took the information, picked up her bag and sauntered out of the office with false confidence in her step.

'I'll be back to check out some marina flats next week.'

Slipping a hand inside her bag, she felt around for the rabbit's foot and stroked the fur.

Nice and safe. Exactly where you'll stay.

Chapter 20

The house was beautiful. Perfect views of the sea, with a short walk to access the beach area, with its green and white Victorian style beach huts, brasserie, surfers cafe, and tennis courts. Two small car parks with pay and display machines didn't detract from the beauty of Langland Bay and from one of the floor-to-ceiling windows, she admired the vista below. The glazed atrium with its internal garden, planted with small trees and palms, was ideal for relaxing, and the modern cubed features of the house had won architectural awards. Open-plan stairs would provide the fear factor for the first few climbs, but Grace was determined to overcome it.

Would Rhys like this place, or would it be too far from the centre of his world, the rugby club, and the suburban feel of their area of Swansea? He may love it for a short time, but she feared he'd grow bored with living in a large, open-to-the-elements box, a showpiece where not one engine part would creep onto any kitchen floor or surface. He'd say the sea was grey and miserable, and he missed the greenery inland, and the drive to the rugby club was too long.

He was a 'bloke's' bloke.' A middle-of-the-road, centre-of-the-street, semi-detached type, happy to wave to the neighbours, borrow a lawn mower, open a can across the fence with the man next door, while discussing any shock sports results and the reason electric cars were a waste of time.

'How the hell will they deal with all the batteries? It's bloody daft. Do you have *any* idea of how much lithium they'll need to mine, to run them?' He'd discussed it with someone down the pub. Grace Googled it and found he was right.

Rhys was a blue jeans and shirt man, not the trousers and jacket type. She couldn't see him living happily or comfortably in a house like this for long. Too big, too many windows. She could hear the complaints already.

Marcus, however, would command this space, with his designer suits and well-groomed exterior. Grace doubted he knew what an engine looked like outside a bonnet, never mind allowing one on his kitchen floor. When servicing came around, the garage would pick up his car. The nearest he'd get to cleaning it would be from behind the wheel using his phone while a team of young men used sponges and buckets outside.

Why are you even placing him here? You barely know him.

'You have a hot tub on the terrace, a small indoor pool, plus a sauna in the gym downstairs.' Miles informed her as they wandered around the property.

'When can you get back to me on the rental aspect, and if we were to buy it, how long until completion?'

'I'll speak to the owner and call you back?'

'Do you think it would be possible to get in here quickly under rental?'

'It might, depends on your deposit, really.'

'OK, I'll wait to hear from you. Look into it please, I have any deposit you need.'

With the viewing ended, Miles left her at the gates and as the buzz of excitement ebbed, she drove down to the car park near the beach huts and headed to the little Surfside cafe above the beach, and ordered a coffee before finding a seat on the outside terrace. Spoiled for choice between the upmarket Langland Brasserie a short walk away, and the casual feel of the daily papers, dogs and log fire in this corner retreat, Grace relaxed and surveyed the surfers in the water. There must have been at least twenty, riding the fast sets of rollers hitting the beach criss-crossing as they broke formation waiting to catch a wave. They were so close as the tide came in, and sitting watching from the outside terrace drew her eyes down to swimmers and sunbathers on the shoreline. Dog walkers sat nearby, waiting until October to be allowed back on the beach, anxious pets gazing at the sand with an excitement which must wait a few weeks to be satisfied.

It would be easy to stay here forever; the sound of the sea, the chatter and laughter of adults and youngsters enjoying the last of free summer days before school term recommenced. Calm descended as the bracing sea scent formed by coastal bacteria delivered a much-needed hit of happiness.

WhatsApp Cocktails Group/Ffion

OK girls, get your glad rags on. Let Saturday night fever begin. We'll start off in the Bras @ 7 pm. I'll book a table but I need to know who's in. Quick, quick, chop, chop, please.

I'm in. I'm going to iron my glad rags right now.

Actually, girls, I'm never going to be ironing anything ever again. Somebody else can do it for me. I bloody hate ironing.
Over the next few minutes, seven responded with positive emojis and thumbs-up signs plus the usual series of flowing hearts, fireworks, and clinking glasses.
I know. I'll order a load of champagne and have it delivered to our table, and tell the waiter to pretend it's from a secret admirer. We can celebrate together and have a giggle trying to work out who sent them.
The phone trilled into life and 'Estate Agent' flashed across the screen.

'Hello Mrs Lewis, Emma here. We've spoken to the owner, and he's happy for you to take on the property whenever you're ready. There's just the paperwork and deposit to sort out, and he's prepared to do what's effectively a rolling contract until you decide if you want to purchase.'

'That's amazing, thank you. Shall I come in first thing in the morning? Will you accept cash?'

There was a silence and some hasty discussion in the background before Emma answered.

'Yes, that's fine. We can hand you the keys late afternoon.'

This was good, this *feeling* was good. She smiled broadly and a woman sitting at the next table looked at her.

'Good news, is it?' She asked. 'It's a lovely day for good news.'

'The best.'

The woman winked and made a signal with her hand symbolising pregnancy.

Grace laughed aloud, a burst of unexpected joviality, eyes sparkling, smile broadening with humour.

'Not that kind of news. I'm too old, anyway.'

The woman shrugged and laughed.

'I had twins when I must have been a decade older than you love. You have a glow about you.'

That ship has sailed. It's on course for the edge of the world. Oh, my god, I forgot yesterday's pill. It's only one. I'll be fine. But I know exactly why there's a glow.

'Hi, I need a car from Monday morning, please, something really special. Probably for at least two weeks. What do you have?'

'Our top premier model would be a Mercedes E class. Is that suitable?'

'Sounds good. What do you need from me?'

'Driving licence, credit card.'

'Great, what time can I pick it up?'

'We open at eight. Can I take a name please, and I'll need a deposit?'

'No problem. One more thing. Would it be possible for someone there to drive my old car back to my place of work? I can follow them there and bring them back. It's only by the docks.'

'That's nearby, I can't see any problem, and you're hiring our top-of-the- range. We'll see you Monday morning.'

'One last thing. Do you have it in red?'

'I'll see what we can do.'

Hell, I'm getting a Mercedes. It'll be like a long test drive. I can leave it on Mam's drive and get a taxi to drop me off every day until I work out what's what.

Chirp
MarX
Hey gorgeous girl, what you up to?
                    Thinking about you Englishman.
Are they decent thoughts?
                              Nope.
No answer to that, is there?
                         None. Hwyl. xx
Not even going to ask.

4.00 pm.

A gilt-edged mirror suitable for the interior of Cardiff Castle reflected her image from the wall a few feet away. Behind it, black, gold, and floral wallpaper with curled sconces provided a gothic backdrop.

'OK Grace, what are we doing today?'

'I want hair extensions, Lawrence, long ones, down to mid-back length please, and I want them a mix of browns, Ombre or Balayage or whatever you call it.'

'OK, we can do that, blend a few in, colour your own hair to mix in perfectly. How does that sound?'

'Go for it. I'm sick of one colour. I want it to look amazing. I don't care what it costs.'

Grace relaxed back in the chair and studied her reflection. She looked tired.

'You do Botox here, don't you?'

'Yes, there's a nurse coming in at six. Late night *tweakment* time. Do you want me to see if she can fit you in?'

'Ooh Yes, please. Do you know how long it takes to work?'

'A few days to kick in, then it just gets better, but you've barely got any wrinkles.'

'Thanks, but I'm thinking ahead now. Does she do lips, too?'

'She does it all. You're looking for big changes, girl.' He laughed, picking up a hairbrush from the nearby trolley.

'My friends have been having it for years. I've never found

time or inclination. But prevention is better than cure, as they say.'

'Is everything OK with you, Grace?'

'Couldn't be better, but thanks for asking.'

'As long as you're sure. I'll just go mix up the colour, and James can do the extensions once you're rinsed and dried. Coffee, was it?'

As the hairdresser sidled deeper into the salon, he caught the eye of an assistant, raised an eyebrow and shrugged, tapping the third finger on his left hand with the forefinger of his right, before mouthing 'Trouble in paradise, methinks.'

7.15 pm

On the way home, Grace slipped five hundred pounds in cash and a note into an envelope, parked a few yards up the road from her mother's house, burglar-crept to the front door, and silently eased the wad through the letterbox before stealth-walking away in her driving shoes.

> Mam, buy yourself one of those posh bags they sell on board. Work bonus, don't tell Rhys. X

Chirp

Mam

I can't thank you enough, and of course, I won't tell Rhys. What a lovely present. Xxx

> Good, didn't knock, was late finishing.

A smile spread from cheek to cheek. This first act of sharing felt ridiculously small but extravagantly pleasing.

A few more little lies, just tiny ones. But this is your mother, Grace. They're white. Don't worry about it.

Chapter 21

Friday. The train to Cardiff wasn't busy, but it gave Grace respite, being among people not engaging directly with her. Gazing out of the dusty windows, she watched the countryside speed past, passengers boarding and alighting at stops along the way, the trackside fields cloaking sheep, horses and ponies knee-deep in their greenery.

Neath and Port Talbot flickered past in a semi-industrial daze, until Bridgend, when the level of excitement rising matched any International rugby game in the capital, where throngs of fans wearing red poured off the train, the sight of the signs for Cardiff Central setting off another bout of joyous singing which she'd joined in so many times as the great Welsh wave broke and spilled over the platform.

Delilah, Hymns and Arias, Bread of Heaven, and *As long as we beat the English* would rise over their heads to the heavens as the march on Saint Mary Street and the Principality Stadium began. *Calon Lan* may slip in there on a late train home, after endless weaving queues to reach the platforms. Gratefully received foil emergency blankets and red plastic rain protectors were thrust into shivering hands. Spring weather and the Six Nations tournament were seldom an ideal mix.

Grace smiled at these memories. Thronging along the heaving streets of the Capital City towards the stadium, joining in the singing of the Welsh National Anthem, now famous for raising goosebumps around the world, and fodder for many YouTube vloggers.

But this will be better than any Wales game, surely? Don't be daft, Grace, nothing beats Cardiff on an international day. With a dragon flag dress, a foam daffodil hat, and a Grand Slam in the bag.

Her hands shook again that morning as she'd applied her make-up, and tried to ensure the beautiful red lipstick she wore outside working hours was perfect, and it took a few swipes with a tissue to blend away tiny errors. No part of her body was immune to the excitement of the past few days, and the shaking appeared in various limbs at differing times.

Russian Red, you'll do for me. I can't ignore you because of a war. Ruby Woo, you stay in the drawer.

Glowing and perfectly made up, she noticed how different her hair looked, longer and thicker, as she'd often dreamed, and it made her smile. Her new reflection was growing on her. Although she'd stopped short of having her lips plumped, she'd followed the Botox aftercare instructions to the letter. Time for those tiny eye creases to vanish completely, and those number eleven lines between her brows to fade into oblivion.

Too much scowling over a steering wheel, too much concentration on roads and traffic conditions. Too many upset tearful grimaces into late-night pillows.

Now it's time to spend some money.

While her mother and her friend Amanda travelled on the earlier train, there'd been no risk of bumping into them and inventing last-minute excuses. Mentally listing the shops in the Capital, she knew they would offer more than her own second city, with its many post-pandemic closures which were still not replaced. Grace didn't know what she'd buy, but it was a good place to start until the new credit cards from the London bank accounts being opened were in her hands.

Miranda was on top of everything and Grace would need to take the train to London the following week to be present when everything was completed, collect her cards, provide proof of identity, and sign paperwork at the branches.

Grace hung onto the beaming, screaming smile she dared not allow to erupt across her face. If it broke free, she'd be up in the aisle, arms in the air, yelling to the carriage:

'I've won the bloody lottery! And I'm shagging a toy boy. Yes, me! I'm a cougar.'

A new me stepping off into a new world.

Me and my Botox, strolling down the avenue…

As she descended onto the platform at Cardiff, Grace took a deep breath. Wobbly legs returned immediately her feet touched the concrete, and swept up in the flow of people heading for the exit steps.

'Oh, my god oh my god oh my god.' began its loop. She was feeling rich. A beautiful cream silk dress flirted with her body, swinging lightly around her knees, a lightweight tonal coat over the top, and cream leather heels completed the outfit.

One hundred million. Why am I in Cardiff?

Because you daren't risk anyone finding out yet. Act normal. Normal women jump on the train to the Capital and get home in time to watch the news while eating an M&S weekend special with their husbands and families. They don't jump on flights to New York or Dubai without a word to an unsuspecting partner. Besides, you need to spend some of it on home soil.

Wales needs you, Gracie!

Even with her organised lifestyle, she didn't have the slightest concept of what was ahead, following the meeting with the advisers, and hearing what seemed to be endless cons as opposed to the pros of ownership of this amount. Still difficult to accept, yet there it was. More money than any average person would ever know what to do with. Trying to recall their words, the phrases intermingled.

'You should start up some businesses to make the best use.'

'You should consider a charitable donation.'

'You should only give away cash.'

'You are best advised to own any properties you give to your family and pay all the bills under your name.'

The list was endless.

I just want to spend some, to see if it's real.

She began walking towards the station exit; her stride

extended with confidence, and once through the barrier, stepped out into the sunshine and breathed in the air, smiling.

'Oh, my god! Here we go!' she said aloud and headed straight for the shopping centre. Where to start? John Lewis, home of all things designer, and a place she briefly scouted around when she was in the city, shocked by the clothing prices, wondering who on earth would pay two hundred pounds for a jumper? Realising now she, Grace Lewis, no relation, would doubtless spend at least that, possibly double.

Wandering through the brands she lifted hangers and studied the materials and patterns, the styles and quality, before wandering over to the handbag section. Grace never owned an expensive handbag. Maybe it should be her first purchase? Or a monster-sized bottle of super-expensive perfume?

Searching online for designer shops while sitting on the train took up the hour needed to get there. Naturally, she'd wander through the labyrinth of departments at historic Howells, Chanel at The Hayes, Hugo Boss, Zandra Rhodes. As she passed a small independent jeweller at the end of the street, she stopped and stepped back to look at the window display and caught sight of an array of antique diamonds glinting in the sun. With the newly gained confidence which arrived with the enormous win, she pushed open the door and stepped inside.

It was a small shop, hiding a treasure trove of jewellery. Not the new extra shiny branded diamonds she'd seen in luxury magazines down the years, backed up by perfectly photographed posters on the walls and counters within, but certainly pieces which were pre-worn, pre-loved, and now consigned to a small independent jeweller. It drew her eye to a large square-cut diamond in an old-fashioned setting to the right of the window display.

'Hello, how can I help you today?' the gentleman wearing a tweed suit behind the counter asked with a smile.

'Can I see the enormous diamond in the window, please? I can point it out to you.'

'Yes, please' he smiled, and they stepped towards the arrangement on show to the public.

'There, that one!'

'Ah, yes, a beauty,' he remarked, 'just over two-carat

weight, set in fourteen-carat white gold, and let me see the size. It's an 'N'. Do you know your size?'

'Afraid not, sorry. Do you have some sort of ring gauge I can try?'

'Of course, but you can slip this on your finger first and we'll take it from there.'

He walked back to the interior counter and laid the box with its old-fashioned paper and string price tag on the glass top counter.

'Here we go, give it a try.' He handed her the ring.

Grace held it and looked closely at the stone. The diamond was beautiful, much larger than anything she owned, apart from some fun costume jewellery. Twisting it in her fingers she caught sight of the price written on the tag now on the counter in front of her.

Three thousand, five hundred and fifty pounds. Tears pricked her eyes, but she blinked them back. *OMG* began its loop. *I can afford a three-grand ring. Just on a whim.*

Holding out her right hand, third finger, she slid it on.

'Oh well done!' the man smiled 'A perfect fit. After all these years of watching ladies trying on rings, I hoped I'd got this one right.'

Grace looked at it, turned her hand to see it sparkle, compared it to her left-hand rings and stood gazing at it.

'It's definitely real?' she queried nervously.

'Yes, of course, madam, only the one inclusion. This is a family business, we've been buying and selling jewellery for over forty-five years. Do you like it? How does it feel?'

'Perfectly lovely. Not loose or tight. It's like they made it for me.'

He handed her a jeweller's eyeglass and suggested she look closer into the stone and the hallmark. Grace peered at the flashing lights deep inside, dazzled by the luminescence.

'It's gorgeous!' she smiled. 'My mother takes me to antique fairs. We adore hunting out old jewellery, although we seldom buy. Look!'

She opened her bag and pulled out the rabbit's foot.

'My lucky rabbit's foot. The best gift ever given to me. Two quid at a Boot sale.'

'Very popular in their time.' He smiled 'Let's hope it brings you luck.'

Grace beamed.

'It already did. Yes, I'd like to buy this. You still take cash?'

'Of course, always a pleasure, although there seems to be a movement towards cards only. Not here, anyway. Let me wrap it up for you unless you prefer to wear it?'

Grace studied it, debating with herself.

In the box, out of the box. On the finger, not on the finger.

'Yes, I'll wear it. Why not?

'Let me give it a quick polish for you.'

Grace slid the ring from her finger and handed it back. As the man buffed the ring with a soft cloth, Grace opened her handbag and withdrew a large pack of cash. The ten thousand once hidden in the sofa cushion needed to be spent before she pulled out her credit cards. The proprietor said nothing, used to sizable cash transactions, and put the ring box and a handwritten receipt into a small rope-handled bag.

'I'll have to run the notes through the checking machine, then it's all yours.

Grace replaced the band on her finger as he made idle chit-chat about the weather and fed the notes through the machine.

'Oops, fifty pounds too much.' He said, handing her the extra note as it finished its job.

'Please keep it, I'm feeling happy today. Donate it to your favourite charity. Thanks for your help.'

'Thank you very much indeed, have a lovely day.'

Folding the note, he pushed it into a charity tin alongside the till. She smiled as she turned to leave and picked up the little bag with the ring box. The sound of an old-fashioned door chime ushered her into the sunlight, as she headed out into the street. The ring was even more beautiful in the dappled light of day.

It looked antique, and if Rhys commented, it was a cubic zirconia picked up at a Boot Sale.

Oh wow. First purchase made. This is going to be fun.

She must buy something for him. But what? A Lamborghini? He'd soon have the engine on the kitchen table. With the thought she *could* actually buy one, she remembered a used dealership somewhere in the area. But for now, the Hamley's store in St David's Centre would doubtless have sports car models.

Chirp
MarX
How's things, beautiful? Can you talk-talk, if I call you now?

Yes.

The phone rang immediately, and her stomach flipped as she slid the answer icon. A smile coerced its way across her cheeks.

'Hello gorgeous.'

The chocolate voice. Her knees weakened, and she leaned against the nearest wall.

'Hey Englishman, how's life across The Bridge?'

'Struggling along. Earning an honest crust. Pick your favourite cliché. It's lovely to hear your voice. Where are you today?'

'I'm up the 'diff.'

'You're *what*?'

'Not up the *'duff*, up the 'diff. Car*diff*. That's its nickname.'

The sound of light laughter reached his ear.

'Phew.'

'No panic, I'm not carrying your love child.'

His laugh was relaxed. 'Let's do FaceTime. You're worrying me. Give me a minute, I'll call you back.'

Grace stepped to the nearest empty bench a few yards away and sat uncomfortably.

'You look amazing!' He said 'Your hair's different.'

'Extensions. I've always wanted them. New job, new me and all that.'

'Wild. I love it.'

What did Rhys say last night? Been to the hairdresser? Again?

'Where are you today?' She asked.

Marcus turned the phone around in a semi-circle, showing a room with an office set up, bookshelves in the background.

'Working from home for a few hours. What are you doing in Cardiff, shopping, or chasing other toy boys?'

'Hey, I'm not that much older than you!'

'Only kidding, besides I love you've got a couple of years on me. All that experience.'

A couple? Charmer. But I suppose it's not that bad.

'I needed to get out of Swansea for the day. You've broken me.'

'Then why are you still smiling?'

'I honestly don't know.'

'You've worn me out, Welshwoman. Are you there all day?'

'I'm here till I fall off my heels or they decline my card, then I'll get a train back.'

'OK, no rail strikes then?'

'Not today. They knew I was coming.'

'I thought that was my special skill?'

'Marcus!'

He laughed loudly.

'You walked into that one! Let me call you later. Can you grab a wine somewhere around four o'clock? That bench doesn't look comfortable.'

'I'll find somewhere quiet indoors.'

'What time train are you getting back?'

'Maybe around six. Although John Lewis is open until eight. I think the last one is at eleven, so I'm not in a rush. All depends on my stamina.'

'Great. *Laters* then. You really look amazing. I hope some of your smile is my doing?'

Grace winked, pouted, and hung up.

Fifteen minutes later.

Chirp
MarX
Suggest Royal Hotel. Comfy lounge. Near the station. By the way, you're driving me insane. Hundred per cent cliche.

Oh my god, he makes me feel like a teenager. I could bounce around the pavements, even in these shoes. Why did I wear heels? I'll buy some flats, just in case.

'I'm going to need a new diary to keep everything in order. This is going to get complicated.' She said to no one in particular.

Stop talking to yourself. People can hear.

Grace marched into the nearest bookshop, fondled a beautiful and expensive A5 page-a-day Aspinal gold pebble diary, paid, and tucked it into her handbag, where it fitted perfectly. The ideal tool to keep her life and lies in order.

In Zandra Rhodes, she bought two stunning dresses and a pair of shoes. In Pandora, she chose some charms and a couple of bracelets to hang them on. One for her mother, the rest to please herself.

Trinkets. The good stuff comes later. I'm not going completely mad just yet.

In Hamleys, she found a perfect die-cast Lamborghini Sesto Elemento for less than twenty pounds and smiled as they slipped it into a gift bag for her. So she'd bought Rhys a fancy sports car. It may only be a model today, but she wondered if she'd ever hand him the keys to the real thing. Or if their marriage would still be alive by the end of the year.

There was little to be done to rid herself of the image of Sian, wearing tight leather trousers, swinging into the passenger side in her place. Or hearing Rhys's response to her pleading.

'Grace, if you'd told me straight away, maybe I wouldn't be leaving you now, with fifty million quid in my back pocket.'

Or maybe you would have been anyway, with the short blonde who's already been deep in your pockets. And slid open the zip in between.

She discovered the expensive Samsung flip phone in the desired rose gold, and watched as a phone shop staff member inserted her old sim.

'Is it charged fully? Will it last the day?'

'It should. You'll need to transfer all your stuff from your old one onto it, but it can wait until tomorrow.'

Back at John Lewis, she raided the shoe and clothing department, and in Chanel, bought a small black *Boy* bag. *This is fun, but with a hundred million, I really should be in Harrods. Next week. Maybe I'll spend the night in London. I need to go up to open the bank accounts.*

At half-past three, with her purchases cascading around her feet in their branded bags, Grace sat in Cafe Nero at Howells, savouring the experience, while the hot liquid revived her. Seeing all the designer carriers around her table, the thought arose she was an easy target for theft. It would take little for someone to rush past and scoop some or all of them from her hands and run off into the crowd. She collected them up and headed for the luggage department. There were barely any customers browsing as she descended on the salesperson.

'Hi, I need a suitcase to hold these bags. And I need it really fast.'

Marcus would call at 4 o'clock and she needed to get to The Royal, grab a drink, and find a comfy seat. Towing a case meant she needed to act with speed..

'Of course, madam, let's see what we have.'

The young assistant in his mid-twenties found a rose gold model with four-way gliding wheels.

'Let's try this, see if they fit.'

'I love rose gold!' Grace beamed.

As he unzipped the case and placed it flat on the floor, a broad smile cheered his face.

'Ooh, you've had a great time today! Next time you're shopping, pop in and give me a yell, and I'll come and carry them for you. You look stunning in that coat, by the way.'

Grace laughed happily.

'Will do, but I've got to get these back to the station without being mugged. And fast.'

Between them, they placed everything inside with minimum squish.

'Let's get you through the till poste-haste.'

Grace nodded rapidly, and as she handed over the cash, and thanked him as he snipped off the sales labels, and handed her the receipt before heading out into the world once again, now looking like a traveller towing a suitcase, instead of a target.

How things have changed. I've spent a hundred quid for a suitcase to get my shopping home and almost as much on a four-month diary. What happened to fifty quid sprees in TKMaxx? Why am I even getting the train back? I should just get a taxi. Keep it sensible, I've already got a day return ticket. No need to be wasteful.

3.50 pm

Grace settled herself into a comfortable armchair next to an unoccupied table in a corner of the lounge of the Royal, crossing her legs and gently swinging one relaxed foot in time to the quiet background music. Placing her wine on the table, she rested her phone alongside ready for his call then pulled the suitcase closer, aware of its valuable contents. The next train was in under an hour, so would be easy to catch, allowing for the walk, ticket machines, lift platform checking, and enough time to talk.

Taking a soothing sip of the Pinot Grigio, the scent of apples and peaches tickled her nose, fast-fading aromas of summer. Soon the crisp white would change for the soft plummy tones of Merlot as the Welsh winds blew through the autumnal streets of towns, cities, and valleys.

Elegantly withdrawing a fresh bottle of perfume from her handbag, she admired the beautiful red glass and golden neck flower design before spritzing herself in Gaultier's La Belle, the bergamot aroma headier than the wine. With fragrance evocative of moments and memories, this newly discovered, never worn bouquet would ensure she would remember this upcoming conversation with every future spray.

Exciting times ahead.

The death of others.

Chirp
MarX
Are you there yet?
                              Yes.
Would you prefer champagne, madame?
                    Lol, ask the barman to deliver.
No need, it's on its way.

144

A slender champagne flute descended gracefully onto the table as Grace raised her chin to see floppy blonde hair and sensual lips smile down at her.

'Hello, Welshwoman.'

Two sets of eyes flashed as they met.

'Oh, my god what are you *doing* here?'

She rose, the blue butterflies exploding inside her, as he pulled her towards him, and kissed her gently on the cheek.

'I thought I'd surprise you.'

'Don't you mean stun me? Look at you, all sexy in your civvies.'

A pleased smile crossed his face as her eyes scanned the length of his body. Wearing light blue denim jeans, a white chambray shirt with a brown leather jacket draped easily over one arm, he stood elegantly casual before her. Grace's hand drifted gently from his elbow to wrist, feeling the intensity of the material beneath her fingers, the sinews under his skin, before interlocking with his own in an affectionate squeeze.

'I've only seen you in posh suits.'

Marcus laughed.

'Posh suits. Straight to the point. Surely a Welsh thing.'

He briefly scanned the half-empty room.

'I presume nobody knows you around here?'

Grace raised a brow and shook her head, understanding his meaning.

'Good.'

His arms wrapped around her, as he pulled her so close the aroma of cotton material mingled with the faint scent of mandarin and cardamom.

'You smell divine.' She closed her eyes as the fragrance washed over her.

'So do you, but you *look* a million dollars. Cwtch me.'

They hugged tightly for a long, swaying second, cheeks touching, completely entranced in their embrace.

'What are you doing here?' She finally breathed as they parted.

'I thought I'd take a quick drive over the Prince of Wales Bridge, as you're nearby. '

'Severn.'

Those strong brows knotted.

'How many?'

'The Severn Bridge. The Bridge will always be the Severn to any true Taff.'

'Not a fan of name changes, I take it?'

'Nobody *really* likes change. We're all creatures of habit.'

He nodded, thoughtful. 'Well, I found a couple of spare hours, and here I am. I crossed the blue just to be with you.'

She laughed at his poetic injustice.

'That's insane. What if I'd got on the train with a glass of wine from the buffet?'

'I'd have raced down the M4 and dragged you off at Bridgend.'

'But where have you come from?'

'Oxford, a sweet city with her dreaming spires. It's a quote, not me being posh. Or too English.' He winked and smiled, then spotted the suitcase, and his voice lowered markedly. 'You haven't left, have you?'

'No, it's full of shopping. I needed new luggage, so I'm using it for today's haul.'

Phew, that was a good buy. Imagine if he'd seen all those expensive designer carriers? He'd think I'd been embezzling.

'We must have been paying you too much. Any Agent Provocateur in there?'

Grace shook her head.

'Give me a proper kiss.'

'But my lipstick is red.'

'Not bothered. Besides, we have a room with a mirror and a list of every return train. Now, kiss me and walk this way.'

Grace raised herself onto her toes to reach his lips, feeling the intimacy of two mouths connecting, lingering longer than expected. Then Marcus was smiling, his mouth tinged red as he handed her the glass and reached for the suitcase. To outsiders, they were a well-dressed couple about to spend a night in the city as they headed towards the lift.

'We look like vampires.' He grinned, seeing their diffused reflection in the metal doors. Pushing the button he squeezed her hand while they waited for the sound of its arrival.

This is wayward wild. He's raced all this way to see me. And he's booked a room.

The barman stood behind his counter polishing glasses, watching as the couple across the room got up, hugged, and headed for the lifts. Observant as ever, he noticed the wedding bands and diamond rings on the hands of the woman, while the man's fingers were bare. To a casual observer, they appeared to be any young couple off to spend time on a city break. Except these two weren't married. Married couples didn't fall into each other's arms like these two. They didn't gaze into each other's eyes. With a final flourish of the cloth, he placed the sparkling glass alongside a row of others and picked up the next.

This pair is going to hit problems, is my guess. Someone, somewhere, is going to get hurt. And it doesn't look like it's one of them.

Chirp/Rhys.
Sorry love, I'm needed again tonight, more dire emergencies. Stay over at your Mam's if you want. You won't have to worry about making noise in the morning and I'll be going straight to watch the game after I get up.

As Marcus inserted the keycard, she placed a hand on his arm to stop him, and tapped a response as he watched her studying the screen.

Wife.
OK, meeting girls later for quick drinks. Won't come back before you go in. Out tomorrow night too. See you as and when.

Last week, those excuses would have stewed for hours, every nuance, and angle queried. All that mattered today was she didn't need to go home.
My lucky rabbit's foot.
'Anything wrong?'
Deep breath girl. There may be a partner waiting for him. Just like you have a husband. Just because there's mad attraction doesn't mean there aren't obligations.

147

'Can you spend the night with me?'

She studied those gold-flecked eyes closely, frightened of the answer. The tiny frown etching his forehead relaxed.

'Can we cwtch, Welshwoman?'

Was it the champagne, the depth of his voice, or the knowledge of what was to come that made her legs weak?'

'Like crazy.'

Marcus tried a Welsh accent.

'Oh, there's lovely!'

Grace exaggerated her own. 'Bloody hell, boyo, you said that just right.'

'You make me smile, you really do.'

Leaning in, he kissed her until Russian Red further invaded their chins, then fully inserted the keycard, pushed the door, and slid the suitcase inside. Lifting her right hand, he kissed the back.

'Nice ring, sparkly. Just like you and champagne. Shall I order us a bottle?'

'Let me. You've paid for the room.'

'If you're sure. I like you better when you're under the influence. It loosens inhibitions.'

He nuzzled her neck. 'If the aunt of the vicar has never touched liquor, watch out when she finds the champagne.'

'Do you always impress women with fancy sayings?'

'Rudyard Kipling, and sadly in my Uni days, we created a quote club. It's supposed to knock the girls off their feet. It rarely works. You're not impressed?'

'I find you impressive.'

Grace smiled with humorous innocence at his next words.

'Even if I organise a sizable *deliveroo* tonight? Maybe we'll arrange a break out for brunch tomorrow.'

'Am I a prisoner now?'

'Oh, I think so, don't you?'

He leaned back on the bed, balancing on his strong wrists as she drained the glass, and watched as she picked up the room phone, dialled reception, and ordered a bottle and two glasses.

Marcus laughed and reached out for her.

'Come here sexy, smeared with lipstick, yet still so businesslike. Have I got time to fuck you before it arrives?'

Grace's heart leaped, and a familiar, excited sensation

spilled into her abdomen.

'Depends how quick you are.'

I sound like a whore. He sounds like a player. This is mega-wild.

She stood in front of him, a vision in cream and high heels. Her eyes held his gaze, as she slowly eased her dress up around her waist, revealing a tanned abdomen and long, shapely legs, broken only by a triangle of white lace.

Why am I wearing cloud colours? Like a virgin? Jesus, what are you doing, girl? This is porn star territory.

Marcus groaned, pulled her towards him, and buried his face in her white panties, one hand moving the triangle of lace aside as his tongue teased her. As she stood there, legs parted, balanced on her heels, her eyes closed, and her head tilted back in rapture.

'Fuck, Grace, look at you.' he moaned, falling back on the bed and taking her with him, one hand fumbling with his zip as his hips wriggled enough to let his solid erection bolt free.

'You make me so hard.'

In a second he was deep inside her, white triangle pushed aside, both fully clothed as he thrust quickly, feeling the hasty, unavoidable rush of fluids from them both spilling onto his jeans, soaking him.

'Jesus, Marcus, what are you doing to me?' she moaned, voice hoarse, mouth dry, gasping as she buried her face in his shirt, the waxy lipstick stains smearing the cotton, her lower body still trembling.

His arms flopped to his sides as his chest heaved, while she covered his torso with hers, rising and falling with him in a tangle of disarrayed clothing. 'Anything you want, baby, I'll do anything you want.' he breathed.

❦

Chapter 22

Marcus drove Grace to Swansea the following afternoon, trailing along the coastal scenic route, avoiding the stresses of motorways which up to now, regularly filled both their working lives. Sitting alongside him as he manoeuvred skilfully along the A48 through Cowbridge, Southerndown, onto Ogmore by Sea, felt completely natural as they talked and gazed at the countryside and coastline passing by.

She studied his hands on the wheel, and his ever alert eyes despite a night drinking champagne, with little restorative sleep. The comforting interior of the car smelled of newness, perfectly pristine, yet she could sink into the leather upholstery and relax completely, occasionally touching his hand as he changed gear.

'I'm glad I skipped work for the afternoon. Major management decision.'

'I'm glad you drove two hours to surprise me. And you keep spare clothes in the boot.'

Marcus cast her a sideways glance as he changed gear. 'Goes with the territory, thankfully. Was it worth it?' He caught her hand gently, before returning his own to the steering wheel.

'What do you want me to say?'

'Let me think… tell me I'm a stud, that you'll want me forever, and you'll dream about me nightly.'

'I'll let you know next time. Will that do?'

'It'll have to.'

Where is this lunacy going? It's not madness, Grace. It's playful delight.

The taxi from the rank outside High Street station, waited outside her mother's house, while she hid the suitcase in the utility room, removed a few items to take home, and hopped back inside for the final stage of the journey. When she stepped inside her own porch, a parcel sat on the side table awaiting her.

'Well hello, Kat Maconie.'

With a beaming smile, she tore at it and drew out the two boxes of shoes. Paper and cardboard rustled in the quiet of the lounge as she tossed them onto the sofa. The waft of leather and other materials filled her nostrils.

'Look at you, Rafi! You're beautiful. Tonight, you're going to Wind Street.' Grace lifted a black patent high heel, ankle strapped artwork, with its huge gold flower above the toes, and traced a finger along the gold edged heel. This wouldn't end up in the pavement cracks.

It's like Christmas has come all at once. Actually, Gracie, it's come a few times. Behave yourself, you're turning into a horny bitch. Isn't that what frequent sex does, make you want more? Especially following a dearth. But I feel the happiest I've felt in months.

Avoiding the expensive new clothes, Grace chose an outfit from her existing evening selection. An obvious high-end designer outfit may raise eyebrows, especially once the bubbly reached their table under the guise of an *unknown admirer.* These girls were savvy. It wouldn't take long before curious glances between the champagne bottles and expensive clothing began adding up to something interesting.

'Has someone left you money in a Will?'

'Had a lottery win, beaut?'

'What's with all the new clothes?'

It was disappointing not to slip into the exquisite Zandra Rhodes gold fluted trousers with the intricately decorated, slightly see-thru blouse with huge sleeves which screamed 'Buy me, buy me' from the rails, but also yelled 'I'm hideously expensive and shamelessly high-end.'

The ring, however, would be on her finger. If anyone commented, it was cubic zirconia, a monster bought at a car boot sale. Diamonds weren't a top priority among her friends, who spent their money on clothes, cosmetics, holidays, mortgages, and looking after the handful of children between them. The Chanel bag was going too, with an excuse already lined up.

I shouldn't have to lie, but I don't want to upset anyone in these difficult times. So Grace Lewis, what's the actual point? If you can't wear what you've bought, and you don't want to change your life, you may as well give it all away. Or find a new set of friends. And how's that gonna work? Put an ad in the local paper? Well-heeled friends wanted so I can wear my good stuff? But I want to change my life. I just haven't decided how.

Soon she would party with lively voices, and despite the secrecy of the celebration, they would make merry around the table. The bonus for Grace was Marcus lurked nearby. Left to his own devices for a few hours, they'd parted with excited words.

'Try Morgan's hotel for a room. It's where we usually finish the night.'

'Not the Marriott?'

'I'm not walking over there in heels, and I hate queuing for taxis.'

Omg, I have a booty call lined up. Grace Lewis has a toy boy for the end of the night. For once, I'm excited.

They booked the table for seven o'clock; the champagne paid for, and as she clambered into the back seat of the cab at half-past six, cream satin flared trousers caught in one of the weirdly shaped heels as she sat with a thump. The weather may creep towards autumnal, but summer clothes were wearable in the warm September temperatures. Her loose gold chiffon floaty elbow-length blouse covered just enough of her arms to keep away any chill, and the long fashionable chains in various lengths around her neck reached elegantly to waist length. New bracelets hung around her wrist and a simple gold-coloured lariat necklace nestled in her cleavage. Grace was a vision of creamy glistening colours and tanned skin at the end of summer, her cheeks illuminated with golden highlighter.

'Off to Wind Street love? It's busy down there already.' The taxi driver asked as he pulled away from the house.

'Yes, I'm meeting friends at The Braz. Girls' night out again. You're only young once.'

'You enjoy love. Back in my day, Wind Street was nothing like it is now. It was all up on The Kingsway then. Full of clubs. Nothing much left there now, except on Northampton Lane.'

Grace hung onto the grab handle as they swung around a corner onto the main road, accompanied by the crackling voice over the intercom from the booking office.

'I've heard all the tales from my mother. She used to love The Valbonne and Martha's Vineyard, and Harper's piano bar.'

The taxi fell into traffic headed directly into the city, the low hum of the engine a backdrop to their conversation.

'Yes, those were the days. Not the same now, of course. The music is all rubbish, not like back in the eighties.'

'My Mam's heyday, as she calls it.'

'Mine too, love, it was the best decade. I used to work the club doors back then. All the mad fashions you girls wore. Those were the days. Fantastic, *mun*. Just think, I might have danced with your mam!'

'Well, she does love to dance, so it wouldn't surprise me.'

Grace's phone emitted its usual incoming sounds.

Chirp/Rhys.
Don't get drunk and let those girls lead you astray.

OK.

Chirp/MarX.
I've found a room in Morgan's hotel. I'll either see a film or lurk nearby until you can get away, I'll enjoy myself looking at all these gorgeous Welsh girls. Wink emoji.

If you must. Horrified emoji.

Well, you're a good-looking, glamorous lot, I must say.

It's the rain. Keeps the moisture in the skin. Xx

Chirp/Rhys
Watch you don't trap your stilettos in the pavement cracks again.
You'll ruin another pair of heels.

I'll try not to.

Grace's sadness was palpable, sitting alone in the back of
the Yellow Cab, watching the houses make way for the city
centre buildings, nursing her gigantic secret and immersed in the
frightening first flushes of an attraction so intense, guaranteed
upsets were ahead. An unwanted message from a husband. A
desired line from a lover. *It's all backwards.*

At the end of Wind Street, Grace handed over a generous tip
and smiled sadly.

'Cheers, *Drive*, don't work too hard.'

'Have a good night, lovely.' he answered in his lilting
Welsh way.

'Oh, and say '*Shwmae*' to your mam.'

'*Iawn.*'

Chapter 23

'Champagne should be cold, dry, and hopefully, free.'

Christian Pol Roger

Grace stepped out into the pedestrianised street and surveyed its length. This was going to be some night, her first proper celebration. Crowds of revellers in the early stages of the evening milled outside the various pubs, bars, and other venues. Now the pedestrianised hub of Swansea's nightlife for nearly two decades, people filled its breadth, the trees lining its length sprinkled with fairy lights.

Standing stoic at the top end, the remains of Swansea's twelfth-century Castle lay siege to revellers winding their way down from the railway station and taxi ranks, watching over the diverse age groups who came to socialise on the main street and side alleys. Following a destructive three-night blitz during the Second World War, only the castle and the Tudor-style 'Cross Keys' pub remained a stone's throw from their ancient walls.

The No Sign bar, a once favourite haunt of the poet Dylan Thomas, varied between lunchtime food trade, where patrons sat comfortably next to open fires while Dickensian portraits and stencilled walls showed its age, to more vibrant weekend evenings where live music entertained and the underground cellar bar became packed with party people.

Along with its recent additions of outside seating, planters, and a rainbow crossing, spread the various hostelries, everything from Coyote Ugly, to Jack Murphy's, the new Founders and Co, a mish-mash of bar, street food, mini shops, and a coffee area, and of course, still at the bottom of the street, only a stone's throw from Morgan's hotel, was La Brasseria. Popularly shortened and pronounced as *The Braz.*

Favoured by the business owners of the city for decades, plus those who liked to rub shoulders with the *crachach,* Swansea's famous actresses and singers popularised this much-frequented Spanish restaurant, on return visits to their home city.

Waiters fandangoed among the dark wood furniture and the wine label-covered walls and alcoves with their basket wall lights. A hard flagged entrance floor led to the interior ground floor and upstairs, while the bar displayed endless bottles of port and wine and the food selection tempted in a chiller at the far end, everything from the freshest fish to the finest steaks, it was simple but effective fayre in a great atmosphere.

Inside, Grace found her cocktails group, drinks in hand, on the large wooden table by the window. The Spanish ambiance of the place transported them to the Mediterranean in an instant.

'Hola chicas!' Grace called out as she approached their table.

Her closest friend Ffion rose from her chair and hugged her. 'Hey beaut, lookin' fleek, come and sit, we're starving. Cracking pair of shoes!'

'Online sale, Ffi, first outing. Plasters in my bag, just in case.'

'How've you been?'

'Long week. Endless meetings, but all the better for seeing you lovelies. Spill the tea girls.' she laughed, placing her bag over the back of the chair.

'Wow, lush bag, Grace!' came one compliment.

'Mam's been to Thailand again, don't look too close.'

'Fake it till you make it, eh?' Ffion laughed before veering straight into gossip.

'I was just saying before you got here, Cheryl from next door, is having another affair. I swear, it's unreal.'

'Who is it this time?'

They leaned in conspiratorially.

'Some guy from the north of England works down here midweek on a building contract, stays in a hotel Monday to Thursday, then goes home at weekends. So while her hubby is away driving his lorry all week, and home on Friday nights, she's getting the best of both worlds and both men crisscross on the motorway. Absolutely no chance of getting caught out.'

Ann gasped. 'Oh my god, have you seen this bloke?'

'Yep, sneaking in after the kids have gone to bed. He's handsome, a bit of a Tom Ellis type. You know, the Cardiff bloke in 'Lucifer? Then he's gone really early for work before the kids get up. It's lucky we live at the end of the street and I'm never tired.'

Helen chimed in. 'It's because you never close your curtains!'

'She gets that teenage girl a few doors down to babysit some nights and goes to his hotel.'

'How do you know all this?' Grace asked.

'Because she bloody well tells me!'

'No!'

Squeals of laughter spilled around the table.

'Yes! She'll come around for a 'coffee' or ask me to pop over there and out it comes. It's not like I'm going to say 'Hi Nick, you know Cheryl's shagging some fella from 'Oop North?'

'No, you've gotta live next door to them!'

'Hundred per cent. I mean, I know we've been friendly, but I think she's extreme. This must be the third affair in three years.'

'I'm amazed at these people who lead double lives.' Helen twisted the stem of her cava glass, watching the bubbles in the light.

'It's gotta be an addiction, surely? You know, those guys who have two families in different parts of the country. Now and then, you'll read about one getting caught out. Most of them aren't even wealthy, just normal blokes with jobs that keep them away from home. For the few that end up all over the newspapers, imagine the percentage who get away with it?'

Grace topped up their water glasses, listening intently.

Ffion shrugged. 'I suppose not all of them are bigamists, either. Make it easier if they weren't going to marry. But can you imagine? Finger dents from wedding rings could give you away in a second.'

Of course, they would. Where would Rhys have hidden his? In the car door? In his back pocket?

Helen carried on. 'Yep, wild stuff. Imagine the intrigue and planning. School holidays and hospital stays, anything that's going to throw a spanner in the works. I s'pose they think they're brilliant minds, but the stress of it must get to them. Just imagine, two wedding rings to swap over, two phones to jiggle, or at least a double sim phone.'

Ann smiled, her eyes lighting up as she imagined the next steps.

'Then you'd have to keep your hand on it every waking moment, just in case the wrong woman saw the wrong message. You'd need two bank accounts, and you daren't go on social media. Oh, my god, I'd never cope with the subterfuge!'

Jo laughed loudly. 'Blimey, that's a big word for a Saturday night!'

'Yep, I'm full of big words. I don't get to use them around Harri, he's a three-sentence-a-night man. These days he does everything in threes. Three minutes soak for his tea bag. And sex too. Three minutes, if I'm lucky'

'Oh my god, I hope he doesn't let that soak for three minutes!'

The squeal of laughter made nearby diners glance their way.

'I'm going to be living two lives, girls.' Grace announced nervously.

'Oh, do tell!'

'Well, I'm leaving L&B. Got a new job.'

A cacophony of congratulatory responses sounded, accompanied by the clinking of glasses.

'I'll still be on the road, but there'll be lots more travel. I'm going to be away for part of the week, too.'

'Oh wow, so cool. Anything more glamorous than all that man cave shite you sell?'

Grace faltered.

'Can't tell you yet, but it's still a nationwide company, and all I can say is I'm glad we don't have kids because it would be impossible to do otherwise.'

'What does Rhys think?'

'Oh, he's OK with it, he'll enjoy the peace, and having no one to tell him to shift his oily engine parts off the kitchen table. I dread to think what the house will look like midweek.'

'Well, congratulations beaut.' They clinked glasses and toasted her repeatedly as she smiled, and realised she would never get to see their reactions to her actual news. A new job must suffice. But now she'd lied to her friends.

Ffion laughed loudly. 'Don't go meeting any flash men on your travels, or poor old Rhys will be the down south lover and you'll be keeping *your* rings in the glove box!'

Grace pulled an amused face.

'Can you imagine?'

They cheered and giggled. She looked thoughtful, then winked. 'Do you reckon I could manage it, girls?'

'I reckon you could manage anything life throws at you, babe.' Ffion raised her glass yet again. 'Take any fun you can get. Marriage wasn't so great for me, was it?'

Grace caught Ffion's eye and noticed a strange expression flicker across her face.

'One life we live. Think Love Island.'

Yells of 'I've got a text!' and a resounding echo of laughter followed 'Hashtag No Regrets'.

The waiter reappeared.

'One more thing ladies, you've got a secret admirer tonight. The boss asked me to deliver seven bottles of champagne to this table. Lucky seven.'

A round of whoops and cries of delight broke the atmosphere. Disapproving glances cast their way, but the cacophony of noise remained high.

'Wow, really?' Ffion squealed.

'Unreal! Who is it? Point him out.'

'Sorry ladies, I'm sworn to secrecy, but I'll bring a couple over to get you started, and make sure the rest stay chilled in the fridge.'

'That's lovely, thank you so much!'

'What the actual fuck?'

'Oh, my ruddy god'

'How lucky are we!'

'One of us might have found our prince and we don't even know who he is!'

'It might be a woman!'

'Anyone swing both ways?' Ffion screeched.

Another bout of laughter peeled around them as the food orders arrived and they settled down to eat and pop the corks on the first two bottles. Grace silently celebrated her newfound luck and her building excitement knowing Marcus was somewhere nearby.

'Iechyd da, pawb' She toasted.

Good health, everyone.

Glasses clinked repeatedly. Never having to worry about money was joyful. Forget the electricity bill or the length of numbers at the base of her card statement. Never again would they cause a moment of angst. Even the four thousand, four hundred pounds bottle of Chateau Petrus 1990 Pomerol red wine locked within the display cabinet nearby could be hers if she signalled to the waiter.

Dare I? Shall I buy the expensive wine? The girls needn't know, and there's enough for a glass each.

Don't you dare. Talk about wasteful and showing off. You know you wouldn't.

But it's a hundred million!

As they drained the last bottle of fizz and dropped it loudly back into the ice bucket, Grace realised she needed to send a bottle to Miranda. It was she who'd handed it to her on a plate, after all. Maybe she could send her the expensive bottle of wine instead?

I doubt she can accept gifts. Company policy, probably. Where is this going to lead?

Wherever the destination, there were few adverse emotions around the journey.

'We're all on the road to ruin, but some are further ahead than others.'

Nobody noticed the diamond.

'Let's finish in Morgans?' Ann suggested, picking her handbag off the chair and standing up.

'OK, although it's probably packed now. It's almost ten.'

They tottered over the crossing at the end of Wind Street and headed into the popular hotel, as busy and noisy as expected, and fought their way to the bar, splitting into pairs.

'I love being out!' Ffion yelled to Grace over the jostling bodies, avoiding drinks passing across shoulders to recipients at the back.

'Don't we all!'

'I never want to get old.'

'Don't think about it, live in the moment.'

Ffion waved her debit card at the barman.

'Local brew, beaut? Doubles?'

'Let me, Ffi.' Grace pulled out her own and eased away her friend's hand.

'Two double watermelon AU's please.'

Soon they'd sidestepped to safety where they stood with their green vodkas, chatting and speed-flirting with strangers.

'Hold this a minute!' Ffion thrust her glass at Grace and pulled out her phone.

With a studious expression, she looked at the screen, a finger moving until she stopped and glanced towards the entrance. Turning to Grace, she reclaimed her drink and leaned in. 'I see you're already keeping those wedding rings in the glove box.'

'What do you mean?'

'Don't lie, my lovely, I have a memory like an elephant.'

'I don't get it. What?'

'Grace, can you tell me why the hot bloke from your Spring Ball is leaning against the entrance pillar and keeps glancing your way?'

Grace swallowed. *Keep calm.*

'The English bloke?'

'Yes, the English bloke. You shagging him? Why else would some hunk from hundreds of miles away be down here alone on a Saturday?'

'Why do you think it's him?'

161

'I've just scrolled back through those photos on WhatsApp you sent me, and it's him. Not someone who *looks* like him, it's *actually* him.

'Remember, we joked about it?'

Acting skills needed. Do I have any?

She glanced towards the entrance and there stood Marcus, sipping from a beer bottle, observing the room. Grace smiled, despite a tiny churn in her abdomen.

'Oh my god, it is him! You're right. He must be down for the weekend.'

He looks amazing in those clothes he's bought. He's obviously hit the shops. Moda, maybe? Expensive. Designer.

'But *why* is he down for the weekend, Grace?'

'He does work for my company, Ffion. He travels all the branches. Let's find out.'

And with a forceful effort, she jostled through the crowd, Ffion struggling in her fast-closing wake. Grace reached Marcus, her eyes flashing wildly.

'Marcus, what on earth are you doing here?'

Her friend sidled up to them both, waiting and listening.

'Hi Grace, fancy meeting you here! What a surprise! Girls' night out?'

'Yes, most weekends we have a few lively hours. This is my friend Ffion.'

They exchanged greetings, Ffion's expression perplexed.

'So what are you doing here?'

'John and a few of the guys from the office just left. I'm down anyway on Monday, and they're always telling me how great Swansea nightlife is, so here I am. It's bouncing. I think we've done the length of Wind Street, both sides.'

Grace laughed at his pronunciation.

'It's Wind Street, as in winding you up, not Wind as in blowing on you.'

Ffion burst out laughing. 'Grace!'

Marcus joined in, the flash of white teeth showing.

'*Oi*, you two, stop it. Blame the champagne. My words get jumbled on the fizzy stuff.'

Marcus winked knowingly.

'Where are you staying?'

'Here, actually. But it's a tad early to go to bed yet, and they've all gone home to their wives. Joys of being single.'

'Well, it's central at least. Shame they've left you, but I've met some of those wives and if they don't get home soon, there'll be fireworks.'

'I can imagine. I've never met a Welshwoman without an opinion.'

It was Grace's turn to laugh.

'We tend to say our piece. Anyway, great to see you, have a good weekend.'

'Will do. Laters.'

Marcus turned away and walked towards the bar, easing through the throng.

'What a hunk. But he could have bought us a drink!' Ffion pouted.

Grace sighed with relief.

'We have drinks, and we've had too many, anyway.'

'Hey, do you reckon he sent us the champagne? He may have been sitting at another table. It's only across the road.'

'Who knows?' Grace teased.

Ffion scrutinised her face.

'That's an awful lot of champagne to send our way for someone down on an audit. Nobody I work with would send me one bottle let alone seven.'

'We don't know it was him. Let's find the others.'

Ffion surveyed her, uncertain.

'Are you sure there's nothing going on?'

Grace managed a withering look.

'Well then, maybe I could?'

She grabbed her friend's arm and steered her towards the champagne bar.

'Forget it, Ffi, he lives hours away.'

'But he's bloody gorgeous. My bed's empty tonight.'

Ffion turned towards the bar. There was no sign of Marcus. *And there he was, gone. Phew. That was a lucky escape. But it is Saturday, my third Capricorn lucky day. Not that I'm superstitious at all.*

Ffion gave an inebriated hiccup. 'I think the girls headed up there.'

The phone vibrated in her bag. It must wait until Ffion wandered to the *Ladies* or found someone to flirt with. Checking on the rabbit's foot nestled in the inner zip pocket, she stroked its fur, a warm glow rising inside. When she finally opened the message, the words were simple.

Room 32. You look so hot in those shoes. I want you right now. But I'll wait until you can get away.

I'm leaving them on.

He noticed the shoes. He noticed the diamond. He noticed everything about her.

Chapter 24

The noise of music on the television penetrated through to the kitchen, accompanied by the sound of the Sunday newspaper being flicked through with speed, open on the table as Rhys stood above it before his late afternoon deep delve into the newsprint from the comfort of the sofa.

'Sit down Rhys, I need to tell you something.'

'Ooh, right Cariad, what is it?'

The screech of chair legs as he dragged it from beneath the table grated, but they settled opposite each other as Grace prepared her thoughts and words.

'Come on, hit me! But think of my heart condition.'

'What heart condition?'

'I might have one in ten years, if you keep surprising me with news.'

Still makes me laugh. But so does Rhod Gilbert. A comedian who knows his way around a Hoover. Unlike Rhys.

'True. But nothing like your surprises.'

The moment the words left her lips Grace regretted them. She sped on, ignoring the hurt that flashed briefly across his face.

'Anyway, I've received a job offer I wanted to run by you.

It's what I want, so this is a sales pitch to convince you I'm doing the right thing for both of us.'

Rhys sat upright and perused her face. His serious expression belied what came next.

'If you were after a new job, why didn't you apply to air-sea rescue? They're always looking for people.'

Oh my god, how does he get these things out so fast? Does he have a joke book under his pillow?

'Hilarious, hahaha.'

Leave the sarcasm out of it, Gracie. Nobody enjoys hearing a spoken laugh.

'OK, go ahead then, I'm all ears.'

'L&B may be in trouble. There have been comings and goings from head office. I think there's a risk of redundancies.'

If Marcus is 'endless comings and goings' then my imagination is running riot. Although there have been quite a few comings.

'That's not good, love, but it's happening all over. Between Brexit and Covid we're fucked as a nation.'

'You're right, and I wanted to be ahead of the curve just in case. I've been keeping an eye out for these past few months, and I did an interview last week, and an offer yesterday. I was last in with L&B, so I reckon I'll be first out if they're cutting staff. If it's worse, and it's full closure, I'd still be jobless.'

'True, well done you, for thinking ahead. You never really liked all that *man stuff* you're selling anyway, did you?'

'No.'

'So are you flogging handbags at dawn, or shoes at sunset?'

'It's service aimed, what I'd prefer to be doing.'

'OK, what's this company called, and when do they want you to start?'

Grace drew a breath. A name, created in haste, sat on her tongue, but the realisation he may start searching and find nothing, was not considered.

'They're called Sunrise Solutions, but they're a subdivision of an umbrella company. No direct advertising. I'd need to be away, though. Training for weeks and head office is in Manchester, so there's going to be a few months when I'm away Sunday to Friday.'

166

'Oh.' Rhys was crestfallen.

'Ultimately, I'll be Sales and Service Manager for Wales, but they need to find an office here first. I'm assured it will be before Christmas.'

Rhys nodded, thoughtful.

'Sorry, it's all the training. Nothing unusual there in the world of sales. Besides, these endless night shifts and the rugby season will keep you busy and we're *ships passing* when it's on. It's a four-hour drive on paper but you know what that motorway is like.'

Rhys flicked the edge of the newspaper back and forth.

'I'll be getting an increase plus a really nice company car. It's exciting, I'm moving up the ladder.'

'How many rungs?'

'Probably five.'

He finally forced a smile. 'But you'll be able to see up the leg of the fireman's trousers?'

'That'd be a stroke of luck.'

'A few extra rungs means a few extra bungs. Think of all those new handbags, Cariad.'

For once there wasn't a hint of sarcasm.

He's a natural. He laughed me into bed fourteen years ago, and he can still make me laugh. But mostly cry.

'So, I go for it? We'll open something fizzy and celebrate?'

Rhys slowly looked her up and down as she stood and pushed the chair back into place.

'My wife is a high flyer. Yes, go on then. I'll find something cold in the fridge. You're bound to have some fancy prosecco hiding in there. Well done.'

He got up, leaned towards her, and kissed the top of her head.

Phew, that was relatively easy. No great drama, and complete acceptance. But what is it with the top of my head?

'I'll just whip outside and phone the recruitment guy, tell him it's on. He told me to let him know anytime over the weekend.'

As she turned away, a hint of filmy mist clouded his eyes. Was it a veil of proud tears, or sadness? *Or is he thinking about Sian? Weeks away, lonely nights in an empty bed. Am I putting temptation right back under his nose?*

Outside, Grace faked the call, and inserted a few light-hearted quips, as she paced up and down on the lawn within earshot.

Returning to the kitchen door, she caught sight of Rhys watching her through the window, a bottle of prosecco already in his hand. He stood quiescent, inert, observing her until her eyes met his, then moved to set the bottle down and began unscrewing the muselet to free the cork.

Grace would have two weeks of free days to set up home, make some day trips, and work out her plans for the next few months. Closing the door she walked across to take the offered glass of bubbles.

'Done, I'll hand in my notice tomorrow.'

'Cheers and congratulations, you little beaut!'

Rhys tapped his glass against hers, then quickly put an arm around her waist and pulled her close. How long since he'd done that? Since she'd let him do it? It felt uncomfortable, being this close to him.

'You kept that quiet you minx.'

'It would have been a disappointment if I didn't get it, so what was the point of telling you?'

Rhys shrugged.

'Kiss!' he demanded, heading for her lips.

For once during the long weeks which trailed them, Grace responded, instead of pulling away, and the discomfort melted into the familiar feel of the years of intimacy that passed between them.

But not now, I don't want this now.

'By the way, I have something for you.' She pulled herself out of his arms and stepped towards a storage cabinet, the disappointment on his face unseen, as she pulled open a drawer and lifted out a shiny, corded blue bag with the Lamborghini model tucked inside.

A quick, sad smile replaced his distress as she turned towards him, holding out the gift.

'There you go. Who knows, one day it may be the full-size version.'

'What is it?'

Rhys peeked into the bag, and his smile broadened.

'Wow, nice. A Lambo. Thanks love, keep doing the lottery and you never know. One day it may be the real thing sitting outside.'

He paused, swallowed then added. 'And I don't want you going off up there thinking things.'

Grace looked him in the eyes. Rhys' eyes were brown, dark, and brooding.

Never trust a man with brown eyes, Gran used to say. But Gran said a lot of things.

'Thinking things, Rhys? What things?'

That you'll be gone by the time I get back, and there'll be a note on the worktop saying 'Sorry, Cariad, I tried, but it didn't work for me.'

Rhys put the gift bag down, and moved towards her, a perplexed look on his face, and took hold of her hands.

'You know what things. I don't want to drag it up again. There will be no *things* to think about, I promise.'

Rhys, at this moment I couldn't give a toss about your things. I have my own things to think about now. And pleasurable things they are too.

'OK.'

❦

Chapter 25

Grace's secret life began with the aid of the beautiful diary bought in Cardiff, leaving daily for the 'office' the first fortnight while her mother was away, by taxi. With the unfortunate 'catastrophic breakdown' of her company car on the way to work that Monday, and a lack of spare vehicles to continue her appointments, it was 'decided' she would travel into work by taxi, and be 'dropped home' by one of the staff members on a rota basis. It *was* only two weeks, after all. Not worth the cost of a hire car as she was leaving the company, anyway.

Rhys nodded as he absorbed this tale and its intricacies and returned to perusing the newspaper, believing she was to be at a desk, cleaning up accounts, calling in quotes, and saying farewells to customers over the phone. He would never know the taxi waiting outside at eight in the morning would pull up at her mother's house minutes later, where Grace watered the plants, shooed away dust, and then slid into the gleaming red Mercedes to drive to Langland Bay.

Weaving through the traffic on Monday morning, she was relieved the car hire employee asked no questions.

'All OK?' She asked furtively as he slipped into the passenger seat next to her, around the corner from L&B.

'Yes, I handed the keys and the briefcase to a bloke called John. No questions asked. Just eyeballed me and mumbled something, then walked off.'

'Thanks so much. You're a lifesaver.'

She dropped him back at the depot, and headed on her way, mentally ticking boxes as she drove. The Wi-Fi and a large screen TV remained in place at the house, plus the existing heavy furniture. Stopping at the M&S food hall in Mumbles, she picked three bouquets of fresh flowers, a couple of bottles of champagne for the fridge, plus a few other necessities including instant coffee, tea bags, and milk. The joy of discovering a whole new area to live in, one infrequently visited for a few hours on a sunny day, meant this daily chore would become an extra pleasure to browse shops usually seen through a windscreen.

Quivers of excitement arose as she pulled onto the private winding driveway of the property, turned off the engine, and stepped out into the fresh, sea-scented morning air. Gazing around, she surveyed the house exterior, with its tall trees to the sides and rear. Her eyes settled back on the red shiny paintwork of the Mercedes. Birdsong and silence, except for the distant sound of waves crashing. Tears welled, but she swallowed to deny the forecast of further wet cheeks. This is it. I've arrived.

Home from home.

Space just for me.

Opening the door, she checked the code on a slip of paper, turned off the alarm, and stepped inside, emitting a brief scream of excitement. 'Oh my god, is this real?' echoed into the white-walled space.

Without the company of Miles and the stream of questions, answers, and discussions, the silence welcomed her in with a stolid embrace. Large, modern, beautifully furnished rooms lacked only accessories since the owner moved out, and the basics Grace knew she was unlikely to change unless she made an offer on the property. The echoing, mausoleum quality was a surprise as her heeled footsteps on the tiled floor tip-tapped around her. She would need to play music or put the television on for some comforting voices. But this was a trial, after all. A dummy run.

Could I live here alone if my marriage is actually over?

Leaving the front door open to allow in fresh air, she returned to the boot of the car and struggled to remove its contents. The rose gold suitcase hiding its trove of treasures, recently buried in her mother's cloakroom, followed in her wake along with the shopping and flowers. Stopping to gaze around once more, she tried to visualise Rhys living here with her but saw only trails of toast crumbs wandering between rooms, and discarded clothes draped over expensive sofas. She realised how very different they were; her preferring tidiness and order, him content with stepping over car parts and any other exterior belongings he felt needed to drift inside.

This was a single woman's place. A rich *single* woman. Not a wealthy *married* woman, with all the baggage and rings accompanying.

And this is going to work. This is bloody surreal. My life is becoming a Frida Kahlo masterpiece. Without the unibrow. Here, I can really sort myself out.

The day's haul was due to arrive between midday and two o'clock, and she'd spend the afternoon opening endless packages from the online shopping sprees made over the last couple of days, converting the space into somewhere filled with her own presence.

There would be casual wear for lounging, more lovely dresses, footwear, and a pair of Wellington boots for those walks to the Surfside cafe and beach, plus a few all-weather jackets. She thought of Marcus, and how she'd left him yesterday afternoon as he headed back to Oxford ready for his week's work. His face happy and sad, his hug all-enveloping, masculinity imprinted on her. She pushed the thoughts away and concentrated on the task at hand.

Opening the case on the floor of the gargantuan lounge, she pulled out her very first purchase, the *duet* of Kat Maconie shoes, and danced them onto a glossy Italian-style white cabinet, displaying them as objets d'art. The soles of the worn pair were meticulously wet-wiped at the end of the night and hidden away from Rhys in the packaging. His words were the same anytime he spotted an oblong box in a carrier bag. 'More shoes, Cariad? Haven't you got enough?'

Women never have enough shoes. Or lipsticks. Why don't men understand this? We can't own three pairs of shoes to cover all occasions. It's impossible.

A pair of Loewe Rose heel slingbacks, which extracted thirteen hundred pounds from her credit card, would soon stand tall next to them, forming a triptych of heels, pride of place in her mini galleria.

She skipped light-footed into the kitchen, and examined the impossible-to-operate coffee machine, and then headed up the gasp-inducing open-stepped staircase to the enormous bedroom with the best vista of the sea she selected while viewing. Moving along the wardrobes, she slid the glossy doors open and peeked inside. Plenty of space, and expensive matching hangers. Empty, just for her. A team of professionals studiously cleaned the place shortly after the owner left.

Pulling off her jacket she grabbed one of the interior hangers and stripped, making sure everything she removed was ready for exit. A quick change into some new casual items draped over her arm and she would be ready to return downstairs to continue unpacking. Tackling the staircase with a suitcase was not an option. Especially alone.

Grace jiggled into a pair of Dolce and Gabbana crystal rose and heart covered jeans, over two thousand pounds worth of madness, followed by a bright red silk comfortable oversized shirt with a French tuck, and black crystallised trainers taking the place of the work shoes discarded so easily. They were stiff, but expensive and stylish. Looking at her reflection, she realised she was already a different person. Weekend lips appeared, with a slick of Ruby Woo.

On point, Gracie. Rock Goddess. Well, maybe not quite. But definitely a 'cooler' version of the Nine-to-Five me.

'I don't work anymore!' she yelped and bounced on the bare mattress before heading downstairs.

I must order some bedding before I can spend the night. What size is this bed? Super king? I better call Emma and ask. It's huge. But there's always the sofa. I'm used to sleeping outside the marital bed.

It was only ten o'clock. If the delivery was coming at lunchtime, she'd head down to the cafe or Langland Brasserie for mid-morning brunch. But first, it was time to plan. Pulling out the notebook and eraser pen, and settling in the big bay window seat with the view of the sea, she began scribbling notes, interrupted only by a message.

Ping
WhatsApp/Mam.
We're in Sicily!' Those Italians are certainly cheeky. No political correctness here, my bottom's been pinched black and blue. I may buy a bag today, they're having a sale onboard tonight, and there are plenty of designer offerings. Hope all's well your end? Having an amazing time.

A few photos of the cruise companions followed, delighted divorcees, enjoying the Mediterranean sunshine. Grace laughed aloud at their face-pulling and silly poses. They were having fun. Boisterous, lively, decades younger than their ages, fun.

Good for you, girls. Because that's what you are at heart.

Contact was sporadic when her mother was on a cruise. She refused to pay for expensive onboard Wi-Fi, waiting until she found it free in onshore cafes. *Like mother, like daughter.*

Yes, all fine here Mam. Has Amanda ravaged the Captain?'

Still trying!

Fabulous photos!' I can't believe you have a blue sky and it's grey over here. Again.

Never mind love, I'll let you get on with your work. Enjoy the day.

Then she was gone. Telling her mother the full truth would be impossible. She loved to chat to everyone, and Grace didn't think she'd hold on to a secret so big. Much as she wanted her to benefit from this good fortune, the mortgage on her house was long ended. *Maybe if I say I've won three million and am giving her five hundred thousand? But Rhys wasn't to find out? Would it work? It might.*

She would hardly want to risk her daughter's financial future if anything were to bring the marriage to an end. Three million was a small amount by today's standards. Grace scratched her forehead. So much thinking, so much planning.

The sky and sea may have been grey the first week of September, but the air was relatively warm. An early fire crackled in one corner of the cafe and a table was free on the outer terrace. Grabbing one of the daily newspapers, she ordered tea and a bagel melt with bacon brie and cranberry and waited in the fresh air for its arrival.

Grace pondered over how the staff at L&B might have reacted to her speedy departure, and what gossip may be circulating. And whether Angela guessed if it was anything to do with Marcus.

'Did you see them on the dance floor at the Spring Ball? Oh my god, he was all over her. I doubt they slept much that night.'

Office machinery would crank into high gear, spilling endless versions into the printing tray.

'I heard they were having difficulties at home. You know.' Accompanied by a wink.

'I never liked her, anyway.'

'She wore too much make-up. And those heels? Who was she trying to impress?'

Grace saw the throw-away shrugs and arched eyebrows and wondered if anyone would get around to saying she'd been pretty good at her job, and was pleasant to have around. Or any compliments at all.

She would miss the occasional office get-togethers around the coffeepot, but not the daily mileage, traffic jams, fighting for parking spaces, or the long lonely days discussing boring products with relative strangers. The thought finally brought a smile to her face.

It was at an end.

I've 'taken early retirement.'

But look at what the future would hold. She would make new friends. The world would become her oyster. Painting, photography, dance classes, travel. The promise of a completely different future sprawled ahead of her, the clamshell which held her tight, slowly releasing its grip.

There weren't any surfers to watch in the calm water, but the tranquillity borne by the sounds of lapping waves and the occasional dog bark was enough to relax and bring a smile to her face. It was a lonely situation, and a large, unshareable burden to be carrying. Grace once imagined announcing to friends 'You'll never believe it, I won the lottery! Big time! Millions!'

Something in her mind knew those 'Wow, no way' and 'Oh my god, you're so lucky!' comments bubbling at her from beneath showers of confetti and champagne sprays, wouldn't be coming with a complete generosity of spirit. They may shout and yell in the moment's immediacy, but by the time the first glass of celebratory fizz emptied, and the screaming died away, they would regard her with envious eyes, as human nature constructs, and friendships would fall by the wayside. Behind their own doors, vitriol would spill and their personal troubles magnify in the wake of her good fortune. The words of Miranda and the financial advisors echoed through her head.

'Be circumspect about telling anyone. If you have to, don't tell them the amount. Say you managed some life-changing luck on the lottery, nothing too grand, enough to pay off your mortgage and to give up work for a few years to travel. That way, when they leave your sphere, which people do in the wake of a major life change, you'll be relatively safe from targeted scams. Sadly, few friendships survive these big wins, even when you hand out financial gifts. It's jealousy and human nature.'

The bagel arrived with her cup of tea, and Grace sat nibbling it, aware she looked more like a rockstar in her outfit than the dog walkers in their wellies and jackets. No longer confined by the constraints of who was thinking what, she tilted back her head and smiled.

If I want to dress like a celebrity on a small Welsh beach, then why not? Life is what you make it, after all.

At half-past eleven, she left the terrace and headed back to the house to await the deliveries. Champagne chilled in the fridge, smoked salmon plus a small tin of Royal Siberian caviar, which she was determined to grow to love as much as her favoured Welsh laverbread, the seaweed delicacy which tasted

176

exactly the same from a tin as it did when bought fresh from the stalls of Swansea's indoor market. Much as she wanted to open a bottle of the fizz, she would need to drive home that evening.

Grace looked forward to the nights she would spend there alone once her 'notice' period was over, and she left for 'up north.' Then she would do what she liked, whenever she wanted, before going home for the weekend on alternate weeks.

She would go out with the girls in Swansea, and Rhys wouldn't know a thing. Maybe they'd go to Cardiff in a Limo. The wine bars of Mumbles were a short taxi ride away if she was brave enough to visit them alone at night. She did it easily during the day, mingling with an entirely unique set of people, and with a Kindle or device to help her blend into the background.

Marcus, in Oxford, was almost three hours away. The diary would need constant reviewing to meet up with the frequency they both desired and there were plenty of hotels that could pass as an overnight company perk.

Hearing the delivery van she headed for the door to greet the driver. There were plenty of packages, and by the time he'd removed them from the back and placed them at her feet in the vestibule, his curiosity showed.

'You'll spend all day opening this lot, love!' he commented, handing her the electronic device she needed to swipe a pen across.

'Not all for me' she answered carefully. 'Hubby will open some.'

She sensed his eyes scouring the property, then scanning her clothes.

'Have fun then!' he turned to leave.

It was then Grace saw the reality of the financial advisors' words. Anyone, anywhere, would size up her situation.

Best he leaves thinking there's a husband here too. He may deliver more stuff in future.

Grace decided she would drive to the nearest shops in Mumbles and buy a pair of men's wellies from the ironmonger to leave in the entrance. She would dirty them and stand them on an old newspaper, remembering to move them occasionally.

Is this paranoia setting in? Already? You can't be too careful, especially when you spend nights alone here.

Don't be ridiculous Grace, many people live alone and you have great security.

Locking the door behind her, she set about carrying the parcels into the vast lounge and dumped them at the foot of the eight-seater sofa where she would chill and open them at leisure.

Isn't this what every woman wants? Endless purchasing power and luxury items sprawled at our feet? The nesting instinct, the homemaking gene. Build your castle strong and fill it with beautiful things.

With a hasty decision, she headed for the fridge. One glass wouldn't hurt and it would be hours before she needed to drive. Besides, she'd bought a champagne fizz-saver. Tomorrow she'd have another. At this rate, it would last the week. Maybe tomorrow she'd get a taxi down and back and drink an entire bottle.

I'm supposed to be celebrating this win. And I know exactly where.

The pop of the cork echoed through the house with a loud ricochet. Pouring a glass, she moved past the lounge and around the back of the ground floor towards the indoor pool. A couple of wicker loungers placed alongside the rectangle of blue water held cubes of white towels folded on thick cushions ready for use. The pool filters moved the water in flowing circles and the sound of the pump was a comforting background drum as the water tinkled in flute-like harmony.

Placing the glass on the small side table between these recliners she looked outside. Tall trees and a private semicircle of garden filled the view through the floor to ceiling windows. Inside, terracotta tiles interspersed with circular designs and wall lights filled the area, while tall potted plants created an ancient Mediterranean style.

Grace kicked off her shoes on the mosaic-tiled floor and picked up her phone. Selecting portrait mode, she took a selfie, arm stretched up high, capturing part of the blue lagoon behind her, smiling into the lens. Posting it to her Facebook account, she selected friends only, then dropped the phone onto a lounger. This could be any spa in any area.

She stripped slowly, folding and draping her clothes alongside, until she was completely naked, standing gazing at the water. Remembering Emma's instructions that the pool cleaner let himself in every Tuesday morning and to never use glassware in the area, she shrugged. Lifting the crystal flute, she stared into the fizzing golden depths, before moving down the curved Roman steps leading into the water, slowly descending, a graceful bronzed goddess, as the tang of chlorine and gentle heat coming off the water filled her senses.

'Sorry, Emma. I'll be super careful. Call it my christening. And you certainly don't use plastic at those. To the Green Goddess.'

Filling her mouth with glorious bubbles, she felt the warmth of the swirling water rise above her breasts and moved towards the centre of the pool.

Chapter 26

Grace spent the weekdays feathering her new nest, opening further deliveries, perusing holidays, playing loud music, going for lunch, trying on items from her new wardrobe, walking the beach, or driving into Mumbles or the city and wandering around the shops and indoor market. Glorious mini solo adventures.

During the evenings, while Rhys was next to her on the sofa at home, the television distracted him as she discreetly continued the absorbing online browsing or ate half of the takeaway curries that appeared when the mood took him. There was no time for lengthy day trips if she was to maintain the charade of working out her notice and arriving home at the usual time unless he worked a night shift. Then she would allow herself a few extra hours before returning home.

There were almost daily video calls with Marcus, who believed she'd taken a couple of weeks off before starting her new job. The Botox kicked in, vanishing away those imperceptible frown lines and freshening up her reflection in the mirror. Grace watched a decade fall from her face the first week, knowing her budget for maintaining *anything* that needed tweaking in the coming years was immeasurable. The diary and the new handbag-sized Chromebook nestled together, always nearby in one of her expensive designer bags.

Those first two weekends, Marcus drove to Swansea and booked into the Marriott once again, as Grace arranged further fake Friday nights out with the girls, they met at the hotel and ate dinner at El Pescador, a short walk away.

Marcus was relaxed, but Grace remained alert to someone recognising her and Rhys finding out they had seen her *in flagrante delicto.* They maintained a businesslike distance between plates of calamari, octopus, and speciality garlic bread, the hot cloves bubbling in melted butter, ready to meet the fresh bread plunged into its golden centre. Near their table, the portrait of a dark-haired dancer, red dress blossoming into a large rose as she flounced into a powerful flamenco move, watched over them.

They avoided physical contact while the aromas and music of Spain accompanied them over the bustle of the popular marina eatery, until they wandered back to his room along the almost empty promenade alongside the beach, comfortably holding hands in the darkness and exchanging kisses reserved for the newly enamoured.

While it tinged the first Friday with sadness as news of the Queen's death the previous day enveloped the country, they watched the news coverage in bed before giving in to passion and switching off the television. The full harvest moon shone down on them through the undrawn curtains bathing the room and their naked skin in a luminous glow.

Grace told Rhys she was spending those evenings at her mother's as he often worked nights on Fridays. The first Saturday morning as they crossed the car park to look at the view of the Bay, a cheery voice called out to her.

'Excuse me, do you remember me?'

Grace's heart sank until she recognised the member of housekeeping who retrieved the rabbit's foot. *Oh, thank god it's not someone I know. Swansea is so small.*

'Of course! How are you?' she held onto Marcus' hand as she smiled at the beaming woman turning up for her working day.

181

'I have to thank you' she began in a rush 'because you were right about the charm. I bought some scratchcards like you suggested and won ten thousand pounds! Within hours of touching it. Thank you so much'

'That's unreal, I'm chuffed for you!'

Bloody hell Gracie. How much money does this thing have at its beck and call?

'I have to go now' she grew flustered 'or I'll be late, but you were a lifesaver. Thanks again.'

Then she was rushing towards the staff entrance before disappearing from view.

Marcus frowned. 'What was that about?'

'She found my rabbit's foot in your room. I gave her a reward and told her…well, you heard what she said.'

'Hmm, that's a nice little pick-up. Maybe you better let me hold it.' He laughed, unconvinced.

'Later, my handbag's still in the room. Let's look at the sea before you have to leave.'

'Maybe we'll trip over a black cat instead.'

'But I'm not superstitious at all.

'So why do you carry it for luck?'

It was Grace's turn to laugh.

'An unwanted gift from my mam. I didn't like to say no. But I suppose it got me a new job, and brought you into my life.'

Marcus leaned in close to her ear, pecked the lobe, and whispered 'I'd have found you with or without it. Eventually.'

Grace's diary filled up with times and dates and creative lists of excuses for being absent in the future; shopping with Ffion, a baby shower at a friend's house, being blocked in a car park for two hours, keys left on shop counters, flat batteries, road diversions, accidents holding up traffic, a lost purse and the need to get to the bank and sort out new cards. Every time an idea would form, she would grab the book and write it down. *Be prepared.*

She spent further time at the estate agency with Emma in the office and with Miles viewing Maritime Quarter properties.

'We don't have any townhouses at the moment, but the second one comes in, I'll let you know.'

'Thanks, Emma, but I may just decide a Flat would be better, if it's big enough. I like the idea of hopping in and out of a lift instead of endless stairs. Plus, my mother is getting older, and she'll be visiting frequently.'

Emma laughed. 'We seem to call them apartments these days. We've gone all American in *downtown* Swansea.'

It wasn't long before they found a suitable seafront penthouse with the desired lifts and direct access to the promenade and beach, and while Grace continued the rental of the luxury bay house, she began signing for the purchase of the property.

I'm actually buying bricks and mortar of my own. And look how fast it's happening. Me. Grace Lewis. In a gorgeous seafront penthouse, with a short walk everywhere. Wow.

Back at the Langland Bay house, It wasn't long before she came to a thought-provoking conclusion, as she sat on the pool steps, twirling a half empty champagne flute, a new daily ritual as the bubbles swirled between her toes.

I could live alone. I'm not sure if I could do it here, without neighbours or friends close by, but I could certainly manage it in the thick of life at the marina.

With its multitude of residents and eclectic mix of nationalities, cycling along the prom all the way to Mumbles would take barely any effort along the flat sweep of the bay, and where the city centre, with its shops and nightlife, was just a few minutes walk. And the meandering M4 motorway, Cardiff Wales Airport, and the vast, undiscovered world beyond, a leisurely drive. For a rich, solo woman.

Ping
WhatsApp/Mam
I bought a Michael Kors! It's gorgeous! Thanks love.

Send a pic!

OK.

It's lush, Mam.

Grace mused as she studied the handbag her mother bought. It wouldn't be one she'd choose for herself, but definitely her mother's safe, solid style. A neutral tone. Large. Lacking fussy adornments. It could do with a silk scarf tied around a handle, something bright and colourful. Beige was now banished from Grace's new life.

Balancing the glass flute with its traces of Buck's Fizz breakfast pulp carefully on the etched, uneven, ceramic tiles, she placed her phone alongside and lowered herself into the water, her bright coral and gold metal trimmed bikini sinking under the gentle undulations along the surface. She'd dressed for the occasion. It was late Tuesday morning and the pool cleaner was due.

No nakedness today. But at last, someone to exchange a few words with.

Outside, heavy rain trickled down the windows between her luxury water feature and the grey exterior of autumn in Wales.

As Grace sat cross-legged on the bed at home, booking the train and hotel tickets for London, she wondered what to wear for the journey. Something comfortable but nothing too light, train seats even in first class, weren't squeaky clean. With excitement building about her solo adventure and pressing 'pay' she bounced off the bed and smiled as she selected a pair of light pink silky pyjamas bought in those ultimate days of the Debenhams closing down sale.

It never failed to amaze her how a piece of clothing or jewellery brought back memories. Something recovered from months or years hidden in a wardrobe, or drawers evoked a special place. A holiday. A concert. She wondered how it was possible to part with these items at all, how others managed this in ever-burgeoning modern homes. All those times placing beloved items into bin bags for donation, only for them to be retrieved in a last-minute panic before delivery, leaving only the easily parted with bundles.

Removing things from life was difficult.

How do you do this with people? Colleagues. Friends you've known for years.

Men you've married.

How is it done so easily by some, who can move on in a minute, and not look back?

She studied the label of the pyjamas wistfully. An absolute bargain on the penultimate day before the department store closed forever, along with white summer shorts and pieces of jewellery from the once bountiful counters where perfumed air tickled the nostrils, and the colours and textures of iconic beauty brand packaging stimulated the eyes.

Grace queued with distinct sadness along with dwindling lines of others waiting to pay at the chaotic tills. Handfuls of clothes hangers in enormous boxes scattered around what remained of ground floor concessions, marked 'for sale' and the sheer ire of this beating heart of the city being no more at the start of the following week.

'It's awful, I can't believe it's going!' one woman announced to anyone prepared to listen.

'Yes, terrible. It's the only reason I ever come into Swansea. It's been part of our lives for so long.'

'The poor staff' A woman resembling a scarecrow, with one large sun hat perched on her head, its price label tapping wistfully against one ear as her head jiggled as she spoke, arms stuffed full of dangling last minute bargains 'they've been here since I was a teenager. It's like losing your best friend.'

Grace agreed and a lengthy interment began while they waited to present their final offerings at the sepulchre of the tills. Heads bowed, sadly shaken, mutterings and even a tear spilled by those who knew and loved this monument to fashion, beauty, and home.

'I can't believe there'll be no more coffee and cake in the restaurant'

'Or their Christmas displays.'

'The January sales.'

'I'm going to miss the make-up counters' Grace mourned as the service concluded and they drew close to the last farewell at the pay points.

'Julien Macdonald. Those fabulous clothes from our own Welsh designer. It's a sad day, ladies.'

'There's always online.'

One older lady whispered her final psalm.

'You can't shop with your friends online, and you can't feel the quality through a screen.'

With the final epitaph, Grace handed over her credit card and sympathised with the distressed faces handling these last transactions as they handed her items over.

'I'm so very sorry for you all. Good luck for the future.'

A few shattered voices muttered their thanks, before turning to deal with the next customer. As she slipped into the pyjamas, the bereavement was intense.

How quickly life changes.

When everything you know and love comes to a shuddering halt when you thought your foot was firmly on the accelerator. A shop, a TV series, a celebrity death. A pandemic.

A marriage.

Better go downstairs and spend some time with him. This may come to a swift end at some point.

In the lounge, Rhys opened a bottle of beer and slumped into the comfy sofa, remote control in his other hand. Selecting the sports channel, he kicked off his shoes and settled himself back for a night of TV. Grace needed to spend a few days in London before heading up North. *Company policy.* He would have the remote control all to himself, and without watchful eyes, could order an Indian takeaway every night. Or any other door-to-door delivery he desired.

Chapter 27

'A luxury good enriches our lives...it's like going to the opera. Those three hours, for which you're willing to pay a great deal, are so much more intense than an ordinary three weeks. They heighten your reality.'

Remi Krug

The morning spent opening accounts around various private London banks, covered hours of meetings and passport presentations with cards and apps arranged and issued, and Grace realised what a fish experienced once netted and dumped on a heaving deck.

She easily understood the ancient idiom as she navigated the banking houses, alone by Tube, taxi, and on foot, and fought off the various investment discussions offered by those institutions until a time when she was ready to consider any next steps.

Not today, thank you.

Next time I'm in town.

She hailed a taxi to Knightsbridge, where she stepped out to meet the frontage of Harrods, world-famous department store with its green and gold awnings, Edwardian Baroque and Beaux-Art Architecture. There were barely any casual conversations with the drivers. The last one turned up his radio when she'd tried to chat. *'Drive'* wasn't so friendly in this neck of the woods.

Grace surrendered to the smile threatening her lips as she surveyed the entrance. Mac's Ruby Woo red was the colour of the day, and it highlighted her blue eyes perfectly, making them brighter than usual.

I have an account with Coutts. I'm banking alongside royalty and every other rich person in the land. And I'm outside the most expensive shop in the country. I'm Grace Lewis, ex sales rep, from Swansea. Whatever happened here, then?

It was empowering to be in London on a rare visit, and despite the traffic noise and bustle of the crowds on the pavement, it was good to see people busily going about their day, some still wearing facemasks, but the majority back to normal. Her first tube journey in years was amusing, spotting advertising posters for *'Swansea Bay'* on the walls of stations, its beautiful Gower beaches tempting anyone in need of some ozone and rock pooling away from the metropolis, for a weekend or longer.

'Where do I begin?' she whispered, as she studied the nearest window displays.

The Moet and Chandon champagne bar with those enormous gold bubbles covering the glass to tempt me in?

'Well, it's a good place to start, a delicate glass of champagne to prep me for the hours ahead.'

A passer-by gave her an odd look as he whipped in front of her and entered the main doors.

Stop talking to yourself, Grace.

There's nobody else to talk to. Not in London. You're in for a lonely day. And a night of clean sheets.

Well, you either have an evening in a really expensive hotel alone or risk explaining to Marcus just how you can afford this beacon of luxury. It's only one night, enjoy it. Just lie.

Her eyes lifted to take in the facade in all its splendour.

Go from floor to floor, Gracie, you have all day. Enjoy yourself, this only happens to a small percentage of the world's population. This ability to waltz inside and not even cast a glance at price tags is unreal. Your luck has been amazing. Run with it.

Her hand slipped inside her cross-body bag and felt for the

rabbit's foot, soft beneath her touch. Here we go, then.

Pob lwc. Good luck.

First though, ride the Egyptian escalator to the top, even if you have to go back down to start again. Be a kid.

As she stepped onto the central escalator, the glory of art déco Egypt accompanied her to the top, resembling the interior of a pharaoh's tomb. The succinct beauty of the panelling, columns and heads of gods and snakes slipped past as it headed to the upper floors. The wonders of the azure-edged ceiling panel with its hieroglyphics, stars and sphinx below glowed above her. Weaving from floor to floor, she made selections in the designer clothing and accessories departments, mentally adding up the cost and trying to square it against her usual spending, the euphoria felt at the door dissipated.

I have this money. I have to spend some of it. This isn't Cardiff, this is mega-spending. How do people afford this kind of shopping and, more to the point, how do they do it without guilt?

I suppose if you're born to it you don't mix in guilt causing circles. You don't see need on a grand scale from the windows of a private jet, or the ski slopes of the French Alps. This is going to be difficult after elation has passed.

Do I really want furniture? This is overwhelming when you can't share it. £128,000 for a crystal and gold camel with a 'thing' on the top? I have no idea what the 'thing' is for, anyway. Utterly gorgeous and I love a camel. But I don't need it.

I want some of it, but bloody hell, I don't need any of this stuff. I don't know what I'm doing here. This is mad.

A hundred million, Grace, you have a hundred million. Picture it. All those bank notes piled high in a vast vault, except of course they're digital these days. Numbers on a screen, really. Until you want some cash. Fifties, twenties, tenners all falling over your head. Spend some of them. Spend lots of them.

In the Cartier department, she struggled to select a Panthere de Massai ring for her mother, a simple, stylish yellow gold, green jewel-eyed panther which fitted partially around a finger. Not much change from ten thousand pounds. A timeless classic according to the Sales Associate, and in a selection of designs, including gemstones.

At the Tiffany franchise, she bought a return to Tiffany's heart bracelet for Ffion, then began searching for herself. In Bulgari, she tried on a selection of bangles and bracelets and bought the rose gold Serpenti viper bangle with matching earrings from the B zero 1 collection.

I've just spent twenty grand on two pieces of jewellery for myself. What if I lose an earring? Am I mad? Well, you do talk to yourself a lot. But they suit my skin tone, and others were trying things on. I'm not the only one spending this sort of money.

Stop it Gracie, people buy here all the time. This brand has been in business for over a century because customers are constantly buying high end. Get used to it. This is supposed to be a pleasure. Stop your silly nonsense.

A further thought struck her.

What can I get for Rhys? And Marcus? I must buy them something. It won't feel right otherwise. What if I buy Rhys a top-end watch and tell him it's a super-fake from Turkey, and a guy in the office was selling it? They even come in a box with leaflets. I could get Marcus a tie pin, or cufflinks. He might not even know the value? Fuck, Gracie, you can't actually buy him anything, can you? Shit, where's the champagne bar? I need a drink. I'm getting stressed and sweary.

With a flute of Moet in one hand and her phone in the other, she contemplated her surroundings. Beautiful and luxurious, naturally. She snapped a close-up and shared it to Instagram with the hashtags #champers #chillax #harrods #justlooking. Rhys wouldn't know how to use Instagram and showed no interest in what he considered a girly app full of makeup tutorials. Grace didn't know if Marcus held an account.

Ping
WhatsApp/Ffion
What you doing in 'arrods, babe?

Slumming it for a change.

Nice. Pick me up a tin of beans and some biccies.

No caviar?

Hate the stuff.

What you doing stalking me?

Bored at my desk.

Issue some bloody licences, girlfriend.

Ooh, is that what we do in the DVLA?

Hysterical. Speak soon.

OK

By the way, entered us into a Tiffany jewellery competition.
Cross everything for luck. Well in your case, maybe not
everything.... mwahahahaha xxxx

Uncalled for. If only. Don't get the chance. lol

Beans and biscuits. Normal people's stuff, despite the joke. This was Ffion. Feet on the ground Ffion. Divorced for two years, on and off boyfriends, but no offspring, and back living with her parents, which she swore was the best option as they spoiled her like she was a ten-year-old.

Grace laughed quietly as she sipped the champagne. Ffion was going to be surprised to discover she'd won a designer bracelet at the end of the following week. Complete with a faked cover letter informing her thus.

Omg, I'm never going to be part of this world, no matter how much money I have. A tin of beans and some biscuits is the level we're all at in my little circle. You need to be born into this, to know people, have friends who do the things rich people do. I don't ski. I don't know how to get an invitation to a catwalk show, and I can't stand in the middle of Harrods waving a fistful of money shouting 'I'm rich now, please show me what to do.'

❦

16.06pm/Green goddess
How's things?

All the better for hearing from you Xxx

Miss you xx

Where are you today?

London. Big meeting. Xx Can you get here tonight? I have a room at the Bulgari in Knightsbridge. We can dirty some sheets.

Posh and naughty. I can try Sweetie. Laters Xxx

As Grace lounged in the subterranean spa at the Bulgari, recovering from a rare massage, scenes from 'How to Marry a Millionaire' flickered in glorious technicolour through her head. Three beautiful, penniless American women seeking rich husbands. There were Texan oil barons, fancy dining rooms, glorious gowns, Marilyn Monroe hiding her spectacles, blind as a bat.

'Men aren't attentive to girls who wear glasses.'

Another world from a decade in the distant past. Schatze, Pola and Loco entranced her with their on-screen chicanery and the film held a special place in her heart as she'd watched it over and over with her mother, after her father left them.

'It's my only hope now, Gracie' she would laugh, ruffling her daughter's hair as they sat on the sofa. 'Your Mam needs to meet a millionaire.'

But mam remained alone, except for short-term romances and a support group of friends. Grace watched her lonely mother during those years go from home to work, work to home.

In a favourite scene, two of them considered letting Loco join the hunt, by proving she could buy lunch with whatever was in her purse.

'There's a fine contribution to a million-dollar proposition.' Lauren Bacall complained loudly.

'One whole quarter.'

'Maybe,' Marilyn simpered. 'But she's awful clever with a quarter!'

Grace pulled the fluffy robe close, the comforting aroma of coconut oil wafting through the luxury cotton, and sighed.

I'm going to have to be awful clever with a hundred million.

Chapter 28

The airport was busy as Grace and her mother headed to the lifts for the top floor. Next time, she'd hire a limousine and arrive the same way as rock stars and millionaires. Instead, she'd booked the private lounge with priority boarding and they dragged wheeled cabin bags from the car park along with everyone else, leaving the new 'company car' she'd leased, in the pre-paid parking zone. Grace missed the hired red Mercedes, but for the next few months she needed to maintain the charade with something believable for work.

It was a last-minute rush, but they were going. Off to Spain on a mother-daughter midweek break, with a few days to enjoy themselves and for Grace to peek in estate agents' windows as desires for her own place in the sun surfaced. Previously unseen daytime television programmes fuelled her with ideas, one of them a luxury villa in the hills around Marbella. Anxiety crept along her spine, something rarely experienced during her busy working life. Her palms and forehead damp with sweat.

Is this a panic attack? I've read about them. What are you anxious about? You have everything. Filthy, obscenely rich. The end of your anxieties not the beginning.

Her mother studied her with concern. 'Are you alright, love? You look hot.'

Grace nodded, the back of her hand rubbing her forehead. 'Yes, I'm fine Mam, just haven't flown in ages. You know what Rhys is like with holidays, he'd be happier if I went alone and he could play around.'

'Now you've got to let it go, Grace' her mother berated 'you can't keep picking at it forever, not if you're ever going to be happy. It's behind you now. If it happens again, well that's a different story.'

'I know. There's something I need to talk to you about this trip, but it will wait until we're sitting somewhere gorgeous with a cocktail.'

Grace didn't mention Rhys thought she was up north working. She would explain when they arrived at their destination, along with the house in Langland Bay.

'Ooh, OK. But let's make use of this V.I.P. lounge. Comfy seats, free food and wine!'

'OK, don't rush, we don't want to look like we're desperate for freebies. Let's just saunter.'

Grace winked at her mother, who grinned back. They burst into laughter, speeding up their footsteps, wheels rumbling along the tiles beside them. They arrived at the desk trying to control their giggles.

They handed their boarding passes to the girl who welcomed them into what was once an extra expense on top of any budget holiday price. When Grace took short breaks with *the girls,* they would be out on the concourse, running between airport shops testing the wafting scents from the perfume counters, eyeing up handsome weekenders headed to the golf resorts along the Costas, the incessant din of milling crowds, and the atmosphere around the pub areas. Grace doubted they'd enjoy being surrounded by couples and business travellers, eyes glued to laptops and tablets, quietly engaged in the day's business.

With an unwelcome intense anxiety creeping through her, the understanding that everything had altered, meaning tough decisions ahead, unsettled her. A shrill voice over her shoulder repeatedly told her 'Once a cheater, always a cheater.'

The voice wouldn't go away. Neither would the chocolate

toned one which called her *Welshwoman.*

Grace watched her mother's face closely over the table at the Eurostars Oasis restaurant. Purposely avoiding going out to eat, in case they needed to go back to their room quickly under the sheer excitement of the news, Grace contemplated how her mother would react and stayed close by, asking for a table as near the exit and lifts as possible.

'OK Mam, I have the news I wanted to share with you.'

This was the moment, and as she studied her mother, tanned and glowing, happy in the candlelight, her beautiful coral dress set off with a stunning shell necklace and matching earrings, Grace raised her wineglass. Her mother always knew how to dress for sunnier climes with a bright selection of clothes which would seldom see the light of day during a Welsh summer.

This is going to be weird.

How will she react?

'Now, Mam, I want you to keep calm, that is top priority. And please don't yell or get loud.'

'Good lord Gracie, what are you about to tell me? Anyone would swear you'd won the lottery.'

Grace fell quiet and stared at her mother, trying not to smile too broadly.

'Well, go on then, tell me.'

Her mother scoured her face. Grace remained silent.

'No. Is that *it*?' She lowered her head towards the table. 'You've won the lottery?' Her voice dropped to a whisper.

Grace slid a hand into her bag and lifted out the rabbit's foot. 'Remember what you said when you bought this for me?'

Her mother sat bolt upright as Grace slipped it back into secrecy.

'Oh my god, no. Really? The lottery?'

The volume level was rising. Grace nodded and grabbed her hands across the table. *Whisper it.*

'Yes Mam, I won the bloody lottery. Now just keep your voice down, please. Don't yell.'

Her mother nodded repeatedly, eyes shining with tears. 'Oh Gracie, that's fabulous, I'm thrilled for you. Is it enough to pay off your mortgage, love? I worry about your mortgage.'

Here it comes. What am I going to tell her? She thinks it's

thousands, not millions. Just like I did. In McDonald's car park.
With a seagull on the bonnet instead of the Spirit of Ecstasy.

'OK Mam, remember what I said. No yelling. I'm going to tell you now, but you must, and I mean this, you *cannot* tell a soul. Not Amanda or anyone else. I'm deadly serious. There are good reasons, Rhys reasons. It has to be kept quiet. OK?'

Her mother took in her daughter's words and nodded slowly. 'I see. Yes, yes, of course.'

'OK then, well, because of the state of my marriage, you're the first person I'm telling. Rhys doesn't know. I can't risk him running off with half of it to that girl of his, or any future squeeze. I can't tell any friends. Can you imagine the gossip? Swansea's a small city. Do you get it, Mam, is that OK?'

Grace saw the cloud of realisation falling across her mother's face. 'Oh god, yes, I see. Oh, my. Who'd have thought it? How much have you won, Gracie?'

Reaching into her bag, Grace pulled out the A5 notebook and pen, opened the front cover, and wrote the number 20 M inside. Then, she turned it towards her mother and watched as her expression changed from delight to shock.

'Oh my god, Grace. Oh, my god.'

Then she sat back with her hands flopped in her lap, speechless.

'Breathe, Mam.'

Her mother managed only a nod.

'Have a sip!' Grace pushed the wineglass in her direction. 'Quick now, a good long glug.'

Her mother raised it to her lips, and it spilled down her chin, then grabbed at her napkin and dabbed at the mess.

'Do you want to finish dinner or shall we go up to our room?'

A splutter led the response. *'Room.'*

Grace gripped her mother's elbow as they tottered to the lifts. The trembling and muffled sounds of joy she tried to hide as they waited for the doors to open were palpable. When they were inside her mother finally yelled like a child, and flung her arms around her daughter, jiggling her up and down with joy, the lift jiggling with them.

It reminded her of the first visit to The Marriott, when she, too, stumbled, but unaided, to the lifts, shaking and desperate to get into a room, any room, away from the gaze of onlookers.

'Oh my god, Gracie, you're set for life! No more worries. As long as you're careful, you can give up work! Maybe try some IVF.'

There was a less-than-pregnant pause.

'If you're still thinking along those lines.'

'Mam, I've never thought along those lines.'

Finally, after what seemed like an endless moment, Grace joined in, and it swept away the worries that plagued her since the phone call with Miranda, and she, too, was jumping and hugging and spilling copious tears of joy. At last, she could share the moment with someone. This finally felt real, not some dream she'd been wandering through alone. Time to let go, time to have real fun with a co-conspirator.

'I know, Mam, it's unreal. I can barely believe it myself. I've been in a daze.'

Her mother's eyes shone with tears after hearing about Miranda's call, the room at the Marriott, the courier, the financial team, and their advice. Marcus remained a secret.

'I'll get some champagne sent up.'

Her mother threw her hands in the air, laughing, and doing a quick twirl.

'Bugger that, love. Let's go out and have some. Oh, Gracie, I'm so pleased for you, I really am. Twenty million. Twenty bloody million. That's amazing. I can see why you don't want anyone to know. Especially Rhys. Much as I care for him, with that amount in the bank you're right, he'd be tempted to take half and who knows where he'd end up.'

'Exactly.'

'So why are you still working, love?'

'Oh come on Mam, I'm not working. I gave up the day I won, but I've told Rhys I've found another job, leased a decent car, and have the days free to myself. It's been wonderful. But if this gets out locally, it wouldn't be long before he found out. And you're right, there's every chance he'd be gone and someone else would step into my very rich shoes. Even if he stayed, women would fall over themselves in the rush. Half of twenty million is still a lot of millions, especially in Wales.'

'We have to work this all out, love. Sit down with a plan and I'll have to cover for you.'

'Thanks, Mam, you're right, we will, and I've been doing lots of planning. But first, I have something for you.' Grace withdrew a velvet pouch from her bag and offered it to her mother.

Her expression was joyous as she undid the ties, took out the Panthere de Massai ring, and slipped it on her finger.

'Ooh Gracie, it's beautiful. *Diolch*, I love it.'

Thank god it fits. It's the first of many, Mam. Anything you want is yours.

They spent the rest of the evening wandering around Spanish bars, eating tapas to fill the gaps from the missed dinner, and drinking Cava, as Grace's mother insisted on the cheaper, homegrown version following the first bottle of French champagne.

'Spend wisely, Gracie, it all tastes pretty much the same, anyway!'

Grace wore a beautiful multi-coloured silk maxi dress, which wafted in the late-season breezes, despite the still warm evening. For once she could wear some of the expensive jewellery, beautiful shoes, and designer handbags which were packed in her case. She smiled at her mother's reasoning, but agreed.

Grace threw back her head and laughed.

'But tomorrow we are going to buy you loads of stuff you don't even know you want yet. A complete new wardrobe. And a suitcase to put it in.'

'I wouldn't say no to a new frock or two.'

'We'll hit the Banus boutiques, and the *Spanish Harrods* you like.'

'Oh, El Corte Inglés. You'll love it, Gracie.'

They laughed loudly, toasted endlessly, and hugged repeatedly before her mother returned to her room and Grace flopped into bed to contemplate finally letting the cat out of the bag. Here, it was an emerald-eyed jewelled leopard from a velvet pouch. No longer alone in her deception, Grace knew her mother needed to use guile to shield her secrets. Maybe for a lifetime. Drifting into a champagne and cava-infused sleep, her last whispered words to herself swam giddily around her head.

Oh, please remember this can go no further, not even to a stranger on a train. We know how that ended.

At breakfast, they both ordered a Bucks Fizz and sat smiling at each other across the table, nursing celebratory hangovers, the only fix a top-up of those bubbles and extra large americano coffees. The exterior terrace fans spun above their heads, the warmth of the morning made bearable by the end-of-season drop in temperatures, while the occasional sparrow hopped hopefully from table to chair, waiting for crumbs from *tostadas con tomate* to drop to the floor.

'I've barely slept all night!'

'I had really weird dreams. Vivid.'

'Must be all the excitement.'

As the *camarero* poured their coffees, Grace smiled up at him.

'Sin leche para mí, gracias.'

'Oh Gracie, what does that mean?'

'It means without milk, senora.' The man smiled back 'And your accent is very good senorita.'

Grace smiled broadly, knowing he was flattering her. She, too, was a senora.

Maybe it's the Botox.

'Gracias senor.'

He smiled and nodded. As he walked away, her mother tipped her head, impressed.' Well done love, it's nice to learn a few words of the language when you're abroad.'

'It's just a phone app. I haven't got very far with it. Thing is, Mam, I'm thinking of buying a villa here, somewhere we can get some sun anytime we want.'

They were far enough from the nearest occupied table to talk freely.

'Ooh love, sounds amazing!'

'Yes, I'm hoping to look at a few while we're here. It's up to you if you want to come with me or lounge by the pool. You know me, I enjoy the odd day on a lounger, but I prefer sightseeing.'

'Gracie, I've been thinking. Why not just give Rhys half anyway and tell him to go, if you're not happy with him? You could live very well on ten million.'

Grace's heart dropped into the pit of her stomach. Here it was, the suggestion she knew would ultimately spurt from her mother's lips in the cold light of day, and the one she knew would make her question whether she'd done the right thing telling her. She clasped her hands across the table, her expression stern.

'I thought of that, Mam, but I've done lots of research. Many big lottery winners end up losing it within a few years. Now, I hope it won't be me. I'm way too careful. But what if it was Rhys? What if he went and spent the lot on fast cars and fast women and a mad lavish lifestyle? What if the money ran out?'

Her mother pondered these points and nodded slowly in agreement. Grace raced on.

'Even if we were divorced by then, I'm pretty certain he'd come running back to ask for more. I don't want that pressure to think about through life, constantly wondering if he was going to pop up again in a few years. Ten million sounds a lot, but it's not really, not by today's standards, is it?'

Her mother sat back, and Grace let go of her hands before she folded them in her lap.

'No, you're right. Even a fancy house would probably cost him a couple of million, and he loves his engines, and cars, and any woman he met would want to spend lots on holidays and all the other stuff people want. You're probably right. You'd be the goose that laid the golden egg. He knows you're sensible with money.'

'Exactly. I daren't tell him. Obviously, he'll benefit from it as we go along if we stay together because my 'new job' will see to it. Rhys isn't a great one for holidays. But if he knew, it wouldn't be long before there'd be some expensive sports car that devalues the minute you buy it on our new driveway, and with all the hours of the day to waste on it, there'd probably be a second, then he'd want to go racing it or something else stupid and expensive. I can't trust him with women, and I can't really trust him not to go mad with money, either. It changes people.'

'True. They go over the top from what I've read over the years. The more money they win, the worse it is. I suppose if you're born into it, that's a different story. You know how to handle it.'

The *Camarero* returned to top up their coffees, and the aroma as it splashed into their cups provided a gentle, heady break from the seriousness of their conversation until he moved away among the other tables.

'Mam, I want to use this money carefully, so you and I are OK for life. I don't want it spoiling us, but I also want us to live really, really well. Now, I will give you cash weekly to spend as you want. If you need more, just ask. I can also buy you a house if you want, or get a lovely apartment on the marina, easy to maintain, right in the middle of the social area. It's up to you.'

'Sounds great, but I think I'd prefer to stay in my house.'

'OK, well I'm buying a place down there anyway, and it will be our secret. We can use it as we please, and both have a key. It will be an investment, as well as a bolthole. You can have one bedroom and me the other, and leave clothes there too. So anytime you want a night out, or a weekend by the seaside, stay there. Or book yourself into a hotel. Whatever makes you happy.'

Her mother's excitement was palpable.

'What about Amanda?'

'Amanda can stay there too, just tell her it's a friend's flat. Maybe one with benefits. She can't know about the win. People talk to strangers, it's human nature to gossip. We don't have to have anything there that shows who owns it, no photos on display, no bills hanging around. Pretend it's their Airbnb and they let you use it when there are a few gaps, in exchange for running the vacuum around and cleaning the fridge.'

'Sounds wonderful, Gracie. I've always fancied a Flat in the marina. You should definitely do that.'

Grace laughed, tossing back her hair, sunglasses gleaming in the sunshine. The *camarero* caught her eye across the tables and winked.

'Apparently, we're calling them apartments these days. I know you love your cruises too, so there'll be plenty of those to go on.'

'I'd still have to share a cabin with Amanda, we can't risk her wondering why I'm suddenly in a fancy cabin and she's paying a single supplement. But she's fun, I'm OK with how things stand there.'

'Good, that's easy then. Of course, we can do lovely cruises together too. Then we'll go 'posh' class.'

'That would be nice. Rhys isn't keen on them anyway, is he?'

'Rhys and the sea are not the best of friends. He barely went in when we went to the Maldives, and you could walk around our island in ten minutes.'

'So what shall we do after breakfast?'

'We're off to Puerto Banus later for some shopping. Then we'll have lunch and look at all the super yachts.'

'You're not buying one of those, are you?'

'No chance, Mam. They cost a million a year to maintain! Maybe I'll buy one of those seized Russian ones. I'm sure they'll be in the sales soon.'

She smiled and pulled at a piece of fresh baguette on the table. Her mother took a smiling selfie and posted it to Instagram.

'I didn't know you did Instagram?'

Her mother raised an eyebrow and pulled a silly pose with her hand on her cheek.

'Oh, of course, who doesn't? What's the point of all those travel selfies if no one's going to see them? Hardly anyone looks at my Facebook page, so I went to Insta. Hashtag glam travel, hashtag women on tour!'

'My mother is the hashtag queen?'

'Now don't you dare follow me, a mother has to have a few secrets.'

'Grace winked and they both burst into a round of laughing which brought tears to their eyes.

'I don't think you'd quite afford one of those super yachts though, love, even in the sales!' her mother dabbed at her eye with a napkin.

I probably could. Just a small one. But it wouldn't go through the lock into Swansea Marina. Maybe I'll buy a boat in Swansea. At least it would fit.

❦

Chapter 29

Chirp
MarX
Can't wait to see you and give you a cootch.

It's cwtch. Don't text and drive.

Layby, Welshwoman. What hellfire jumble of letters is that?

The Swansea devil's own lol

Swansea has a devil? Xxx

In the museum. xx

Grace waited at the top of a flight of grand stone steps outside the Bath Spa hotel as Marcus pulled into the car park. Wearing a long cream wool coat over light blue denim jeans and a loose cream blouse with matching ankle boots, she swept down the driveway to greet him in the car park, arriving at his driver's door as he turned off the ignition.

'Hello gorgeous, you look like a snow angel in that outfit. Wow, this place is nice. Has Christmas come early?'

'Special weekend rates.'

'Corporate deals, they're the best. Now, give me one of those bloody Welsh *cwtches* you do so well. I've missed you.'

His arms were around her, his face close to hers as they hugged tightly.

The cool of early evening caressed her cheeks as he swung her gently from side to side in a slow dance that brought a smile to her lips.

Still takes two to tango.

His lips brushed the side of her cheek, and his chin rubbed against her hair.

'You smell like luxury.' He breathed in deeply, holding her tight a moment longer, before releasing her and finding her mouth with his own.

'I've booked dinner for half seven, assuming we can make it that far?' she ventured, taking his hand and tightening her fingers through his.

Marcus laughed. 'I'll try to control myself for an hour, or so. Let's get inside and chill. It feels like ages since I saw you.'

'Well, now we can have three days and nights together.'

Marcus let her go briefly to unload his weekend bag, then took her hand and led her back towards the steps.

'And that, thank goodness, is the end of my working week. Let's grab a drink. I want to sit and look at you, and talk.'

Grace settled at a table with two comfortably upholstered chairs in the smaller lounge, while Marcus ordered at the bar, her eyes taking in his height, the handsome, confident stance, the thick blond hair, before he turned towards her, carrying a bottled beer and a glass of gin and tonic. Her insides executed a double backward somersault with an end pose worthy of Olympic gold, at his easy, confident gait.

Gracie, you're getting feelings for this guy and I don't think they're all lust. You mustn't, he's too young. He doesn't want to be embroiled in a triangle of trouble. His life is calm and easy.

He doesn't know what it's like to be married. Oh, what are you thinking? With a hundred million in the bank, any man would take on any of your fast-growing foibles.

'So, how have you been? Are you enjoying the new job?' He sat and placed their glasses down.

'It's fine so far, but let's not talk shop.'

'OK. I thought you could unload, and tell me you wish you hadn't left us.' An arm slid around her shoulders drawing her close.

'Not there, yet.'

He glanced through the window behind them. 'The air's getting a nip and the trees are turning. You should see the colours I've been passing on the road.'

'Now you're being very English, and talking about the weather.'

'Change the subject, you said.' He grinned and winked.

'Where have you been today, Englishman?'

'Nowhere near Swansea Bay, but I've heard they're missing you down there. Gareth's got your patch, so he's happy.'

'Good, I felt sorry for him. His wife and kids barely saw him. And all those bloody tractors.'

'Tractors?'

'I've covered for him, and trust me, there are tractors, cows, and sheep on those roads. They hold you up forever. We're talking shop again!'

'I'm going down there on Tuesday. I've learned the hard way what you Welsh get up to after a bank holiday.'

Grace's face fell. 'Yes, but this is a sad bank holiday, not the usual kind.'

Marcus slid his hand down onto her thigh and squeezed it. Grace covered it with her own. Nothing further to add to a nation in mourning for a monarch.

'Seriously, I've missed you loads. Being far away from you is tough.'

'I know, I've missed you, too. We're getting gooey here, aren't we?'

'Does it bother you?'

'Nothing wrong with a bit of goo now and then.'

He kissed her affectionately on the forehead.

206

'Shall we take these drinks to your room?'

'Our room.'

'That's nice. *Our room.*'

Their room housed a gold canopied four-poster bed with matching curtains and cushions, a tonal armchair, and pleated folds of material spilled down the back as a headboard dressing. Comfort and cosiness, a degree of olde-worlde charm, and a desk provided all they needed.

'Give me a proper hug, Grace.'

He pulled her into his arms and gripped her tightly. 'I think I like you in jeans, my blue goddess. You look like you live by the beach with a surfer dude boyfriend and an open-air fire.'

Is he psychic?

'Are you a surfer dude, Englishman?'

Marcus flicked back a lock of hair about to tackle his right eye, a movement she found enthralling.

'I've been known to hit the beach on a board, if that gets you going?'

'Wetsuit or bare chest?'

'Whatever you prefer. I've done both. Manscaped.'

'I thought I was supposed to be the funny one?'

'Let me take your coat off, let's chillax.'

They made themselves comfortable on the bed, resting up against the thick, plumped pillows, her head on his shoulder.

'This is nice at the end of a long drive. I need ten minutes later to upload some paperwork, then I'm completely done.'

Uploading paperwork, orders, results. Thank god that's gone from my life. Now, I just have endless secrets to keep on top of.

'You don't mind me not ravaging you straight away?'

'Not at all. This is lovely. You smell all manly, with a tinge of autumn in your hair.'

'And you smell like perfume counters, French, and way too expensive.'

Grace laughed and snuggled into his chest.

'It's Coco Chanel. It *is* French.'

'So how are you getting away with this, if I may ask?'

'Spa weekend with the girls, and of course, the state funeral on Monday.'

'Subterfuge suits you, my little secret agent.'

'Well, Bath is famous for its spa.'

Marcus picked up the TV remote and flicked to the news, showing wall-to-wall coverage of the Queen's passing peppered with ticker tape of other grim events. He pressed mute, and the pictures told their silent story in the background.

'I can't believe we've known each other for such a short time.'

'Feels like forever.'

'We met in May, we're halfway to October.'

'That's cheating. We've barely been together.'

'Doesn't feel that way. I lusted after you for weeks, coming to Swansea to see you. And there you were, gone.'

He laughed loudly, and his face lit up.

'Did I get it right?'

Grace ruffled his hair. 'Vast improvement. I'll teach you some more, *now in a minute.*'

'Welshisms. What'll my mates think?'

He kissed her, let out a sigh, and closed his eyes. 'I can't wait to show you around my old Uni city. I did my business studies degree here, you know.'

'Really? So you know all the pubs.'

'Naturally. It's what students do first. Map the booze route.'

'So what's your idea of the perfect job, if you weren't doing this *Man on a motorway stuff*?'

Marcus laughed. 'Great description. I seem to spend most of my life on one.'

He contemplated for a long moment.

'I think in an ideal world I'd be running a surf school somewhere, getting up each morning, pulling on a wetsuit, and heading out onto the water, teaching people to get over their fear of the sea and letting them discover the thrill of riding a wave.'

'Wow, not just an occasional passion, then?'

'Well, it is these days. Oxford isn't exactly coastal. But I can hang ten with the best of them when I get the chance.'

'I believe you.' Grace laughed. 'Have you ever surfed the Gower?'

'Never, but one day I will. I've seen those Swansea tourism posters on the London underground. *Fancy riding a different tube?* It stuck in my mind. With you down there, perhaps you can show me the best spots. Maybe I'll enter the Welsh Surfing championships?'

'I didn't even know we had any. Are you that good?'

Marcus nodded a few times, enthusiastically. 'Absolutely. Not.'

Grace burst into laughter.

'I'm seeing you in a completely new light.' she added.

'Oh?'

'Yes, you're no longer my man in a suit. You're my man in a wetsuit. Action man.'

Marcus leaned in close and kissed her earlobe. 'I like the 'My man' bit. There's not much action going on here though, is there?'

Do I rise to this challenge? It's usually him taking the lead. Be brave. Modern woman and all that.

'OK, let me change that before we eat.'

Sliding her hands over his buttocks, they headed for his zip.

'I thought we didn't have time?' he murmured as his lips touched hers.

'So we're a bit late...' the words vanished under the force of his kiss.

While they reconnected among the fine lawn bedding, the air outside grew cooler, the sky turned darker, a quick swirl of wind rose from the west, and a flurry of leaves tapped an irrational rhythm against the windowpane. There was no irrational rhythm from Marcus, who took perfect control of Grace's warming body until they both reached the point of melting into each other and the comfort of the bedding beneath them.

'Winter's on its way, Sweetie.' He murmured, as they nestled back against the pillows, arms woven tight around each other, breathing slowing. *I know, and I'm relying on you to keep me warm, Englishman.*

Over the weekend, they visited the Roman Baths and Spa, under the scrutiny of the goddess Minerva, whose gold head enthralled them both as they studied its beauty, immersed in the city's history. They swam in the hotel pool, lounged in the spa, and ate at quirky restaurants, cementing their attraction with constant bonding and touching. It was on the last night Marcus brought up the subject of Rhys as they lay bound in each other's arms in yet another tangle of bedding, Sunday night television with the lying in State scenes and funeral preparations barely audible, but flickering as the background wallpaper most of the nation saw on their screens.

'I dread to ask, but how are things at home?'

I'm finally having badly needed space. If only you knew how much space.

'I've been away more than I've been there, but the best they can be, I suppose.'

'OK. I felt I should ask. I don't need to know the ins and outs unless you want me to.'

He wants to know if you're still sleeping together, still intimate.

Tell him. Go on, tell him.

But he'll think you're just seeking revenge.

Tell him anyway. This doesn't feel like revenge.

Grace shrugged and played with the fingers on his left hand, twirling them gently and rubbing her fingertips against his buffed nails, before taking a deep breath. The eternal signal something far-reaching was to be revealed.

'It's the usual. He had an affair.'

Marcus dipped his head.

'Difficult to get past, especially now you are too.'

'I tried not to.'

'That's my fault. I'm sorry.' He gave her a peck on the cheek.

'Too late to worry about it now.'

'Do you know if he's still seeing her?'

'Not a hundred per cent, but at the moment, I don't really care.'

'It could be worse.'

How? What's worse than sharing someone else's body?

'What if he was an alcoholic, a gambler, or violent? All difficult things to recover from.'

It didn't even cross my mind. And he's right. They would be definite deal breakers.

'Unless, of course, he's a serial type, and won't stop at one.'

'That's yet to be revealed. What about you? Have you ever lived with anyone, been in a long-term relationship?'

Marcus laughed gently.

'Yes, of course. Who hasn't? I wondered if you were ever going to ask me.'

'Sorry, I didn't mean to be nosey.'

'That's fine, it shows you like me a little, to want to find out this sort of stuff.'

I like you a lot.

A big Tesco trolley full.

Marcus pulled her closer to his chest.

'I lived with someone who left me for my best friend. Her name was Georgia. It was a few years ago, but it taught me a lesson. If there's a steam train on the tracks, get out of its way.'

I didn't expect to hear that at his age. Isn't unfaithfulness the preserve of the bored, married forever age group?

Georgia. Very public school.

He was still talking. 'Life happens. You can't wish it was different, or wish *you'd* done something else. If people are leaving, step aside. They may not always go. Some get over these things.'

Get out of Rhys's way? But it's over, isn't it? But would it be if I hadn't confronted her? He's still my husband, the one I married, the one older by five years, the grounding influence. The one who should have known better. The one who will require half my fortune as payment for his infidelity.

And I'm still in the arms of a lover.

Marcus traced a finger across her lips, and she bit it playfully, so he gently pinched the end of her nose, leaning in to steal another kiss, murmuring as their lips caressed. Then he pulled back, his face serious, his eyes darkening. Grace followed his lips as words formed.

'You may not want to hear this now, Mrs Lewis, but I have some bad news for you.'

Her body tensed.

Mrs Lewis? Oh god, what? Not the end already?

A breathless pause.

'I'm afraid I've fallen in love with you.'

Then, ensnared in his arms, she was a bug in a web of sticky, shimmering gossamer.

Fuck.

The silence lingered, except for his breathing against her ear.

'Oh god Marcus, really?'

'One hundred per cent. Sorry, but you must have known this was coming?'

Grace was silent.

'I know this is quick, but I think I've been in love with you since the night of the Ball, so for you, it's just weeks, but for me, months.'

He slipped a hand through the front of his hair, down to the nape of his neck, his elbow high in repose.

'So, Sweetie, what now?'

She struggled up, looked at him lounging against those marshmallow pillows, and leaned in to kiss him, this perfect specimen of manhood, who declared his love for her nanoseconds ago.

'I'd say thank you for not dumping me, or 'that's thrown the cat among the pigeons.'

Sometimes only a worn-out old cliche will do, and you're full of those at times, Gracie. It's your Gran's inheritance. Her generation stored them neatly in their navy handbags ready to pull out for any occasion.

A flood of unexpected tears coursed down her face. Marcus pulled her close, rocking her back and forth.

'What is it, Grace? Tell me. I didn't mean to upset you.'

What the hell is happening to me? He's going to think I'm completely mad. Pass the smelling salts, Mr Darcy.

'I'm sorry, I don't know where that came from.'

Marcus was calming. 'I think you're under a lot of stress, travelling and change. You're tired and life's complicated. Add in all this sadness' his hand flourished towards the TV 'and most of the nation is at a pretty low ebb.'

'Yes, I didn't think her death would affect me this way.'

'Likewise. Maybe we should stop all this sex. It's very tiring.'

Her surprised expression drew a wink and a smile. 'But now I want to tell you again. Grace Lewis, I love you. It makes *me* happy, so just cwtch me. You don't have to feel the same, but I think we're good for each other, however long it lasts.'

However long it lasts? But I want it to last forever. Unlike our Queen.

Change the subject, Grace, change it fast.

'You're still coming to Windsor tomorrow?'

'Yes, of course I am. It's history.'

Then he was kissing her damp face, her eyelids, her lips, and her arms were creeping around his neck.

'Oh, Marcus' a sob left her throat 'make love to me again. I need you right now.'

'All night, if that's what you want, baby.'

Of course, it's what I want. To be glued in your arms, and never melt. But I can't tell you this right now. There's this huge thing to deal with. Bigger, even, than a State Funeral.

Chapter 30

Rhys answered her call on the third ring.

'Well, did you wave goodbye to Queenie?'

'Where's your sense of respect, Rhys?'

'Sorry, Cariad, I watched some of it on the telly. Very sad.'

'Yes, it was.'

'Did you get a good spot?'

'Yes, we were on The Long Walk, we were so close to the hearse it made it worth the walking and standing. The guard opposite fainted, but I'm glad I went.'

'Will you be home for the weekend?'

'Yes, of course.'

'Good, I miss you, you know. Even with all the wild parties and beer cans I've been tossing around the lounge. It will be nice to have you home. Just don't look at all the chaos.'

I know he's teasing, but he knows how to annoy me.

'I think it's time we got a cleaner in twice a week. I'm going to be too busy to keep on top of all your mess when I'm home.'

'OK, boss woman. Can she wear a French Maid's outfit?'

'In your dreams.'

And my increasing nightmares.

Grace's phone was ringing but there was no name, just a jumble of numbers.

Call centre? Better answer anyway.

The voice on the end of the line was male, older. An English accent. Unknown region.

'Hello love, is your name Grace?'

'Yes, that's me.'

'My name is Graham Bolt. You may know my son, Marcus?'

'Yes, that's right.'

Dads never ring girlfriends.

This dad is ringing this girlfriend.

Grace was aware of the tremble in her hand, and a dryness in her mouth. A somnambulant pause wavered before he finally spoke and she understood why it was so drawn out.

'I'm afraid it's not good news Grace.'

A second hesitation. A voice noticeably tinged with despair.

He doesn't want to say the words.

What words, Grace?

What words will he use?

'I'm afraid Marcus was involved in a motorway accident yesterday.'

My man on a motorway.

Sinking. Knees weakening.

Sit, Grace. Something is coming that will need a chair.

215

Chapter 31

With her head resting on Ffion's shoulder, Grace's friend held her tightly as sobs wracked her body.

'Oh my god Gracie, I have no words.'

They slumped in the front seats of Grace's car, Ffion behind the wheel, on a grey, chilly morning, adrift in the middle of England. Through the windscreen, the cemetery still showed signs of a funeral drawing to a close. An empty hearse sidled past, people milled around the entrance waiting for the next, and flowers from earlier services rested against the exterior wall as the celebrant waited for another cortege to arrive.

'His poor parents.'

Grace nodded, attempting to wipe away the tears, regaining her posture only slightly.

'I can't believe it, Ffi, I can't bloody believe it.'

'I know, beaut, it's tragic. I'm so very sorry.'

Ffion's perfume was the only comfort. The familiar aroma of iris, patchouli, and vanilla her friend always wore, filled her senses, as strong as the blooms left in full view at the exit.

La vie est belle

You smell French and too expensive Marcus said, the weekend he told her he loved her.

'I couldn't tell you, Ffi, I just daren't. So much has gone on with Rhys, you'd never know.'

'I'm so sorry, Grace, but I tried to warn you. I sent you a letter. I couldn't tell you to your face.'

Grace sighed heavily. 'So that was you?'

Ffion nodded, a tear sliding down her face.

'It doesn't matter now, I'm past caring about my old life.'

'Did you *love*, love him Grace, or was it just sex and affection?'

Just sex. Those words again.

'As close as can be, in all my confusion.'

'Oh bless you, I really don't know what to say. What about him, did he love you?'

'He told me a few weeks ago, and every day since. I can't believe I'll never see or touch him again. Oh god. It was a full on whirlwind.'

'Let's find this pub and get you a few drinks.'

A gloved hand tapped the driver's side window. A man about Marcus's age, face pinched, eyes red, motioned for Ffion to lower the glass. She pressed the button, and cold air flooded their warm space.

'Do you ladies want to follow me to the pub? I'm in the yellow Honda just there.'

'Yes please, we'll get lost otherwise.'

'It's not far and there's a car park. Plenty of food and drink laid on, and a roaring fire. I think you and Grace need both.'

'Thanks, yes, I think you're right.'

'It's been tough, today.'

'Yes, it has.'

Grace closed her eyes as they pulled out of the crematorium onto the main road, the wracking pain of loss, overwhelming. As the car travelled over the uneven surface, she closed her eyes to shut it all away, and drifted into exhaustion as the engine noise and vibration jostled her into slumber. *Ffion had my back with the letter. Please be a long way. I can't deal with this. I need to sleep, forever and ever.*

I think I might want to die.

☙

Chapter 32

Grace opened her eyes. Rubbed them. Focused. It took a moment to realise she was horizontal, sheathed in the comfort of warm folds of bedding. *What the hell? Am I at home? Where's Ffion? Explaining to Rhys? What will she be saying?*

'I don't know what happened Rhys, she fainted when she saw the price of those boots she fancied. An assistant had to bring her a chair. Seriously, I don't think she's well. All the insane mileage she does. She looks totally peaky to me.'

The indent of her husband's body was still visible on his side, the duvet pushed back. Grace sat up, acid sickness rising so quickly in her throat that she escaped the bedclothes and rushed towards the en-suite. The sickening sound of infertile retching and coarse burn of stinging reflux brought tears to her eyes.

Oh, Marcus.

You can't be dead.

You just can't.

Her husband's distant voice responded to the cistern flush, as he called up the stairs.

'Do you want your coffee in bed, Cariad?'

My phone, where's my phone?

Grace dashed back to the bedside table, heaved her phone from the charger, and entered the security code, hands trembling.

7.20 am
MarX
Morning gorgeous. Have a lovely lush Sunday down in Welsh Wales. Xxx

Today. This arrived earlier. Is someone playing tricks?

'Yes or no?' Rhys again. With a squeak, she responded. 'No, I'll come down.'

'Ok'. Don't forget you're going to the Boot Sale with your Mam.'

Rushing back to the ensuite she closed the door and locked it, ran the cold water tap, sat on the toilet, and pressed the call symbol alongside his name. Three long, interminable rings. Then the melting sound of chocolate, spoken with the accent which now blended beautifully into her life.

'Well hello gorgeous, this is unexpected.'

'Oh, my god Marcus.' she whispered, then burst into great heaving sobs she struggled to muffle.

'Grace, what's wrong?' his voice dropped in response to her whisper.

'I dreamt you'd died.'

The chocolate solidified. 'What?'

'It was so vivid. I just woke up. Ffion was driving me to your wake at a pub. It was awful. It was so real I've just thrown up.'

'Oh gosh Sweetheart, I'm very much alive, I promise. Try to calm yourself, take a minute. I really am fine.'

The sobs slowed.

'I'm so sorry. I don't know why it felt so real?'

'I can't say I've ever suffered a nightmare. Did you eat cheese last night? Doesn't that cause them? I hate hearing you so upset.'

Grace shook her head. 'Pizza, there was no cheese on it.'

'Pizza without cheese? You heathen.'

Grace smiled as his words lifted the mood.

219

'You're had a long week. I think the funeral may linger in your imagination. Not that I'm any expert.'

Grace sighed.

Of course it has. It was the biggest funeral anyone will ever attend. No wonder it's affected me.

'I'm so glad it was just a dream.'

'It shows you care.'

'I have to go now, I'll ring you later.'

Legs jiggling fretfully, feet cool against the tiles, she dropped the phone into the sink with a clatter which reached Rhys downstairs.

'Do you want this coffee, it's getting cold?'

It was just a dream. It's already fading now.

'I'll be there now.'

In a minute.

That was awful. Awful. Awful. And hasn't it told you something, Gracie?

It has. But it's hard to leave a marriage, even with all the money in the world.

Well, end it then.

You know this can't go on.

Why can't it go on?

I've no idea.

Pulling the phone from its ivory grave, she padded into the bedroom, pulled on a silky dressing gown, and headed for the stairs leading down into the reality of cooling coffee and a talkative husband. As her foot touched the top step, two unspoken questions touched her lips.

So this means it wasn't Ffion who sent the letter? Then why did my subconscious think it was?

❦

Chapter 33

'Come brothers, hurry. I am drinking stars!'

Dom Perignon

Remember, remember the fifth of November, gunpowder, treason and plot.

They spent late afternoon on Bonfire Night at the marina, listening to live music amongst fairy lights in an eclectic bar named after the buoy way out in the Bay. As they sat in The Swigg, patting dogs lounging around their feet, toes tapping in time to weekend music, Halloween decorations still hung high around them, mixed with lamps and stringed lights, YouTube fires on the wall screens flickered an added dimension of warmth among the liveliness. Grace looked happy, eyes shining bright, despite the wintry weather outside, inside was warm in the red brick, converted industrial building in keeping with the National Waterfront Museum alongside.

When she first suggested Marcus come to Swansea for the Guy Fawkes Night fireworks display across the Bay, he booked the Marriott, their safe corner of the city, and arrived late on Friday night. Grace joined him soon after, while Rhys was home believing she was staying up North.

When news arrived via social media that the event was cancelled due to an incoming storm, they ambled back to watch the fireworks whistling into the sky from households around the city, disappointed when the storm failed to materialise with the expected velocity. Strolling around the marina basin and headed back to the hotel around seven o'clock, the whoosh of launching rockets and Roman candles and smell of cordite hung in the surrounding air. Grace shivered under her coat as they laughed their way back to the seafront.

'Let's sit on the outside patio and watch the fireworks over Mumbles. It's a great viewpoint in all directions. I think they still have some benches we can sit on.'

'As long as you're warm enough?'

'Yes, I'll be fine.'

They sat and gazed at the lights twinkling around the Bay, interspersed with the bangs and colours of multiple extravaganzas spilling down over the water. Marcus pulled her close as they gazed at the beauty showering over them.

'This is great, it feels like we're on a cruise ship looking at the sea and the reflections.'

'Shame they cancelled it, it's pretty spectacular, especially with the music. Thousands turn up, and there are bonfires on the beach.'

'There's always next year, Sweetie.'

Grace swallowed. Next year. So easy to say. Where on earth would they be next year?

There was something else which needed to be said, and that moment, huddled against him in the cold, hair whipped around her face by frequent gusts of wind, Grace reached out and touched his cheek with a red leather gloved hand and took a deep breath. Marcus looked into her eyes and smiled as he caught reflections of fireworks in their depths.

'Sorry Mr Bolt, but I need to tell you something.'

A hint of fear reached his eyes. 'No…Grace.'

'Yes, Marcus.'

A cascade of golden fireworks burst high above them, sprinkling the glittering waters of the bay with light and sound, as Grace Lewis finally told Marcus Bolt she loved him.

Chapter 34

Geneva was beautiful in early November. Days after Bonfire Night, she watched the Jet d' eau in the centre of the lake soar high into the air, splashing back to the mirrored water below. The chill was palpable, but Grace was on a mission.

This is exciting. My first solo adventure. I can't wait to make my first personal expensive purchase. I'm going home with an Aquanaut on my wrist.

The taxi from the airport dropped her in the centre, and from there she wandered around the shops, stopping for coffee and a cake at Patisserie Sofia, ordering a hot chocolate and a genoise biscuit with ganache then heading off to find the Patek Philippe salon before checking into the Hotel d'Angleterre for the night.

Dinner overlooking the lake, and the menu looks exceptional. But it's British. The England Hotel. You messed up there, Gracie. Marcus would laugh his posh socks off if he knew you'd forgotten your schoolroom French. But it looks amazing.

Grace booked an exclusive lake-view luxury room shortly after organising her flights. Two days and nights instead of the original one-day excursion planned at the Marriott. The hotel website was more than tempting, and her first solo foray abroad needed to be sumptuous, safe, and welcoming for her new life of travel. The Leopard Bar. The Cigar Room. Windows Restaurant. It all looked and sounded amazing. By the time she arrived at its doors, the sporty white watch wound around her wrist, joining in the luxury lifestyle ahead while the peak of Mont Blanc, a little over forty miles away, peeked at her in the distance.

At the Patek Philippe salon, staff introduced her to the collection. This spur-of-the-moment decision to buy herself a sought-after timepiece brought a delighted smile to her face as she viewed the counters and cases displaying the famous styles and models they produced.

After an hour of browsing, the disappointment at the revelation she was unable to buy any of the models, stung. Trying to hide her pique on hearing the words, she produced a cool smile.

Do they know I'm rich? I can't bloody well tell them, can I? Only hint and pout. Waitlist? Or find a dealer somewhere? These things are like gold dust.

How embarrassing. You have no clue about the ways of the wealthy world.

Now I want one more than ever.

Escaping into the sunshine, she bolted to the hotel, covering her chagrin at Reception. Delighted with her lake view room, and free of her cabin bag, she returned to the streets of the city and went clothes hunting instead.

You'll need another suitcase, Gracie. You're getting trigger-happy with these credit cards.

Passing the tourist office, she went in and studied the leaflets on display, paying attention to the day trip to Chamonix and Mont Blanc. The woman behind the counter regarded the collection of designer shopping bags cascading over both arms haughtily.

'You can take that trip tomorrow and be back late afternoon, madam. It's well worth doing, and you can ride the cable car to the top.'

Grace lingered before pulling out a credit card, unsure if her fear of heights would allow her onto one. Chamonix at the base appeared pretty, so it would be worth the time on the coach.

'In euros or pounds?'

'Euros, please.' Wasn't that what the TV gurus advised?

With all your money, it doesn't really matter. Now, buy a Mont Blanc pen instead. They're expensive. Better than a fridge magnet. Make up for the epic fail with the watch. All the money in the world and still things you can't buy.

A good life lesson.

A myriad of tiny moisture diamonds sparkled and flickered in the air around her as it snowed at the top of Mont Blanc. Skiers flung themselves off the precipice in a madness she could only imagine. The height of the ski lifts and the wet floors of the carriages were danger enough for Grace on the ride to the summit, while the whoops and cheers of the skiers at each stop on the journey produced by an exaggerated swaying motion, made her cling on tightly. Although she joined in with the laughter, while putting on a brave face, she'd secretly prayed they wouldn't fall from the sky and tumble to the mountain floor below.

Ski lift disasters are as rare as plane crashes.

It should have helped with her fear of heights.

Gracious relief swept over her as she stepped off and made her way onto a solid rock with the group of passengers inside the cafeteria and viewpoint at the top. Some were tourists like herself, others were ready to slide down the slopes of the peaks in a quest for adrenalin and the perfect run. Grace never considered skiing lessons, despite her love of the white powdery stuff nature provided bountifully in this area.

Grace and Rhys made frequent trips to their nearby Brecon Beacons whenever there was a report of snow. Rhys would endure her requests to enjoy the pristine, silent scenery, as snow seldom landed near the coast, taunting them in the distance from the peaks of the Dark Sky National Park.

Standing with her face in brilliant sunshine, taking in the beauty of the surrounding mountains, newly bought Gucci sunglasses tipped up to allow the warmth to cover her cheeks, she marvelled at it all, and what her newfound wealth was enabling her life to become, while the Aiguille du Midi skywalk remained firm beneath her feet.

A pair of Spanish skiers stood awkwardly taking selfies while struggling with their equipment. Grace signalled a shutter press with a hand, amused at their irritated conversation.

'Please... thank you... perfecto.'

As she took their phones, the sting of cold touched her hand when she pulled off a glove. Ensuring there were a few well-composed shots, she handed them back and replaced it with haste.

'Ooh it's so cold!' she laughed 'I hope they're OK.'

The two men studied her efforts and gave a thumbs up.

'Si. ¡Gracias!'

Gazing around at the white brilliance of the snow nestling in the folds of the rocky peaks, she marvelled how they'd even built this on top of a mountain, and how long it must have taken to get everything needed to the summit. The flat viewing walkways were easy, if not slippery, but the steps she avoided, fearful of feeling light-headed at such altitude.

Being alone, it wasn't worth the risk of fainting. The guide told her she may be affected. It depended on the individual. Some felt it more, others less. Either way, spending too long at that height was ill-advised, so she allowed herself an hour at most before taking the cable car down to the first swap over point, where altitude sickness was less likely.

The discovery that she didn't miss Rhys came as a surprise. She texted and called, and it was always nice to hear his down-to-earth Welsh accent, but like reaching the end of a favourite television series, you missed the characters in the aftermath, but not enough to turn it back to episode one and start over again. It could wait another year or more before the desire to rewatch arrived, if it ever did. There was always a newer, fresher series, with livelier characters waiting in the wings. And Marcus was never far from her thoughts or her phone.

'Oh my god this place is amazing!' she enthused to the girl handing her a mug of hot chocolate inside the cafe.

'Pretty cool, eh? Have you stepped into the void yet?'

She couldn't place the accent but the English was perfect.

'What's that?' she asked, dropping her change into the charity box alongside the till.

'Just through there' she pointed.

'Oh, thanks, I'll take a look later.'

Grace headed towards a table, took off her new fluffy fake fur and sat down.

Well, this is incredible. I'm over fifteen thousand feet in the air, drinking a cup of hot chocolate on top of a mountain. Unreal. Yet I'm alone, and I like it.

'The world is my lobster!' she laughed aloud.

Lobster. Oyster. I can afford either.

Just can't get my hands on an Aquanaut.

Sipping the rich chocolate, she pulled out her phone, raised the mug, adjusted her fluffy headband and posed with the phone at an angle. It was a beautiful photograph. Grace noticed her skin glowing, her eyes shining.

While she mused and finished her drink, and checked her social media accounts and emails, she grew aware of a creeping wooziness.

Sliding her arms into her coat, she left the table and faltered toward the cube with the dramatic name, hanging invisibly out over the vast drop into the snowy valley almost five thousand metres below.

With a lifelong fear of heights, whatever bravado she thought she could muster, and despite the encouragement of the people standing around the area with their beckoning arms and smiles, she declined and stepped back after glimpsing the reality, a sharp bitterness rising in her throat.

I shouldn't have had that hot chocolate. I feel sick.

Nearing the edge of nowhere was enough.

Stepping onto an overhanging glass cube with nothing but a transparent panel beneath her feet, was something Grace couldn't contemplate. Seeing and hearing the crack appear beneath her feet, she felt the silent scream rising.

Into the Void? Not for me.

As she turned to walk back towards the cafe, her legs wobbled, her body gave way, and she spiralled to the cold floor.

❦

Chapter 35

The doctor was frowning. 'You were on top of a mountain?'

'A high one. Mont Blanc.'

'Understandable why the medic didn't consider the outcome we seem to have now.'

Grace bit her bottom lip.

'Under normal circumstances, the pill will work ninety-nine per cent of the time. Have you suffered any sickness recently, or forgotten to take any?'

Grace thought hard, then remembered the Marriott and the return home.

'It's rare, but if you were sick, or forgot to take a pill or two?'

I threw up at the hotel an hour after taking it. Oh my god, after seeing the financial advisors I drove home and forgot completely.'

'I've missed two pills.'

'There's your answer, I'm afraid.'

But I can't be pregnant. That's never been in my plans.

'But surely I'm too old, doctor?'

'We deal with many geriatric pregnancies these days.'

'Geriatric?'

'Thirty-five plus is advanced maternal age if you prefer that term.'

'The father is younger, will it make a difference?' The words were out before she realised how foolish she sounded.

The doctor raised an amused eyebrow.

'Only in the conception phase. Naturally, it's a numbers game and I presume being a younger man…well, the more tries scored, the more likely you are to win the game.'

Oh god. Gracie, you're pregnant. Up the bloody duff. Deep breath. Deal with it. It's not the end of the world. You have options.

'But I've been taking the pill since, is that going to cause any harm?'

'There's absolutely no evidence from decades of women doing the same thing.' She began filling in a form on her desk.

Grace ploughed on. 'What about alcohol? I've drunk champagne, wine, the odd gin and tonic.'

The doctor peered up from her keyboard.

'Well, stop immediately. There are risks, but unless you were drinking heavily every night, I wouldn't worry excessively.'

'The last major occasion was within a few days of conception. I was celebrating a major life event.'

'In that case, I hope this is an agreeable surprise and not one that's going to ruin your plans?'

She means do I want to discuss those options?

'It may be troublesome in the interim, but I'm sure the outcome will be satisfactory for everyone.'

Jesus, Grace, you sound like a Sales Rep, not a woman with a baby in her belly. There. Baby. You've said it.

The doctor studied her carefully, then shuffled some pamphlets.

'Good, here are some leaflets and I'll make an appointment for you with the antenatal clinic.'

Grace wasn't listening. Grace was remembering.

We'll show it to our kids.

Or will I be the only one showing it to mine? Either way, this doesn't feel like the diabolical disaster I always imagined. It actually feels a little bit amazing.

Chapter 36

As they entered the hotel foyer, Grace slipped one hand into her bag, fingers briefly caressing the rabbit's foot nestled inside. *Please look after me. If there was ever a moment I needed you, it's now.*

The sound of her heels against the marble tiles echoed around the empty seating areas as she discovered they had the place to themselves.

'G&T, or would you like the good stuff?'

'I'm really thirsty, English. Can you just get me a glass of iced water?'

Marcus shrugged, amused, and headed for the bar. While Grace warmed her hands by the roaring fire in the corner of the lounge, outside, dusk was already falling amid dark rain clouds, despite the large wall clock showing only four o'clock.

They made themselves comfortable on an antique burgundy leather Chesterfield in the centre of the room, a large colourful oriental rug below their feet. Antique paintings of racehorses filled the beautifully decorated walls. Grace, drawn to the small bronze horse's head sculpture on the marble table where their drinks rested, studied the elegant arched neck.

This is as good as anywhere. Classy.

It was Friday and a weekend on the edges of the horse racing town of Cheltenham lay ahead.

'Marcus, I have some news.' Her face was pensive.

Relationship-changing news.

'Are you OK, you're very pale?'

She nodded, a brief series of urgent jerks. He placed a firm hand on her thigh as he loosened his tie with the other and slumped into cosiness beside her. 'What is it, Welshwoman?'

'It's a lot to take in.'

She studied his expression. The mini frown was in place.

'Sounds rough. Do I need to be worried?'

'Depends what you want from life.'

There was a deep breath, his chest rose and fell, and a hand rubbed his chin.

'Pretty much what every man wants. Football, beer, fast cars, fast women. And pizza. There has to be pizza.'

'Hilarious.'

'OK, break it to me. My loins are well and truly girded.'

Oh, I know they are.

His eyes rested on hers in a mutual gaze.

'I'll start with Cardiff, then.'

His brows moved in the opposite direction.

'Remember when you called me before we met at the Royal?'

'Yes, when I knew I was going to taunt every speed limit to reach you?'

Grace smiled, a tentative tilt to her chin.

'But do you remember what I said on our very first call?'

Marcus lowered one brow.

'Let me think. Nope, it's gone.'

'You thought I said I was up the duff?'

He relaxed and laughed. The chocolate sound reverberated around the empty lounge.

'Ah yeah, that would have been a miracle.'

Grace smiled knowingly and laughed back.

It only takes once.

Didn't you have biology lessons at your posh school?

'I joked I wasn't carrying your love child?'

Her hands twisted gently together, eyes on his. 'Well, it

seems that was an inadvertent, if lighthearted, lie.'

His eyebrows crashed together above confused eyes. Grace held her breath.

And here's the unwanted, pregnant pause.

Or the unwanted pregnancy pause?

Grace recognised every emotion as they flickered across his face. Shock, confusion, disbelief, then slow edging towards acceptance.

'Grace… really?'

What if he walks away?

What if I was just excitement?

No ties, no strings. No babies.

'Please don't panic.' she offered 'This needn't affect your life.'

He pulled her into his arms with stunning speed.

'You've *become* my life. But are you absolutely certain? Have you done a test?'

As she devoured his Black Orchid scent, the freshness of his hair and clothes, her senses rose as her face rested against him, the cool clothing fibres tickling her skin, the leather of the sofa a distinct background base, the faint creaks of the hide as they moved, a comforting sound.

This will be fine. Surely?

Lengthy tendrils of beach-curled hair fell across his chest as a relieved breath released itself into his shoulder. No further words left her lips. This was his moment. To speak when he was ready.

His breathing slowed as the silence between them grew, yet his arms held her comfortably, unmoving. There was no distance between them. There was quietude.

Marcus sighed. 'Give me a minute to take this in.'

Grace waited seconds.

'I know this is quick, but honestly, I can take care of this.'

Gentle fingers lifted her chin to observe her expression, the frown back in place, a raw edge to his voice. 'What do you mean, take care of this?'

232

'Not in *that* way.'

'I hope not. At least not before discussion.'

'I just need you to know there's no pressure on you. For anything.'

'I'm not afraid of pressure, Grace. Gosh, are you one hundred per cent on this?'

She nodded, scared to smile.

'So I'm going to be a father?'

'Physically, yes. Practically, only if you want to be.'

She paused, uncertain.

'Please don't doubt you are the father.'

He nodded, taking in her last words, and waited a while before answering.

'Of course I want to be involved. It's just your situation… I mean…. what happens now?'

'What do *you* want to happen now?'

An agitated foot tapped swiftly against the Turkish rug. 'Me? I want you to pack your bags and move in. We can be at my house in an hour and a half. I wish you'd stay with me just once. It's not a hellhole of pizza boxes and paperwork. I'm very tidy. You might actually like it.'

He doesn't understand why I can't stay at his house. I'd end up mentally moving in before I've had my alone time. It's a worse betrayal than hotels. A Sian level betrayal.

Grace smiled. 'Marcus. I'm not even showing yet. We have plenty of time for those types of decisions, but first I have to sort out *my* situation.'

His foot stopped tapping, and his shoulders relaxed. 'Oh god, Sweetie, Being a parent has always been in my dreams for the future. Looks like we're about to do it in reverse, but who cares?'

Grace let out an imperceptible sigh.

Thank god. I don't want to do this alone. I know I can, but I really don't want to. I can't be my mother. I'm not that strong.

A relieved breath touched her ear as his arms pulled her closer.

'Do you remember what I joked about that night at the Marriott?'

Grace moved her lips close to his neck, her own breath

warm against his earlobe.

'You said we can show it to our kids. It made me giggle.'

He nodded, his hair teasing her cheek.

'Then you fell asleep, bare-faced and gorgeous. I knew you'd become my life, married or not. It was written in the stars.' He added with haste 'Not that I believe in that nonsense.'

They both laughed and the fleeting frown she'd grown so fond of, vanished. Smiling broadly, she held his face in her hands, just as she'd done the first night in her hotel room. It felt good then, better now, a comfort to them both.

'This is nothing we can't work out.'

He nodded, thoughtful.

'I have to ask how? I know we forgot the condoms, but I assumed you'd be on the pill.'

'Yes I am, well I was.'

Going to lie again, Grace. Suck it up. You're past the point of no return on that front.

'I was upset over the argument. Rhys wasn't happy about the job, and I ordered a bottle of wine in my room. I threw up in the bath, but I'd taken my pill a couple of hours earlier. It must have come up with it. I completely forgot about the next one. Your fault. You were all I thought about.'

Not quite all, Gracie. There was another exciting reason, the one he can't know about yet.

'Good to know you thought about me.'

'Looks like the sex was very productive.'

'Blame me. I was pretty insistent we kept going.'

'You were. Your little swimmers can live for five days, so it could have been Cardiff or Morgans.'

Marcus laughed. 'There's no holding back with you, is there, Welshwoman? Tell it like it is.'

Grace shrugged. 'Don't confuse me with your English Roses. There's a fiery Celt in me you haven't seen yet.'

Marcus produced a smile she'd never seen before. A comforting, all-enveloping, everything will be fine, smile.

'That's it then. If it's a boy, we're calling him Morgan. Very Welsh, I think.'

'Well, we can't call him Marriott, and certainly not Royal, although I'm sure he'll be a real little prince. What about Owain

Glyndwr, old Welsh royalty?'

Grace looked serious, but a tiny tremor of a smile struggled to be contained at the corners of her mouth.

'I could never pronounce it! Bloody hell, Sweetie, who was he?'

Grace burst into laughter, blue eyes bright.

'The Prince of Wales, the original, true prince, and I'm only kidding about the name.'

She pulled out her phone and began typing quickly, searching and scrolling.

'If it's a girl, she can be Morgana.' she proclaimed, turning the screen to face him.

'It goes back to Welsh mythology, too. We'll ignore the Arthurian bits. The English bits.' She winked and slid a hand onto his thigh.

'So I'm going to have the real Welsh Mam experience soon. It'll be interesting to see you in action.'

Grace laughed happily.

'Be careful what you wish for.'

He held her tightly, silent for long moments, before allowing a deep sigh to escape his perfect Greek God chest.

'I'm sorry, I should have used condoms. It was just so long since...well ... you know...I didn't think either of us was at risk of anything else. Pregnancy was the last thing on my mind.'

'I think we were both so out of control, it wasn't going to come up.'

They looked at each other for a long second, then burst into spasms of laughter.

'Oh, it did, repeatedly. All your fault, Welshwoman.'

'No wonder I've been having vivid dreams. It's a pregnancy thing. I didn't even realise that throwing up after that awful nightmare was morning sickness.'

'Oh my darling, poor you.' He hugged her tightly. 'Now I know why you only wanted water to drink. I can't believe I'm holding two of you.'

'How does this make you feel?'

'It's amazing. Is everything alright?'

Grace nodded quickly, relaxing completely in his arms.

'Yes, I've had all the advice from my doctor. I wanted to be certain before telling you. It's happened to millions of women. None of us know we're pregnant on the actual day and life goes on as normal until we find out. Which includes booze, smoking, and the pill. I haven't been drinking much lately because I'm always driving, and I've never smoked.'

'Didn't you notice from your period?'

'My pill didn't give me one. It was just more convenient, you know, having a job where you're driving all the time, in and out of male-dominated places. It's difficult finding toilets, plus I didn't get the monthly pain. You need one hundred per cent concentration on the road.'

'Oh Grace, I never even considered it. You meddle with your body, just for work?'

She nodded and shrugged nonchalantly.

'You boys don't know how lucky you are.'

'Cwtch me and tell me you love me. I don't hear it enough from you.'

Grace draped her arms elegantly around his neck as her face followed, her cheek against his warm skin, her chin on his collar.

'I love you, English.'

There was a concord of peace as he savoured the words before he spoke. 'Are we shortening it now? Am I Lawrence of Arabia?'

'You've lost me.'

'My dad's favourite film. And by default one of mine, I suppose. Someone called him 'English.' We'll watch it together, and I'll catch you when you fall asleep from boredom.'

'Camels? I do love a camel or two.'

'Deep golden deserts, rolling into the distance. Sunsets and romance. Actually, no, there isn't a single woman in it. Strike the romance.'

'So no fashion or shoes?' she laughed, twirling her ankle to show off her latest purchase.

'Bedouin chic. Stripes and flowing robes.'

'Isn't that a really old film?'

'Yep. A guilty pleasure. The man was an Oxford legend, but born in your fair land.'

'Really? My old films are hats, frocks, and songs. I've no idea why, but it is what it is.'

Marcus laughed and lifted her head to kiss her deeply.

'We barely know each other, really.'

His lips are so pliable and warm.

But what about his parents, what will they think? Oh, my god. This is getting scary. So many unravelling threads.

'But we have plenty of time to discover the dark, dirty little secrets.' His laugh was mirthful. She shifted, tensing against the aged, supple leather.

'You've given me the best news ever, Sweetheart. I love you madly, but now we *really* need to talk.'

Grace murmured as she closed her eyes and rested her head back on his shoulder.

Dark, dirty secrets. Filthy lucre.

And I have to tell Rhys.

How on earth do I do that?

'I know, but let's just cwtch here for a while. I need a nap. It's been a long day, and this Chesterfield is *so* comfortable.'

Arms encircled her. An early five o'clock shadow pricked against her scalp as she stretched, sighed, and nestled closer, eyelids drooping. A cresting wave of exhaustion washed over her at the relief of sharing the news, and the fear of what was ahead.

'I'm not going anywhere. You just rest my beautiful Welshwoman. I bloody love you, see.'

Grace laughed at his Welshism.

This is going to bring changes I'm not ready for. Fast changes. Something's got to give, and they never finished that film.

Poor Marilyn.

Poor me.

Poor Rhys.

Three-quarters of an hour later, a member of reception staff leaned close to his ear.

'Can I get you a drink from the bar, Sir?'

Marcus turned his face towards her.

'A double brandy, thanks.' His voice remained low as other guests now occupied the lounge. 'And will you keep a lookout for a flower delivery, and have it sent up to our room, if you don't mind?'

She nodded, and tip-toed away smiling, as he continued reading his screen.

'*Capricorn women think deeply, use their logic, and explore all plus and minus points before making commitments. They will never make impulsive decisions for the sake of excitement, their security is too precious for them to take such risks. These practical women are very concerned with family values.*'

'Really, mate? You're reading this tripe now?' he muttered as his finger curled gently around one long tendril of dark hair sweeping across his shirt front.

'Accurate, though.'

❦

Chapter 37

Marcus lay naked on his back, expression confused.

'Grace, are we OK to be doing this now?'

'Of course we are. I want you inside me, now. It's been ages.'

Grace pulled herself up from a kneeling position on the floor, her hips headed for the erection she'd instigated with her mouth and tongue and nimbly slipped on top of him, a hand guiding him urgently between her legs, and let out a huge moan as she began moving rhythmically back and forth.

'Oh god, I love you so much.' he breathed as his hips caught up with her, hands cupping her breasts as she moved above him, the lustrous hair tangling in his fingers as she slid repeatedly, her eyes closed, lips parted. He slipped a finger inside her mouth as she sucked on it, biting the tip gently teasing him.

Marcus groaned, then swiftly tipped her over as he mounted her and she lay languorously beneath his powerful chest, her legs slithering tightly around his back, his arms pinning hers to the pillows behind her head.

'I can't believe we're here' she breathed 'how did we get this far this fast?'

He thrust deeper inside her, his lips coming down hard on

hers, his tongue probing her wet mouth, his skin feeling the dampness spreading down her thighs as his erection dived deeper and deeper.

'Who cares? 'He managed before they exploded into relief within moments of each other, the moans and soft cries of spent passion dissipating beneath biting mouths and sweating necks as they nuzzled together, their first encounter since she'd broken the news. Resting, breathing coming in heaving desperation, Grace felt a tear fall and touch her skin.

'Marcus?' Her eyes darted to his face. He rolled onto his back, damp hair stuck to his forehead, and caught her hand in his.

'Don't worry, they're tears of happiness. Hundred per cent.'

'I hope so.' She looked concerned.

'I mean it, don't doubt it. It's just been such a surprise. Really. I love you. I'm just fearful of what's ahead. It's going to be upsetting for you, and complicated.'

In the morning, mingled with the scent of the beautiful blooms he'd ordered one-handed from his phone as Grace slept in the lounge after telling him the news, Marcus awoke to sounds of retching from the bathroom and leapt out of bed to stand naked in the doorway.

Grace was throwing up repeatedly into the toilet, tears running down her face under an endless, debilitating onslaught. A steadying arm went around her while the other pulled her hair back from her face until the heaving subsided and he helped her back to bed, a hand towel pulled off the rail in passing.

'Hell, Sweetheart, is it like this every morning? That's horrific.'

He handed her the towel, and she nodded.

'It's awful, and they won't give me pills because of my age. I'm classed as ancient.' She attempted a laugh.

'This is going to weaken you so much. You've already lost weight.'

'It's not just the morning. I've eaten lunch and thrown the whole lot up.'

He slid an arm around her, pulling her close. 'How will you manage with work?'

'I don't know. I can't eat so I go all day on a couple of ginger biscuits.'

She rested her head on his chest until the drift into exhausted sleep was complete.

The moment she was motionless at his side, breathing regularly, Marcus fumbled for his phone and searched morning sickness and pregnancy websites. While he scrolled, he would check out work-related issues so she would know exactly her lawful position. It was quarter past seven, and he was going to do his best to look after her all weekend.

There was one more vitally important thing he needed to do, and his nimble fingers typed efficiently, before a lengthy, thoughtful pause, then he pressed *send.*

Marcus
Hi mum and dad. Just letting you know. You'll be meeting my new and very serious girlfriend soon. Hopefully, before Christmas. Xxx

Mum.
About time you moved on from Georgia, darling. We'll look forward to it immensely. Dad sends love. xxx

Grace was in the throes of a nightmare. Marcus dozed alongside until her moans and twitches alerted him into wakefulness. Shaking her gently, he murmured. 'Sweetheart, come on, you're dreaming. Wake up.'

It took a few more, firmer shakes before she finally opened her eyes and focussed on his face. He smiled happily, taking in the sight of the dishevelled beauty at his side.

'Good morning gorgeous. I think you were dreaming.'

He touched the tip of her nose with his forefinger. Grace stared at him, confused, before throwing back the duvet and escaping the bed. He frowned as she ran to the ensuite, wearing his shirt she'd pulled on in the middle of the night.

Marcus sat up, put his hands behind his head, and sighed. This was grim. Seconds later he was striding in her footsteps. Again, the tear-streaked face and continuous retching.

'This can't go on.' his arms curled around her 'How long is it supposed to last?'

As she rinsed her mouth after the final retch, she shook her head.

'A few weeks, maybe?'

'This is ridiculous, can't we see your doctor together? There must be something they can do? You're wasting away. I thought you were supposed to put on weight when you're pregnant, not lose it.'

She nodded, leaning against his chest.

'I'm so tired. I want to go back to bed.'

'Come on then, let's get you tucked up. You're not doing anything today.'

When her eyes closed and her breathing slowed, Marcus pressed his lips together, his jaw tightening. She should be back at work tomorrow, as should he. Grace needed to take a week off to get medical intervention agreed. But without this sickness problem resolved, she may need further time off. It wouldn't bode well for her future employment.

She can stay at my house, I'll take a week off too. She can use an Oxford doctor, without going back to Swansea. Maybe they'll prescribe where hers won't.

It must be time to tell her mother about the pregnancy and about their relationship. Before Rhys bore witness to any sickness and realised his wife was pregnant.

With a Welsh Mam at the helm, he'd be happier going back to work. With nursing and ambulance strikes affecting the country, and doctor's appointments nigh on impossible to get, worrying about Grace needing emergency medical attention was something he could do without.

What a bloody state on a country. And where the hell are we going now?

❦

242

Chapter 38

Rhys,

Your wife is having an affair with a young guy who works for her company. His name is Marcus, and he lives in England.

Anon

A finger pressed a button, and a sheet of A4 slid out of a nearby printer. Folded in half, it was pushed into a long white envelope, the name and address already printed on the front. It would pass as official, to be opened by the addressee only.

Chapter 39

Rhys opened the envelope and pulled out the bill. Only it wasn't a bill, it was a handwritten sheet of paper. It took a moment to register what he was reading. Then he shook his head and swore loudly in Welsh.

Is this why she's gone to work in an office in England? Fuck, that's it. She's found someone else, and it's all my fault. Bloody Christmas. Bloody booze. Bloody Sian. For fuck's sake, mun.

Rhys Lewis' life unravelled before him. The house was empty, the furniture halved, his beautiful unappreciated wife gone, future uncertain.

'What the hell happened, you twat?' he yelled. 'No wonder she barely makes any effort to come home.'

Wiping away a tear, he scrunched up the paper and threw it at the wall. 'Marcus, eh? Well, let's find out exactly who you are, *boy bach.*'

Rhys picked up his phone and tossed it from hand to hand. Finally, he stood up, rammed it into a back pocket, grabbed his keys, and stormed out the door. The raffia mat skidded away, casting further loose strands across the tiles.

This isn't the wisest course of action, boyo, but it might make things clearer. If she's at home.

Twenty minutes later he parked outside Sian's house, switching off an over-revved engine. Knocking hard on the door, and leaning a finger against the grubby buzzer, he waited, knowing this was precarious.

When it creaked open, there she stood, the small blonde with the package that delighted and entertained him for the early part of the year.

'John!'

'Alright?'

'So-so. What are you doing here?'

'I need to ask you something.'

'Come in then.'

'Are you on your own?'

'Yes.'

'Maybe I better stay out here.'

Don't you trust yourself even now, you dickhead?

Sian pulled a face. 'Whatever. What do you want to know?'

'Did a woman come and see you before we broke up?'

'You mean your wife?'

'Yeah, sorry about that.'

Sian glowered at him.

'Yes, she came to see me. I can't believe you're married with kids and she's pregnant.'

A deep scowl altered his features.

'What?'

'She showed me your photo, John. But that's not your name is it?'

Rhys shook his head.

'Middle name. But we don't have kids, and she's not pregnant. We can't have kids.'

'Oh.'

Sian's face changed. Her voice grew angry.

'Well, then she was doing a fucking good job of trying to save her marriage if that's the case. I ended it with you because I thought you had a family.'

'We don't, honest.'

Sian folded her arms in front of her.

'She's a talented actress! Or you're telling me more lies. Now who do you think I'm going to believe?'

'Can I just ask you, did she give any signs she was with someone else too?'

'Are you kidding? She was heartbroken. Tough, though. Businesslike. Didn't even cry. Finding out her husband was unfaithful, coming up here and confronting me. I felt so terrible I phoned you to end it in front of her.'

'She listened to it?'

Sian nodded. A large tear formed in one eye which she wiped away with a swift, angered movement.

'Of course she did. I wouldn't have been seeing you if I'd known you were married, and with kids. She needed to know it was over. I thought she may end up having a miscarriage if she got upset. She must have been *tamping* inside, but *Chwarae Teg*, she didn't show it.'

'I'm sorry. I really am. I was stupid. I'd better go now.'

'Yeah, well, that's why I didn't call you to tell you she'd been here. Stupid doesn't cover it, does it, John? Or Rhys, whatever you are these days.'

As he strode down the steps towards the car, a voice sounded to his left.

'Excuse me, young man.'

Rhys turned to face Sian's neighbour.

'If you're back up here again when you have a lovely wife at home, well, you're *twp*. You need your head examined. Go home where you belong and leave this girl alone. She's years younger than you. Let her find someone single instead of wasting her time. You men are all the same.'

Before Rhys formulated a reply, the woman disappeared back indoors. Sian, too, with a heavy slam of ageing wood and he stepped onto the pavement alone under hostile fire.

'What the actual fuck has been going on here? Grace? What the hell have you been doing?'

Getting back behind the wheel, he headed back to the motorway, drove frustrated for fifteen minutes, and turned off at the sign for Swansea Docks. He knew whatever she was doing was his own fault.

Parking in the visitors' space outside L&B, he turned off the engine and ran a nervous hand across his mouth. This was a daft idea. But it was a franked letter so it must be from a workplace. And that workplace must surely be here.

Shouldn't I call their head office and ask if there's a Marcus working for them? Don't be a twat. There must be hundreds working for this lot, and they're not going to tell you.

Glancing around, Rhys realised he'd never visited this place where his wife spent three years of her working life. It wasn't ideal for someone as well put together as Grace. The age of the building, and the unloved exterior, all spoke of a workplace only staff inhabited. Nothing fancy for visitors and no need to put on a glossy front for kerbside traffic. There wouldn't be much passing trade.

Rhys pushed open the heavy doors, headed towards the reception desk, and pressed the yellowed buzzer. It was Angela who slid back the faded opaque corrugated glass window a long minute later. It took a moment before the surprise on her face became noticeable.

'Hiya, it's Rhys, isn't it? Grace's husband? What can I do for you?'

'Yes. Look, er… Angela?'

She nodded nervously.

'I know we've met in the past and Grace has left, but…' Rhys ran a hand through his dark hair and scratched his head. 'I've been told something and I need to know if it's true.'

Angela leaned sympathetically towards him across the scuffed, unloved counter.

God, this place is dire. They haven't painted these walls in years. All it needs are some nude calendars and here's your man cave. No wonder she wanted out.

'What do you need to know?'

'I've been told she's having an affair with a guy named Marcus. Does he work here?'

Angela's partially restrained smirk faced him. 'Really? I'm sorry to hear it. But we don't have a Marcus at this branch, Rhys.'

'So are you saying there's no Marcus at all, or just not in this office?'

Angela crossed her arms, looked at him directly, then deftly changed the subject.

'How is Grace, anyway? We were all upset when she never came back in to say goodbye. Just upped and left, didn't even bring the car back herself.'

'What do you mean, upped and left? She did two weeks' notice.'

'No, she didn't. Just never turned up for work and some guy from Head Office called to tell us she was finishing immediately. She let a courier drop everything off on the Monday morning the week after the bank holiday.'

'You're kidding?'

Rhys' right leg fidgeted.

'No, we were all pissed off, to be honest. Three years with us and not even a goodbye.'

Angela leaned across the counter and whispered. 'You didn't hear this from me, but there is a Marcus. He's a few years younger than Grace, fantastic-looking. He lives somewhere in England but travels the entire country. One of the National Managers. They were on the same table at the Ball in May.'

'Ball?'

Angela's eyes flashed.

'Didn't she tell you about the Ball at the Celtic Manor?'

'Just about a conference.'

'You didn't see any photos?'

Rhys shook his head. Angela pulled out her phone, made a few exaggerated movements, and showed him her screen.

'Here you go, group photo of this branch.'

Rhys looked at the image in front of him.

'So you haven't seen her wearing *that* green dress?' Angela teased, as Rhys saw his wife wearing the gown for the first time.

'Marcus did. So did everyone else. She looked stunning, don't you think?' Angela zoomed in on Grace for better effect. 'Sorry to be the bearer of bad news, but a few of us thought something started that night. You know what office gossip is like.'

Rhys didn't respond. Rigidity set into his facial muscles.

'Personally, I'd say there's something going on judging by the number of times he would drive down, probably to see her after work. Then, poof, in a wink... she was gone. No longer working for us and now we don't see him either.'

'What's his surname?'

'I can't go that far. Data protection crap. Why don't you ask her? Mind you, they often post pics of the bigwigs on the website.'

Rhys looked her directly in the eyes.

248

'Did you send me the letter?'

'What letter's that, then?'

Rhys glowered.

'This place needs a clean-up. No wonder she left. See you around.'

The heavy-meshed metal door slammed behind him, shaking the entrance. Angela closed the ancient opaque glass sliders and leaned against the frame. Rhys, with his typical dark-haired Welsh heritage, was a handsome bloke. The sort of fella she was missing in life, as yet unable to find. What a shame this was likely to end badly for all three of them.

Angela smiled. A *tidy* result and the visitors' book remained unsigned. He was never there.

Someone sitting in the swivel chair his wife used to occupy glanced out of the window, briefly noticed him opening his car door, and casually swung it back to attend to whatever they were dealing with. In the visitor's space outside L&B Chemicals, Rhys thumped the steering wheel.

And boy did it hurt.

Unknown number flashed as a call came in.

'Is this Marcus Bolt?'

A man's voice. Welsh accent.

Swansea office?

'Yes, how can I help?'

The words came fast, a cannon blast through the speaker on his desk.

'Are you having an affair with my wife?'

The lengthy silence confirmed it.

'How did you get this number?'

Fuck, even this bloke's voice is good-looking. Just like his website photo.

Marcus was calm. Dealing with people was his forte. Although a furious husband would be an unfamiliar experience.

'Someone from your office phoned me and told me all about it. They gave me your number.'

Marcus exhaled slowly through his nose.

No, they didn't, mate.

'So now you know, where do we go from here?'

Marcus heard the sharp intake of breath as the shock of confirmation hit home.

'Is it serious?'

'If you mean are there feelings involved, then yes.'

'Well, bloody embroider it a bit. I need to know.'

Marcus paused. This guy needed careful handling. Man-to-man or business-speak?

'Why do you need to know? Didn't you have an affair? It seems Grace wasn't party to that.'

'It's over.'

Marcus took a potshot. 'Well, maybe in future this will be.'

'What? For fuck's sake, man, what are you planning on here?'

'I suggest that you talk to your wife, but in the interests of full disclosure, it will be Grace who needs to decide.'

Hearing Marcus speak her name was rough. This was his wife. The one that he'd cheated on with a younger woman. Repeatedly. Wilfully. Wildly. Shagging for the sake of it, at any rampant opportunity.

'But you live in England!'

'And Grace works here most of the time.'

'So are you telling me you love her?'

'I am.'

'And does she love you?'

'You really should ask her.'

 Silence.

'I told Grace if she was trying to save her marriage, I would step back. Which was many weeks ago.'

'Is she with you now?'

'No, she's not.

Rhys sensed this wasn't a lie. The truth was, another man was in love with his wife. A good-looking, successful, *younger* man. One who wore a suit, who never worked night shifts, who drove a flash car, with his photo on a company website. A man with clean, oil-free hands who never picked up a takeaway in case leaks trickled onto expensive upholstery.

Rhys hung up.

Marcus stared at his phone and ran a hand through his hair. He couldn't bring himself to call. A text was quicker. Grace was at work. But she would read it. The message didn't appear as he wanted, but under the shock, he couldn't remember how to spell her husband's name.

Chirp/MarX

> Sweetie, he knows. I've just spoken to him.
> Someone from L&B told him.

🍂

Sitting in her mother's autumnal garden as Grace broke the news about her relationship with Marcus, she sat back against the smooth wooden slats of the garden furniture.

Well, that's a relief.

'And Rhys doesn't know? Oh, my god Grace what is going on? What are you planning on doing?' her mother asked.

'Mam, I don't know yet. Neither of them knows about the money.'

'Well, that's something, at least you know this new guy isn't after you for it.'

'He's not a new guy Mam, he's the man I'm in love with. He's going to be my future.'

Her mother leaned back into the chair.

'Of course, I'm not thinking straight, this is all such a shock. I didn't think you'd met anyone. I hoped you'd manage to fix things.'

'So are you happy for me?'

'How can I not be? You're set for life and have a new man. You know I never wanted to see you alone. Despite all these modern single girls racing around all over the place, all happy to be doing so, or pretending to be. I know what that's like. I just have this sad feeling for Rhys, which is silly, I know, as he's

251

been the catalyst in this. He's still my son-in-law after all.'

Grace looked away into the trees, and the squirrel hanging off a bird feeder, trying desperately to steal something which wasn't his.

'I know, Mam, but not for much longer. I'm sure there'll be room for you to have a relationship with him, although for me it will be *out of sight, out of mind*. Never stay friends with your ex, they always say.'

'*They,* whoever they are, seem to say a lot of things these days. We're always being told what we can and can't say. So when will you tell him?'

Grace looked down as her phone chirped, read the message, shivered, and then her eyes lifted to meet her mother's.

'It looks like he already knows, Mam.'

Chapter 40

'I'm worried you may want to stay with him because you're scared of moving on. I know this is difficult and I know about surging hormones. I get it you'll be thinking of security and finances, and all the other stuff women think about. I may be a handful of years younger Grace but believe me when I tell you I love you, I will look after you both, I have a good future ahead and I'm not that young guy who just wants to go surfing and travelling, and mess about for the next decade, although with you and our children alongside we can do it all if we want to.'

Children? He is thinking plural then. Like the night at the Marriott. Serious, Deadly, all-encompassing commitment.

'We never need to worry about finances, trust me on that count.'

He raised a puzzled brow, uncertain of her meaning, but continued.

'I'm scared to leave you with all the mileage I do, and in this state.'

Grace squeezed his hand.

Of course he's terrified, I'd be too. But I'm completely calm. Decision time, Grace.

'I have my mother and my friends if I need help.'

He nodded quickly. 'I'm more than grateful to them. I know it's early days but they seem to be the worst days.'

'Marcus, everything has changed. I can't feel the same

about him now, not when I'm in love with you and carrying our child. I've clarified my confusion. Yes, it's sad, and yes we lived a life together, but he gambled with it and in the end, it was me suffering the aftermath. Until you came along and put a smile on my face, and made me happy.'

Marcus pulled her close and hugged her tightly,

'This has been a whirlwind for both of us, I know. But that's how people end up as couples. Some take longer, for us it's been really fast. Blame your damn rabbit.'

She laughed, a sound missing in recent days.

'Don't you dare take his name in vain.'

'He has a name?'

'I meant him to have one, but I never got around to choosing it.'

Chapter 41

They stood on the driveway of the Langland house.

'Marcus, I'm going to be living here.'

'Wow, it's amazing.'

'I want it to be ours. Do you want to move in with me?'

'How can you afford this place, if you don't mind me asking?'

'It's my father's. He lives in Thailand, so rarely visits. We're not very close, but I'm next of kin and looking after it. It'll be mine one day. He has more than enough to cover every whim for his conveyor belt of girlfriends.'

'Is that why you weren't keen on having kids, because of your father?'

'He dumped my mother, leaving her with me to bring up. Spent all his time roaming and working around the world, and stayed on the other side of it ever since.'

Marcus raised his brows, surprised.

'Don't you speak much?'

Grace shrugged.

'I get a birthday card from one of those companies who print and send, sometimes a Christmas card. If he remembers.'

'So you didn't think your husband would make a good father?'

'I wouldn't give him the chance to find out. I was right by

the look of it.'

'Do you think maybe he wouldn't be tempted if you had kids?'

'I know plenty of solo women with them. Their partners left to be with others.'

'What about me? Do you think I may leave in the future?'

Grace looked him in the eyes.

'I have no idea. Not much I can do about it, anyway. Ours was a happy accident.'

'True. But you knew how much I loved you beforehand.'

'I know, English. Give me a cwtch.'

Marcus folded his arms around her, holding her tight, kissing her hair, her eyelids, her nose, and the tension growing between them vanished.

'I have never felt luckier in my life since meeting you my darling. Get a divorce, let's get married. We can live happily ever after like those bloody fairy tales we secretly believe in.'

Grace grimaced.

'No proposal on one knee, then?'

'How can I propose to an already married woman? It doesn't seem right.'

'Only kidding. I love your sense of propriety.'

He eased her to arm's length, as his expression grew serious. 'I just want you to know what I think from now on. Blame my business brain. I need to focus on every aspect of my life in case I mess up. I can't bugger this up, you're too important to me.'

Grace nodded, absorbing his sentiments.

'OK, my mother and I bought an apartment in the marina as an investment for weekends, holiday lets, that sort of thing. I'm thinking we could stay there during the week? It would save at least half an hour in the mornings, to get you onto the M4. I'll have to finish work but I can rent out this place as an Airbnb for an income. I just can't go driving around the country with a huge bump, and my company doesn't have an office in Wales.'

Still not going to tell him about the money, honey? That he can give up work and spend all day surfing? If I do, I'll have no 'me' time, ever. It'll be the frying pan into the fire. There's plenty of time for the big reveal. It's not as if anyone knows. Or there's been any publicity.

'I'll have to think about it. England's pretty central for all my travels. I thought maybe you'd come and live with me? You could rent it out, or keep it for weekends?'

'Oxford?'

'Why not?'

Why at all? No sea, no beach, nobody to talk to.

'Keep your place and use it in the week, or a few days of the week? We'd both have some space that way, at least for the foreseeable.'

'True.'

'And we have months before we have to decide on anything more permanent.'

They strolled down the hill to the Bay, wrapped up warm against the frigid November air, as the sun shone on the sea creating a perfect winter's day. Marcus let out a low whistle as he took in its full beauty.

'My god, this place is amazing. It's so Victorian with all these beach huts, and there must be thirty surfers out there.'

'Yes, they're often there. It's a great place to surf. A photographer's dream, really.'

'Are you into photography, darling?'

He's replaced sweetie with darling. It sounds very English. A more permanent option.

'I put a few things on Instagram now and then, but I'd like a decent camera instead of my phone. I love watching them.'

'Come on, I'm ravenous, let's get in this Surfside Cafe you keep telling me about.'

'You've got to have a bagel melt with bacon, brie, and cranberry. They're amazing, but they drip down your chin if you're not careful.'

His sweeping gaze of the bay returned to her face, a smile lighting up the gold-flecked eyes.

'Hell, Wales is full of hidden gems, but you, my Green Goddess, have to be the diamond.'

She groaned.

'Flatterer, but you haven't seen Caswell yet. Or Three

Cliffs, Oxwich, or Rhossili. All part of the coastal path. We're completely spoiled with our Gower beaches. Come on, there's an open fire inside.'

'Sounds great, but you, Welshwoman, will not be traversing any coastal paths for the near future. *'This shall forbid it.'*

He grinned and winked. 'Shakespeare. Juliet, no less.'

Grace laughed. 'Your parents must have spent a fortune on your education, posh boy. Just for you to quote me love stories.'

'Oh they did, and you have no idea of the awful things I'll treat you to on cold winter nights when we can't afford to turn on the heating. Richard the Third, Hamlet, Macbeth, and our very own Winter's Tale.'

'Couldn't we just watch Netflix and chill?'

'If we must. Now, give me your hand, these steps don't look easy.' He led her towards the sand and the terrace.

Marcus breathed in lungfuls of cold, salty, air and smiled as he surveyed the rocky shoreline revealed by the tide.

'I could get used to spending weekends here, Sweetie.'

'I have to warn you we're the wettest city in Britain.'

'Lucky I'm a keen Pluviophile. It was raining when we first met, remember?'

Grace laughed and squeezed his warm hand. 'Speak English. We learned Welsh in school, not Latin.'

Sweetie's made a comeback, vying for position with darling. Just never call me Cariad.

Grace pulled a small box from her bag. 'Before we go in, I have a silly present for you.'

His face lit up.

'What do we have here?'

As her eyes reflected the shimmers of the sea, she handed it to him. 'Open it.'

Pleasure touched his face as he lifted out the inner cushion of the box and his eyes drifted from what nestled in his hand, to the gathering of boards and riders out among the waves.

Silver surfer cufflinks.

'I love them, thank you Welshwoman. They're perfect.'

He kissed her full on the lips, leaving traces of Ruby Woo on his mouth. She stroked them away with a thumb, laughing, as he drew her towards the cafe.

How can I possibly tell him the truth now? All these lies, these stories. I'll have to keep them going until they peter out. Pretend to win the money in a few weeks' time. That's what I'll do, get past Christmas, and tell him in the New Year. I'll say I've won twenty million. Him and Mam will be on the same page.

But not the full amount.

I can't ever tell him that.

Money changes people.

Look what it's done to me.

Chapter 42

'Oh, it's you again! How was the Ball? Did the dress wow everyone? Did you get laid?'

'I have so much to tell you.'

'Really? Get going then, I haven't got all day, I'm a busy inner voice.'

'I won the bloody lottery.'

'Yes, I noticed. No more TKMaxx for you. Don't you miss it?'

'I have popped in a couple of times.'

'So what's up this time?'

'My life's upside down. I'm throwing up daily, the nightmares won't go away, and I have to make a huge decision.'

'So what's the problem?

'I don't want to leave Wales and move away somewhere trendy, well-heeled and glamorous.'

'I don't blame you.'

'Do I really need to be in a vast mansion outside London or Oxford? I don't even know anyone there.'

'You don't need to tell me.'

'Everyone I've ever known is here, except Marcus.'

'Of course they are.'

'There aren't any beaches..'

'But the shopping would be better.'

'I can't shop forever.'

'Exactly. Wales has all you need, with the exception of endless sunshine. But you can get that in Spain when you sign for that villa you've just put a deposit on.'

'You know about it? Of course you do.'

'Naturally. I'm not asleep at the wheel all the time. Just some of it.'

'And everyone talks to everybody else here. You know what the Welsh are like. Nosey and chatty. The Martini mother tongue Mam calls it. Anytime, anyplace, anywhere.'

'Why does she call it that?'

'Some old 80s adverts. You forget it was her era. Ultravox and the New Romantics.'

'Tragic taste in music. Anyway, you won't get that in England. Nobody speaks in London.'

'I know. I'd miss it. And they'd laugh at my accent.'

'Why do you need to up sticks to England?'

'I have no idea. My head is full, and I'm not coping. Maybe it would feel like running away? Hiding my new status among all the other rich people.'

'You've a lot going on. Sounds like you have a touch of 'Hiraeth.' But have you decided on a pushchair yet? And a pram? Do people still use them?'

'I have absolutely no idea what people use.'

'Remember, change is good. It pushes you along.'

'You think so?'

'Every day the clock resets.'

'I'm not sure I want a reset.'

'Someone once said 'Change is inevitable. Growth is optional.' Although in your case, you're going to be growing a fair bit.'

'So what do you think?'

'I think you're boring me now. Catch you next time. Oh, wait. You were going to tell me about the Ball. I can spare a few minutes to hear about that. If it's worth it.'

'One hundred per cent.'

Chapter 43

'Life is too short to not have oysters and champagne sometimes.'
Christie Brinkley

They held the Spring Conference and Ball in Wales on the last day of April, which was a bonus with the venue less than an hour from home. The Celtic Manor, host to major golf events, presided over presidential visitors, film stars, and everyday people and companies as they passed through its portals daily. The resort centre boasted spas, pools, cabins, and woodland, as well as function rooms of all sizes.

Close to the junction on the M4 which carried traffic across from England, its ease of position made it a better choice than many other conference centres across the two River Severn crossings. When Grace arrived at her table, those seated were flowing with compliments on her dress and mask.

'And who is behind all these lovely disguises?' she returned the compliment.

Names and branches were forthcoming in a hubbub of chatter, as they poured the sparkling wine. It was impossible to recognise anyone even if she'd met them in the past.

When a man in a dinner suit arrived just as the waiter handed her a glass of fizz, he'd taken the seat to her right while the chair to her left remained empty. In moments she was face to face with gold-flecked hazel eyes peering at her from beneath a beautiful peacock feathered bird-beaked mask, and with each movement of the strong-jawed face, the light danced among the variegated colours, and she wondered exactly who was hidden below them.

'Good evening, who do we have under this beautiful red creation?' a voice like Spanish hot chocolate poured over her, thick enough to dip in a finger and lick it clean.

'Grace Lewis, Sales Rep. Swansea branch, covering everywhere between there and here. But who's under there?'

He captured her hand in his and lifted it gently to his lips, where they touched the ends of her fingers in a light kiss.

'Marcus Bolt, Head Office, Company spy. At any given moment you'll find me at a Motorway Services or lurking in a branch checking up on all of you. I'm like 007. Nobody knows what I do, or where I'm headed. It's Top Secret.'

Then he emitted a laugh that broke the awkward mood of strangers meeting for the first time in a formal environment and took a sip of the fizz in a glass next to his place setting.

'Good evening everyone, here's to a wonderful night, good food and drink, and masks of a completely different kind to those we've suffered in recent times.'

Everyone joined in a toast, some with groans, others with cheers. Finding herself seated with strangers was a surprise, but it meant a chance to get to know new people, meet voices only ever heard on a phone, mingle, and enjoy this event in the corporate calendar without spending the evening with staff from their own branch, gossiping and giggling.

The preamble of chatter was easy, much of it work orientated and the wine and prosecco flowed freely across the crisp white tablecloth, crystals spilled with abandon around the place settings and cutlery. With everyone booked into the hotel overnight, there were no concerns about travelling long distances home.

Marcus tilted his head and leaned in her direction, as she found herself the centre of his intense gaze.

'I don't think I've met you before, have I?

'No, I'm out on the road early.'

'I must get down earlier to catch you and grab a coffee, you can tell me all about your area. Maybe I'll come out with you for a day, see how you work your territory.'

Their eyes met and remained locked in the moment and Grace knew the wave of attraction emanating from him was about to surge over her.

Wow, what's this? I haven't felt this sensation in years. Did my uterus just contract?

As they discarded disguises around the table alongside the first course plates, Marcus and Grace unmasked in unison, counting down from three, and sat smiling at each other as they fiddled with the ties holding them in place.

'Well, hello again.'

The expression which crossed his face, and the subtle wink that accompanied it, showed her they'd met before. It took a few moments for recognition; a brief muddled mix-up at the entrance doors of the branch when her laptop case became caught up in his umbrella handle, ending up on the floor in a shower of raindrops, as she left the building as he arrived.

They exchanged only a few words, the usual apologies and amused comments about 'meeting like this' and 'entanglements' before she was flying out of the doors not to be late for her first appointment on waterlogged roads in pouring rain.

'It's you! Man with a brolly!'

'It is indeed. And it's you, babe with a briefcase.'

Amusement lit up her face, fuelled by the prosecco bubbles.

'I'm not sure that's suitable workplace talk.'

The blue eyes narrowed, framed by dark lash extensions which intensified their colour under his flirty gaze, as she fluttered them coquettishly.

'It's not, but we're socialising, and I thought you deserved to know you are, indeed, a babe.'

They laughed together.

'Did you by any chance, ask to be seated next to me?'

'Is it that obvious?'

A further wink as he topped up her glass with the remnants of a prosecco bottle.

'It might be, now you mention it.'

'Well, in that case, I'm glad. Although I wouldn't have admitted it off the bat.'

'And what about this empty chair? There's no placeholder. Is the invisible man joining us?'

'You got me now. I didn't want anyone alongside you to steer the conversation away. Privileges of management, I wanted your full attention.'

'What if I'd changed the placeholders and sat on the other side?'

'You didn't. Cheers. To entanglements.' He lifted his glass and touched the side of hers, already mid-way to her lips.

Oh, Gracie, this is fun. Way too much fun.

He thinks you're a babe. And he wasn't afraid to say it. Did he engineer this discreet side of the table, behind the enormous flowers and balloons, near the curtains at the edge of the room? He's obviously a man who knows how to get what he wants.

Once the remains of the dessert course vanished, and the band took the stage, the lights dimmed. Most got up to dance, leaving them discreetly at a darkened curve of the large circular table.

Marcus was even more handsome unmasked. At some point he'd removed his jacket, draped it on the back of his chair, and loosened his bow tie, while a waft of expensive aftershave crept into her nostrils.

'I love your fragrance.' she breathed in, heavy lashed lids dropping low on her cheeks.

Marcus leaned closer.

'Tom Ford. Luckily I'm well paid.'

'It smells like leather. Expensive leather.'

He slid his chair nearer to hear her voice over the volume of the music and whispered 'It's Fucking Fabulous. The name of the fragrance.'

Grace raised an eyebrow.

'You're kidding.'

'I'm not.'

She laughed as they moved even closer in the dimmed light. Soon they were deep in conversation, the heady mix of wine and perfumes moving them into a private bubble no one nearby dared burst.

When they finally wandered across the dance floor, admiring glances from the sidelines went unnoticed as they immersed themselves in the music. His hand drifted low down her back as they did a slow dance, and while she wanted it to remain there during their time on the floor, when the band finished and the DJ took over, wilder beats produced a sea of waving and gyrating, forcing them to blend in.

It was a quarter to the witching hour when they giggled their way back to the table and removed their masks for the ultimate time. Grace sat, smiling, but Marcus remained standing and leaned in close. She peered up at him beneath tilted lashes, eyes confused, and her smile vanished, long neck and décolleté stretched to perfection beneath his lowered gaze.

'It's been a pleasure getting to know you Grace, but I'm going to head back to my room now.'

He caught the disappointment in her eyes.

What's he doing? He's going? But there's chemistry. Damn, it's early.

Leaning even closer to her ear, his soft breath blew a tendril of hair as he whispered 'I can't take a minute more being this close to you without touching you, and that's impossible in a room full of colleagues.'

Grace's change of expression brought a hint of a smile to his lips.

'It's 233 in case you want to join me.'

Her eyes locked on him in silence.

'I really hope you do, but wait ten minutes before following me. If not, then you've been amazing company. You are a truly gorgeous and fascinating woman. Never forget that.'

Their gaze didn't waver, but diplomacy and discretion showed on his face. Lifting her left hand his lips touched the back, skimming the rings in unspoken recognition of her marital status.

'Two three three.' he repeated slowly.

Grace smiled as he drifted away, suit jacket draped over one shoulder, saying goodnight to those still at the table. She sat with her thoughts a few moments longer, before moving into the empty seat next to the woman from a Scottish branch, and poured herself another glass of wine as they exchanged a few pleasantries. If this was going to happen, she needed a top-up. The excitement building called for extra Dutch courage.

It's been a long time, girl, are you sure?

Angela appeared, swaying from out of the flashing disco lights, and plonked herself heavily alongside Grace's chair with nuggets of gossip from the London branch, waving her wine glass capriciously before an excess of alcohol saw an emergency run towards the Ladies' Room.

'Don't leave, I'll be back to carry on our chat' she hiccuped.

Grace smiled and nodded. *No chance. I'm invited to another exchange of pleasantries. Where I foresee little talking.*

Making her excuses to those left seated, she weaved her way discreetly towards the exit in the flashing semi-darkness of the vibrating function room. The DJ continued his set and as she headed towards the lift doors *'I gotta feeling'* by the Black-Eyed Peas began playing as a thunder of feet headed back towards the dancefloor in her wake.

With a smile bordering on a smirk, Grace muttered under her breath 'I've got one too. I think tonight is going to be a very good night in room 233.'

As she pushed the metal button and waited for the lift doors to open, the TKMaxx conversation came to mind.

'Different lifts, different times. No Bridget Jones knickers.'

She'd followed orders completely. Wandering barefoot and slightly worse for wear through corridors and floors in search of 233, heels swinging in one hand, mask and bag in the other, her dress rustled around her spray-tanned ankles. She met with bemused attention from a couple of inebriated male employees, giggling as she cheerfully fended them off.

'Wow, you are *gorgeous*!'

'Come home with me, I want to marry you!'

'Already spoken for, but thanks anyway!'

Two three three was repeated until she finally stumbled upon it, knocked lightly, and leaned against it to steady herself. She barely registered ten past twelve on her watch before It opened so fast she fell straight into his arms, bag, mask, and shoes tumbling to the floor. Marcus closed it sharply behind her, as he pinned her gently against the heavy wood, wrists above her head under a powerful hand.

There she remained while they kissed against the fire regulations, his free hand touching her face, her hair, his breath catching in his throat until with a few backward steps, he twirled her purposefully into the room.

'I know you're married, are you certain about this?' he whispered into her ear as her hands crept down to his cummerbund.

'*White rabbits.*' she breathed.

'What?'

It's past twelve. A new month.

'Never more sure.'

Feeling his erection against her through the expensive material of his trousers, her head spun with prosecco and pleasure.

It's been years since I felt like this. This rush of endorphins. Never more sure. Bloody certain, in fact.

White rabbits, white rabbits, white rabbits white rabbits.

'Thank Christ for that, you've been driving me insane.'

As he eased her down onto the bed, raising her dress up around her waist, he kneeled on the floor, hands spreading her thighs gently as his face nuzzled into her knickers. Grace moaned loudly as she stretched fully on the bed, a dark halo of hair cascading around her head, while the tsunami of bubbles floating around her body drenched her in one overflowing cascade of giddiness.

'I wasn't sure you'd come.' he rasped.

'You knew I would.' she uttered, the room swaying pleasurably.

'I *hoped* you would.'

A thumb hooked under the flimsy material and pulled it aside, and before she managed a gasp, his tongue was already licking her, encircling her engorged folds as her head swam and her body endured sensations absent for eons.

Grace raised herself up and cried out, the fastest release made him pull her up towards him, enfolding her tightly in his arms.

'Oh my god Grace, hold on to me. You're shaking.'
They remained clutched together until the sensations subsided, his lips touching her hair, kissing her forehead, murmuring soft words she barely heard, until her breathing slowed, her head stopped swimming, and she managed to speak.

'Sorry, it's been a while.'

'Don't ever be sorry.'

Then he was kissing her again, his lips soft, then more urgent, rougher as she responded to his tongue inserting itself deeper into her mouth, his hand holding her chin, slipping down to her throat.

'It's been a while for me too.' He nuzzled the words into her neck.

It was Grace who pushed him onto his back and unzipped his trousers, a hand creeping inside to grasp what hid in wait, and it was his turn to moan, his handsome face barely visible in the semi-darkness.

'Wait... condoms...'

She covered his lips with a hand, slipping a finger gently into his mouth, and tracing the outline as she withdrew it. Then she straddled him, the moisture between her legs allowing his stiffness to slip inside her with ease, as the green dress rustled rhythmically against the luxe material of his trousers, his hands moulded around the satin, still holding her breasts firmly hidden from his eyes.

'No need.' she breathed, gyrating faster as she felt his length fill her needs.

'Bloody hell, woman.'

Sweat formed on his forehead as she slowed rhythmically, back and forth, back and forth.

'Don't stop, don't you dare stop.' she breathed, eyes closing as the sensations grew.

'I won't.'

Marcus didn't cease until he rolled her over on all fours, bundled the dress up onto her back revealing a shapely bottom and tanned legs in the dim glow of a bedside lamp, and plunged into her from behind, harder and faster until she was crying out in desperation.

'Fuck me. Harder.'

A low roar came from his throat as they climaxed together, quivering and falling in a heap of panting and fluids.

'Oh, my god Grace.' he heaved.

'I have to get this dress off' she choked. 'I can barely breathe.'

He rushed for the zip, feeling his way amongst the folds of satin, and pulled it down swiftly, lifting the material over her head, revealing a matching bra, just as rapidly removed. He flung the dress to the floor leaving her naked and glorious on the duvet, her breathing coming in great heaving pants, her breasts rising and falling temptingly.

'Better?'

She nodded furiously.

So much better.

'You are so beautiful.' His lips descended on a breast, tongue encircling a nipple as it raised to meet him, her back arching towards his body.

Arms snaked around his shoulders and pulled him savagely into her abdomen as his lips traced her breasts and belly, before working his way back to her breathless mouth, mumbling words against her skin she barely heard among the rush of intoxicated bubbles fizzing in her ears.

I'm sinking into this bed, what's he doing?

Oh god, these sensations. I've drunk too much.

She tugged at his trousers, open but taut around his powerful thighs, pushing him onto his back. He lay still, eyes closing, shirt partially undone, allowing the aroma of his fragrance to free itself into the air, the spicy warm leather mixed with florals sexy and masculine to her senses as she inhaled it deeply.

Oh my god, this guy is incredible. Younger, fitter, he makes me feel amazing.

She straddled him nimbly, as she undid the remaining buttons, leaving the whiteness of the shirt outlining his muscled torso. tugging his trousers off and onto the floor, where she disappeared with them over the waterfall of the bed, onto the maelstrom of the carpet as her red-stained and smeared mouth closed over his penis.

'Oh god, woman! Deeper.'

Their desperation rose into a crescendo as she raised him back to life, the taste and smell of him filling her senses.

What the hell is happening here? You're possessed. And so is he. Enjoy it. You're never getting sex like this again.

Six o'clock was the exact time Grace stumbled back into her own room, the door on the evening's events closing for the last time behind her as she threw herself on the bed fully clothed, and fell straight into a languorous sleep. It was half past ten when she finally awoke and stripped off the gown he'd so patiently helped her back into, his lips touching her bare shoulder as she walked away into the empty corridor four hours earlier.

'Doubt anyone will be around now' he said as she collected her heels, mask, and bag and he kissed her briefly for the ultimate time.

'Drive carefully, lovely lady.'

Distracted, unsure, awkward, his confidence of the hours before now vanished into the night behind them.

So that's it? Nothing to be said? This is what a one-night stand feels like? Well, you wanted it.

With a scrabble of fingers, she found paracetamol in her overnight case, and took a couple with a long glass of water, before the aromas and fluids of the last ten hours were washed away under a hot shower.

Studying herself in the steamy mirror, she set about cleaning off the remnants of smeared red lipstick that clung to her lips, chin, and neck, fingerprints from her crime of passion.

Grateful she didn't have to share a lift back to Swansea, Grace wanted to be alone with her thoughts and delight following one incredible night and to yell it loudly without witnesses, over the steering wheel, through the windscreen.

Revenge was sweet, yet the mirror revealed it was the furthest thing from her mind. There were no unknown messages on her phone. Her number was easily attainable to anyone in the company. A brief WhatsApp from the cocktails group asking if she'd enjoyed her 'posh do' arrived.

'Of course. It was amazing. Table decorations were *totes lush.'*

Searching through her photo gallery she found a suitable snap of the balloons, centrepiece, and table crystals, and sent it. Then another of her with Angela, and Gareth, plus a group photo taken at the bar before they moved on to individual tables. She scrolled back and found one of her and Marcus seated, smiling, taken by the Scottish woman. He was so incredibly handsome. She would have to be careful in future if he visited the branch, although she'd only seen him in passing once, during all her time at L&B. Even less reason for him to come now, nursing his morning after embarrassment.

I've done the walk of shame. Call me Cersei Lannister. Oh well, something to remember when I'm ninety. Best not delete this one by mistake.

With a sad smile, she sent it to the group.

My table companion last night.

In moments, a string of raucous expletives flooded the screen alongside queries and rude emojis.

Is he free and where does he live?

Grace didn't have a clue. Nowhere during the night did he mention a partner, or where he lived. Their chemistry was so strong, it seemed others seldom entered the conversation and his phone remained silent and dark, no messages blighted their intimacy, and they took only a few photographs of the group at their table.

Young, free and single as far as I know. But you'll need plenty of petrol money to visit this one. He's somewhere in the middle of England.

Ping.
WhatsApp/Ffion
So did you?' Wink, lips, fire emojis.

Church and bride emojis.

Boring. What's his name?

Marcus. It means dedicated to Mars. Born in March, Polite, and shining. I just Googled it lol

Well, you should have been polishing it in that case.

You're incorrigible.

100%

Marking the photo as a favourite, she moved it to a new, private album.

I'll never forget last night. Married or not.

And you, my beautiful green frock, are headed straight to the dry cleaners.

Chapter 44

The expression on her husband's face was telling. Rhys came towards her, hands clenched into tight balls, jaws clamped together until he spat out the words. 'What the fuck's going on Grace, tell me. Now.'

She silently sucked in the deepest of breaths as he stood immovable in front of her, a frightening wall of emotion released after days of hiding, awaiting her return.

'What do you want me to say, the same thing that went on with you?'

Her insides shook. This was a different Rhys to the one she'd known for fourteen years. A simmer ready to boil.

Oh, my god what if he gets violent? I've never seen him like this.

His eyes pleaded. 'Is it? Is it the exact same that went on with me?'

'I think it must be.'

My stomach is in knots. This is scary. He's so angry. The baby.

Rhys closed his eyes. 'So is this just shagging? You're shagging this *Saes* twat?'

Grace paused long enough to ignite fear in his eyes.

I can't tell him there's a baby. I just can't.

'No. I'm sorry but it's not 'just shagging.' And he's not a twat.'

The anger was visible, sinews in his hands and lower arms shaking.

'So what is it then, are you in love with this bloke? Are you just getting revenge for Sian?'

Grace closed her eyes as a response left her lips. 'Don't mention her name in this house. Everything that's gone wrong between us is because of that girl. And your inability to keep it in your trousers.'

The birds fell silent outside, their home hung leaden between them. No sounds at all. Heavy air and a waiting silence.

'Well, were you in love with her?'

'No, I wasn't.'

'If it doesn't work out, give me a call, I'll miss you.?'

Grace watched and waited. 'Do you remember that? Hardly the words of someone without feelings.'

It was then Rhys did the unthinkable. He burst into helpless, heart-wrenching tears which spilled down his face in a torrent, his chest heaving. Grace could only step forward and put her arms around him as his body shook, words incomprehensible.

'Rhys, calm down.' she murmured, 'Please, calm down. We have to talk now, sensibly and quietly, don't you think?'

Green Goddess.
I've told him it's over. I'm going back later to pack my things. He's working nights so I can have the place to myself.

MarX.
Hope it wasn't too harrowing for you, sweetie. Let me know when you want to talk. Did you get your pills? Love you Xxx.

Yes. Will call you later. I feel bad. He was so distraught.xx

Understandable. Xxx

Stepping back into her house in the suburbs, the first sound Grace heard was the fluttering of wings. In the lounge, a tiny bird flapped its way across the furniture, from carpet to dresser to dining chair to lampstand. Grace tiptoed to open the patio doors and moved away, allowing the creature to find its way out.

'How on earth did you get in here, you little *dwt?* You're so pretty with your gold head.'

You left that patio door open while you paced up and down in the garden.

The tiny bird stopped and looked at her, perched on the lip of the lampshade. It held her stare for long moments.

'Off you go birdie, you're not safe indoors.'

As the words left her lips, Grace shivered, thinking of her grandmother. The goldcrest turned away and flew into the garden. She rushed towards the doors to close them, and keep November's air outside.

The bird was no longer to be seen, but staring in at her from the lower branch of the Rowan tree, sat a beady-eyed magpie, still seeking the last red berries clinging to the bare branches. They planted the tree soon after moving in, at her Gran's request.

'It's the Celtic tree of life, Gracie, it's very lucky. Everybody used to plant them in the old days. The fruit has the shape of a pentagram. It protects.'

As she remembered her grandmother's words, parts of the magpie rhyme she hadn't thought about in years, came to mind.

One for sorrow, two for joy…five for silver, six for gold, seven for a secret, never to be told…

And birds indoors are bad omens.

Chapter 45

11 pm
Chirp
MarX
Did you take the pills?

Yes, as directed. Xx

Good Sweetie. See you soon. They may knock you for six. Xxx

Hope so. Need sleep. xx

Grace discarded the phone and settled into the pillow of her marital bed. Rhys was working a night shift after their earlier confrontation, still upset as he left her there in the lounge with a slam of the door and the sound of an over-revved engine and squealing tyres.

Let's hope these do the trick. I can't face any more throwing up. My ribs are showing, and those suitcases are heavy. I'll be gone before he gets back in the morning. He won't even know I stayed.

03.06

The phone rang, as the projection clock's laser-red eyes scowled in the crouching cavern which lurked at the far end of her old bedroom. As she searched in the darkness to answer, a slurred *yes* was her response to a query by a vague voice in the distance.

'This is Paul at the factory, I'm so very sorry to tell you but Rhys has been in an accident on site and has been taken to Morriston Hospital.'

Nice try, hormones, but I'm ready for you this time.

'Ok, thanks for letting me know.'

Grace pressed *end* and let her hand fall onto the duvet, the phone nestled in the crumpled folds.

As if they'd be able to get an ambulance these days. I need to drift off to sleep and you want me to drift off to a hospital?

03.15 the red-eyed digital display flicked over.

Her phone was ringing through the duvet, muffled but audible.

'Grace!' It was her mother.

'What Mam? I'm trying to sleep. You know I'm dreaming, don't you?'

"Grace, wake up now!'

'I can't. Too tired.'

The phone dropped onto the carpet, the familiar voice echoing her name as it landed with a soft thud, screen face down.

03.35 glowed steadily across the ceiling.

The doorbell rang repeatedly, accompanied by a loud rapping on the etched glass which allowed the sun to warm the anonymous pink envelope she once held in her hands.

Oh, for god's sake, what now?

Grace stirred, dazed, and slithered off the bed to stand upright, wobbling in the darkness.

'Ok I'll play along, just give me a minute.'

In her dream, she drifted down the stairs and reached the porch, bathed by the luminous mist of a UFO streaming a halo around her, so bright, yet more broken threads of raffia scattered on the cold tiles beneath her feet.

That damn mat needs chucking out. What a mess. Why hasn't he thrown it? And the memory with it.

'Who is it?'

Will it be some film star I used to fancy, or a green alien ready to beam me up?

'It's Mam, open up.'

The door opened to blinding headlights.

'Grace are you drunk? Didn't you listen to your calls?'

'I'm not drunk, Mam' she slurred.

'I'm exhausted and pregnant and this is another nightmare.'

'What on earth?'

Her mother's arms enfolded her,

'Gracie, wake up love, it's not a dream, this is serious. Come on now, wake up. It's Rhys, he needs you. He's in the hospital.'

'He's not, Mam. Marcus was dead and buried, but alive again in the morning.'

Her mother reached for a coat, draped off a hook on the wall, and fought to get her daughter's arms into it, covering her silky, thin pyjamas.

'Grace, Rhys needs you now. Where are your shoes? We need to get in my car.'

Grace rubbed her eyes. 'In the lounge, by the sofa.'

Her mother rushed to find them, spotting the suitcases lined up, and returned just as swiftly. Pushing her towards the car, the cold of the early hours shocked her bare feet as they touched the paving slabs.

'Put them on inside, we don't have a minute to lose.'

Grace struggled into the passenger side as her mother secured the front door and started the engine allowing the warmth of the interior to revive itself with the heater once more on full blast.

Oh thank god, I can sleep again, and all this nonsense will be gone by morning.

'The manager rang me saying he couldn't get any sense out of you. It's lucky I'm down as an emergency contact, that's all I can say. Grace, are you listening? Do you have Rhys' mother's number?'

With her head settled back against the comfortable upholstery, Grace drifted straight back into the arms of Hypnos. Ten minutes later, outside the accident and emergency department, there was nothing her mother tried which released her from the grip of the tireless god of slumber.

As she begged a paramedic waiting outside a pile-up of ambulances to look at her, the exterior of the hospital was manic.

'I can't wake her up, she thinks she's dreaming. I don't know what's wrong but her husband is here, he's been in a serious accident. She needs to be with him. Awake.'

'You best go into reception, give her name and see if they'll tell you from the computer if she's on any medication, and find out where your son-in-law is. I'll keep an eye on her. It's a nightmare in there, though. Just warning you.'

'She just told me she's pregnant, but I'm not sure if it's part of her dream.'

'Does she take drugs?'

'No, of course she doesn't take drugs. Do *you* take drugs?'

The anger in her mother's voice was palpable, and the paramedic lowered his eyes.

'I'll look at her.'

❦

♥

14.40 pm.
Green Goddess.

Rhys is dead. I have no words.

♥

Chapter 46

Grace's phone remained switched off during the week following her husband's death. Her mother insisted she stay in her guest room and together they journeyed through the shock, the visits from friends and family, people from the factory, and the private doctor who called to monitor Grace while her sickness eased.

'There is no known risk of miscarriage due to shock or upset in pregnancy.' he told them. 'Rest as much as you can during this terrible time, naturally, as you come to terms with your husband's death. My condolences.'

Grace spent much of the time crying or asleep during the day, venturing down to the lounge at night, under the safety blanket of the darkness outside, where they ate homemade comfort foods from trays on their knees.

'Mam, can you try to get the funeral arranged quickly, I can't wait the weeks it takes these days. Pay double. Money talks.'

The meeting with Rhys' family proved difficult. In their upset and angst as they hugged and comforted someone rarely seen, her own responses were stilted, unresponsive, secretive. Spending the week wearing loose dark clothing, hiding imagined signs of her early pregnancy, she coped with the onslaught of his friends and her own appearing as and when they could manage, with guilt and despair.

If you'd told him about the money, he wouldn't have been at work. He'd still be alive.

Stop it, Grace. This was an accident.

You weren't to know this was going to happen. That this man you married was going to fall from a height and die of his injuries as you slept in a cold car in a dimly lit hospital car park. While his mother and mother-in-law were inside dealing with the tragedy.

'Grace, did Rhys know you were pregnant?' her mother ventured carefully.

'Of course not Mam, he was devastated when I told him I was leaving. I've never seen him so upset. That was so hard to do. I had to spare him that, at least.'

Grace's mother nodded wisely.

'Yes, that would have been dreadful. But you've been unhappy and as tragic as this is, you have to look to your future soon.'

Grace drew her legs up around her chin as she sat on her mother's old sofa. 'Mam, I haven't spoken to Marcus for a week. I turned my phone off.

'You mean he doesn't know?'

'He knows. I sent a text then turned it off. I can't face him.'

Her mother rubbed her forehead. 'Don't you think he's worrying about you, love?'

Grace shrugged. 'I can't go off driving around to meet him in this state. I don't even want to go outside. I feel like everyone knows all the awful details.'

'Nobody knows anything, how could they? He can come here to see you.'

Grace shrugged, her pale face lacking make-up, hair tied up in a ponytail which had barely seen a hairbrush.

'Why did you have your suitcases packed? You could have just bought everything new. Why put yourself through that? I would have packed them for you and donated them.'

'I didn't want him to face opening my wardrobes and doing it himself.'

Her mother nodded tersely.

'I'll get the cases, save you going back there again. You shouldn't have been lifting them, anyway.'

'I didn't, I opened them in the lounge and brought armfuls down at a time. It was safer and easier.'

'I think you need to ring Marcus, love. I thought you'd been speaking to him, up there in the bedroom.'

She shook her head sadly. 'When I'm ready, Mam.'

Grace sat on the edge of the bed and lifted her handbag onto her knees. With a vast sigh, she reached inside for her phone, and switched it on. While she waited for the week-long preamble of app loading and updates, she slipped her fingers into the zipped compartment and drew out the rabbit's foot.

Oh my god, what the hell?

Only part of it sat in her hand, loose hairs spreading across her skin. With a careful rummage, she removed the remains of the charm, pulled apart through age and the constant movement of her handbag, and sat looking at the two halves in her palm.

Is this why Rhys died because you broke apart? Did you get rid of him to make life easier for me?

You're losing it, Gracie girl. It's an old bit of tat, a crutch, not a living, malevolent creature.

She closed her hand gently around it and rushed for the stairs blinded by another bout of tears.

Slowly, don't fall, you can fix this. Take your time. Nothing bad must happen now.

'Mam, I need glue!' she called out.

As she appeared in the kitchen doorway, her mother glanced at the open hand held towards her and her daughter's distraught face, huge tears dropping onto the ceramic tiled floor.

'Oh love, what a shame. Don't upset yourself over it. Come here.' She wrapped her arms around her.

Grace pulled back. 'Are you kidding? We have to repair him, or my luck will run out. Look what happened to Rhys.'

Her mother frowned heavily, her voice dropped softly as they parted. 'You don't really believe that, do you, Gracie?'

Grace moved to the worktop and placed the rabbit's foot carefully on the surface.

'I need glue. We need glue. You bought it as an heirloom. If we don't repair it, imagine what else could happen?'

284

Her mother nodded slowly, studying her daughter's face. 'Ok love, let me think. I'm not sure I've got any but next door might, they've always got the grandkids there. I'll ask.'

As her mother closed the kitchen door behind her, Grace vaguely heard a phone ringing somewhere in the background and ignored it.

❦

Chapter 47

When her mother answered the door, a tall, handsome, agitated man stood in front of her.

'Are you Grace's Mum?'

An English accent, the word 'mum', and the worried expression meant she knew who it was.

'Hello Marcus, you'd better come in.'

'Thank you.' He stepped into the hallway.

'Sit in the lounge, *bach,* and I'll tell her you're here. Sorry we're meeting under these circumstances.' She pointed to the doorway and the sofa in view beyond.

Upstairs, she knocked and entered the bedroom. 'Grace, Marcus is here, love.

'What? How?'

Her mother was calm as her eyes drifted to the black trouser suit still hanging on the wardrobe door and the shoes cast adrift at the base.

'I phoned the office and asked for him. He's the father of your child, and I know yesterday was terrible, but it's over now. You can't keep hiding in here forever.'

Grace stood and smoothed imaginary creases from her plain black jeans.

'He looks very upset, shall I bring him up, or are you coming down? I'm going to pop next door for a cup of tea, give you both some space.'

Grace ran a hand through yesterday's washed and styled hair. 'Give me five minutes to make myself presentable, and I'll come down.'

'Ok love, I'll make him a cuppa.'

'He only drinks coffee Mam.'

'I'll get the good stuff out.'

As her mother turned to tackle the stairs, she added quietly 'This isn't some sort of punishment from above or beyond. It's just bad timing. Plain and simple bad timing. Remember that. Grief does terrible things to people.'

❦

Chapter 48

Visitors Space L&B chemicals, Swansea.

Marcus switched off his engine, contemplating recent events and the speed at which they'd unfolded. A sad smile touched a face now showing the merest trace of a faded summer tan. Autumn ushered in a season of rapid changes, some faster than the leaves flurrying around his feet those mornings as he stepped outside his Oxford home, the Boston Ivy trailing his door frame, the green flashed with red and purple, reminding him of Grace, the dress and her lipstick. And now they were heading into December and winter.

As she fell into his arms in her mother's lounge, his relief was overwhelming. They'd sat on the ageing sofa, arms wrapped around each other in a never ending *cwtch,* tears flowing down both faces as words remained unspoken for an interminable length of time. Her words when she spoke, forever ingrained in his memory.

'*He was so upset after finding out about us, he shouldn't have gone into work. Whoever told him is completely to blame.*'

The ravages of recent events showed on her face, while the black blouse drained her skin of colour. Showering her forehead, her hair, her fingertips with kisses in the only show of compassion he could muster, he avoided her lips.

The lounge door had been gently closed as darkness fell, and still they remained unmoving together, with the occasional exchange of brief softly spoken words. Sounds of crockery rattling and a radio echoed somewhere from the wall behind them, until there came a gentle knock on the door, and Grace's mother reappeared carrying a tray balancing three mugs of hot, aromatic coffee, her face showing a sympathetic smile.

'Come on, love' she'd said 'You can't keep this handsome fella to yourself all night. It's time we met properly.'

Swansea was growing on Marcus. People spoke to each other like they were best mates. There were no strangers. Everywhere was laughter and the lilting Welsh accent rose above buoyant, easy chatter. 'Alright?' became a passing greeting by pedestrians, not a question.

'Everyone's so smiley!' he told Grace days later.

'Welcome to Wales. *Croeso y Gymru!*' she smiled back. 'We'll keep a welcome in the hillsides.'

This morning, as they awoke in the penthouse apartment overlooking the sea, he ran a palm gently over her abdomen and smiled as he felt the beginnings of a soft swelling, then made them both coffee, kissed her on the head, and set off to the Swansea office, a short drive from the marina. He beamed as he passed *their* Marriott Hotel on the corner and headed to McDonalds for breakfast.

A throwback to his Uni days, it was a rarity which must be done occasionally. A reminder of less serious times when groups of mates discussed cheap student nights out, over hash browns and McMuffins, wearing their Gorgon's head Bath University hoodies. Fun days, study days, Georgia Days. Unlike the present.

This is one minuscule benefit of you leaving us, Grace. I get to use the visitors' space. You stole it whenever I visited, and I never even knew it was you. I should have complained, that would have been amusing.

When Angela from accounts asked how Grace was, long

after she'd left, he realised she knew about them. How, was a mystery, but it was a good guess and offices were notorious for gossip.

She must be bloody psychic. Or watched us at the Ball.

Quick thinking with his response, a casual reply slipped off his lips. 'Hasn't she been in touch since she left? I thought you were all good friends here in Swansea? Say *'Hi'* from me if you bump into her. She was a genuine loss until Gareth took over.'

The glint in his eyes as he spoke, a warning.

Marcus covered any important meetings on Gareth's old patch, until a replacement was found, and handled all primary interviews on the territory. The new representative needed to live somewhere in the large, rural area and so far, from the handful interviewed, none appeared suitable. But it kept him coming to Wales regularly, with a genuine excuse. A bonus.

Marcus glanced towards the first-floor window and the desk where Grace once sat. He imagined her there, spinning slowly in the creaky swivel chair he now commandeered on these visits, before racing out into the world.

I must remind John it needs a squirt of WD40. Furniture farts aren't a great impression should someone walk in unannounced.

During their first fleeting contact, crossing over in what passed as a 'Reception' area, he didn't consider his entanglement with a Rep. from an outlying branch would lead where it had. It was *something* at first sight, despite Grace barely registering him in her preoccupied state.

Those eyes. So beautiful. What the hell is she doing here? A little Welsh daffodil lighting up the grey of a so far lousy, soaking wet morning edging the docks.

When he asked the manager about the woman in a suit racing to leave the building, John responded 'Oh that's Grace, Swansea and Cardiff Rep. always in a rush to get on with her calls. I don't think she likes being in the office much. Don't blame her though, our surroundings aren't exactly salubrious.'

John gave a self satisfied belly laugh. Marcus' face was quizzical.

'Sorry, but we have a little walkthrough in Swansea called Salubrious Passage. Been there for centuries. Bit whiffy late at night, all the pubs and clubs run alongside it. Stay over one Friday and me and the boys will take you out for a drink. It's an eye-opener. Very lively.'

'Sounds like a plan.'

'You can walk in the illustrious, inebriated footsteps of Dylan Thomas. Take a selfie by his suit in the visitor centre. Mind you, he didn't have your taste in menswear. It's got turn-ups. And you'd dwarf him for height.'

'You're an aficionado, I take it?'

'Me? Nah. I don't read poetry. Love Undermilk Wood, of course, but I hear Johnny Depp is a huge fan. Who knows, maybe one day he'll pop in?'

Marcus laughed. 'So you think I'd find myself a nice Welsh girl on this night out?'

'I'd say. The girls on Wind Street would love you.'

'I'm sure I'd love them back if your Rep. is anything to go by.'

'A cracker, our Grace. Swansea girls are 'beauts' as they say around here. They do like their glam stuff.'

Marcus showed no further interest, due diligence done, discretion the better part of valour. With the Conference and Ball in the company diary, and mixed tables planned allowing branches to mingle in the pandemic's wake, it would be easy.

To nurture connectivity.

He smiled to himself and knew exactly who to talk to for those seating assignments to be arranged in his favour.

If you want to get ahead, get a hat.

Or a mask.

Spotting the rings on her finger as he sat was a setback, and he considered excusing himself and moving to another table to avoid the dismay ahead. Until she smiled. Then spoke. Those luscious scarlet lips moved gently in a musical accent below a cardinal-coloured mask, as his eyes plundered her shoulders, breasts, and slender arms emboldened by an emerald jewel of a dress that oozed beneath the folds of the tablecloth in a liquid river of satin.

Wow.

Just wow.

I'm not going anywhere.

The comfort of knowing they'd be together by Spring, with a son or daughter of his own, made the next step child's play. In business you needed certainty, and the steps to gain it needed to be dealt with efficiently. No room for error. Fearless action.

Check her address and next of kin from staff records.

Type, print both letter and envelope at home, take it to Swansea, and run it through the franking machine.

Post it.

No regrets.

You took a colossal risk. It was old school, but you had nothing to lose. A man has to take charge when life is changing fast. Would she ever forgive me if she knew it was my fault?

Marcus stirred his coffee and reached for today's copy of the local paper found forgotten and unopened at reception. Settling into the swivel chair, he unfolded it as the creaking began.

With a big delivery out back, this floor of the office was empty as staff gave a hand with the boxes. He glanced briefly through the grimy window and wondered what elegant, beautiful Grace thought when she scoured this industrial view, before turning his attention to the front page.

The headlines were large.

`100 Million lottery winner lives in the Swansea Bay area.`

Raising his brows, he let out a low whistle. 'Lucky bastard!' and casually scanned the columns below, blowing gently on the hot brew.

`The record-breaking amount for Wales was won over the August bank holiday. The lucky lady lives in the suburbs and is in her mid-thirties. She discovered her massive prize days later.Let's hope she's spending plenty of it around the city.`

Marcus set down his coffee mug with a clatter. Brown

liquid scalded his fingertips as it spilled onto the desk. 'Damn!' he shook the affected hand sharply.

Mid thirties. Tuesday. August.
Champagne on a 'school night.'
Resignation.
The Money Shot.
Fuck, Grace.
Is it you?
If it is, are you ever going to tell me?

With rising trepidation, he folded the paper and tucked it in his briefcase. No one at L&B needed to see this. By tomorrow, it would be yesterday's news. Tomorrow there may be a dramatic change to his future.

❦

Chapter 49

'Champagne makes you feel like it's Sunday and there are better days around the corner.'

Marlene Dietrich

In the seafront Penthouse apartment leading directly onto the promenade, soon to become a second home during the week, Marcus placed the newspaper on the coffee table, front page up, and gazed at the Bay sparkling in winter sunshine. As the tide crept towards the sand dunes, a pale blue sky touched the grey horizon in the distance. Mumbles pier and lighthouse edged to the right of this vista while the nearby ancient West Pier which channelled the river Tawe towards Trafalgar Bridge, gripped the Bay in its claw-like curve.

Fishermen and surfers used this breakwater, and he watched with envy as they flung boards with fearless abandon from on high, into enormous waves on turbulent days, followed by their owners who leapt in, fiercely straddling them. Van loads of surfers in wetsuits arrived at the dunes car park on surfing days, and Marcus yearned for time to buy a board and join them a short walk from the front door.

The more he studied the headline, the more it fell into place. And the more his stomach knotted.

Complete game changer if it's true. But surely she won't be working, pregnant, miles from home? Face it, mate, there's no way that's happening. All those upmarket hotels we stayed at, I don't even get those and I've been with L&B for years.

Marcus sighed and sat on the sofa. Nobody would tell someone they just met how a hundred million pounds would hit their bank account in the coming days. Resting his forehead in one hand, a foot jiggled on the thick carpet.

That's probably my saving grace. No woman would trust the actions of a man who knew the truth before beginning a relationship.

Numquam… pecuniam…nubere?

That's me kicked from the quote club.

Never marry for money, but marry where money is.

One hundred million?

Jesus Christ.

Green Goddess
Just leaving my mother's. Home soon. Xx

Marcus studied the text. *Home.* He smiled, his eyes drawn back to the newspaper headline.

It doesn't make any difference. Kick arse amazing, but no difference. No man is an island. No man lives alone.

When Grace walked into the apartment, she knew by his expression, something was amiss. He stood up as she dropped her handbag on a chair and headed towards him for a hug.

'What's wrong English?' A sad, uncertain smile and a frown creased her forehead as her arms slipped around him.

Marcus didn't reply, but responded to the kiss she planted on his cheek with one on her lips, and slid an arm around her, before steering her gently towards the coffee table. In silence, he pointed to the headline and waited as she picked up the paper and absorbed the words.

'Is this you, Grace?'

Oh, my god he knows. The amount, too. His voice is shaky.

Grace scanned the columns then dropped the paper and turned to pick up her handbag. Marcus watched as her fingers dipped inside and withdrew the repaired bundle of fur with the metal pin now wrapped in a soft cotton handkerchief. She turned, reached for his left hand, and slipped the rabbit's foot into his palm, closing his fingers gently around it.

No saying you've won twenty million now. You're done.

'You never touched this the night we bumped into the girl working at the hotel. But it's never been far from you when we're together.'

Her face clouded. With a disconsolate sigh, she told him the truth. 'Yes, that's me, Englishman, and that's our future together taken care of. It's a biggie, don't you think?'

Thank god mam hasn't bought today's edition. She'd be yelling 'Kidnappers!' loud and clear.

Marcus remained silent.

Time to be businesslike, Gracie. He's never seen you in corporate mode.

'I don't need to point out there was no way I'd have told you, a relative stranger. Only my mother knows, and Rhys never found out. It's only you two who know now, and just you the amount. And obviously this.' She pointed at the paper. 'But I think data protection probably covers that.'

Marcus remained silent. Grace raised a single eyebrow.

'I'm sure this is difficult to take in, so I'm going to wander across to the Marriott and order a *driver's* cocktail, while you let it sink in and decide if you can survive my subterfuge. I planned to tell you on New Year's Eve. A fresh start. I wanted everything behind me, and time to come to terms with it myself. It's a *huge* amount.'

Grace studied him, completely calm.

'Follow me when you feel able, and we'll toast again in the

first place I celebrated.'

Placing both palms on the sides of his cheeks, she kissed him gently on the lips

'Nothing's changed English, except our lives will be wonderful.'

Then she whirled away as Marcus stood in silence, a spot of blood staining the handkerchief as the pin of the rabbit's foot pricked his hand.

It's one hundred million, Gracie, he's not walking away because of a few lies.

Money can't buy me love?

In this case, it probably can.

Even though it didn't need to.

As she sat at the bar, non-alcoholic cocktail in hand, Grace dialled Miranda's mobile number. The line was no longer in use. She called the lottery switchboard and asked to speak to her directly, to be told:

'I'm sorry, we no longer have that person employed here.'

How old are you? Wasn't that what Miranda asked? I told her mid-thirties. That's what the headline says. And she seemed so trustworthy. But she warned you, didn't she? Trust no-one.

Grace glanced at the sporty white Aquanaut on her wrist. *My expensive fake. But everything comes to she who waits. And soon.*

Half an hour passed since she ordered her drink. At the corner table where they'd first held hands and eaten gigantic garlic prawns, the chairs stood empty. She signalled for a second glass, and moved to sit where he'd led her that night, the butterflies pounding in her throat. She slid into Marcus' seat and watched the entrance. As she waited, fingers tapped her screen.

Here you are again. Same hotel, about to order shoes. Yet more *Designer shoes. Chanel espadrilles. Flatties? Grace, you hate flatties! But I'll be needing them now. Can't risk falling over these coming months. What if there's no one to pick me up? Of course there will be.*

'Grace.'

I know that voice.

Chapter 50

Delighted, Ffion smiled. 'I'm glad you've told me about Marcus and I'm thrilled for you both about the baby, but I didn't send you the letter. Not even with the best of intentions'

Grace frowned and added milk to her cup. They were relaxing in the lounge at Swansea's Grand Hotel, sharing a magnificent afternoon 'Cream Tea' piled high with cakes and sandwiches.

'Who the hell sent it then? I have no idea.'

'I didn't know about Rhys until you told me. But I knew about Marcus, by the way he kept looking at you in Morgans. And your WhatsApp after the Ball. Dead giveaway. Oh sorry, beaut, that was thoughtless. I meant it was obvious.'

'Don't worry, Ffi, slip of the tongue. Maybe it was just a stranger, or even someone at his work. But how would they have known? It's not like people publicise an affair. Marcus and I didn't tell a soul.'

Ffion shrugged, taking a bite from a salted caramel and popcorn eclair, which registered pure delight on her face.

'Chance?' she wiped a morsel from her lower lip. 'Someone in the right place at the right time? Working at the factory and overhearing small talk? Oh, my god this eclair is lush…maybe the girl told someone about Rhys in all innocence and they worked it out?'

Grace sipped the Earl Grey tea as the tiny stringed paper square holding the tea bag in the cup spun in a breeze from a foyer door opening.

'She knew him as John. Nobody would put two and two together unless they'd seen them out.'

Ffion sighed. 'Then maybe Rhys *was* telling someone. A mate? Men gossip too. We all do it. Remember my neighbour? They're still at it, and I'm still hearing about sex toys and positions over a cup of icky instant coffee.'

Amused eyes met over the cake stand.

'Well, I'm not likely to find out now, am I?'

'No, I doubt it. You'll be alright with Marcus by your side and I know grief has to take its course, it's natural.'

Tears crept down Grace's cheeks.

'I feel terrible. Rhys complained for ages about defects in the machinery. Things were always breaking down, but I didn't expect this to happen. He went into work that night so upset, what if that's what caused the accident?'

'Gracie, you can't blame yourself. Shit happens all the time. I'm sure Health and Safety will be all over it.'

Yes, and any compensation will go straight to his family, with extra on top.

Ffion hugged her, and the memory of the nightmare returned.

'We've done this before in a nightmare, Ffi. We were cwtching after a funeral. Only it was Marcus' funeral. It was awful, too realistic. Pregnancy hormones, it turns out.'

'Oh, that's grim. Sorry.' she pulled away. 'I don't want to add to your troubles.'

'You'd never add troubles to my life. You add joy and laughter on our nights out, and keep me sane. I'm glad you managed to get away from work early.'

Ffion laughed. 'Flexitime, beaut. But I worry about you so far away. I know it's all modern woman's stuff, but you should be nearer home now.'

'I will be, Ffi, I'm taking early maternity leave, or I may just hand in my notice.'

'Good. Plenty of other jobs for your skill set. Oooh....I didn't want to tell you before the funeral, and you'll never believe it, but I won one of those big morning TV programme competitions. You know, a two-quid text entry?'

Grace smiled. 'No way, what did you win?'

'A fabulous new BMW and fifty thousand pounds cash! On top of this Tiffany bracelet I won when you entered me in Harrods!' She rattled her wrist, and the heart jiggled against the pearl and silver chains.

Grace beamed happily. 'Oh Ffi, what fantastic news. You've always wanted a BMW. You're on a lucky streak. Keep entering things. Just imagine what you could win in the future. That reminds me.'

Grace opened her bag and pulled out the book on manifestation, her diary sliding out with it. She pushed it quickly back inside.

I don't think I'll be needing you much longer, my beautiful, expensive organiser. You're getting too big for my much smaller handbags.

As she handed the paperback to Ffion a few grains of Swansea Bay sand spilled onto the table between them.

No need to throw any of those over my shoulder for luck.

'Ooh, Ta beaut. Glad you remembered to bring it. Baby brain not kicked in yet?'

'No, but I hope you get further with it than I did.'

Ffion smiled happily. 'Best part is, I don't really remember entering. But I must have, because a courier delivered the money last week, and the car arrives tomorrow! Mind you, I'll never be as lucky as that local woman who won a hundred million. Lucky bitch.'

Grace's breath was sharp.

'That's bloody fantastic Ffi.'

Fan-tas-tic. Little by little.

And you get to keep your friends.

Grace hugged her tightly.

'So, I'm buying the drinks. But alcohol-free wine? Yuck. Breaks my bloody heart.'

'If you knew how ill I've been you wouldn't want me drinking the real thing.'

'My sister was like that, sick as a dog for months. Instant diet. Looked like Kate Moss for weeks, then turned into a total whale.'

Grace's jaw dropped. 'Oh no, I hope I don't turn into one.'

Ffion winked. 'I think you've already had your Free Willy moment, beaut.'

They burst into the usual round of raucous laughter which always accompanied their get-togethers.

'By the way, Ann and the girls send their love and look forward to seeing you for a night out when you're up to it. Do you want to tell them, or shall I?

'Will you tell them Ffi, I can't cope with any judgemental looks at the moment? By the time I see them, we'll all be used to the idea.'

Ffion looked thoughtful. 'I just *wish* we knew who sent us all the champagne that night.'

Grace studied her hands, the nails now Winterberry red. No further need for classic French manicures.

'Maybe it was that hundred million lottery winner, and she fancied one of us. Wasn't it you who asked if anyone swung both ways?'

More laughter followed as Grace picked up an elderflower and lemon drizzle cake.

Seems we both have strangers we'll never know, sending us stuff.

301

Chapter 51

Grace stood on Deidre's doorstep, her complete lack of emotion a revelation. Sian's house, footsteps away, stood quietly in the brief natural glance taken in its direction. No sign of life. No cars outside. With a purposeful averting of her eyes, Grace took a deep breath.

Should I even be here? This feels daft, really, but then she was so kind to me. And I think we really liked each other.

It took a few moments before she pressed the bell, but not long until the older lady opened the door. Deidre's expression showed only a momentary lack of recognition, soon replaced with a beaming smile.

'Oh my dear, how are you? How lovely to see you! Come on in, please.'

'Thank you, Deidre, that's kind of you.'

Grace stepped into the chilly hallway. 'I've brought you some flowers, and something naughty to eat.'

She handed over an enormous bouquet filled with beautiful, scented colourful blooms and a luxurious box of unopened chocolates bought on her foray to Harrods.

'Oh, there was no need, you know, but thank you so much, they're beautiful.'

'My pleasure, it was the least I could do.'

Grace stepped inside the house and shivered as the lack of heating became apparent. No doubt she would soon be back in the chair she'd sobbed in on April Fool's Day while caressing a hot Elvis with her fingers.

'Let's have a cup of Glengettie, shall we?'

Grace nodded. Tea was always the answer to life's troubles.

'Sorry it's a bit cold in here love, but you know, these days I daren't put the heating on until the evening. All these awful price rises, will they ever stop?'

Grace nodded and sat absorbing the room full of grandmotherly attributes, something missing from her own life for many years, and the large Welsh dresser where The King still sat on his throne out of harm's way. A cheap daily tabloid, a thin women's magazine, unopened bills, and an old black handbag paid obeisance at the base.

What do I say, do I tell her all of it? She's the only one I can tell, really, except for the money part. Or will a thank you do?

Diedre reappeared minutes later, with two steaming mugs and some Welsh Cakes on a plate not dissimilar to the one her mother laughed about at the Boot Sale where they'd unearthed the rabbit's foot.

My lucky rabbit's foot?

'Here we go my dear, this'll warm us up. I thought we'd stick with mugs again, just in case.'

She winked, a simper at her lips, and pulled her cardigan closer around her body. Grace nursed a more expensive floral, white china version, obviously reserved for 'best' and emotion-free days.

'So how are you, my lovely? Has everything worked itself out?'

Grace blew gently through her lips, relaxing into the upholstery of the ancient chair.

'Yes, but not all in a good way.'

'Oh dear. I have to tell you that husband of yours was up here once more that I saw, not too long back, either. Sian showed me a photo and told me all about your chat. He didn't go inside, mind you, just talked to her on the doorstep. But I have to say I went out there and gave him a piece of my mind. I hope that was alright? Is that what this is about?'

303

Grace tried to smile, but it didn't appear.. Why was Rhys there? An attempt at rekindling the affair? She shook her head sadly and pushed away the thought.

Doesn't really matter now, does it, Gracie? Forget it. It's passed. He's passed.

'I'm afraid my husband died recently, Diedre. He was injured in a factory accident and died in hospital the same night.'

'Oh dear god, I'm so sorry to hear that. So, so sorry. Oh dear, I can't quite believe it. And with Christmas so near.'

Grace managed a few brief nods.

'Neither can I.'

'You poor lamb. I don't know what to say.'

'Things have changed so fast since I was here in the Spring. I tried my best and I think he did too, but it was obvious I wouldn't get over it. Then I met someone else. And fell in love.'

'Well, that's wonderful my dear, I'm happy for you, but sad at the same time. Life is cruel. So tragic. Too young.'

'We'd only just separated.'

'I understand. You'll always have feelings towards a man you've lived with. That goes without saying.'

Grace dug out a tissue from her bag.

'The worst part was, I was actually asleep in his bed that night. I'd gone back to clear out my things, and he was working a night shift. I slept there one last time, to say a silent goodbye to my old house and my marriage, and leave first thing before he got back. I didn't even believe the phone call in the early hours.'

'Middle of the night phone calls are never good. Bless you, have a Welsh Cake, I made them this morning. Or shall I open the chocolates?' she offered the plate but Grace shook her head.

'No thanks, I have to be careful these days, things keep making me sick.'

Diedre's eyes slipped to her waist. 'I see.'

'Yes, I'm pregnant, and no, it's not my husband's.'

A sad pause hung between them before Deidre issued words of common sense.

'In a way, that's good, love.'

Grace took a deep breath. Yes, it was good. *No child never knowing its father.*

'It feels strange, but I'm here to say thank you for your kindness that day, and because I'm not sure if I should tell Sian.'

Deidre considered the words before she answered. 'It's a kind thought, my dear, but maybe you shouldn't. I think Sian has a new boyfriend now, I see him coming and going a lot. Maybe leave it to me. I'll drop it into passing conversation.'

Maybe Sian wouldn't be bothered. Months have passed.

'She probably won't ever find out. I can't imagine her checking the obituaries. My mother always reads them, and more often than not there's someone in there that she knows. But I don't, and I'm older than Sian.'

Sian. How can I even say her name? She's responsible for all that's happened, all this angst and upset and grief, all this change I'm undergoing. No, she's not, it was Rhys. She just happened to get in the way.

'Yes, that would be a better idea, thank you Diedre. You're wise, and my bump isn't showing yet.'

'It's a difficult time for you. Have you decided what you'll do? '

'I'm working in the North of England, so I'll probably move up there, and you know what life is like, people come and go from it all the time.'

And I'm still lying, even in front of a harmless stranger I'll never see again after today.

'Yes love, friendships vanish just as quickly as you find them. Life isn't always straightforward. Your new man, is he good to you?'

'The absolute best. But he's a few years younger than me.'

Diedre nodded and smiled.

'Lucky you. I'll cheer you up and let you into one of my little secrets, shall I?'

They exchanged brief, silent, bemused glances. Grace wondered what the cloak and dagger mystery would be, what shrouded reminiscence would a woman Deidre's age have stored away which would jolt someone in her mid-thirties.

'If you want to, it's safe with me.'

'Well, my dear, you remember me telling you about my husband, and me staying with him after catching him out?'

'Yes, of course.'

'Well, the reason I did, was for revenge. He never knew, of course, but I couldn't have stayed with him without some comeuppance. I started an affair with his younger best friend, just for the hell of it. I know it must sound terrible, and in fact, you are the only person who knows this, but he deserved it, and his friend was very handsome, very willing, and very…how do I say it, athletic?'

Grace burst into laughter.

'Oh Diedre, you naughty girl, that's so funny. I hope you enjoyed every minute.'

They giggled together, age gap of no consequence.

We women never forget. We never forget our youth, the beauty we possessed, the fun times, the sneaky times, the wild times. We may go on to hide it behind granny facades, below tweed skirts and charity shop cardigans, but the memories live on. Good for you, Deidre. Good for you.

'There were many minutes, my girl, many minutes. It saved my marriage, but I enjoyed it, and it went on for months until they offered him better-paid work in Cardiff. And in those days, getting about wasn't as easy, so it came to its natural conclusion.'

'You must have missed him when he went?'

'Yes, I'm afraid I shed a few tears when I was on my own, for too many weeks than I care to admit. I never saw him again. Men and their friendships don't last as well as ours do, and once he'd left, life moved on. There was no further contact. But he was so blinking handsome, it made it worthwhile for me.'

Her eyes drifted across to the photo of her children dressed in school uniform, taken decades before, and without even having to ask, Grace made the connection. Deidre didn't need to say 'but my son was the spitting image of him.'

That remained her secret.

'Do you think your husband ever guessed?'

Maybe he, too, saw it daily in the boy's face.

'Well, if he did, he never said. But to be honest, every so often I would drop the occasional hint, mention his name a few times, you know the sort of thing. And as it's always said, my dear, revenge is definitely a dish best served cold, and although he went on to have other affairs, I was content with just one.'

There you go, then. Tit for tat leading to more tit for tat. A daily reminder that Deidre'd taken revenge every time he looked at the cuckoo in the nest. Is that why he carried on? Or was he one of those serial types, anyway?

Diedre folded her hands in her lap.

'Ah, the good old days. You're bringing it all back to me now. I haven't thought about him in years. Do you know, I never even took a photo? We just didn't use cameras much in those days, not like now when you all have them on your phones. Do you have a picture of your young man?'

Grace pulled her mobile from her bag and flicked through her gallery.

'Actually, Diedre, let me show you one nobody else will ever see, as you've shared a secret with me, I'll share one with you. This was taken that night in Swansea when we met months after our first time together. Look.'

Diedre's face broke into a smile.

'I can see what's been going on there!'

'He actually said 'We can show it to our kids.''

'Oh my, he was keen then.'

Grace paused reflectively.

'Yes, I suppose he was.'

'Very handsome. I can see the attraction.'

'Only one problem, Diedre.'

'What's that, dear?'

Grace took a slow, dramatic sip of tea.

'He's English.'

They looked at each other, two sets of blue Welsh eyes twinkling in the gloom of an unlit room, and began laughing loudly. The older woman winked. 'Oh well, nobody's perfect.'

Oh, Deidre, you love 'Some like it hot' too.

Chapter 52

Winter, 1st December

White Rabbits, white rabbits, white rabbits.

Lounging on her mother's squishy new sofa, Grace watched as she dusted her collection of ornaments. In one corner of the room stood the large Christmas tree they'd spent hours erecting and decorating that morning, after struggling to walk the sizeable box in from the garage. It was usually Rhys' job.

Eclectic baubles brought back from her mother's travels filled the boughs, complete with realistic pine cones dusted with fake snow, while empty storage boxes and tissue paper cluttered the floor. Bright lights glowed and twinkled in the darkening afternoon.

'I swear everyone's putting up the Christmas decorations earlier each year. There's not much point really, living alone, but I love fairy lights and my tree ornaments.'

'It looks lovely Mam.'

'Just yours to do next, whenever you're ready, let me know. That's if you're bothering.'

Grace's mother wore a brightly coloured new Hermes scarf, and the wafting scent of Moncler perfume filled the room, fighting with a Diptyque Snow candle burning on a side table.

'Your Gran would have a fit if she was still here. 'Tree up twelve days before, tree down Twelfth Night.' I was never really sure of the rule.'

'Well, you get the most out of it this way, as you're going on your Christmas cruise with Amanda. Besides, half of Swansea already has them up.'

'Do you mind me going, Gracie? Amanda is really looking forward to it. She's alone otherwise.'

'Of course I don't mind, it will be lovely for Marcus and me to spend it together. We've got loads to sort out.'

Her mother sneezed as a cloud of dust tickled her nose and laughed. 'If I'd done that two years ago I'd be petrified of failing the Covid test at the port!'

Grace laughed, hopeful that it was now in the not-so-distant past.

'It's understandable you and Marcus need to be together, but you could come with us, you know? I'm sure they'd have a suite available. You could do with some sun. Plus, it's your birthday on the twenty-eighth. We can all celebrate together.'

A first Christmas with Marcus, and a birthday celebration in one. We could ask his parents along. We have to spend time together sooner or later. A long way from the heartache.

'I'll suggest it. Might be nice, now that I think about it.'

'Good. Now you're over your sickness, you should be fine at sea. But don't leave it too late. Christmas cruises are popular.'

Cruising around the Caribbean. No rain, or howling December gales to drag the lights off the Norwegian Spruce outside the Langland house. Palm trees. Steel drums. Family. The travel you wanted so badly. Before the baby arrives and it's all a nightmare of luggage, nappies, and bottles. You can wear the Chanel espadrilles on deck. Stroke of luck you ordered them.

'Mam, how old are kids before they have to go to school? By law I mean.'

Her mother considered for a moment.

'I think you started about five. Can't you Google it?'

Grace laughed and pulled out her phone, her slender berry-tipped fingers typing in the request. 'Yes, you're right. Five.'

Five years of globe-trotting ahead. What an education for any child.

As her mother moved to the kitchen to make coffee, Grace closed her eyes and visualised the future. Floppy hats, white silk maxi dresses, beautiful flat sandals, and huge raffia bags, with a baby bouncing on one hip. She daren't risk tripping on any ancient cobbled streets they wandered along, despite the safe hand of a tanned Marcus, head to toe in white cotton, guiding her safely along, one hand low on her back.

Heels would be restricted to dancing and expensive restaurants in cities around the world, while 'Nanny' looked after the baby. Where seeking new red lipsticks would be *de rigueur* as she discovered the upmarket department stores of South America and the Far East, with furniture shipped back to fill whatever nook in whichever home it suited.

Stop daydreaming Gracie.

I'm not. This is reality.

Her mother reappeared with two mugs of instant coffee and settled at her side. 'Shame it's not a Bailey's this year, love. But Nadolig Llawen anyway.'

Her mother clinked her coffee cup against Grace's with the Welsh Christmas toast.

'I saw something on TikTok which said that's really not etiquette, clinking glasses. But sod it, Swansea's not big on etiquette, anyway.'

'Clink away, Mam, I love the sound it makes. Everybody does it. Can you imagine a wedding without clinks?'

'I can't imagine yours without them, love. Have you had a scan yet? Do you know what you're having, or don't you want to know? Oh, this is so exciting. I'm going to be a Gran, a Mam-gu.'

Grace shook her head, averting her eyes to the poinsettia already dropping leaves on the coffee table.

'Mam, why did you call me Grace, and not a Welsh name?'

'Oh, that's an easy one, love. It was your Dad. He loved musicals, and one of his favourites was High Society. When you were born, you were so graceful, he took one look at you and said 'Look how elegantly she stretches her arms. That's our Grace Kelly.'

'Really?'

Her mother nodded. 'He loved the songs, the smart suits the men wore, and of course the vast mansion and cars. Mind you, it *is* a lovely film. He would put you on his lap to watch it and you'd point at all the fabulous hats and clothes and the look on your face was adorable.'

Grace raised her brows.

'Really? I'm named after a Princess? Of Monaco?'

'Yes, it's always on the telly around Christmas. Don't you remember it?'

'Yes, of course, but I haven't seen it in years. I remember the song about a boat.'

Grace's mother studied her and smiled.

'The True Love.'

'Shall we watch it? I'm sure it's somewhere online. It will cheer us up after all this sadness.'

Her mother reached for the remote to the enormous brand-new smart TV hanging on one wall disguised as an Old Master painting and Grace caught her discreetly wiping away a tear.

'It'll be fun, this sound system is brilliant. Your Gran would have loved watching films on this. She called you Calamity Jane, you know.'

Grace yawned and stretched, the morning was tiring and they were heading out for a late lunch in an hour to celebrate their endeavours.

'You were always into mischief, falling over or moving ornaments around when she babysat. She loved singing The Deadwood Stage to you, because it mentions Adelina Patti, you know, from the Patti Pavilion on the seafront? You loved it and tried to sing along, but it always came out as 'tricktrackleday' instead of 'whipcrackaway'.

'I never knew that! The opera singer?'

'Yes. The most famous in the world, when she was alive. It was her Winter Garden.'

'How do you know all this Mam?'

'Social media history groups. Full of stuff you never knew, and old photos. People *love* all the memories. Especially this time of year.' Her mother gazed at the tree, lights sparkling, lost

311

in her thoughts.

'I saw Queen there, you know, before they were famous. Or was it the Brangwyn Hall? I forget, it was a long time ago and they're right next to each other.'

'You really were a bit of a rocker, Mam.'

'Trouble is these days, I've forgotten most of the things I did back then, with my menopausal memory.'

Grace closed her eyes and drifted back three decades. The beautiful red-bottomed model boat glided effortlessly across the swimming pool, launched on course by elegant hands. Vague spoken lines about a father hurting both mother and daughter and Grace Kelly, a goddess in a white flowing robe, broke through the scene.

She sat upright. 'Yes, let's watch it tonight. When it gets dark and the tree lights are on.'

Seems I might be a bit of a daddy's girl after all. Should Thailand be on my travel list? Maybe I should email and tell him about Rhys.

And that he's going to be a grandfather.

❦

Chapter 53

A pair of wrinkled, age-spotted hands plumped up the cushion on the chair where her guest so recently sat, not long after washing their mugs and setting them carefully on the draining board.

'Well, what's this now?'

Rheumy eyes held up the scrap of fur in a red net bag to the light and a slow, thin-lipped smile appeared.

'Oh, I haven't seen one of these in years. She must have left it by mistake. Oh dear, I forgot to ask her name, and there's no way of returning it now. Never mind, I'll give you a good home, *bach*. Who knows, you may bring me some luck at the bingo.'

Deidre gently stroked the fur and placed the rabbit's foot in her yawning handbag, resting on the dresser.

'Now, how did you get open? I must have the clasp tightened in the Market. I'm sure there's a repair shop by the laverbread stall.'

As she snapped it shut, the thick envelope tucked inside, with 'Merry Christmas Deidre xx' in scrolling letters, and the means to pay those unopened bills for years to come, hid unnoticed for now.

Elvis observed royally from above, a hint of a smile on his face. An out-of-the-blue urge to sing a line from one of his songs made Deidre's lips move, her weak voice finding only a title to hum.

You're the devil in disguise.

Chapter 54

Grace returned to the marital home with a carton of milk balanced under one arm and picked up letters off the still-shedding mat. She kicked it away and closed the door, stepping into an empty lounge, knowing it would never be full again. No curries on trays on their knees. No Evening Posts littering the coffee table. No arguments over food shopping. And no hearing Cariad in his deep Welsh voice. When the door closed behind her as she left, it would be for the last time. The house *sounded* empty, despite the furniture. Those loud echoes heard in unfurnished properties, where every tap of a heel or creak from a floorboard reverberated around her. Where their Christmas tree stood, its lights twinkling through the dark December nights, was an empty, unlit corner.

Upstairs, wardrobes were clear of clothing, with drawers devoid of possessions. The local charity shop had collected Rhys' clothing and Grace's suitcases a few days before the funeral, their wedding photo in the ornate frame from the hallway now in the care of her mother.

The house was ready for the Estate Agents. Emma and Miles were due within the hour to take measurements and photos of the property named 'Cartref.'

Home.

Grace sighed and sat on the sofa, hugging the *woman with the golden tears* cushion once more, and shivered.

'If you can keep it furnished for now, it's better from a selling point.' Emma advised over the phone. 'People aren't always capable of visualising where their own furniture will fit.'

'No problem. But I want it on the market before Christmas, and I don't really want to set foot in it again once I've given you the keys.'

'Understandable. Don't worry, we'll take care of it all. You can enjoy your cruise and we may have sold it by the time you come back.'

The heating timer which Rhys always set to five o'clock, allowed the end-of-year chill to pervade the midday air.

You were such a stickler for that damn temperature gauge. We always fought over a few degrees. Like many couples. Toilet seats left up, lights left on, food left on worktops, unwashed takeaway containers in the bin instead of the recycling. I was the stickler for that. You were hopeless.

Come on Gracie, it's time for your last tears to flow. You had good times. So many down the years. They just seem so long ago. You need to cry them here and leave them here. Step into your new life with some sense of happiness. For Marcus. And Morgana.

Careful, girl. That's a surprise.

Grace leafed through the letters, salty tears falling again on the envelopes of condolence cards and bills. She read each one, wiping away further droplets at the kind words inside, and taking solace from the beautiful designs. With the last one withdrawn, she stiffened.

Sorry for your loss. Such awful news. Condolences from all at
L & B

Angela & team. Xx

They remembered me. Maybe I'll call in and apologise for my swift exit. But what is it about this card that's familiar?

Sorry.

One spectacularly curled S.

Grace didn't need to move. She simply unzipped the cushion now by her side, reached in, and removed the crumpled letter which landed on the mat on the first of March. Smoothing out the creases, she set it on the coffee table alongside the white card bearing four embossed geese flying into distant clouds, and the truth stared up at her.

The same hand wrote those singular words of regret, remorse, distress, and sorrow.

Sorry you don't know me, but better coming from a stranger. Only not a stranger.

Everyone lies Grace. Everyone.

Nine months. A gestation of a trial, waiting and wondering if the offender would ever appear. Judgement drew to a close as the evidence affirmed itself on the bench before her. Angela had been *somewhere* at the right time. Chance. Zemblanity.

It's not worth a confrontation.

Tea will fix this.

Tea fixes everything.

As the kettle boiled, she set out three decent china mugs, while the sensation of a hundred butterflies grew deep inside. Frowning, she sank against the countertop, cradling her abdomen until the fluttering ceased. With pursed Ruby Woo lips, she pulled her phone from her coat pocket.

'Dial Marcus.'

The night at the Marriott, those insects rose high in her throat, choking speech before settling around her ribcage. These were different. The blue and black beauties were vibrant shades of rose and pink. Three rings and his chocolate voice melted into her ear.

'Hello Welshwoman, what's up?'

'Not a lot. I only wanted to tell you I've just felt the first flutters of our baby.'

'Grace!'

She could *hear* his smile.

Alone in the emptiness of the kitchen she once shared with her husband of twelve years, she studied the single enormous solitaire diamond now pulsating with the light of neutron stars on her left hand. Inches away on her wrist, the tiny diamonds edging the face of the newly acquired *genuine* Patek Philippe sparkled like a halo above it as her fingers moved upwards to toy with the wedding rings nestled against her décollète, hanging from a simple gold chain.

During the coming months, she would slip those marital mementos into the deep drawers of a jewellery box with a sad sigh of regret. One day, they would turn up under the glass viewing counter of a charity shop or antiques fair, where customers seeking bargains would point, query prices, and ask to try on. Or maybe on a trestle table at a Car Boot Sale, the decaying box filled with broken, discarded treasures from the decades ahead.

It's difficult to throw anything away.

'So, English' she mused, phone flat against her cheek, lips in a close kiss to the microphone, 'have you resigned yet? Or are you still my man on a motorway?'

His laugh was gentle as her toe pressed the waste bin pedal, while her free hand pulled the diary from her handbag, and dropped it into the empty bin liner with a muffled thud.

Must remember to put you in the recycling when I leave.
Sometimes, you just have to let stuff go.

The End

About the Author

Dawn Llewellyn-Price splits her time between the South Wales coast and South East Spain, wedged between the national parks of Sierra Espuna and Sierra de Las Moreras.

As a columnist for magazines and newspapers in both countries, including the South Wales Evening Post, she's also published in specialist scuba diving magazines. A return to fiction writing, long after a first short story in 'Best' women's magazine, begins here.
Loves sunglasses.

 dawnllewellynpricewriter

 dawnllewellynpricewriter

 dawnllewellynpr

The follow up to this story is underway...

If you enjoyed this novel, please consider leaving an online review at Amazon.
Many thanks.

Printed in Great Britain
by Amazon

39214015R00182